SEQUELA

by Cleland Smith

Published by Gauge

ISBN 978-0-9927202-0-9

For my beautiful sons,
who will always be too young to read this.

Acknowledgements

Acknowledgements are due to Gary Gibson and Hal Duncan; without their encouragement and advice, this book might never have seen the light of day. My family and friends have been endlessly encouraging – thanks for your enthusiasm and support. Special thanks go to my Mum and my Mother-in-Law who both helped by giving me baby-free time at crucial points in the writing and editing process. Finally, the biggest thank you of all goes to my husband, Matthew, who has been an invaluable reader and sounding board throughout the writing process.

sequela /sɪˈkwiːlə/ *n*

1   the long term effect of a disease.
2   any complication of a disease.

Chapter 1

When Farrell opened her mouth to speak, her tongue was black. Kester glanced at the two male members of the interview panel. Their mouths were closed. Farrell tipped her head back, revealing two lines of sores that stretched down from beneath each ear and disappeared under the band of her broad-knotted cravat. Kester recognised the patterning: she was wearing Emerna-B, a mod of a street STV, cultured in-house to provide a more focused patterning. It had been commissioned by the MD of V Global in New York and had only been spotted on two or three wearers since. All were internal to V and all were high-worth individuals. It was evidence of Farrell's selective promiscuity and she was wearing it like a diseased peacock tail, her feathers raised and shuddering.

Kester tried his best to look impressed – Farrell was clearly powerful. Within a few months the mod would make it back down the shag chain to the streets, perfect evidence of the desirability and ambition of everyone in its infectious family tree. Along the way it would cement relationships, ease promotions and secure interviews. When the MD's exclusive contract ran out, wearers would rush to buy it from the Pigs in the hope people would think they'd caught it from a prestigious individual, but for now it was the equivalent of a catwalk disease. Farrell was the principal interviewer and Kester's prospective new boss. She would expect him to want it.

Kester tried his best to smile. The collar of his shirt was getting tighter. He wasn't used to wearing a suit and tie, and could feel little raw patches developing at the sides of his neck. He pushed from his mind the image of the fukpunk he had seen shooting up under Waterloo Bridge, Emerna-A sores weeping where his studded necklet was rubbing. It was the heat; the sweat. The sun was blazing in from the glass wall to Kester's left and he was trapped in a wedge of sweltering light. The air-conditioning blew over him every few seconds, but only served to remind him how hot he was. He wanted to bare himself and stand beneath the unit, or open his shirt and press his chest and cheek to a cool, shaded portion of the giant window before him.

The three panel members sat in the shade, protected from the sunlight by a tall partition, backs to more glass. Looking at them was tiring. Avoid their visible skin and he had to look at their clothes. Their corporate clothing line was as busy with adverts and logos as any in the City. Kester wasn't used to holding conversations with people who were dressed this way, never mind who wore, though he saw people who did either or both all the time down by the Embankment. His eye was constantly drawn to the seams, pockets and panels that were given over to advertising: Brinkov, Virgin, Herschel, Sony, Smith & Smith. He moved his eyes away and focused between two of the interviewers on a slice of simple clear sky. V's London headquarters was the tallest building in the City and seated as they were on the top floor, there may as well have been nothing out there. They could have been sitting in a skyscraper in the desert.

Kester struggled to remember the questions he had noted down before the interview. Would V be the first company to produce wholly designer STVs? Would they continue to produce street-mods? Where was the growth in what was currently a niche market? How many wearable STVs did they hope to release within the department's first year?

'I'm interested to know a bit more about your motivation, Doctor Lowe.' Mrs Farrell's black tongue flashed as she spoke. 'There's a lot of money being poured into this new department and I need to know that the person running it is 100% behind V. Why do you want to work for us? This is a big move for an academic.'

'Yes, it is a big move. But then V is an extremely…by which I mean to say V is an extraordinarily…' Kester wished he'd had more time to prepare. This wasn't the informal chat he had been expecting. Department head was a senior role, but he felt like a grad trying to claw his way into an internship.

'I understand that scientists who move from the public to the private sector can sometimes come under scrutiny from their peers.'

'It's true. The truth is, Mrs Farrell, I'm a bit tired of – a bit dissatisfied with the package. I've spent seven years at the Institute and, put it this way, I'm currently working on a research project developing new viruses and...'

'Exactly what you trained for, I believe.'

'Yes and no. It's true my thesis was on viral design, I'm a virology expert, so yes they're my thing, but the viruses I'm developing now are...' Kester stopped himself. Many of the viruses were destined for the military arena or for social control. To explain his distaste for them would be to break the Official Secrets Act and risk court action or worse. 'They're boring...it's not what I wanted to do really.'

'Boring? Working at the Institute?' The fat man to Mrs Farrell's left finally broke his silence. 'I understand. Discretion is something we prize in our employees.'

His name and the name of the third panel member had slid through Kester's brain without leaving a trail, not a first letter, not a sound. Mrs Farrell, on the other hand, had stuck with Kester from the moment he had seen her image online. She was highly made up so that her age was hard to judge, but her picture was attractive, in an artificial sort of way. In person, in motion, she looked as if she had a stolen sweet in her mouth and was sucking on it, toying with it. If you could see past the logos, her tailored suit flattered her angular figure. From what Kester had heard about interviewing in the big City firms, he had better start seeing the sexy side of her quickly. If the rumours were true – he stopped and reined in his runaway thoughts – the rumours probably weren't true, but at least he had come prepared. And after all her hair was nice; her lips did look experienced.

'I notice you aren't wearing any viruses,' the third panel member said, running his eyes across Kester's visible surfaces. 'Not that I can see.'

'No. It's not really done in academia.'

'I know, I know. Just never understood it. Why wouldn't you? Nice international pool of ambitious people given the perfect excuse to shag.'

'To be honest, most people think it's vulgar to crack your nanoscreens.' Kester watched the thinner man to see his reactions. He betrayed none; just stared. 'And nobody uses the delay function on the latest generation screens. It's just not seen as attractive, so I suppose it's not worth the risks or the looking...diseased.'

This wasn't the right thing to be saying to a panel of habitual wearers. Mrs Farrell laughed.

'Some people,' Kester said, swallowing.

'Vulgar? To wear a street virus, perhaps, but to wear an exclusive, something that demonstrates that you're moving in the right circles...' Mrs Farrell smiled, shaking her head. 'How, then, would you demonstrate your success? By wearing an expensive suit? Surely that wouldn't be vulgar?'

She must know as well as him that academics couldn't afford to wear expensive clothes – not by her standards. Now that she was facing Kester head-on again, mouth closed, he wouldn't have known she was wearing. He stifled a bitter laugh and looked down into the lap of his weddings-and-funerals suit.

'No. I mean no, I wouldn't wear expensive clothes to show my status. In academia it's all about citations. Some of the super-competitive profs wear citation clickers round their necks – I don't suppose it's really fashion though and to be honest...'

'You wouldn't do that either?' the fat man asked.

'To be honest, sir, it's only impressive once you reach a certain stage in your career. If you find that sort of thing impressive.'

The fat man laughed to himself. He was wearing too. His eye-sockets were dark, purplish, a symptom of one of the newest mods out there. He was completely bald, must have alopecia Kester guessed, and the virus he was wearing had the unfortunate effect of making him look like a corpse, albeit a reasonably fresh one. Kester swallowed a shudder. The virus was too new for the interviewer to have gone to the Pigs to get it, which meant someone down the short chain from the commissioner must have actually slept with him. You had to give it to the new high-flyers; they were blind to beauty where power was involved. Of course he may have paid for it. Kester felt suddenly uneasy for thinking this right in front of the man. Don't judge, he thought; maybe he's a nice guy, a legend in the sack.

'So money is your motivator, Doctor Lowe,' Mrs Farrell said.

'Mostly.'

'Mostly.' She nodded slowly. 'Well, money isn't a bad motivator. It certainly means good performance in my experience.'

'It's not just money,' Kester added and shifted in his seat, drawing himself up, trying again to remember the notes he had scrawled the night before, 'it's the achievement.' All three of the interviewers seemed to speak only in perfectly-formed, polished sentences and it was making Kester feel like a madman on the rant, struggling with fractured theories. He took a deep breath and tried to explain. 'I've always liked making things, fiddling and adapting the existing to improve it or change it in interesting ways – and it's a big achievement when it works. Even those who are opposed to the current trends in biotechnology and soft nano are fascinated by what we are doing with disease. It may seem foreign to them, even wrong somehow, but that doesn't mean they don't appreciate the science behind it, the art of making it work – their faces…it's like seeing your father's Savile Row tailor looking at the latest Haute Couture Brinkov. They don't "get it" but they can still admire the artistry.'

'You've found your voice, Doctor Lowe. You get quite passionate when you're being honest, don't you?'

'Well, I enjoy success as much as anyone and, you know, the challenge of…creating something new.' Kester tensed. That was a lousy answer. He'd lost it again; he should have just said *yes*. Next time he'd just say *yes* confidently.

'Let's take a break,' Mrs Farrell said. 'I want to make a phone call.'

Kester smiled to contain his surprise as Farrell left the room. He sat squeezing his hands for a few minutes while the interviewers took some lazy notes on the panels in front of them. She wasn't making a call at all: he could hear her small-talking with someone in the open plan office beyond the sliding doors. Was he supposed to be able to hear her? She had him on a spit, had left him over the fire to see what happened. He took a deep breath to calm himself. He had to get out of his seat, had to get to the window. It was the closest he could get to leaving the room.

'May I?' he asked, leaning forward in his chair and indicating the window.

'Of course,' the large man replied with a smile. 'Hot, isn't it? You must excuse Alexis, by the way – interviews are a sort of hobby for her.'

'Not at all.' Kester got up from his chair and walked to the window. 'She wants to make sure I'm the right man for the job. That's fair enough.'

London rose up before Kester. He had never seen it this way

except in pictures and was struck by its geometry: concentric circles of ever taller buildings rippling out from the palace, a pebble dropped in the centre of the city. The buildings rose outwards and upwards from it, shaped into a scoop by line-of-sight laws and planning restrictions, and stopped at their highest point in a ring where the Green Belt began. London was a splintered splash of metal, stone and glass contained in a beaker.

The further out you came, the newer the buildings and the higher the towers. Laid out at Kester's feet was 'the City', London's finance and big business district. Here, there was evidence of frenetic building work, with the effect of the Green Belt multiplied by the constraints of the City's secure perimeter. Cranes leaned out from halfway up buildings, corseted in place, stratifying, building across and on top of existing structures; skeletons of buildings reached spindly into empty space, waiting to be fleshed. Canary Wharf, the Shard, the CloudCatcher had long since been swallowed into the illusion and the building bias towards the City set London on an eerie tilt.

As it extended outwards and upwards, the architecture grew more ostentatious in colour and form, jostling for attention. Each building strove to be unmistakeable in the skyline, some crafted into physical representations of logos, others so distinctive that they stood themselves as the company's identifier, many failing and becoming just another ledge in the bowl of construction, empty folding seats swallowed in the crowd. On a cloudy day it would resemble a renaissance vision of hell, but in today's raw sunshine it was a fabulous glittering stadium with towering stands and Kester was standing in the sponsor's box.

'Doctor Lowe.' Farrell was back.

Kester returned to his seat holding the City inside him, enlarged by it. Once Farrell had taken her seat, he smiled his most convincing smile, looking only at her. If he was to signal anything, now was the time. He hoped she couldn't see him bracing himself as he set to unbuttoning his cuffs. The two men craned forward and watched with greedy eyes as he rolled up his sleeves, doubtless expecting to see the symptom of some new virus. There was nothing. Pale, blue-veined flesh on the underside of each arm; delicate fair hair and freckles on the other. Kester was suddenly aware of his relative youth, his appearance – dishevelled hair, left its natural brown, soft-looking compared to the slick manes of the two hirsute panel members: cold silver, lion blonde; power colours. If only he had a strong nose, less button-like – he thought of his mother.

The second man on the panel looked up and leaned forward. Byron – the name returned to Kester. But Byron what? It was something that fitted with his appearance – Tall, Long, Haggard? He didn't look as if he was wearing, but Kester had noticed him scratching himself under the table from time to time. He had an oddly diseased look about him too. Perhaps it was his lean frame, or the fact that every few minutes he would raise a hand and whisk it around his head as if warding off flies or wafting incense. He slumped back in his chair, his lascivious smile fading as he realised that Kester's arms were bare.

'I may not be wearing anything today,' Kester said, smiling what he hoped was a reassuring smile, 'but I have brought a little something with me.' He rolled his sleeves up further, then clasped his hands tightly in front of him to steady their shaking. 'You can't see it on me because I have my nanoscreen set to suppress but not eliminate the infection. This keeps it present at a level which is useful for our purposes today but prevents it from presenting fully – like I said, I don't wear.' This was it. Kester swallowed and then looked up at Farrell. 'It doesn't present for a good thirteen hours, but I'm happy to share it with you.'

'Your balls are showing, young man,' Byron said, casting a glance at Mrs Farrell, his smile returning.

Kester's hands jerked in the direction of his flies. Diverting them at the last minute to his pockets, he laughed, too loud.

The two gentlemen had seen what they needed and left. Kester managed to shake each of their hands without visible recoil. Back at the window, he tried not to listen to their mumbling as they took leave of Mrs Farrell, talking about the timings of the following interview.

He stepped toes to the glass and looked down. There were few buildings on the edge of the City that were a single piece like this one. Kester knew a couple of people who worked in construction and they were always moaning about how hard it was to get permission to demolish the older buildings. Stratification was often the cheapest and quickest option. The V building was iconic because of its singularity and its prodigious height, not to mention the cantilever glass shelf that jutted out of the back of the building overlooking the Green Belt and the conurbation beyond. Kester had seen it in umpteen pop videos. He toyed with the feeling of vertigo as he looked down. Shifting his weight forward, he let patterns emerge in the movements of the dots below, people, all uniform at this distance. The glass was spotless, near absent, and the air-con created the illusion of a breeze; he felt at any moment he might fall.

'Well, now.'

Kester jumped. Farrell was right behind him. He turned to face her and she put an arm out on either side, hands against the window.

'Shall we pick a spot?'

He was an insect trapped within glass, against glass.

'I meant a description.' Kester glanced side to side for an escape route. 'When I said I could share it with you I meant I could show you my concept notes.'

'No you didn't.'

'I've got my notes here – if I can just get my Book.' Kester slid his back down the glass, ducked out from underneath her arm and dashed over to his bag. Picking it up he sat back down and put it on his lap, beginning to rummage in self defence.

'Did I get rid of the others for nothing? Why not show me properly? Or would you prefer I call one of them back? No problem. Who's it to be?'

Kester fumbled his Book out of his bag.

'No, thank you, I don't –'

'You don't go both ways? I suppose you think that's alternative do you? Not religious are you?'

Kester looked down at his Book and pressed his thumb to the base panel to switch it on. In the bright light its transparent body was made solid by smears and fingerprints. He ignored Farrell's jibes.

Taking his Book in one hand and wiping it on his trouser leg, he continued, 'I don't think it's a good idea. It takes more than half a day to present and much longer to reach full virulence and you don't want to be waiting around to make a decision. You don't want to expose yourself to something not knowing what it will look like. I could have anything.'

'Come on, Doctor Lowe, this is the '80s. I have a nanoscreen like everyone else.'

Kester felt himself shrink. She said *Doctor Lowe* as if she were a lawyer; the opposition's lawyer.

'Call me Kester.'

'Kester,' she said his name with a kick, violently. She smiled at it as if it were quaint, a nickname. She stalked around the desk and perched on its front edge, directly in front of him.

'With all respect, your nanoscreen can't recognise this virus unless I give you the uploads.'

'Which you will. Which you wouldn't travel without.' Mrs Farrell stared at Kester until he looked away. 'These make you uncomfortable,' she said with a patronising smile, indicating the sores on her neck, and then untied her vanilla hair so that it flowed down over her shoulders, covering them.

Kester clasped his hands and glanced down at his Book. The base part of his brain was taking over. She was older than him, probably knew a few tricks. This was so wrong.

'You'd better not be one of these types who comes in boasting and has nothing to deliver.'

'No, I've just put it on this morning, it's new. But like I said, it won't present on me.'

'We've got other people crying out for this position.' Farrell smirked.

Distracted by his Book again, Kester was caught off-guard. 'I know – but I'm the best. Wait until you see...' He realised that his hands had stopped shaking.

'Oh, finally a bit of real confidence.' Mrs Farrell pulled off her cravat and pinched open the first few buttons of her shirt.

'I don't want to boast.'

'I want you to boast. You're supposed to be boasting – this is an interview. Everyone boasts and most people lie. You're not lying to me are you?' She loosened the tie at the top of her culottes.

'No, I swear, I've done private trials.'

'Private trials!' She giggled at the lewd connotations like a girl, and then turned serious. 'You're not screwing with me?'

'No.'

'Not yet.' Her mood flicked again into aggressive flirtation. The front of her culottes slid down, revealing a flat creamy stomach.

Along the seam of each leg, running up from the corners of her Hollywood to the top of her hips, was the shadow of a line of sores, together making a proud V, a deliberate exaggeration of her shape. 'I'm a company girl.' She nodded at her naked groin.

Kester was burning up despite himself. He forced himself to look her in the eye and left his chair. As he stood, the cityscape rose back into view, its tilt making him feel as if he was falling towards her. With her hair down, Mrs Farrell's face was softer. She batted her eyelids like a cartoon and held out one hand towards him.

'Come closer. You won't see them,' she said. She flicked the crumpled front panel of her culottes down over the edge of the desk, exposing herself completely.

Kester felt his focus narrowing, his mind shutting out all other concerns. He walked forward and felt her hand slide round behind his neck, pulling him faster towards her. The city swelled up, breaking against the skyline. Kester's body was in conflict: sinking stomach, rising erection. This was so wrong. She pulled his head forward and down until her lips were at his ear and his eyes looking straight down the front of her shirt. Wrong in such a teenage way.

'It doesn't bother you,' Kester mumbled into her hoisted-up bosom, 'mixing business with pleasure?'

'At V, business *is* pleasure.'

Kester let out a strangled laugh and lumped his hands to her waist as she grappled with his trousers.

'Damn these old-fashioned flies.' They had ruined her practised routine. She laughed as she undid his belt and fumbled with his button and zip. 'You protecting something special behind this fortress?'

'I hope so.' Kester lifted his head. Committed now to a cause, if not the one he'd walked through the door for, he kissed her hard on the lips.

'Oh.' Farrell started back as if he had broken some unspoken rule of interview, and then recomposed herself. 'Bold.' She laughed, slid his trousers down over his hips and yanked him in close. 'We need to get you down to our corporate tailor for something a little more easy-access.' Reaching down, she found what she was looking for, found she'd had the usual effect and smiled. She wriggled forward, sliding her other hand to the base of his back, kissing him in return as she lined herself up professionally. 'Much more easy access.' She smiled like a predator.

'That's if I get – oah!' Kester's mouth left him as their hips clattered together. The interview had all been foreplay to her.

'If you get the job,' she finished his sentence, hooking her sinewy legs up behind his back and constricting around him.

-o-

Kester had had sex before, but not under interview conditions.

'That's just it, Mum. There isn't much to share.' It rather cut down on how straight he could be with his mother. 'I think I impressed her – impressed them I mean – but you never know with these things, do you?'

There was rain coming from somewhere. Kester quickened his pace – he was almost at the Bloom. The bulging glass structure would provide temporary shelter from the rain. As he drew closer, his eye was drawn by the dark rocket at its centre; what used to be the Gherkin was now its kernel, a building within a building, completely visible only from one angle, as if the Bloom was a great glass fruit with a segment cut out.

'You know how well you've performed, Kester.' His Mum always voiced a belief in him that went way beyond reason.

'I suppose…'

He paused at the edge of the Bloom's North entrance and gazed down the promenade of shops and bars that curled away round the ground floor.

'And you will have done well. You always do.'

Kester's Book beeped, registering the ad he'd stopped beside. *ALL NEW LADYSQUEAL AT THE BLOOM 55!* Finally, the Pigs were catering to women. Below the tagline on his Book's display popped up a list of eight viruses that were loaded for sale. Some were classics and some were new, commissions for which the exclusivity contracts had lapsed.

'Nobody does well all the time, Mum.'

Kester looked up at the full size ad. A businesswoman rodeo-riding a mechanical pig. The smell of rubber filled Kester's nostrils, an olfactory memory bursting open like a nasty liqueur sweet.

'*You* do, Kester. Don't talk yourself down.'

Kester made a noise. He was back in the branch of the Pigs he had visited as a teen tourist, green from his life outside London: close pink rubber walls, a grubby plasma screen above a hole in the wall, a stack of rubber blocks to stand on, worn grab-handles.

His mother took his silence as the need for more encouragement. 'You're the best at what you do, Kester.'

When he'd visited the Pigs there had been nothing to catch; it was just a quick release for the oversexed and the undesirable, for gentlemen who tired of the palm. Kester snorted to expunge the smell from his nostrils. He had only done it for a dare.

'I said, you're the best at what you do.'

'Mum, I'm not the best – I'm good, but you know. You never know who you're up against.' Kester had a little smile to himself. Mrs Farrell would have liked that one.

'You, Kester, are creative – you always have been – and I'll bet that's what they see in you.'

Kester laughed at the idea that creativity might have anything to do with his success or otherwise. It had been more a case of the classic quickie – pretty functional. Then again, it had been popping up in his brain like a forgotten set of keys ever since. Popping in and out. A sudden flush and he got all muddled; he could hear Farrell's hair, smell her hands. He looked back up at the rodeo-riding executive, then walked on.

'You're not just one of these lab people,' his mum said. 'You've got it all going on up there.'

'Lab people?'

'Like those folk of yours at the Institute.'

'Those are my friends! They're good people.'

'They're good lab people.'

'Oh come on, Mum, apart from Dee you've only met them two or three times.'

'That's right and I thought they were perfectly nice lab people.'

'Mum, *I* work in a lab – I'm a lab person.'

It's not that calling someone a lab person was particularly offensive. She could have been calling them anything – it was the way she said it. Kester had heard her use it with all sorts of job titles, from sales attendant to managing director, and she could make all of them sound like they were just playing at work. He could imagine the look on her face, as if she had tasted them and found them sour.

'Mum, some of those lab people are eminent scientists – far better than me!'

Kester was aware of a few passersby looking at him. He thought initially that their attention had been drawn by his tone, but then he noticed that before each person looked at his face, their eyes were darting up and down his body, automatically scanning for logos and ads, and failing to find them.

'Hm. We'll see about that, when you've got a top floor office in the tallest building in the City and they're still plugging away in the old world.' She flitted onto her favourite subject. 'How is Delilah?'

'I keep telling you, Mum, it's Dee now. She hates Delilah.'

'Well, it's the name her father gave her and Lord knows that man knew what was what.'

Kester recalled his mother's admiration for their neighbours' memorabilia collection and the mortification it caused Dee. How her father's judgement had any bearing on whether Delilah liked her name or not was a mystery to Kester.

'Delilah will keep you on the straight and narrow. She's good for you, you know.'

'Mum, how many times, she's just a friend.' Kester emerged from the other side of the Bloom to a fleeting dry spell.

'Can't friends be good for one another?'

'Yes, I suppose so.'

'So, what will you be doing in this new job?'

Kester toyed with the idea of trying to explain to his mother what it was he was going to do and then dismissed it.

'It's pretty much the same as I do now, Mum.'

'Oh I see, good…that's good, isn't it?'

'Yes, Mum.' Kester knew she had never got farther than the title of his thesis, but it touched him that she wanted to understand.

'Yes, pretty much the same but with better money, better perks, better location, better everything really.'

'Better lab people?'

'Better colleagues?' Kester hummed and hawed. 'That remains to be seen.'

'I'm so proud of you Kester! Give my love to Delilah. Bye, darling.'

The phone call ended abruptly, as they always did. His mother had got what she wanted from the conversation, so that was the end of it. It irked him sometimes, but not today.

Kester's mind wandered, blurring time as he weaved through the streets to the Blackfriars City checkpoint. This morning, walking through the City towards V, he had had a curious shrinking feeling as the buildings around him increased in height almost exponentially. Now it was he who grew as the City fell away, becoming larger than himself, dwarfing the buildings around him.

The checkpoint had been fashioned from an old archway, rescued in pieces from the rubble after the riots in the early part of the Century. It was one of the largest of the City boundary checkpoints, a classic example of the fusion of old and new, stone and glass, that dominated the aesthetics of the City and a neat reminder of why the City had been securitised in the first place. Kester glanced up as he passed under the archway and caught sight of a plaque showing a list of dates: 1840 – the building of the original archway; 2017 – the year it was burned down; 2047 – the year the permanent checkpoint was erected. He passed through the wide glass doors. They would close automatically if there were ever a break in the stream of pedestrians.

Up ahead, there was a scream. There was a temporary hush and everyone looked towards the source – a man trapped in the barriers.

'I've had a haircut!' screamed the man, before launching into a tirade about securitisation.

He gripped the top of the barrier, holding himself up as his legs failed, their muscles disabled by an invisible NTS beam, triggered when the bioscanner failed to recognise him. Two guards, holding Bruzless batons, marched through the crowd to the barriers and dragged the offender to a door at the side of the hall. There was a thick wave of snuffing and humfing and the commuters continued on through the barriers.

Kester readied his Book as he approached the barriers, paranoid that it wouldn't be read. A brief tone sounded between his biometrics being scanned and the barriers registering the pass on his Book, but the two were matched in a split second and Kester passed through without incident as he always did.

Out of the City, Kester headed down to the river and back west towards the Institute. Under Blackfriars Bridge the fukpunk he had seen earlier was in a deep sleep, crouched, his knees drawn up in front of him, his coloured clothes and hair making him look like a dejected bird, a piece of totem pole sawn off and abandoned.

At the edge of the underpass a few more fukpunks were gathered, a different gang, either more careful or more experienced in their narcotics dosage. Two of the five were bare-chested, showing rashes creeping up from their low waistbands. They looked like twins, had the same side-ways Mohican and bandaged fingertips. The other three were dressed variously in studs and leather with strategically placed PVC windows. They must be hardcore – the viruses weren't even mods, just plain STVs and street mutes that had been going round for donkeys'. Kester shuddered as he noticed a green smear on the window of one boy's transparent crotch-piece. He just didn't get it. They were passing round a bottle of Quicksilver. No wonder. The street drugs they used as painkillers were generations behind those the City wearers used. He looked away as he passed them.

'Fucking nouveau-pox!' one of them shouted.

Kester jumped and took a small skip out of his path as another spat at him.

'What?' he replied involuntarily, hurrying on.

'Where's your pansy bracelet?'

Puzzled, Kester looked down at himself and noticed he was still wearing his V visitor pass.

'Right,' he said, unclipping it and sticking it in his pocket. They'd never do anything to him, but better to walk the rest of the way back in peace.

-o-

Alexis Farrell darkened the glass partition between her office and the rest of the floor.

You'll feel queasy, Doctor Lowe had warned her.

The room was still set up for interview, the desk still in disarray. She walked unsteadily across the floor to the side wall where a concealed door led to her apartment. It sensed her approach and slid back to allow her through. She kept on walking across the wide, glass-fronted room, closing her arms around her body and squeezing her triceps in her sweaty palms.

The light faded up in the wet-room. Farrell flicked a manual switch by the large mirror above her dressing counter. An arch of old-style light bulbs spluttered into life around the edge of the mirror, creating little white windows in the pupils of her eyes. She looked pale. Did she look pale? She put a hand up to the soft surface of her image and watched the small pressure rainbows pulse at her fingertips. Whatever the virus, this happened – the sudden sideways push of anxiety leaving her dissociated, nauseous. It would pass, leaving the real symptoms behind; she knew that, but she couldn't switch off the fear. She automatically pinched the band around her wrist, releasing a pain-relieving shot, though Kester had assured her she wouldn't need it.

At least this time she knew what was happening to her. Alexis clung to this thought and forced herself to remember.

The virus infects only the cells in the border area between your irises and the whites of your eyes – it can't unlock the neighbouring cells, so it's self-limiting.

Alexis had concealed her horror. Her eyes?

In any case I've programmed in a forced rapid shift which means that any tertiary viruses revert fully to the inert form in which they are unable to reproduce. It's also very stable which means the chances of it throwing up a mutation that can spread further are beyond negligible.

She leaned in to the mirror. Her eyes felt different. Did her eyes feel different? She could feel the muscle movements as her focus shifted, could see her pupils contract as she moved closer to the lights.

You'll only need the uploads if you want to reverse or arrest the effect, or if you don't wish to remain infectious; no more cells will be infected or damaged once the effect has presented. And I only work with tissues that can regenerate fully to their pre-infected state so there's no fallout and no scarring. You may experience a blurring of your vision, but it will pass. It's just your irises recalibrating their muscular movement to account for the altered cells – the body's pretty clever like that.

Was her vision blurred? When would it blur? He hadn't said. She breathed in for the count of four, out for nine, in for four, out for nine, willing herself to calm down.

You'll notice bloodspots first, just around your irises. The virus needs to destroy some cells to reproduce – it uses these first cells as factories, which burst, releasing more viruses into your system, but like I said, after three rounds, when the viruses reach their inert form, all they do is enter the cell, express the genes we've programmed them to and remain there. It's a small area and a limited population of viruses so there won't be much bleeding. The effect will wear off gradually as your cells regenerate. The bloodspots will quickly be disguised by the effect in most people and will probably be gone within a day or two.

Alexis looked up at her eyes again. The first bloodspots were appearing in a ring around her irises.

'Oh my god.' She shook her head.

This is really a small-scale demonstration of my approach – once the virus gets stuck in, it will do its work very quickly. I just think that viral displays…well they should be attractive, you know, like the displays of birds.

Sleep was what she needed. Sleep, the only thing that could shut down her anxiety and reset her body to its default. She lay flat on her hard mattress and tapped her Book to black out the windows. It could have been her first time; the corrosive whole-head scent of freshly chlorined public toilets gushed into Farrell's mind, taking her back:

Cold porcelain on the heels of her hands, the burn of a rash rising on her thighs and forearms, a deep itch. In the mirror, Gaunt's reflection behind hers, amused; his Sabotage aftershave, scent of the '70s, flowing out of his sleeve and up over her shoulders, warm and sickening against the rough background of chlorine; his hand steady between her shoulder blades, its heat and weight bleeding through her suit jacket, building like that of an iron left sitting at a child's scream. She had let loose at him.

'Whose fucking idiot idea was all this? This is miserable. Getting yourself on the proof pages is fun – screwing on a helipad, seducing an idiot fatcat – that's fun – this is fucking miserable. Some bored alpha-cock thinks it's a good idea to show you he's been screwing by cracking his nanoscreen like a fukpunk and cutting the crotch out of his Armani and a bunch of other alpha-cocks are impressed by his spotted dick flapping in the wind.'

An acid upward trickle in her gullet; a dry-retch.

'And all because some geek hacker teen fuckwit wants to prove to his mates he's had sex.'

Gaunt had laughed and rubbed her back. 'Well you bought into sex is success, Alexis, just like the rest of us, just like that fine young geek. Why would you be screwing fatcats on helipads otherwise?'

Her throat opening like a forced valve; the splatter of half-digested coleslaw.

Alexis shook her head to clear the memory and employed her

breathing again.

Even the enforced night of the black-out couldn't convince her body to sleep. She stroked her forehead, set the bed to vibrate, counted. She pressed her fingertips against her eyelids and watched as geometric patterns pulsed and churned in the red darkness. Each time she checked the clock, only a few minutes had passed. It was hours since the blood-spots had appeared. In her mind they had grown, they had taken over her eyeballs, she was weeping blood.

Eventually, she gave up trying to distract herself, raised the lighting and walked quickly back to the bathroom. As she approached, she could see that something had changed. Her eyes looked dark from a distance. Her heart rattled. It was blood.

She paused as if unsure whether she wanted to see, then closed her eyes and walked on towards the mirror. As she felt herself drawing close, she reached out. Her fingertips bumped gently against cold marble. She dragged them upwards and slid her hands onto the surface, stepping forward until the cool edge of the sink unit pressed against her belly.

I can make these things better. If they're going to make an impact on the high fashion market, or even the high street market, they've got to be different from what you can pick up on the streets.

Taking a few breaths, Alexis opened her eyes.

They've got to be beautiful.

Chapter 2

Kester watched Dee. She was staring into her coffee. When she disagreed with Kester, or when he had offended her in some way, which he frequently did without knowing how, she grew dry and pale. Right now, she was made of paper-thin porcelain. If he hit her with his teaspoon she would smash like a china mask. There would be nothing inside but cold air and dust.

He recalled a conversation they'd had years ago, before leaving for different universities, the feeling that something hadn't been said, or that he had missed something. She'd had the same look about her then, as if she was thinking, but had left her body and ascended somewhere else to do it. There had been an unusual juicer machine on the counter behind her in the student bar and he had sat, trying to figure out its inner workings, waiting for her to finally explain to him what she was thinking.

She never had. She had spotted what he was doing and they'd had an argument about how he never listened. But Kester had tried listening and had never heard her say anything that helped him understand her better. When they ended up both working at the Institute, Dee's smugness was apparent, as if she had somehow engineered the situation, or as if it was inevitable and only Kester couldn't see this: she had won some unspoken argument begun years ago in a student bar that had a stupid juicer machine.

'Kester...' Dee stirred her coffee and looked past Kester for a moment. 'What are you doing?'

Kester blew on his tea and took a cautious sip. She was going to let him know what she was thinking, this time. A good start.

'Why are you leaving – why are you going there?'

It was less than forty-eight hours since Kester's interview on Wednesday. V had called first thing on Thursday morning to offer him the job. After pretending to consider it for half a day, he had accepted, and by Friday lunchtime he had handed in his notice at the Institute. Though he was between secondments and there was nothing sensitive at the lab, he was still expected to leave immediately. Dee had disappeared on Thursday after hearing about the offer and had only just resurfaced as he was about to leave the lab for good.

'Well,' Kester said, and then he paused. He had known that Dee would take it the worst. People were leaving the Institute all the time to make the move to the private sector and while she never openly criticised them, he could tell that she disapproved. She was never quite as happy for them as the others, who often congratulated their departing colleagues as if they'd effected a grand escape. 'The money is better.'

Dee let out a long breath, deflating and sinking back into her chair, arms reaching forward, hands still cradling her coffee cup.

'And things are changing out there, Dee. We live in a bubble at the Institute. I swear nothing has changed inside these walls since 2010. But out there, there's lots to do, lots to be a part of.'

'Like what?' Dee had a wry smile on her small mouth.

She had a great knack of making you feel like she was intellectually superior, but compared to the people Kester had met since he'd started job hunting in the private sector she was naïve. And she seemed younger. Kester looked at her clothes. They were grown up, but her look had never quite lost the high-street fashion feel of their student days. She looked unprofessional – smart enough, but not...he couldn't put his finger on it. The people in the City looked sharp, crisp, like freshly printed flyers. They had clean edges, their clothes were expensive, tailored, and they just seemed more adult.

'You can't think of anything, can you?'

'Business.'

'Business?' Dee gave a soft snort.

'What do you think keeps the City afloat – keeps this whole country running? Public money? No – it's business. That's an interesting thing to be a part of.'

'But we help people here.'

'Businesses help people.'

'Please – the kind of business you're scrabbling to get into?'

'I'm not scrabbling. But yes, those businesses help people as a matter of fact. There's demand for their product.'

'That's not the same thing.'

'Anyway, who said we help people at the Institute? You know where I was supposed to be seconded to next; you know where the diseases from our department are headed for; you know what they're used for –'

'For the good of the world; for keeping populations under control and keeping the peace.'

'Wow. The marketing department has done one on you. Are you sure you didn't get your doctorate on the blacknet?'

'Ha ha.' Dee took a sip of her coffee and failed to suppress a sneer. 'Fair dos; I suppose *your* track record isn't exactly grounds for a humanitarian award.' She sighed and shook her head. 'It's just I always thought we'd do it, you know?'

Kester was thrown for a moment.

'Make the next generation of screens, like we always talked about.'

'Oh.'

'Look.'

Dee was taking something out of her pocket; a piece of paper, folded down small. She unfolded it on the table between them, handling it as if it were an ancient treasure map. Kester felt a pulse of shock: there was his handwriting. It was the A3 sheet of paper they had covered with their ideas during their first planning session.

He let his eyes wander over the page. It started out serious, a statement of intent. Their screen would be different to Stark Wellbury's. It would be compatible with the human immune system and would not require immunosuppressants. Towards the right hand side of the page, their attention had turned to technical detail: lists of the hard nano components of the Stark Wellbury screens and what they did, a close-up sketch of how the binding sites on their sweeper cells opened up, breaching the diamond coating that made them otherwise invisible to the body.

At this point the page started to look more chaotic – pint glass rings and a couple of dried spills, one transformed by a doodle of a palm tree into a desert island, brought the atmosphere of the bar rushing back into Kester's head. Next to Dee's sketch of the binding site was some of Kester's own artwork, clearly added later in the evening – a cartoon immunoglobin pointing at the open binding site and crying out, 'Antigen! Antigen! Call the B cells!'

On the bottom right hand corner of the page, which had been ripped and stuck back together was more of his handiwork in the form of a shaky cartoon depicting the body and the screen as a kung fu master and his cocky young apprentice.

Kester was shocked that Dee still had this. They had carried on their planning in earnest in their spare time and had applied unsuccessfully for funding on several occasions, but he'd forgotten this document even existed. There was a date written in the corner by which Dee had predicted nanoscreens would be affordable and available to everyone, not just the rich, keyworkers and City residents. It had long since passed. In the last year or so their planning sessions had fallen off, though Dee was always trying to spur Kester on.

'This is what was missing.' Kester took the paper from her and raised it up, balanced on his fingertips like an ancient artifact. He felt Dee's gaze intensify. 'All those funding applications.' He widened his eyes and held the paper out to her. 'If *this* had been on the front page...'

'Come on, Kester.' Dee snatched the paper from him and put it back down on the table. 'This is our dream. You're just going to give up on it?'

Kester stared at Dee's face. Was it real disappointment? Did she really think they would have done it, or would she just miss the discussions?

'You know no-one would ever fund it.'

'Why not? Just because no-one has stepped up yet doesn't mean they never will.'

'Dee – that's exactly what it means and you know why. The screens are big business for the companies involved.'

'And the government? What's to say they won't see sense and step in?'

'Come on. The Minister for Health is on the Board at Stark Wellbury – and legitimately too. I mean the whole reason he's there is to look after the government's interest, but you know he's corrupt.'

'This was our thing Kester; this is what we're here for. We could change things. It's not right, everybody being dependent on one company's drugs.'

'And that's why we have deregulation – soon they'll have a

choice. Plus, not everyone is dependent any more.'

'Right, you mean the people who have been on them so long their systems are shot. Nice.'

'Look, Dee.' Kester could feel his voice getting prickly. 'I would love to do it more than anything in the world – Doctor Dee the immunologist; Doctor Kester the virologist, saving the world together – but it's just not going to happen, I'm telling you. The only way would be to make the money ourselves and set up on our own – and who makes that sort of money?'

'Just…' There was a potent mix of frustration and disappointment in Dee's tone. 'Just help me do one last funding application – this could be the one.'

'Dee, I can't. I mean I can help you with the application, but I can't stay. And anyway, they've said I can do my own research in my own time. I'll have great resources at V, so maybe this is my best shot. I can start working on it in the evenings. Maybe I could get you a pass – we could still do it together.'

'Don't be so naïve, Kester – those bloodsuckers won't let you take an unscheduled piss. And you think I would be seen dead working there?'

'Dee…'

They sat in silence for a few minutes, sipping their drinks.

'Enough.' Dee folded up the paper, stowed it away, sipped her coffee and grimaced again. 'This tastes like dog-ends. Let's get out of here.'

Without waiting for a reply, she got up and unhooked her jacket from the back of her chair.

'Where are you going?' Kester tried to balance the annoyance in his voice: enough to let her know how he felt; not enough to send her off into one of her rages.

'Come on. Come with me and you'll see.'

'Are you going to show me something to make me change my mind?'

'Ha ha, Kester. Change your mind? With that pay cheque on the table.'

'How do you know about the pay deal?'

Dee fiddled with the fastenings on her jacket, pausing a little too long before replying.

'You're the one who's been telling me all about how much better it is.'

'It sounded like you know how much I'm getting.'

'Well…'

'Has my mother been calling you again?'

Dee smiled half-heartedly and shook her head. She took a breath and then relaxed, putting a hand on the back of her chair.

'I don't mind it really,' she said.

'Dee, I'm so sorry. You know what she's like. She gets an idea in her head and she just won't let it go.'

'It's not a problem.' Dee's eyes wandered. 'I sort of like it.'

There was a pause. Kester had known Dee for long enough to know that the pause meant something, but he had no idea what.

'Come on then, get your jacket on,' she said. 'If you want to know where I'm going, you'll have to come with me.'

'Who's going to be there?' Kester said, standing up and pulling on his jacket. 'Is it a pub? Are the guys coming? Will Raph be there?'

Dee's form stuttered and froze as if she was buffering. Surely not another casualty. Kester was just getting to know Raph. He was a great guy, but there had been some drama over him wanting to take a female friend to a Graphene Skin gig and Dee wanting to go with him instead. Kester had done his fair share of listening and nodding. But Dee didn't even like the band and the girl was just a friend. He couldn't see anything in it.

'Did he take you to the gig in the end?' Kester asked. He should duck and cover.

'He didn't take anyone to the gig,' Dee said. She smiled and looked pleased with herself. 'I hacked his account and sold the tickets to a nice man called GigMunky360. He didn't find out until too late. He didn't have anything to wear anyway – I donated his Graphene Skin t-shirt to Aldo to shred up for his lab rats. They were short on bedding.'

'And that's that?' Kester asked.

'Come on – let's go.'

-o-

Dee led Kester away from the Embankment where they always

drank. They walked along Surrey Street and up onto the Strand. She loved this part of the city. It felt like it had stood forever. The buildings were unchanged except by the slow stroke of human presence, moulding objects in its path as a river shapes its rocks. The smoothness of worn banisters under her hands thrilled her. The steps here dipped in the middle, worn away by generations of feet carrying enquiring minds through the streets; minds thinking of who knows what – cures, new technologies, problems and solutions. She felt the presence of all those people, all that knowledge all around her, as if the buildings had memories. They were always warm.

The further they got towards the City, the newer the buildings became. The paving slabs were blank slates, sharp-edged and clean. They knew nothing that Dee cared to learn. Every now and again a small old building, protected by law, nestled in between the ever-heightening glass structures; crumpled old men in spanking new bus stations, settled, looking at their shoes or their bottles, unaware of their incongruity. They were mostly pubs, the occasional jeweller's.

As they walked, Dee felt herself grow warmer, her cheeks flushed against the cold. Kester was talking about her next funding proposal. She only half listened as he trawled over old ground, commenting on where they might have gone wrong in the past. And suddenly, there it was: 'this time,' he was saying, 'our proposal', 'we', 'us'. She smiled to herself. She nodded and interjected now and again, without upsetting his momentum. If he was still thinking like this he could still be persuaded. He wouldn't go. He would bottle it.

Eventually, a digression sent Kester off into a long monologue about his most recent project. Work – proper work – it bored her. If it wasn't about their screens, their baby, she wasn't interested.

Perhaps there should be something else to talk about when the working day was over, but they only ever talked about their research, occasionally about Kester's mother, sometimes about stuff they did when they were kids. Something was missing. What did other people talk about? When she saw couples in restaurants, with fruitful faces, gabbling as if they had so much to cover, what were they talking about? What could they be saying that was so interesting for so long? They weren't talking about work. But then she and Kester weren't a couple, never mind how much his mother acted like they were.

They approached the City checkpoint. Dee braced herself.

Despite working in the City for one or two clients, she never got used to the place. It didn't seem to bother the others. They seemed comfortable enough there, even taking advantage of their passes to frequent the bars.

Kester walked through the barriers ahead of her, looking suddenly awkward as he always did when faced with security. He stopped on the other side and waited for Dee, giving her a series of exaggerated baffled looks.

'Where are you taking me?' he asked.

Dee shrugged, raised her eyebrows and shouldered past him towards the exit.

Out on the street she went onto automatic pilot, defocusing her eyes, seeing only the shapes of people as they approached, the fuzzed impression of their ad-splattered clothing, the occasional striking logo shining through. It was a dance; her shoulders swivelled back and forth, leaving skelfs of air between her and those she passed. Every now and again a quick skip and ball-change prevented a collision. She was aware of Kester bumping along behind her, apologising frequently. How he could handle all that interaction with the wearers was a mystery to her.

An image flashed into her head: her first meeting in the City. The client had been wearing an oral form of some newly modified virus and there were dry sores extending out of the corners of his mouth, giving him a sinister exaggerated smile. She could still feel it: his firm handshake pulling her forward; the scrape of the sores on her cheeks as he planted a kiss on one then the other; the rawness of her skin where that night she had scrubbed it with her nail-brush. If the City wearers had been anywhere near as extreme as the fukpunks and the S&M crew, their bits hanging out all over the place, she wouldn't have been able to come here.

The crowds gradually thinned as they gained distance from the checkpoint and Kester caught up and fell in stride with Dee. They walked in silence for a while, past St Paul's, down Cheapside, and then up Wood Street. A strip of bars had sprung up there for the City workers. Since the City had been securitised and in-living had become the norm, they were open 24 hours a day. The City was now a residential centre again and no longer ceased to exist out of hours; it was always alive, always exciting. The rumours about what went on there were wild.

'Can you believe it about Stark Wellbury?' Kester said, breaking the silence.

'What about them?' They were back onto screen-talk.

'What?' Kester broke stride and started skipping along sideways beside her. 'You didn't read the news this morning? It's finally out – what all that scaffolding was about.'

'What?' Dee remembered some gossip about the front of the Stark building.

'It's a wall of exchange booths, glass-fronted, facing out onto Toulouse square.'

'What?'

'They've gone all theatrical. It's like a massive marketing thing I think. I can't believe you didn't see the reports. It's like some crazed Harvey Nicks window display.

'Every member of staff has to be seen to have sex with a different partner, and a powerful partner relative to them, every day – and I mean literally seen. Think of the size of the offices – that's got to be ten booths across and maybe...I don't know how many up the way.

'Apparently the policy is that they can be used at any time, but every hour on the hour they all have to be occupied at once. That's got to be hundreds of couples at it in the side of that building, twenty-four times a day, seven days a week. How much sex is that? I can't even do that sum.'

Dee stopped and looked at Kester for a minute. He looked impressed by what he had just described. The whole idea of exchange booths, private never mind public, sent an acid burn to the back of her sinuses.

'No,' she said. 'No you're not feeding me this one. It's got to be a publicity stunt or – it's probably a hoax.'

'Come on, who would make this stuff up? It only just opened this morning, but it's already all over the net. It's there for anyone to go and have a gander. And get this – the hourly exchanges are all precisely timed so before and afterwards the rooms are steamed and super-heated all at once and the side of the building glows hell-red for a good thirty seconds. You'll be able to tell the time by it. Apparently.'

'You're talking out of your arse, Kester. I've never heard such –'

'I can't believe you haven't heard about it.'

'Bollocks, bollocks, bollocks.' Dee looked up and saw that they had reached their destination.

He wouldn't be expecting this. She turned off towards the bar and walked through the scattered, empty tables that sat out in the cold. Kester stopped behind her.

'You really don't believe me? You know, after what I've seen –'

'Does it sound like I believe you?' Dee asked. He was spoiling it already. 'I mean I know that some pretty weird shit goes on in the City, but walls full of shagging people? Come off it.'

'I expect they do have to get quite a lot of cum off it.' Kester braced himself to get hit.

'Kester!' Dee made a disgusted face and took a swipe at him with her bag.

What a shit he was. She allowed herself a small laugh. It brightened her mood again. They stood looking at one another for a minute or so. He was so transparent. He was thinking of telling her something, saying something else stupid, confessing something maybe, but he didn't. With a small shake of his head it was gone and she pretended she hadn't seen it.

Dee looked up at the entrance to the bar: a flaming archway enclosed in glass. Inside was a mosaic of logoed shirts, coiffured hair, and hands holding glasses of champagne. It was just like any other bar, she told herself, hot air, laughter and jostling movement.

'We're going in here?' Kester asked.

Dee nodded and smirked.

'Are you trying to teach me some lesson?'

Dee ran back to him and grabbed his hand. A shiver ran up her arm to her throat as their palms slotted together. It stayed, a fluttering thrill in her gullet. If it helped him to see the grotesque nature of the world he was headed for, it would be worth spending some time close to the wearers.

She dragged him almost at a run through the doorway into the stifling air of the bar, weaving under armpits and squeezing between sweaty backs. Everyone in the place was wearing. There were rashes, sores, shadowy eyes, red eyes, tufty hair. It was like midsummer party in the plague ward. She held her breath as they made their way to the back of the bar. There, the crowd cleared a little. She led Kester through an archway into a small back-room.

They were met with screams and hollers. Tucked around a

circular table, clambering up, running towards him, were their friends from the department, silly on champagne and dressed up in shirts and ludicrous ties. They all sported faked symptoms: Betta had a big red nose, John had his hands painted purple, Sienna had bright red spots all over, and Calvin wore a swimming-cap with tufts of his hair pulled through. Kester burst out laughing.

Betta ran over. She kissed and hugged him.

'We thought we'd let you know what you're in for!' she squealed and pushed a glass of champagne into his hand. 'Enjoy it.' She laughed and took a gulp out of her own glass. 'This represents the whole of the tea and biscuits collection for the next six months, so you'd better be grateful!'

Betta lurched and Kester put an arm around her. He looked round at Dee. She shrugged and smiled.

'Dee.' He reached out a hand towards her. 'You?'

'My plan, but everyone really. Dressing up was John's idea – surprise.'

They both glanced over at John. He was swaggering and talking loudly about some imaginary deal he'd done.

'My god, how long have they been here?'

'Well I was trying to get you out of the café for the best part of two hours.'

'And where's your costume?'

'Aha!' Dee beamed. She unfastened her heavy coat, turned away from him for a moment, and then turned back, her shirt unbuttoned to her cleavage, revealing her boobs covered in stick-on scabs. 'Ta dah!' she said proudly. 'I brought you some scabs too.' She looked down at her boobs and saw that they were starting to peel. 'Oh balls – they're falling off.'

'Don't pick!' Kester said, smacking her hand away from her chest.

Dee laughed and picked up a glass of champagne for herself.

'This is it you see,' Kester said. 'It's all so ugly, funny, pathetic, but it doesn't have to be. I can make them beautiful.'

Dee acted as if she hadn't heard him and gave him a squeeze.

'Come on. We've designed some special games for you to play, with lovely forfeits.' She pulled him over to the table and sat him down.

After a few rounds, Kester was starting to look more pliable.

Betta and Sienna were at the bar. Dee could hear a booming voice over the rest of the babble offering to give Betta something 'real' to wear. Calvin had wandered off, presumably to the gents, leaving his swimming cap on the table this time and John seemed away in a world where conversation wasn't the thing. A great deal of the purple from his hands was now smeared on his face. It was time to go on the offensive.

'So, Kester,' Dee said, pointing into the main bar, 'look out into that pit of idiots and tell me why. Seriously.'

'Why what?' Kester asked, then realised that she was back on the subject of the job and made a face. 'I've told you already. It's not just the money – I'm going to have my own lab. I can use it for whatever I like as long as I get the work for the company done too. It's not like the Institute where everything you do is reliant on someone wanting to fund it. I'm going in at a high enough level that I can decide what to do…to a certain extent.'

'We were going to do it together,' Dee said. She must sound confident. 'So stay, let's do it.'

'Dee…I'm sorry. Maybe down the line if I get somewhere with it…'

Dee leaned back and shook her head.

'I might – I will, I promise you.'

Kester knew how much it meant to her; that was clear. And maybe he really meant to do it, once he settled in and got the measure of his new job.

'And I get to have fun creating new stuff for my job in the meantime.'

Then again, perhaps not.

'It's a stupid fatuous industry,' Dee said. Shocked by the venom in her own voice, she took a breath and tried to temper her tone. 'I mean fashion viruses, really.'

'It's not doing anyone any harm.'

'Isn't it? Look at all those young directors that keep dropping dead in the board rooms. Don't you think that might have something to do with the weird disease culture they're building up?'

'I think it's more to do with stress.'

'You do not – it was you that pointed it out to me!'

'Dee, the whole point of my viruses is that they'll be safe. I can make them cool without hurting people.'

'Great. Just what the world needs you to do with your genius – your genius and your sense of "cool".'

'But Dee, that's the fun part, that's not the whole picture. I can make a start on the screens, maybe even start testing – think of the limitless resources I'll have.'

'You think you'll have the time in between making designer diseases?'

'I'm not stupid, Dee, I've told you, I'm getting private lab time written into my contract.' Kester shook his head.

Dee wobbled in her seat, the drink suddenly catching up with her. They were going round in circles.

'Yeah, but they'll own your research,' she said.

'Better than the research not being done at all.'

'Hm,' Dee grunted in an unladylike fashion that made Kester laugh at her. 'Shut up,' she said.

'Show me someone who's going to fund a piece of research at the Institute that I don't have qualms about and I'll stay. Never mind the screens – anything at all.'

'And what next? Where do you go from there, Kester? Five years' time, seriously, where are you?'

Betta and Sienna sloshed a tray of shots onto the table and slid back into their seats.

'Jesus, leave some in the glass,' John said, the life flicking back into his eyes.

'Come on, Dee, five years' time?' Kester said. 'Christ, this is like going through another interview. I suppose I'm going to have to shag you too?'

'What?' Dee said. 'Don't be disgusting.'

'That's what they do,' John said, though it wasn't clear if he was talking to them as he was staring intently at the table.

'They do not. It's just big City talk. He's just being stupid. He's trying to avoid my question because he can't answer it sensibly – it was a serious question, Kester.'

'I'm telling you,' John said, 'you have to sleep your way in at the bottom before you can sleep your way to the top.'

'Oh shut up,' Dee said. 'Has it ever happened to anyone you know? No. So there. Anyway, he wouldn't have been going in at the bottom, they were going to give him his own lab.'

'*Were* going to?' Kester said. 'They *are*.'

John raised his eyebrows, impressed.

'You knew that already,' Dee reminded John.

He slurped down one of the shots in slow motion.

'Those are for the game.' Sienna tried to grab the glass from him, too late.

Calvin arrived back at the table, sat down quietly and closed his eyes.

'Ah,' replied John, a little behind in the conversation, 'but how many people do we know who've been interviewed at V?' He jabbed his finger on the table in front of Kester. 'Just one, huh? Just Kester. And I know what Kester's been up to!'

'He's right. It's true,' Kester said, and then laughed, eyes on the table. 'She made the others leave the room, she dropped her culottes and we did it right there on the desk. All part of the process.' He laughed again, shaking his head.

'What?' Calvin shrieked, his eyes snapping wide open.

'Stop lying!' Dee slapped Kester hard on the arm. 'You're just trying to shock me.'

'Just telling it like it is,' he said. 'That's how I roll now.'

All of them burst out laughing except for Dee. This wasn't going right. He was making a fool of himself.

'That's how you *roll?*' Sienna scoffed. 'You need to sort out your vocabulary. You need to be using words like Target! Achievable! Succeed! Make sure you say them all with an exclamation mark on the end. Oh, I love this song,' she interrupted herself and started singing along to the music.

Dee narrowed her eyes in mock suspicion at Kester. If she played along, he would stop it.

'Don't be mad,' he said.

She added a pout to her expression. She should be mad. He was glorifying everything she hated with his bogus boasts and the others were hailing him for it.

'You're not mad at me are you?'

'You're the one who's mad,' she replied. At least he knew he was in the wrong. 'You're a pig and you know it.'

'I have a new drinking game!' John announced.

'Oh yeah?' Kester puffed his chest out.

Dee knew that look. He had passed the drunk-awareness barrier and believed that he was perfectly fine. The idea that he'd have a hangover the next day would seem impossible to him.

'Yesss.' John listed to the side for a moment and then seemed to perk back up suddenly, as if he'd briefly switched off. 'It's Drink or Dare!' he announced proudly. 'We dare you to do something and if you don't do it, you have to drink.'

There was a pause while everyone looked at each other, and then Dee burst out laughing.

'A new game John?' she said. 'That's the oldest game in the book.'

A deflated looked flitted across John's face, but he brightened again instantly.

'Aha! But it's new to this table.'

'OK, John, since you suggested it, you have to show us how it's done.'

'Nono,' John slurred, pointing at Kester, 'the birthday boy has to do it.' His finger jerked in the air as he pointed to Kester, as if he was riding a train. Kester hawked with laughter.

'My god he's drunk,' Dee said. John failed even to register that she was talking about him.

'Okayokay,' John said, 'here's my dare, birthday boy.'

'Leaving boy,' Kester corrected him.

'You're leaving! Oh oh I know, I knew that.' John smiled slyly to himself as if he had a drunken secret. 'Here's your dare. Kiss! Or drink!'

'What, are you five years old?' Dee asked.

'I am…I am thirty-five years old.'

'You are not,' Kester said, shaking his head, 'you just don't remember your thirty-sixth birthday.'

'Kiss! Or Drink!' John repeated, then began chanting, 'Kiss! Kiss! Kiss! Kiss!'

'Oh god, shut him up will you,' Betta said.

'OK.' Kester leaned across the table and, pulling John towards him by his tie, kissed him on the lips.

'Tuh!' John slumped back down in his seat. 'Not me, chickenboy – one of them.' He swung an arm out towards the bar.

'Well, you're not getting lucky tonight John, not in that state, so take what you can get, eh?' Sienna laughed. She wiped her hands across her face, smearing her spots.

'Your turn John, your turn,' said Calvin.

'OK. What's the dare?'

'I've got one already,' Calvin said. 'You have to get one of these guys' ties off them.'

'Oh no,' Dee said.

'Oh yes,' shouted John. 'I'll have to do it! If I drink any more I shall surely die.'

'Don't do it, John,' Dee said, but he was already half on his feet, holding onto the table while he got his balance.

As John walked out into the bar, it was as if he had a repellent forcefield around him. The crowd seemed to collectively sense how drunk he was and parted around him, forming a two-metre wide circle of disgusted glances which moved as he moved, shifting like a bait ball.

'Hi, oh hi.' John waved to the circle around him. 'Hey, nice tie.'

'Thanks,' replied the object of his concentrated gaze, unsure how else to respond.

'Can I have it?'

'What?' Temper sprung, the man walked towards him, chest puffed out. 'You little prick. You think I'd give you a 300 Euro tie? Coming in here with your stupid costumes – don't think we haven't noticed. What's wrong with you?'

'Nothing,' John said innocently. 'Nothing, but maybe…'

'But maybe what?'

'But maybe I feel a little sick.'

'Sick? Oh god, he's going to puke!' The man put his arms out to the side and stepped back, shepherding his colleagues out of the danger zone and distorting the circle.

'300 euk tie makes me sick.'

'What? That didn't even make sense.'

'You heard me.' John started to pull himself up, to stand straighter.

'Shit,' Dee said, 'we need to get him out of here now.'

'Here.' John was staggering over to the woman next along in the circle, who was wearing sores around her lacquered lips. 'You've got a little something…' He indicated the corner of his mouth. '…just here on your…it's just a bit of…' He leaned forward to wipe at her mouth and her companion smacked his hand out of the way.

Primal instincts kicked in and John launched himself at the man in a bear hug. His target reacted in kind and their shoulders clattered together.

Betta and Calvin leaped into action, grabbing at any bit of John that flailed within reach. Managing to catch the crook of an elbow each, they tried to drag him back, but only succeeded in opening up a target. As the man punched, John's soft stomach collapsed around his fist like a cushion, sending vomit shooting out over his front and punching arm.

'Cameron!' A tall woman who had been making her way across the bar called out above the rabble.

She had no trouble getting through the crowd. A path opened up before her as it had for John, but out of respect, or perhaps even fear. The sick-covered man looked up and the expression of disgust on his face turned to one of guilt.

'Cameron?'

'Davis, sir. Ms.' Davis wiped at the front of his sick-covered shirt with the end of his sick-covered tie.

'You're fired,' the woman said without emotion. 'Go and get your things. I don't want to see you again.'

That voice. Dee saw Kester's outline freeze in what appeared to be fear. The fear spread to her. Her skeleton went cold.

'Mrs Farrell,' Kester said.

'What?' Dee leaned in to him, still keeping an eye on the situation, stepping back out of the way as Calvin and Betta bundled John back into the corner.

'That's Alexis Farrell,' Kester said. 'My new boss.'

'Oh fuck,' Dee whispered, 'sorry.'

'Sorry for what?' Kester asked.

Mrs Farrell's eyes wandered over the group and finally settled on Kester. She took a moment to recognise him. When she did, she stalked straight up to him.

Dee recoiled and stepped behind Kester. She stared at Farrell. She was wearing something in her eyes – metal – gold. Her pupils were wide in the darkness of the bar and the effect was pronounced: a feathery metallic circle round each iris, flecks of blood, rings of eye shrapnel. Dee had never seen anything like it. Those weren't contacts – this was some sick new thing – eye implants. She wouldn't put it past Farrell's type.

'Well, well,' Mrs Farrell said, stretching out her hand, 'if it isn't my newest acquisition.'

Farrell wore a long blood-red wool dress. A strip of colour co-ordinated ads ran straight down from one shoulder to the hem. At first glance it looked quite a demure get-up, until she walked and you could see that it was slit up the side, revealing her long sinewy legs right to where they joined her hips. Easy access, thought Dee. Farrell's her hair fell in exaggerated curls around her face, an attempt perhaps to soften her appearance, but her augmented eyes were hard and intelligent.

Kester reached out and shook Farrell's hand.

'Is this something to do with you?' Farrell glanced over her shoulder at the mess on the floor.

'No,' Dee said quickly.

'Yes,' replied Kester, almost at the same time, 'my leaving party. I'm afraid John can't handle his drink.'

'Being a drunken idiot is one thing; public assault is quite another. So I must apologise for the behaviour of our ex-employee.'

'He asked for it,' Kester said.

Dee shifted her attention to John, who was sitting behind her, grabbing at her knees. She tried hard to stay tuned in to Kester and Farrell's conversation, though the tone was confidential.

'I don't know about you, but if I gave it to everyone who asked for it, things would start to get a little silly,' Farrell said.

Looking back up, Dee bristled. Farrell's smile was charged.

'You'd certainly be busy.' Kester laughed.

'You start a week on Monday?'

'Yes, they seemed to rush me through the security checks. I had no idea it would be so soon.'

'Make sure I'm alerted once you have your induction. I'd like to go through some…ethical issues with you before you get started on your work.'

'Of course. I look forward to it.'

Every time Farrell smiled, Dee felt she was making a joke at Kester's expense. Her lipstick was too perfect, her teeth too straight, too white.

'Anyway, I see you have other business to deal with, so I'll leave you to it.' Farrell made a move to leave, then paused and turned back towards Kester. 'You don't have a costume?'

She indicated his friends, avoiding eye contact with them, smiling with amusement at their faked signs as at a child's toy. Dee realised she hadn't given Kester his stickers.

'No,' he said.

'Not wearing?'

Kester shrugged his shoulders. Mrs Farrell leaned in closer than was necessary.

'You're the only one in here, you know.'

A wave of Farrell's perfume came around Kester and reached Dee. It was warm, nocturnal, the smell of a stranger's bed.

'I know,' Kester said.

Farrell turned so that her hair swished against Kester, and then she disappeared through the crowd, a path opening up before her towards the central spiral staircase. At the foot of the staircase, one of the bouncers whispered into her ear. She looked like she was giving an instruction. He lifted the cordon and she ascended into darkness, leaving the rising noise of the bar below. Dee watched the staircase for a moment or two after she had gone.

'Right you lot.' The bouncer heaved over to where they stood gathered outside the archway. His subsonic voice erased the noise from the bar when he spoke. 'Back in your room. You're lucky you're drinking so much or you'd be out of here.' He winked at Calvin. 'Table service only.' Looking out to the bar, he caught the eye of one of the waitresses and signalled her. 'And do yourselves a favour and take that shit off before you leave. You go back into London like that and the fukpunks'll rip your tiny heads off.'

-o-

Dee bided her time. John quietened down and then left with Calvin. Betta and Sienna weren't far behind them. The night slowly fell to pieces, until just she and Kester were left in the back room of the bar. She drank Farrell out of her mind. They picked out individuals in the bar beyond and laughed about their appearances, talked about stupid things that had happened during Kester's years at the Institute. Dee's confidence grew as she saw nostalgia take Kester over and a latent disgust at the wearers rise to the surface.

'Shall we make a move?' Kester asked when their conversation slowed to closing-time pace.

Dee nodded and smiled. She started picking off the scabs that she had left and sticking them to the table.

'Let's smuggle this last soldier out,' she said when she was done, grabbing hold of the neck of the last champagne bottle. It was still half-full.

They moved swiftly through the crowd, which was as boisterous as ever, constantly renewing itself with workers just finished their shifts or taking illicit breaks. The bouncer clocked the champagne bottle, but just smiled grimly at them as they walked out onto the street.

'Good night!' Dee called to him from a safe distance, smiling winningly and holding up the bottle in a toast.

'Come on,' said Kester. 'Now it's my turn to show you something.'

'What?' She handed him the bottle to take a swig.

'Don't you worry – it'll be a treat.'

Kester took her by the hand, stuck his thumb in the neck of the champagne bottle and started walking, jogging, running.

'Where are we going?' Excitement rose in Dee's chest.

'Now, now – you'll find out soon enough!' Kester laughed.

He led her ducking down silvery glass alleys, lit up screen-stage bright by the office windows above, where the City night-shift worked under sunshine lighting. In the narrow alleys between buildings the darkness tumbled down, heavy velvet curtains falling. Every now and again they would slow down to a walk and Dee would ask the same question.

'Where are we going?'

Kester's answer each time was to take a swig of champagne, hand the bottle to her, take it back and carry on.

They ran past offices and offices and offices, stacked to vanishing point, past long luminous windows full of off-duty workers, chattering and slurping noodles at ranks of low blonde benches, past the happy neon pool-hall entrances to the Pigs.

Outside an old church Kester stopped and announced, 'Here we are!'

Above the church stretched a mammoth glass and steel archway, supporting a stilted skyscraper. A placard, caught in a design vacuum between old and new, explained the origins of the church and showed where the churchyard had been. On the ground by the entrance old-fashioned paper money, dampened by the dew, stuck to the pavement. Here and there free corners fluttered like trapped moths. Kester gave Dee just long enough to see where they were and open her mouth, then cackled with laughter, grabbed her hand and led her on again, now at a shuffling jog.

'Kester, my feet!' Dee let out a pretend sob. Her feet were throbbing and she could feel a blister forming on one heel, but anticipation pushed her on.

'Come on, we'll be late!'

Suddenly they burst out onto a large square. Dee looked up. On the three sides facing her, the walls were lined with tiny figures. Figures sitting at desks; figures walking around. It was as if someone had put a lid on the City and trapped the daylight. In the centre of the square, invisibly suspended, almost at pavement height, hung a glass globe large enough to crush a man, in which the building ahead of them and all the City beyond it was reflected upside down, bringing a muddy orange slab of sky down to pavement level.

'Oh my god, Kester.' Dee stared at the globe in wonder. 'It's beautiful.'

'No no, not that,' Kester panted, as if she were admiring a bollard. 'Look!' He grabbed her by the shoulders and swung her round to face the fourth wall of the square. 'The changeover.'

The whole side of the building was radiating red light. The steel divisions glowed as if they were molten, as if the building was about to slide down into a mass of metal and light at their feet. The Stark Wellbury logo sat at the top of it all like a giant red prawn, towering above the buildings of its competitors, clashing with the orange sky above them.

'It's not...' Dee stared, mesmerised by the colour, her chest heaving.

At first she thought that the shifting hue was an illusion, but as the windows faded from red to green she realised that she was watching the heat dissipate from the building. The outer booths, faster to cool, faded first and the green closed inwards until it snuffed out the building's red heart.

And they appeared: pairs of Stark Wellbury employees, side-by-side, staring out into the square, their symptoms invisible from this distance. Dee heard Kester laugh nervously as if unsure how she would react, as if he hadn't really believed the story either. The figures stood eerily still for a few seconds. She half-expected them to break into some synchronised dance routine. Then, all at once, as if a bell had sounded in the booths, they threw themselves at each other, tangles of clothes and limbs, unwrapping each other like lapsed abstainers overtaken. Some dropped to their knees, some kissed ravenously. There were hands in hair, hands up shirts and in culottes, clothes wriggling off as if it was a race, as if none of them could wait. In seconds, the whole building was writhing and heaving.

Dee and Kester stood side by side, still, as the figures had a moment before. They were still panting from their run. Dee laughed suddenly, shocked at herself, at her desire to see.

'We look like a couple of perverts, standing here panting.' She giggled.

Kester laughed. They stared at the spectacle for a few seconds more.

'I didn't really think...' Kester tailed off.

Dee looked round at him. His cheeks were flushed. His face was tinged a surreal reflected green, like a divine alien. His mouth was slightly open. She felt the space between them keenly; a Perspex wall.

Kester looked round. The wall vanished.

They were on each other, kissing violently. Their arms interlocked, and their feet scuffled back and forth, as if they were struggling to climb through one another. When they disengaged, they both staggered back as if from a fight. Dee squealed. Kester was back; she finally had him.

'What's going on? Where are we! What are we doing?' she said.

Kester laughed, panting again.

'Come on, come on!' Dee jumped on the spot, then laughed and grabbed Kester's hand. A charge passed between them. They ran.

At the opposite side of the square, Kester swung Dee round by the hand. They paused, laughing wildly at the upside down view of the Stark Wellbury building in the glass globe, and then ran on.

On the tube they sat opposite one another, sharing the spectacle they had just seen with their giggling stares, laughing out loud every now and then, swigging from their almost-empty champagne bottle and passing it between them. A space cleared around them, as if they might go off. This was it. Dee felt the intensity of the coming encounter in her buzzing lips, in her eyes. Finally. There would be no question of Kester leaving – leaving her, leaving their research. Out of the tube they ran again, all the way to Dee's door.

Chapter 3

It was quiet in Lady's living room. Cherry sat in the middle of the floral couch. She was slight in build, but it sagged anyway. It had seen so much action over the years, so many buttocks, clothed and bare, that it had given up on supporting weight or springing back in any meaningful way. The antique clock in the centre of the mantelpiece was ticking loudly.

Lady was on her way. Cherry could hear her hollering at seekers through the building. She approached like a school marm with a purpose, chastising here and laughing there, changing swiftly between aspects as she marched through the long corridors.

This place hadn't always been Lady's quarters. It used to be a small children's ward, annexed to the main hospital, but she had now taken it over as the base for her business. In the long hall that ran through the annex some of the bright cartoon paintings still survived, but not here in Lady's sitting room. It was more like the sitting room of a real house. It sat right down the end of the corridor, holding her at arm's length from the rest of the building. 'Lady's rooms' they called them, this collection of small living spaces. Cherry had always imagined that the warden used to live here.

The clock's tick became less and less dominant as Lady drew closer. Soon the laughing and chiding stopped and all that was left to hear was Lady's heels clicking on the linoleum tiles. It reminded Cherry always of her brief time at school, of the sound of grownups walking in the corridors while lessons were on. The sound peeled years off Cherry's age as it drew nearer: twenty-two, twenty-one, twenty…by the time Lady reached the door, Cherry was a twelve year old girl again.

Lady didn't open doors like anyone else. She didn't just come into a room. This was a classic Lady entrance in three acts: the door burst open and she paused in the doorway for a moment; she stepped aside and glanced over her shoulder like a woman being followed; and then she closed the door tenderly, as if to make up for her brutal treatment of it moments ago. She acted as if no-one was party to this performance, ignoring Cherry as an actress ignores the audience.

She went to the window, checked who was outside, then pulled a chair out from the table and set it in front of where Cherry was seated on the couch. Placing her bottom neatly on the chair, Lady straightened her posture, crossed her legs and smoothed her pencil-skirt down along the top of her thigh, her hands meeting and clasping when they reached her kneecap. Cherry had never seen Lady stay still for very long but today she looked as if she was settling in for a long conversation.

Cherry observed Lady's clothing. At first sight she always looked well dressed, well heeled, but if you looked for long enough, the details started to offer themselves up to you – loose threads, lines where an item of clothing had been taken out or let down, dark colouration along the collars of her blouses. Lady's makeup, which was also quite striking from a distance, had an inaccuracy about it, as if over years of applying the same shapes to her mouth and eyes her standards had slipped. Cherry remembered being impressed by Lady's flawless appearance when they had first met, but then that was a long time ago and Lady was approaching her fifties now. Perhaps, Cherry thought, her makeup was still the same. Perhaps it was her face that had changed and the two no longer aligned.

'Cherry,' Lady said. A frown was hovering on her forehead, held back by her tightly-bunned hair. 'You can feel something starting?'

'I feel a bit funny,' Cherry replied after a moment.

Lady exploded up from her chair and back into movement as if Cherry had said the magic word to release her. She paced and let her hands wander around her person, into pockets and out again, up to her face, onto the backs of chairs, across the table top.

'Funny? Funny ill?'

'I guess. Not so much now, though. I just mentioned it to Marlene for something to say.'

Lady laughed a false high-pitched laugh, as if to emphasise how unfunny the situation was to her.

'Not the sort of thing I'd recommend for small-talk, Cherry. Not something to be joked about really. What do you think?'

'I do feel funny...just...I couldn't say how yet.'

'Funny pregnant?'

'No!'

Lady snorted. 'And how would you know? Been pregnant lately?'

'I'm sealed.' Cherry tried not to raise her voice. Even if she hadn't been sealed, raising the subject of pregnancy with her, a seeker of disease, seemed in bad taste to say the least.

'I forget.'

Lady sounded as if she had genuinely forgotten this about Cherry. It was possible that she had. She had forty-two or forty-three seekers working for her right now, a lot to keep a track of. On the other hand, Cherry was the only one from central London. Girls who lived outside the big cities tended not to be sealed. The governors believed that it encouraged promiscuity and so it was frowned upon. This wasn't a problem in the cities, where everyone had nanoscreens fitted thanks to the key workers scheme. They could do whatever they wanted and get away with it, disease-wise – one less disincentive to having sex – so in the name of either population control, infant rights, or youth preservation depending on who you listened to, they would have their female children cervically sealed age ten.

For Cherry, being ex-London had its benefits. The screen made her a good seeker, as it flagged up unknown infections and dealt with known ones. Never mind that, it meant that she was guaranteed a job as a seeker, going out to find viruses, rather than being stuck in the Hospital knocking shop waiting for viruses to come to her. She could get uploads on the blacknet to keep her up to date with all the logged and registered viruses that were out there. A registered virus was worth nothing to Lady and could put a worker out of service for weeks, maybe permanently. She needed one of two things: new mutations of high presentation STVs, or commissioned exclusives caught somewhere down the chain from the buyer, both of which could be sold on to the collectives who ran the Pigs.

Lady tottered round and round, drawing a neat circle about the sofa where Cherry sat, as if there was some invisible line there that she didn't want to cross. Her lips were pursed and her eyes darted around the room, as if she was looking for something.

Cherry looked up to the window. From where she sat she could just see the giant billboards that lined the opposite side of the retail park. She straightened her back to get a better view. They had just uploaded new ads. Staring Cherry in the eye, five times life-size was Galletti, Barcelona's newly signed striker. Creeping down from the outer edges of his eyes were two neat spikes of rash, red raw, as if two triangles of flesh had been peeled from his cheekbones. It couldn't be real – nothing she'd seen was that neat. Then she noticed the Glaxo logo in the bottom corner. It was real then; a paid for exclusive. Airbrushed though. It must be brand new, as it hadn't been featured in yesterday's seeker bulletin. Either that or Lady was slipping behind on her admin.

As Cherry watched, the image zoomed out to show Galletti performing tricks with a Nike football. He was in good company: the next billboard featured the actress Tilly Harrison wearing a sheer gown, blown against her by an unseen source of wind to reveal shadows of red on her thighs. Droplets of Dior *Rash* flew towards her from a giant atomiser as she writhed on the spot, scratching herself. That one would be real. Wearing was rife in the fashion world. To Galletti's other side, New York band *The Itch* were silently slamming away at their guitars, the singer periodically lifting his by the neck to show his fukpunk-style smeary crotch-window. Cherry shuddered.

'It costs me if you're wrong, you know.' Lady stopped mid-circle.

Cherry looked up at her. She wasn't sure if she was supposed to answer. 'I know.'

'Testing has just gone up again.'

'I…' Cherry paused, unsure of the correct thing to say. 'We could wait.'

'Wait? I need you fit to seek at the Global Finance Conference next week.'

'I feel…funny, but I couldn't put my finger on it. I mean it might not even be an STV.'

'Didn't you get your uploads?'

'Yes, but you know sometimes they can be out of date.'

'You should be careful where you get them.'

'I am, but we could wait for some proper signs – wait and be sure.'

'We can't wait. Not if there's a possibility. What if Franco's lot has picked it up? Rumour has it he picked up an exclusive and a mute last month alone. He's got ten girls and fifteen boys now all out seeking. And he's got all the bases covered – sends them all over; sends them to all types of places.'

'Spreads them thin.'

'Did I say that?'

'Yes Lady.'

'Then yes, he does. But he's got more than before.'

Lady started another circle of the couch then paused right behind where Cherry was sitting. Cherry could feel Lady's breaths stirring the hair on the top of her head. She felt for a moment like something might come down on her crown. She braced herself.

'You logged all your encounters?' Lady asked. 'Did anybody claim to have anything? Anybody look like they had something new?'

'There was a guy with sores, but I think it was an oldie. His skin smelled like ointment and I could see the shadow of where the sores had extended originally. I think he was trying to shape them to look like an exclusive.'

'Tosser.' Lady strode over to her door. 'Bring up Cherry's log,' she ordered as she walked in. 'I want to see her account of everyone she's tried for the past two weeks – no, three to be certain. And mark up likely candidates for me. Thank you Ben.'

Lady was already closing her office door when Cherry got up from the couch. She was visible through the frosted glass, pacing up and down. Ben isn't in there, Cherry thought. Lady would never show her emotion like that in front of her secretary, surely. But then she was increasingly frantic these days when she did her rounds. The threat of the big companies catching up and taking all the business in-City was getting to her. Rumour had it that she had had to let Ben go but was too proud to admit it. Cherry watched as Lady's silhouette moved to merge with that of her desk, continuing to fidget.

The ads outside changed again and drew Cherry's eye. Standing, she could see the traffic moving around the busy retail park. She watched as a dad dropped off a clutch of pre-teens at the cinema, parked, then walked a roundabout route to the Hospital, glancing over his shoulder now and again. At the far corner of the park, a trickle of red and white figures started to appear, waving their scarves, dancing and singing. Beyond the crop of housing she could see the top of the stadium rising up. Past that there was nothing until the City's north eastern boundary, its ludicrous buildings appearing from this distance as an impenetrable wall. Time to go, Cherry thought. With the football out and a movie just about to start most of the hookers would be busy – prime time to use the showers.

As Cherry walked to the door, she caught sight of herself in the full length mirror. The mirror here was much better than the one they had in the wardrobe room, which was poorly lit because the windows were rarely washed. It usually had a hoard of girls jostling for position in front of it, too. If you got to see what you looked like, it was what you might look like shouldering for position at a market stall; a portrait in motion.

Cherry looked funny in her terry towelling tunic. Like an inmate of the old children's hospital, she thought. Her hair needed cut. It was starting to look wild. She was surprised that Lady hadn't pulled her up for it. Her pale brown skin looked darker against the boil-wash white of her tunic. The tunic had been laundered so much that she could see the shadow of her nipples through it. She glanced round to Lady's office door. Seeing that the silhouette was still ensconced behind the desk, she grabbed the hem of her skirt and lifted it up quickly to her neck. Her pubes were squint again – she knew it. Barbara was rubbish, or she did it on purpose. One of the two.

Cherry pulled back her long mane of straightened black hair and tried to look objectively at her body. She seemed thinner – just on the cusp of being too thin, girlish. Satisfactory though, she thought to herself, maybe more. Her years on the job had certainly given her toned muscles – that was for sure. And unlike some of the workers, she laid off the junk. But then she had an advantage, the one good thing she had brought with her from the city. She turned and twisted round to see herself from the side, from the back. She was sinewy, tough. Could have been a ninja, she thought.

Her Book beeped: a scan update. Through the glass door, Lady's silhouette stopped and stiffened. Cherry let her tunic drop and took her Book out of the small thread-bare pocket at her hip. H1N1 mute. Flu. Another small-mutation causing delays on her nanoscreen. She sighed, walked over to the glass door and knocked.

-o-

It was a couple of hours until Cherry started her shift. She lay on her back in her runk and stared at the low ceiling above her. She stretched as well as she could, her arms meeting with cold plastic behind her and to the sides. She trailed them bent along the white walls.

'That's just brilliant,' she said to herself. She put on her Lady face. 'Who wants to buy flu, Cherry? Would you want to buy it? Is it sexually transmitted? Does it look impressive on a business man?'

She had the second runk from the bottom in her stack. Most of the workers on the lower level runks were hookers, but there were a few exceptions, chiefly seekers who didn't like heights or couldn't be bothered with the climb. Ten shelves above her was the top runk, most of the seekers' ultimate aim. Cherry understood the ambition though she didn't share it. She had climbed up to visit seekers further up the stack before and had sat with them, dangling her feet over the edge, making paper airplanes to send messages to their mates in the runks across the room, laughing as they flew off course and landed wherever they wished. She liked the slight feeling of vertigo, the feeling that she might at any minute just launch herself out into the air and fall. She imagined them all doing it at once, drifting to the floor like terry-towelling snowflakes.

Cherry sat up and pushed herself into a crouch, then leaned forward to the locker that walled the foot end of her mattress, taking care not to bang her head on the ceiling. There was nothing much in there, really. Her old Book from when she lived in London. It still worked, and though she still used it to update her screenware, it spent most of the time as a picture frame, showing an old photo of her mother.

Her Book beeped, and her mother's face was momentarily obscured by a message reminding her to do her updates. She grimaced, then picked it up and pressed her thumb onto the ID pad. It beeped a welcome and she scrolled the menu and chose 'updates'. The display went slow, then white, and eventually a garbled message appeared. The blacknet update server she'd been using had been shut down.

'Damnit.' She held the Book tightly, restraining herself,

swallowing down the urge to smash it against the wall. She couldn't break it. It would be too hard to get another one that would work with her old screen, besides which the blackmarket versions were expensive and buggy as hell. She started a search on the blacknet for a new update server, adding a few filters and leaving it to do its thing. There was so much information out there now, so many unregulated servers, that it was a slow process. The advertisers and so-called help sites were always one step ahead of the search engines, dominating the results lists. She touched the Book's fingerplate and propped it back up, a picture frame once more.

There was a dull knock at Cherry's front wall. She grabbed the handle on the back of the rigid plastic panel and pulled it up and back along its runners so that it became a second ceiling. There, filling her exit, leaning in from a few rungs up the ladder was Marlene, naked. Using her free hand Marlene lifted her breasts one by one so that they rested on the edge of Cherry's mattress. A higher runk would spare her this view every shift. Cherry tried to peer round her ample friend.

'Hi, sweetie,' said Marlene, then in a deep voice, 'Morning Cherry.' She jiggled her breasts from beneath. 'Thought we'd tell you your favourite dress is still up for grabs.' She continued in her own voice, 'How'd you get on last night?'

'More dead ends.' Cherry glanced over at the picture of her mother and frowned.

'You need to get into the City, get pillow talking with someone at the records office.'

'I know, I know. But I'm fresh out of friends in high places and my guardian angel seems to have misplaced my number.'

'They're notoriously bad for that, though we've never had any trouble with ours, have we girls?' Marlene looked down at her breasts again, then shot Cherry a disturbing grin. 'Anyway, I sent you three planes, but I guess you didn't get them.'

Cherry laughed, then yawned. 'You going out too?'

'Yes.' Marlene gathered her frizzy brown hair with one hand and twisted it over her shoulder. 'Thought you might want to buddy up for the first part of the night. We're both working the airport.'

'Yeah, sure.' It would be nice to have some company, Cherry thought. Seeking in a pair was sometimes easier, definitely safer and always more fun.

'Come on, then.' Marlene descended the ladder and waddled away from the runk stack, beckoning with a bearlike arm. 'Let's get tooled up.'

Cherry hung her legs down over the edge of her runk.

'Hey,' came a shout from the runk below, 'get your feet out of my face, Cherry.'

'Sorry babes.' Cherry jumped down to the floor.

'Jeez, you're going to break my nose one day,' said the girl in the runk below. She was new to the Hospital and still getting used to things. Some of the other seekers would have gone all diva if a hooker had spoken to them like that, but Cherry had never got the hang of feeling superior.

'Come on,' Marlene said, already halfway across the room.

The runkroom was in the old teaching theatre. It must have been circular when it was built, with seating up the sides for the trainee surgeons to observe their masters at work. It had since been transformed into a many-sided polygon by the twenty runk stacks that had been installed around the walls and the narrow ladder panels which ran up in-between them.

Cherry looked around. Most of the doors were closed. The once-white panels had been decorated by their owners in different styles: classical, abstract, graffiti, but mostly in block colour. The room looked as if it had been hung with a patchwork quilt. Here and there a panel was open and the occupant was lounging in their runk, rummaging in their locker at the foot of their mattress, or just sitting, legs hanging out, watching what was going on below.

An open shower unit stood in the middle of the room. Each shower stand had a set of cleanser dispensers, and a large extractor above the showers sucked out the steam. Right now the whole theatre smelled of just-used shower. Cherry liked it. It reminded her of being little, of going into the bathroom after her mother had washed. It was a welcome break from the dreadful changing room aroma that filled the room at shift change: Lynx, Source, Impulse, Sensorra; *Ocean Lotion, Spice it Up, Manjack Musk, Mint Tingle*; a muddy blend of hormone-tinged scent.

'I need to shower,' Cherry called after Marlene.

'Well, hurry up,' Marlene said. 'I'll go down and pretend to try that dress on for you so no-one else snags it.' She laughed to herself, and threw the double doors wide open before her.

Cherry wriggled out of her tunic and put it on the floor at her feet before soaping up. Picking it up again she scrubbed herself red with it, then rubbed and rinsed the tunic itself. She finished just as the water stopped. She wrung her tunic out, then opened it out again and gave it a shake so it wouldn't dry creased. She half danced back to her runk and flicked it over the rail on her closed door.

'You're in a good mood,' the new girl said, smiling up at her.

'Yes! Just woke up feeling good.' Cherry realised she had goosebumps. 'Cold today. I'd better get downstairs.'

Holding one arm across her boobs to stop them bouncing – she'd once heard that running-bounce could stretch them prematurely – Cherry jogged across the room to the double doors that led to the stairs.

The staircase was as it had been when the building was still a hospital: painted two different offensive tones of olive, floored with flaking lino, cold. Cherry took the stairs two at a time, until a door opened with voices on the floor above. She changed her gait suddenly, taking more demure single steps.

What used to be the level three renal unit was now the seekers' dressing room. It was a long room with dirty windows all down one side, minimal and white, a little less clean on the inside than it had been as a ward, but not by much.

It was first come first served. There was no sensible way of having your own clothes in the Hospital, unless you wanted to waste time going out into the town to get them cleaned at the launderette. That cost money too, and none of the seekers really wanted to waste a coin when they could wear what they chose from the communal wardrobe and have it washed for them in the old Hospital laundry rooms.

'Imagine no possessions...' Marlene crooned and then hollered, 'Shop every day at the House of Lady!'

Cherry burst out laughing. Marlene was standing by the rail with Cherry's favourite dress over her head. That was as far as it would go.

'Come on, Marlene,' another girl was saying, 'it doesn't even fit you – you're going to rip it. Let someone else have a go.'

'Fair enough,' Marlene said, hearing Cherry's laugh. She pulled the dress off her head and tossed it into Cherry's arms.

'Oh, come on!' the other girl said, stamping her bare foot and swearing.

'Sorry, honey,' Cherry said. 'How about you have it tomorrow?'

The girl snorted and started rummaging through the rest of her size section of the rail.

Cherry slipped into the dress. It was old fashioned, or classic as Marlene described it, but it fitted Cherry perfectly. It was black satin, with a small print of the kind that you never saw any more. The berries on the print looked a little bit like cherries and though she knew they were too small and a bit too red to be, it pleased her. Its skinny belt fitted her waist perfectly on the tightest hole and the flared skirt swung just at her knees. She thought of it as her dress.

She felt drips from her long wet hair starting to seep through the fabric at her back.

'Will you do my hair tonight, Marlene?' she asked, twisting it up out of the way and tying it in a knot.

'Sure thing, Madame C.' Marlene was round the other side of the rail, trying on dresses that were more her size. 'You know Lady never buys in any new stuff that fits me – still the same five things. I'm sure this one isn't even a dress.' She appeared from behind the rail in a brown sack-like get up. 'I look like a giant shit.'

'You know, maybe with a belt,' Cherry said, but couldn't keep a straight face.

'Oh, like a two-parter, yes, I like it.'

'You're disgusting.' Cherry started to look through the shoe rack to see if there was anything new.

'Hello, ladies.' Tim was leaning in the door, bare-chested. The strip-lights laid a pale halo across his smooth blonde hair. 'Ooh, baby,' he said, seeing Marlene, 'take that off before I cream myself!'

'You always did have a faecal fetish,' Marlene said, winking at him. 'You're as bad as the clients.' She disappeared back behind the rail to pick out a new outfit.

-o-

'So who are we tonight, Marlene?' Cherry asked as she and Marlene stepped off the airport bus.

While Marlene mulled over her question, Cherry took in the

scenery. The sky overhead was gradated: toward the City it was misty with white office light, punctuated by occasional neon bursts where a logo crested a building; over the airport it became a traditional suburban bar-heater orange; further out still it was dark. The walk from the bus stop took them along a bright ring road. There were tall floodlights every thirty feet or so but they were made redundant by the blinding advertising hoardings that fenced the outer edge of the road. On the opposite side of the road was a long strip of airport hotels, the building materials and window design betraying the decade that each was built in. The target client base of each hotel was revealed by the products being advertised on the hoardings opposite.

'We're on our way back from a hen party,' Marlene said. She had a knack of coming up with scenarios off the top of her head. 'The hen works in the fashion industry so we all had tickets to the launch of Dillinger & Bosch's new range in Berlin. We slept with all sorts of people there. We're here on a stopover on our way home to Edinburgh.'

'A stopover flying London to Edinburgh? That seems a little unnecessary.'

'OK, smart arse. Our flight was cancelled so they've put us up here for the night and we're getting on the first flight tomorrow.'

'Fine. Sounds plausible. But what if they ask what Berlin was like?' Cherry had never left London.

'Just say, "Wild, totally wild…" Then let your eyes go misty as if you're remembering something. That should satisfy them. And we didn't have any time to visit anything cultural because we were too busy drinking and shagging and watching the show.'

'Good.' As they passed the Sofitel, Cherry's eye was caught by the Galletti advert she had seen earlier outside the hospital. 'Been in here lately?' she asked Marlene.

'No. Didn't have a great deal of wearers last time I was in.'

Cherry nodded towards the adverts that were showing. 'They're obviously getting a few now. They're starting to recognise me at the Helicon so I need to give it a break.'

Marlene shrugged in agreement and they turned off down the drive. They followed the path around the side of the building where it took a long shallow slope down towards the direct entrance to the bar. Inside, the basement level bar was surrounded by inward sloping mirrors which reflected the view from the sub-basement pool. The décor of the pool, tiny shimmering green tiles, lent the bar a sensuous underwater feel and lit the engraving in the mirror above the art deco style bar, a Muchaesque nymph suspended in water, sheer robes swirling around her. As Cherry gazed at the nymph, the unwelcome image of a fat businessman swam past. She grimaced and Marlene laughed out loud.

'I know,' said the barman as he approached them. 'Not quite what the designers had in mind. What can I get for you, ladies?'

'A Velvet Rope for me please,' Cherry said.

'Straight vodka for me,' Marlene added.

The barman started to prepare their drinks.

'I'm afraid our companions haven't arrived yet, but they said to put it on their tab – is it OK to do that when they show?' Cherry asked.

'Yes, no problem,' the barman said with a sideways smile.

Cherry turned her back to the bar and leaned against the thick brass handrail. There were only three people in so far but it would busy up in the next hour or so. She casually inspected the current crowd. One had a delegate's bag from a pharma conference. Could be ambitious; he looked like he was still working. A beeped tune sang out from his Book and he swore. No – he was playing a game. His bag was probably just stuffed full of freebies. The second was looking at her watch too often. She would have been a good bet but she obviously had a flight to catch and was calming her nerves before she set off for the terminal. The third looked promising. Marlene already had her drink and was making her way over to him. She glanced over her shoulder at Cherry.

'Beat-cha! That's why I never order cocktails.'

Cherry watched as Marlene made her approach. Her target was young, broad and tall, and he had marks on his face where a set of sores had recently healed. Perhaps he had been hoping to pick up something new wherever he had been and had set his screen to get rid of them – wanted a blank canvas.

There was an American feel to his clothing – blazer and slacks, ads concentrated on his upper arms like scout badges – but his scraggy dyed-black hair style betrayed a more alternative look outside his work environment. If he ever spent time outside work. His wearing most likely made him a New Yorker or a Bostonian, unless he worked in a London office long-term and was heading home for a visit some place that wearing wasn't approved of. If so, he should have uploaded sooner.

Marlene had established herself in the seat next to him and they were already laughing together. She looked up and beckoned to Cherry. Cherry picked up the drink the barman had just placed at her elbow and walked over to join them.

'Cherry, this is Brad,' Marlene said and continued talking as Cherry shook Brad's hand. 'Brad's just come back from Berlin – can you believe it? I was just telling him how we were supposed to go and missed it. Can you believe we ended up stranded here in London? These guys – what was your friend's name? Lena? Lena's about to join us – they were there the whole time.'

'Wow,' Cherry said, quickly working through Marlene's revision to their story. 'I'm so jealous.'

'I know,' Brad said with a kind smile. 'It's not something I'd like to miss, particularly when the company's paying for it.'

'What do you do?' Cherry asked.

'I work in merchandising and promotions for the Yankees.'

'That must be quite a job.' Cherry leaned in closer. 'So what took you to Berlin? You were at the show, right?'

'Right. It wasn't so much for the fashion as for the wearing scene. You've seen the new Nike ads?'

Cherry nodded.

'My boss is negotiating with a potential sponsor and he wanted me to try and pick up something exclusive, if you know what I mean, to sweeten the deal. Something our new star can wear in our ads.'

'You wouldn't just commission something?' Marlene asked.

'He's very much of the mind that if we can get something straight off the catwalk or from a high-worth individual, that would be better. Anybody with money can buy the exclusive in the first place. Plus, that sort of money would buy us a top pitcher.'

'Good point,' Cherry said.

'You don't wear?' Brad asked Cherry.

'No.' Cherry tried her best to look innocent.

'You should. Good looking girl like you. It could only do your career good. What do you do?'

'I'm a little scared of wearing to be honest.' Cherry ignored his last question. 'I know it would help me...I'd like to but...I don't know. Did you manage to pick anything up? Do you know yet?' Keep asking questions about him. Cherry had learned that if you questioned people enough and kept them talking about themselves, most of them would happily spend a whole night with you knowing nothing but your name.

Brad glanced down at his Book where it lay on the table. 'Not sure yet.' Just then, a slight woman in an understated grey dress approached them. 'Lena!' Brad said enthusiastically. 'Let me introduce you to Cherry and Marlene. They were supposed to go to Berlin but missed it – long story. Marlene, you wouldn't believe it – Lena got it together with Hetta Campbell, or so she keeps telling me.'

'Really,' Marlene said, with a knowing nod. 'Come on – let me buy you a drink.' She stood to lead Lena to the bar.

'Put it on my tab,' Brad said as they walked away. 'This one's on the Yankees.' He turned his attention back to Cherry. 'I don't know if her story about Campbell is true because I was in a backstage exchange booth with Karl Dillinger at the time.'

'Actual Dillinger?' Cherry put her hand to Brad's then pulled it away quickly. Coy, but not too coy.

Brad nodded. 'He had a brand new exclusive on. A good old-fashioned syphilis mod. Calls it "Der Handschuh" – "The Glove". Tollbooth designed it for him. It's an extension and adaptation of the classic palm rash.'

'Sounds cool,' Cherry said.

She glanced down at his hands. There was nothing there. She tried to gauge if he had any other signs it might be coming on. There were tiny beads of sweat around his hairline, but it was hot in the bar.

'It's very cool. Maybe a good one to start with.' Brad raised his eyebrows at Cherry.

Cherry glanced with mock nerves at the exchange booth in the corner of the room. She should go for it. This was the best lead she'd had in weeks and if she didn't bring in something soon she'd end up spending a week on hooker duty to pay her way.

'We can go to my room if that would make you more comfortable,' Brad said.

Cherry opened her mouth, looking tempted but fiddling with the edge of her dress.

'I'll have another drink sent up for you – it was a...'

'Velvet Rope,' Cherry said quickly and giggled.

'Alright.'

As Brad stood to go to the bar, Marlene looked round at Cherry and winked. It was looking good from both ends then. Cherry gave a quick grin. *Jackpot*, she mouthed.

-o-

Kester woke, disoriented. The ceiling looked wrong and the lightshade...he was at Dee's. He was in Dee's bed! He was in Dee's bed...

He glanced over to his left, moving only his eyes, wanting to keep the moment to himself for now, unsure how he felt about it. Unsure how it felt about him. There she was.

Kester fast-forwarded through the previous night in his head: the café, the bar, the square – my god, the square – Dee's front door, Dee's bed and then yes, a drunken foray of fumbling and apologies. Through the fuzzy memories came the vivid picture of her sharp features looking up at him from the pillow, pale skin and flushed cheeks, her long black hair spread out around her head in wild waves that stretched out past the edges of his memory. A remembered shudder of pleasure shot through him, making him twitch and clearing the pain from his head for a few moments.

It wasn't long until Kester's hangover flooded back in to his head. When he moved the pain sloshed from side to side. Staying still was the only solution. Or...he reached out a hand and felt Dee's warm stomach slipping away from his touch.

'Need some water,' she murmured as she slid from the bed and walked carefully to the bathroom door.

It was still dark, but...Kester let his head fall to the side in search of a clue to the time. The pain sloshed again. The figures on the wall glowed gently in the twilight. 17:30. No, it wasn't still dark; it was dark again. They'd been asleep for...he muddled through the sum...twelve hours...thirteen hours. Thirteen hours, Kester thought. A plunger went down in his throat. Just then, he heard a smash and a sickly shriek from the bathroom.

'Kester…' Dee appeared in the doorway of the room, holding onto the door posts. 'My eyes…Kester…' Her voice was on the edge of panic, her lip trembling. She wobbled across the room towards him.

'Oh shit.' Kester sat up too quickly and sent a giant throb of pain to the crown of his head. The virus. He was still infectious. Thirteen hours – the time it took for the virus to establish in the target tissue. 'I'm sorry,' he said, clutching his head. 'It's harmless. I can get you the uploads. Just let me get my screen.'

Dee fell silent for a moment. She was on her knees at the side of the bed now, staring at him.

'What?' she asked, putting a hand to her head.

'I said I'm sorry, I was still infectious – I didn't give my uploads time to get rid of the virus fully. The upload will deal with it.'

'Kester?' Tears were running down her face. 'You did this?'

Kester felt the panic rising in his chest as the thoughts raced across her face.

'You slept with her. Her eyes…was that?'

'You knew…'

'I thought you were joking.' Her voice was rising. 'I thought you were joking.' She looked up at him, rage carving deep shadows in her face. 'What did you think –'

'It's OK –'

'OK?' Dee screamed, staggering to her feet. 'I'm bleeding out of my fucking eyes!'

She launched herself at him and smacked him in the jaw with surprising strength. Kester cried out, clutching his buzzing face and struggling out of the other side of the bed.

'It's just a few cells – it'll only take a few days for the upload to clear it completely, unless you want to wear it.'

'Shut up!' The words ripped from her throat. 'Get out.'

'But the uploads…'

'Get out!' She climbed off the bed and chased after him, pushing him against the wall.

'My clothes…'

Dee wrestled him out of the bedroom door and pushed it closed against him. He held the image of her in his head: pupils wide with fear, pale belly, perfect landing strip, black and white all over except for the flush of anger on her cheeks and the bloody rings around her irises.

Kester's clothes were in a sad soft heap at the bottom of Dee's couch, underpants nestled inside his jeans.

'What a cock.' He grabbed his head again. He could hear her crying through the door. He looked around for something to write on. Her Book was open on the table and he pulled it towards himself weakly.

Dee, I'm sorry. I thought you knew about the interview and I was just so drunk last night I forgot about the virus. I kept it in case there was a second round of interviews. I just forgot to upload. It won't do you any damage, he wrote. He deleted what he'd written, and then wrote the same thing again. *The blood spots are just temporary and the virus is self-limiting. I'll send the uploads, but even without them it won't do any harm.*

That's not right, he thought. Then, hearing her moving around in the bedroom, talking to herself, he dashed over to his clothes. He'd seen her mad at other people before. She'd be pacing in circles, winding herself into a needled vortex. She'd be looking for things to throw. His jeans on, Kester rushed back to the Book and added, *I'm sorry.* He paused over the last sentence wondering whether to add anything more, then thought better of it.

Fumbling his Book out of his pocket he texted Betta: *I fucked up. Dee's mad at me – I can't explain now – can you go over?* He grabbed his shirt, walked quickly to the door and left.

Chapter 4

Alfred Blotch, Minister to Peter

Blotch polished his badge with the sleeve of his robe and surveyed the room before him: eighty square feet of abrasive blue carpet filled with bank after bank of wood-effect diamond-shaped desk modules. Each module seated four headsetted volunteers facing in towards each other. In front of each volunteer was a keyboard and monitor along with a round palm-sized 'call-ready' button built into the desk. The glowing call-ready button was designed to allow the volunteers to indicate to the system when they were ready to take their next call, turning red when they were on a call, amber when the call was over and green when they had hit the button. Together the buttons provided Blotch and his floor manager with a visual map of call volume and of who was working hard and who was not. Long green pauses indicated a slow day and on busier days, when the buttons hardly showed green long enough to be perceived, a lingering amber glow amongst the sea of red was quick to draw the eye.

It was busy today, a red day. This was good for the Real Church but bad for Blotch's headache. The room had the acoustics of a leisure centre and the slightly sympathetic tone that was required with most calls gave the constant gabble of voices a depressing edge that wore him down across the day.

Blotch started his two-hourly tour of the helpline floor, walking slowly like an adjudicator, hands behind his back. The static built up in his robe as it dragged behind him, the grain of its hem catching and releasing on each rough carpet fibre. Tuning in and out of conversations as he walked, he let each 'hmm', each 'I understand', each 'let it out' wash over him. These were the boring ends of the conversations. Every now and then there was a tantalizing 'Is she still friends with your wife?' or a 'Really, three of you?' but for the most part it was platitudes and comfort.

Halfway through his floor walk there was a blip, blip, blip from somewhere inside his robes. An escalation. Blotch nodded to the floor manager and returned to his office, a few doors along the corridor. This was the only time he got to hear the good stuff himself. And it was usually pretty good – calls were only escalated where the caller was in particularly bad trouble, or where the subject matter of the call was deemed dodgy in some way. Those calls could be enjoyable but even they frustrated him. If he knew that some of the calls had ended well – an averted suicide, an abandoned insurance fraud scheme – that would be something. But even as centre manager, there was no ringing back caller 8592 and asking, 'Did you manage to resist having it off with your brother's wife?' No closure; no job satisfaction. His life was a montage of cliff-hanger endings from cancelled soap operas.

Blotch closed the door to his small office and squeezed in behind the desk, putting in his earpiece as he settled himself in his chair.

'Hello?' he said, hopefully.

'Hello, Minister,' came a voice in automatic comfort mode. 'It's Simon Shaw here. I've got a potential call-back for you.'

A call-back. Dull. And probably nothing.

'Go on.'

'A disgruntled admin worker. Works in the administration centre in St Paul's. He called to moan about his co-workers' wearing. He's being bullied but that's not the interesting part. One of his moans was that they have been using sacred areas of the building as exchange booths.'

Blotch felt his colour rising. 'This is an outrage!'

'Not just an outrage, Minister, illegal too. The installation or use of existing structures as exchange booths is explicitly forbidden inside any leased religious building – I checked. It's a standard part of the template lease drawn up by the Religious Buildings of the City Protectorate after the expulsion.'

'Right, I see. That is interesting. Did you prime him for a call-back?'

'I did, Minister. He's asked that someone call him tomorrow evening.'

'Great. That's great. Good work Simon. Put it in my calendar please and attach the call reference so I can review the call before I get back to him. Thank you.'

'Thank you, Minister.' There was a click and the voice was gone. Simon was a good worker – straight back onto it, no lingering around for praise.

Blotch had briefed the floor yesterday on their new mandate and it was already paying off. This was just the sort of information he was looking for – City people doing dodgy things, wearers in particular, illustrating the need for moral guidance inside the City.

Blotch opened up his email and scanned down the list. There it was – '75th ANNIVERSARY!!!' He opened the message. Somebody called Harmonie was planning next year's Real Church anniversary celebrations and was 'exited' to hear about everyone's ideas. From putting up bunting to serving up world peace, they needed help with everything. As part of its celebrations, the Real Church was running a campaign to re-establish a presence in the securitised City of London and reoccupy the Real Stairway after a 25-year absence. Here, Harmonie had pasted in a picture of the Real Church's landmark church and former City headquarters, the crystal formation-inspired 'Real Stairway'. Its precipitous north face, designed to reflect light and shine a beacon of purity out onto the City, had been digitally defaced. It now displayed the logo of HSBC, the current leaseholder, at the top of a banner of red and black adverts that reached to the ground.

It was the word 'promotion' that had got Blotch interested in the email. Promotion and a solid gold Real Church necklet were to be awarded to the individual who made the single largest contribution to the Real Stairway campaign. Nominations were to be made by the employee's line manager. Blotch took in a long breath, testing the seams of his tunic to their limits. Promotion and a solid gold necklet – you couldn't argue with that.

Blotch moved on to today's unanswered mail. Top of the list was a news bulletin from Reuters. He scanned down the headline list. This was usually as far as he got, but today something caught his eye. 'V set to take wearing market by storm'. He clicked through to the main site.

Global pharmaceutical and technomedical giant V is set to make a late but spectacular entry to the viral wearing market. This morning V announced the appointment of Dr Kester Lowe as head of its new viral design department VDV. Dr Lowe, formerly of the London Institute of Immunology and Viral

Medicine, is widely considered in the scientific community to be one of the greatest new thinkers in the field of viral design. The lack of information forthcoming from the Institute on Dr Lowe's projects and clients is indicative of the high-profile nature of his previous work. Clients the Institute was prepared to namecheck include the UK MoD and US DoD, along with private companies Tollbooth, Rigatronics and Stark Wellbury, where Dr Lowe worked as a consultant to the nanoscreen design department on their delay technology.

Although V is just the sort of client to whom the Institute already provides contract consultancy services, Dr Lowe's move has nevertheless raised some eyebrows in the old-school ranks of the scientific community. Dr Bayliss of the Department of Nanotechnology, University of San Diego, sees this as another nail in the coffin for pure research science in the UK: 'To me the UK has always held a tiny flame of hope – it was a place where the academic's golden dream of no-strings funded pure research still lived on, though of course the funding pool has been steadily shrinking for the last century or so. But when brilliant young academics like Dr Lowe start jumping ship and moving to the private sector you wonder whether they have seen the future and that future spells the end for any kind of pure research.'

According to V, Dr Lowe's remit in his new role is to become the first true 'virus designer' in the eyes of the wearing public. So far, V is being sketchy on the details of how Dr Lowe's viruses will differ from the STV mods currently being commissioned and designed, but its boasts that his appointment will "usher in a new age of viral wearing" are tantalising to say the least.

While V insists that Dr Lowe will be free to assemble his own "crack viral development staff", two existing staff members are already known to be heavily involved in the set-up of the department: the infamous Alexis Farrell, who continues to elude the constraints of any official job title, and Gerald Harper, formerly of V's small viral screening division.

Blotch smiled grimly to himself. This could be good or bad. Or both. He picked up his Book, typed in a number he preferred to hold in his head, then stared at it for a moment. Some air was required. Squeezing out from behind his desk he whipped the waterproof poncho from the back of his door and slung it over his arm. He looked around his office. He didn't need anything else.

On his way through the building Blotch went back past the call centre floor and gave a wave to the floor manager, pointing towards the exit to indicate that he was going out. The floor manager nodded and waved back. Continuing towards the headquarters' atrium, Blotch passed through a glass-sided corridor. It was the main route into the building and the occupants of the flanking rooms were often pointed out to guests by their hosts as if they were rare species in a walk-through aquarium. It was a point of great pride with the Church leaders that the Real Church was the first established in the UK to follow the "American" model; it was a business and wanted to show it.

On one side was the network room, where banks of operators sat at terminals, or walked around with their Real Church branded Books. They were working the net. They wrote blogs, posted on forums, tweeted, mapped on webweb and spent countless hours duplicate tagging on MSAR, iSee+ and Google Reality to make sure whoever won out in the augmented reality market, they would continue to be represented. They talked to other Real Church followers and reached out to those who hadn't yet heard of the Church. The room cast a net around the world and attempted to keep it pulled tight. It was thanks to this room that they were streets ahead of the Church of England and the other traditional churches in terms of reaching a new audience. They had technology on their side, which seemed to hold a lot more weight with most young people than centuries of pomp and ceremony, something which the old churches had either chosen to ignore or failed to notice.

On the other side of the corridor were the fundraising and achievements departments: one bringing in the money; the other sending it out in one way or another. Blotch passed through and entered the atrium. He dodged around the tall concrete tablet that stood annoyingly in the centre of the room, recording the Real Church's mission and values, and headed out of the tall glass doors. As he exited, he came out next to a woman who was swiping her Book at the donation point, a small-scale representation of the Real Stairway with a panel on the front.

'Thank you,' he said to her with a small bow. She scuttled away, smiling shyly.

Blotch glanced either way down the broad avenue where the church sat and then shuffled across, pausing in the middle to give way to a struggling Volvo. At the coffee shop he got himself a cup of tea and then settled at one of the three empty pavement tables. He cursed quietly at the smallness of the metal chairs. The tables were small too. Just big enough to each have three placemat sized displays built into them.

The number was still on Blotch's Book when he took it out again. While the line rang he gazed across the road at the church and contemplated the lasered inscription above the building's faux-crystal doorway, singing out the Real Church's motto in gold leaf: *Bringing Moral Balance.* A small congregation was dribbling out from the entrance to the smaller East Chapel where they held weekday services. He noted how few of its members paused at the donation terminal. It was a hobby of his to watch the worshippers exit. It was always interesting to see where the different people would go next and the coffee shop gave him the perfect view either way down the street with its three bakeries, its upmarket lingerie boutique and its branch of the Pigs. The local Pig branch had been tastefully named *Holes Only* for the nickname of the infection-free suburban branches and the owner was such a fan of puns that he had incorporated a snooker hall on the top floor. If Blotch saw a worshipper disappear in there it wouldn't be the first time. For now most of them had stopped to check the lunchtime lotto on their Books. At least they had the decency not to have them on during the service. Blotch fixed on a man in a depressed green coat that came down to his shins.

'The Hospital: Lady speaking.' The smooth telephone voice sent a shiver down Blotch's neck. He had almost forgotten he was on a call.

'Lady,' Blotch lowered his voice instinctively, 'it's Minister Blotch here. I'm glad I caught you. I've got a favour to ask.'

'A favour? A paying favour?'

'Potentially.' Blotch flared his nostrils. People could be so indelicate about these matters. Glancing up and down the street he realised he had lost the man in the green coat. He looked back up at the church inscription and forced himself to refocus. 'If my memory serves me correctly you used to have a contact at V.'

'Yes.'

'Are you still in touch?'

'The Hospital still uses V's testing centre, if that's what you mean, but you know they're not keen on me shouting it around.'

'I'm thinking specifically of your friend Gerald who runs the centre.' For a second, Blotch worried that he had got the name wrong. He took his Book from his ear quickly and flicked a document icon from the side-menu towards the table-top.

'Oh yes?'

'I don't know if you've heard the news but he doesn't run the centre any more. He's had rather a nice promotion.' Blotch wiped the grimy table display with his sleeve and cast his eyes over the mail. Gerald, yes. He could barely make it out. The display looked like it had been used as a chopping board.

'Yes, I heard.' Lady sounded hesitant. 'Perhaps I could put in a congratulatory call, but it might seem a little odd, since his new department is technically going into competition with me. And I doubt he'll be able to give you any information if that's what you're looking for. It would be helpful to know what it is you're looking for.'

'I'm looking for...' Blotch hesitated. He wasn't exactly sure himself what it was he wanted. 'Eyes on the inside, I suppose. We don't like the idea of these "designer viruses" any more than you do. It just seems prudent to keep an eye on things, don't you think?'

'Hm.' Lady's answer gave little away. 'Let me speak to him and get back to you. Could be a week or more. He's a busy man. He'll be even busier now.'

Chapter 5

Kester undid his tie for the third time. It was never going to look good enough because it would never be a good enough tie to wear to V. However, he thought it was a bit mad to go and spend a load of money on a new outfit when there had been talk of a corporate tailor.

As he flipped the tie back over his head to start again, there was a metallic spang and he found himself standing in the dark. Cursing, Kester left the bathroom and paced around his small flat in an attempt to find some kind of reflective surface. He had thought he would stay in his Lambeth flat when he started at V, rather than live-in like most of the V staff, but over the last few days all the little niggles that he had learned to ignore had started to get to him again: the lack of any natural light source in the bathroom, the noise of next door's boiler kicking in at five every morning, the slight cant of the living room floor, the missing skirting board in the hall. He was preparing himself to say goodbye to the place, nitpicking as he might with a lover when he saw the breakup on the horizon.

Stooping in front of his watermarked chrome kettle, he flattened out the two uneven ends of his tie. How would the morning go? He thought himself in through the revolving doors of the V office. At the reception desk he would say *Hi. My name is Doctor Kester Lowe. Alexis Farrell is expecting me. She said to report to her for my induction.* He would say it in a confident tone, without stumbling over his words or having to check his Book for the details. The receptionist would say *Doctor Lowe – of course! Please, this way.* Nice and straightforward. That bit couldn't go wrong.

Flicking and tucking his tie into a fat knot, he continued the day in his head. Mrs Farrell would be looking over some important documents when he arrived. People would be fussing round her like cleaner wrasse. The receptionist would show him into her office and leave, bowing as she backed out of the doorway. The attendant employees would look up and then buzz out of the room, heads down, leaving just the two of them. *Hello*, he would say.

Where to go from 'hello' was the hard part. She would make some lewd comment. Or would she be different now that he was an employee? With people he knew already he would idly practise conversations in his head before he met them, but then he knew the sorts of things they might have to say to him. Perhaps she would make some comment about John's performance in the bar. *Oh, him,* he'd reply, then follow it with a lie about John – John wouldn't mind. *He's just a guy from the department. He sometimes just tags along. He can't handle his drink. He's bipolar.* Maybe slightly fewer lies about John. *I see,* she'd reply. Then she'd hit her Book and mist up the windows that looked onto the rest of the floor. All the employees outside would give him daggers through the opacifying glass. *Time for your induction.*

There was a beep. His Book. After pacing around for a bit, Kester spied it, sitting camouflaged on the edge of his smoked glass coffee table. The transparent body of the Book was a brilliant innovation – just looking through it gave you an AR view of everything you pointed it at – but Kester always forgot to set it to solid when he put it down and it would disappear into its surroundings effortlessly. Word was there was an upgrade coming that would make it change automatically when you put it down, but it hadn't materialised yet. He should have got the one with the red fingerplate and topline. As he picked it up the round button in the centre of the fingerplate recognised his thumbprint and unlocked. A good luck message from Betta.

Kester thought of Delilah. It had been over a week. Betta had been acting the go-between, but it had all been one way. Dee had met all of Kester's apologies with silence. Betta said she was waiting for him to turn down the job, but he had no idea why he would, or why she would think that he would.

Kester's eye wandered automatically to the picture of him and Dee that sat gathering dust on top of the fridge. He remembered the day it was taken – his eleventh birthday, a Friday in the summer holidays. That morning his parents had been deep in excited conversation when he came downstairs. The kitchen smelled of his Dad's aftershave and burnt toast. On the television they were claiming that the threat of AIDS was over and on some channels that all disease was beaten for good. Someone had invented a nano-device that built itself inside the sufferer's body and protected them from disease, taking over the functions of their broken immune system.

When Kester had finally managed to get his parents' attention, his Dad had jumped in and explained to him what the immune system was. On the television there were arguments raging. Some people seemed to be against the device for some reason and others were saying that scientists had bettered the design of the human body. Kester couldn't follow the arguments, but he remembered thinking that it must be very important because neither of his parents had said *happy birthday* to him. Dee had beaten them to it, bursting in the back door, arms outstretched, chanting *I am the birthdaybot. I have come to install your nanoscreener. Surrender your guts.*

-o-

It was strange being back at the V building. It was only a week and a half since his interview but everything looked different to Kester. He stood looking up at the building, recalling what he had felt: a sickness, nausea, the feeling that he was about to try and fool someone. Why he should have felt this way he had no idea. He had been designing viruses for eight years now, had a PhD out of which had come several extremely well received and now commonly cited papers and articles, had produced viruses for the MoD, the Home Office and large private clients home and abroad, but faced with this new audience he felt like a fraud, despite having the notes on his Book to back it all up.

It had been sunny, he remembered, sunnier than today. The steel structure of the building was exposed. It wore its skeleton on the outside. Above the front entrance sat the point of a gigantic V, whose arms were thrown tall to the top corners of the building. It had been incorporated into the structure and housed the mechanism for the mechanical window cleaners that swept round the building just before dawn. Beauty and functionality went hand-in-hand. Well, reflected Kester, a certain sort of modern beauty. Used to the mothball streets around the Institute, this still looked like the future to him. He recalled noticing how the V-shape was tapered to vanishing point at the top ends to exaggerate the ridiculous height of the building. The sky had been blue and flat. Fine backlit balloon skin stretched tight over the top of the city.

Today it felt stormy. The sky was again blue, but Kester knew it could change in a matter of minutes. He stood before the giant V and looked up. With clouds skittering past fast on the wind, it looked like the immense building was sliding sideways, bending in the breeze. Kester felt suddenly giddy and looked straight ahead. Trying his best to breathe evenly, he walked in a superhumanly straight line to the single revolving door that gave access to the ground floor. As he stepped into the doors he was aware of the enormous V that branched above him. He felt a sudden spike on the top of his skull, a fear that the V might drop suddenly and split him like an anatomical model right down the middle, revealing everything.

The ground floor of V was a real show-off piece of engineering. It was walled entirely in glass, all the way round. The only opaque surfaces were the eight elevator tubes clustered like thick power cables in the centre of the floor. From the outside they appeared to hold up the building. The floor was highly-shined stone so seamless that Kester wondered if the place was built on one huge polished rock. There was nothing there except the reception desk, space, the odd piece of art. Kester made an appreciative face as he walked past a long swoosh of metal close to the reception desk and tilted his head to show that he was considering the piece.

At the front desk, Kester said, 'Hi,' exactly as planned. 'My name's Kester Lowe. Alexis Farrell's expecting me. She said –'

'What time is your meeting?' asked the receptionist with a clinical smile.

'Meeting?' The unexpected question flustered Kester. 'No – I'm sorry – I'm not here for a meeting.' As he fumbled in his bag for his Book the receptionist started to look nervous. 'It's my first day. Mrs Farrell said I should see her for my induction.'

Kester pressed his thumb to his Book and sought out the acceptance note with the instructions to come to reception.

'Let me see.' The receptionist studied the message with a frown. There was an odd metallic sound to her voice. Kester couldn't tell if it was her or the acoustics of the reception. She had tawny hair that was nearly the same colour as her tanned skin. She was a mannequin that hadn't been painted yet. She glanced down at Kester's jacket and failed to prevent her eyebrow from rising. So he was well-dressed enough to be a client but not to be an employee? Kester could feel the colour rising in his face.

'That should be sufficient, sir. A representative from V Division V will be down shortly to escort you to your department. Please take a seat.'

The receptionist indicated the bank of shiny metal behind them. The one Kester had assumed was a piece of art. Was this a test, perhaps? As he walked closer to the cantilever wave, he saw a slightly dulled patch in the shape of a pair of buttocks, the signature of the last person to sit there. If it was a test, he wouldn't be the first to fail. He chose an alternative dip in the wave and sat, straight-backed, wondering if he should get his Book out and load something impressive-looking to read. No. Someone was bound to appear before the jacket ad changed and they'd see what he'd been reading last – a gun firing, blood seeping down the cover, gold lettering too big to hide with his fingers.

As the minutes passed, Kester's mind started to wander. What would happen, he wondered, if whatever was holding the bottom floor together gave? Would the whole building just shunt down a floor and stop there? He imagined the thousands of workers on the floors above bracing themselves suddenly with bent knees and outstretched arms, and then standing up straight and continuing what they had been doing. Would a building be able to take that? No, the glass would break. He replayed the scene in his head. This time, everyone stopped and braced as the glass exploded outwards from the windows; then they stood up straight again and continued what they were doing.

Kester looked around the vast room again, his eyes lingering on the back wall. Slowly, it dawned on him that it wasn't clear glass at all. Of course it wasn't. The whole building backed onto the City perimeter, so if it had been glass he would be looking at a car park, grass, or the back wall of a train stop, not a square full of people going about their business. So how could it look so convincingly like the world continued beyond it? Just a big holoscreen? He was itching to go and look. And that must be what was holding the building up – the wall. He felt a little more comfortable. But was that any way to support a building, he wondered, just down one side? What if something fabulous happened in the square below and everyone rushed to the front windows...

'Doctor Lowe, sir.'

Kester had heard the footsteps but had been away in a dream, half listening for lift doors, but not for footsteps. He stood up to greet the stocky young man who had come to fetch him. The man had an open face and slicked back hair, giving a charmingly old-fashioned appearance. He looked to be about the same age as Kester, perhaps a few years older.

'I'm Gerald.' The man introduced himself with a vigorous handshake.

'Kester Lowe,' Kester said. Then he laughed and added, 'But you already know that.'

To his relief Gerald laughed too. Some people's laughs disappointed Kester to the gut; Gerald's was a little piece of truth that lit up his eyes.

'I've just moved from viral screening,' Gerald said, eyes still sparkling. 'I'll be your head technician. Mrs Farrell sends her apologies. She wasn't able to greet you herself, but she said she will come down to the lab later to see that you've settled in properly.'

It was an odd feeling: disappointment and relief swirling together, mingling like currents of hot and cold water to become something tamer.

'That's great. I'm dying to see the lab.'

'In that case, sir, follow me this way!' Gerald strode towards the lifts.

'Please, call me Kester.'

The doors breathed open and they stepped inside. Kester hadn't noticed the extraordinary quietness of the doors at the interview, but then that day his ears had been filled with the constant *woomf* of his heartbeat.

'You know Farrell really wants us to get ahead of the game on this one,' Gerald said, 'so it's great that you could be involved from the start.'

Gerald's informal demeanour was helping Kester to relax. He realised that he had been holding his shoulders tight up towards the sky. It was a relief when he relaxed the muscles and let his arms hang softly.

'But you already have a viral department,' Kester said.

'Yes.' Gerald nodded. 'But its primary focus has been viral screening and the production of antiviral agents and vaccines. I was getting a bit bored of it to be honest. I've been there a good few years now, so this is a welcome break.'

'Screening? I thought you said that before, but I don't remember seeing that anywhere in my research. Who needs screening inside the City?'

'Mm. I guess that's why they don't normally let me out of the lab. It's not something that we publicise. We provide the service outside the City. It's still a lucrative business, especially with the high MR we're seeing at the moment.'

'MR?'

'Sorry – V-speak – mutation rate. We're seeing an all-time high. In the cities, the mutations are given room to flourish by the screens – so you might see a person who has previously had a virus reinfected, the infection quashed by their screen, but any mutation that has occurred in the meantime hanging around. Sometimes it takes long enough for the screen to report it or the adjusted uploads to deal with it that it gets passed on. Of course we know very little about it until the person it's passed on to happens not to have a screen. The screens report, adapt, report, adapt and so on, but in practice Stark don't have the time or the inclination to document all the new strains outside the database. There's an arms race going on. We just can't see it. Until a casualty pops up extra-city.'

'Yes. I just wrote a related article for New Scientist about how the screens are influencing the presentation of STVs –'

'A subject close to our hearts here. Yes, I read it and I confess it hadn't even occurred to me that widespread facial symptoms were a new thing for sexually transmitted disease.'

'We change our behaviour, we influence which mutations thrive and are passed on. Simple and beautiful.'

'Well,' Gerald said, 'beautiful once we're done with them.'

Kester's mind wandered back to Gerald's screening services. 'So there are more viruses out there for you to pick up in your screening, but presumably that doesn't make it more lucrative?'

'No,' Gerald said. Then he paused. 'But it makes it all the more interesting to us as scientists.'

The lift stopped at the twelfth floor and the doors opened onto a stark white room with a set of sliding doors on the wall opposite. It was very different to the glassy floor where his interview had been held.

'You must excuse the look of the lab. Consensus amongst the designers was apparently that this was what a lab should look like. Their ideas are so clichéd sometimes. Still, better they went down this route than the benches full of bubbling test tubes in the basement route. You ever been to the LayTech lab in old Kensington Palace?'

'No.'

'Hm,' was all Gerald said. He raised his eyebrows and laughed to himself. 'It all looks a bit more V when we get through security. Right, you had your biometrics done as part of the security checks so we should be good to go.'

'Welcome...Gerald,' said the doors in a monotone voice. 'Welcome...Doctor Lowe.'

The doors slid smoothly apart and they walked through into a small anteroom in which hung a row of white coats, each with a pair of boots sitting neatly beneath them. Beside each coat was a tall thin locker. There was a liquid alcohol dispenser on the wall and not much else.

'This is our basic infection lock,' Gerald explained, 'but don't worry, we've got far more thorough screening and scrubdown booths for the higher-risk stuff. Your coat and boots are at the end. Your locker should recognise you. Just be sure to shut it after you're done. They open every time you walk past which is a bit of a pain. I'm sure it seemed very smart to the techies, but you don't always want them to open. Just like you don't always want to leave the room when you come within three feet of the doors. You won't have much call to use it anyway, I shouldn't think, as you'll have direct access to the lab floor from your private quarters. All that can be infection-locked too should the need arise.'

Gerald gabbled on as he pulled on his labcoat. Kester went to his station and put his jacket and shoes in the locker. He felt like he was going swimming.

'Will I need this?' He lifted his bag and looked over to Gerald.

'Not for now. And you can always come back for it if you do.'

Kester put his bag in his locker and pulled his coat and boots on.

'We had nothing like this at the Institute.'

Gerald laughed. 'Maybe that says something for us and maybe it doesn't,' he said. 'Oh – step away from your locker. It'll scan you and open again any minute.'

Kester stepped away a moment too late and the locker pinged open again.

'I see what you mean,' he said with a chuckle, then pushed it shut once again and stepped towards the lab doors.

'Let's go then,' said Gerald and led the way.

'Welcome…Gerald. Welcome…Doctor Lowe.'

'Don't worry,' Gerald assured Kester, 'after a few days you won't even hear the constant welcomes.'

'Nice to be in such a welcoming place…'

Kester's voice tailed off as the lab doors slid open. He had expected to come in at the edge of a room. He put his hands out as if he had lost his balance and looked around to get his bearings. They were stepping out of a central hub. The elevator tubes and the decontamination room were enclosed by a smooth circular white wall.

'A bit disorienting, isn't it?' Gerald said. 'This way.'

The central part of the room was a large open-plan work area with white benches and crane-legged stools. Hundreds of pieces of equipment were suspended from the ceiling on swoop-down apparatus; a flock of elbowed machines roosting above them.

'If you face this way.' Gerald put out a hand. 'That's the front of the building. We did manage to persuade the designers that we needed some sunlight. Of course, it will be misted down to some degree most of the time to help regulate the temperature.'

Kester nodded. The lab took up a whole floor of the building. He felt like he had been unexpectedly kissed and for a moment he swore he could smell Farrell's perfume. He glanced behind him.

'On either side and at the back we've got the viral manipulation rooms and the isolation suites, thirty rooms in all. We thought you'd need somewhere to keep subjects comfortable and monitor them in isolation.'

'Yes,' was all Kester could muster.

He looked around the side and back walls. They too were white and were divided evenly with further sets of white sliding doors. Each one must have been the size of his Institute lab.

Kester suddenly realised that there was something missing:

people.

'Where is everyone?' he asked, starting to walk round the workbenches.

'Farrell wanted you to be the first to see it – except for me of course. I've had to do some basic testing to make sure everything is fit for purpose and built to spec. It's been such a short turnaround.'

'But this must have taken months,' Kester said, looking up at the ceiling in wonder. It was a vast clinical cavern, apparatus suspended like stalactites.

'The floor has been earmarked for a while and we already had most of the kit on order, but Farrell wanted to wait until she took someone on to set out the final spec. This place was empty a week ago, if you can believe it. I wouldn't lean on any walls in case you get paint on your coat – it'll never come out.'

Kester looked at the white walls, then down at his white coat and laughed. It was true; the air had a just-painted chill to it. Many smells of newness mingled: polished metal, new plastic, electronics just unpacked. None of the usual lab smells were there. He remembered his post-interview talk with Farrell. He had raved about his perfect lab. She had asked him what he needed and she had delivered.

'I thought I'd leave you to yourself for a while, let you settle in and get together a plan of action. As you need people we'll draft them in.'

'Great. Thanks Gerald, that's great.'

Kester needed some time to think. The only time he had worked in a large lab like this had been on his various secondments and even then he had worked alone on his projects, or with a couple of postdocs max. He could get so much done with a whole staff. But first he would need a plan.

'Farrell wasn't sure if you were going to live in,' Gerald said, 'but I've set up a corner suite for you just in case.'

Kester walked over and entered the front left corner office. It was like a miniature of Farrell's, with a huge glass desk in the centre, eight feet long at least. Light flooded in from two sides. On the wall to the left was a sliding door which withdrew and welcomed him as he walked towards it. A room twice the size of his Lambeth flat opened up. It was undecorated and unfurnished except for the bathroom suite which was done out in small tiles the colour of brown-trout scales. Kester noted a little shelf at arse-height in the walk-in wet room and smirked to himself. Then he laughed out loud.

'I can't believe it!' he said to himself, turning to see Gerald standing in his office by the desk.

'Mrs Farrell will send someone down to consult you on the fittings and furnishings,' Gerald said, with a slight smile.

'Wow,' Kester replied. He walked back out into the main lab. 'But for now, I'd like to be at the centre of things.'

Kester walked back out of his suite to the central workstation and sat down.

'You'll need this,' Gerald said, rushing over, digging in his pocket. The Book he produced was sleek, next generation. 'It controls everything – just have a play with the menus. Give me a shout if there's anything you can't find. It'll know which workstation you're at, so just tell it what you need. I'll arrange for your personal account to be transferred over.'

'OK.' Kester took the Book from Gerald. He held the fingerplate and flicked the Book left then right like he had seen people do in the adverts. Two wings slid out from the sides, tripling the size of the display. 'Cool. Thank you.'

'Now, if you'll excuse me, I've got some things to finish up in the screening department. I'll be back up in an hour or so. I'll beep you before I come.' Gerald smiled, then his mouth popped open and he raised a finger. 'Just a few housekeeping things – I always forget! Fire escapes are through the corridors at the back two corners of the room – they lead up to the roof. There are escape slides to the back of the building – why escape the building when you can escape the whole City? The facilities are back out in the hall, and the exchange booths are round the central hub. They exit back into the decon room so don't get them confused with the exit – you might get more than you bargained for!'

With that, Gerald smiled his Hollywood smile, turned on his heel and headed swiftly to the decon room.

Once he was sure Gerald had left, Kester took in an enormous breath.

'Yes!' he shouted, then whooped. He leapt up from his stool and ran to the front window to take in the view. His lab was about halfway up the building and the square below was smaller than the palm of his hand. In the buildings that flanked the square he could see tiny people trundling about their business.

This whole space was his. He couldn't believe it. Swinging to face the centre of the room, he opened up his labcoat and ran, holding it out like a cape, up and down between the benches. Suddenly, he worried that someone was watching and stopped, but kept laughing to himself. His colleagues from the Institute – if only they could see it.

Sitting back down at his desk, Kester selected the workstation option on his Book and rested his hands in front of him. An outline keyboard appeared on the surface at his fingertips and quickly recalibrated to his hand size. A wafer-thin monitor swooped down from the ceiling. There was something distinctly dental about the whole setup.

On the monitor the 'housekeeping' information that Gerald had just shared with him was laid out on a 3D rendering of the lab. Exchange booths; so it was true. His curiosity got the better of him. He should at least know what they look like – what to expect, and if not now when there was nobody around…? He laughed, then got up and walked cautiously towards the central hub. 'Welcome…Doctor Lowe,' said the doors to the decon room. He walked on, but caught a glimpse of the room. As the doors were closing, he swore he saw a figure in there. Coats hanging, he thought to himself. He was always spooky, seeing figures in coats and curtains. 'Welcome…Doctor Lowe.' The doors of the first exchange booth parted.

Kester hovered in the entrance. Inside, the booth was lit in a cool pink light. By the door was a panel of coloured buttons, the pink one glowing. Kester touched the green switch and the light faded to green. The booth was small, the size of a double bed. The walls were made of a velvet-finish rubber. The only things in the room that he could see were a ledge at the back with various dips, what looked like stylised rounded hand-grips on the walls, and a sleek oval dispensing machine with glowing buttons advertising Durex Pop-it lube capsules, Dryvul pessaries and a type of V-branded painkiller Kester had never come across before. There was a half-moon black bulb on the ceiling, presumably something to do with the super-heating. Kester stared up at it, his mind wandering – how did it work? There was the smell of perfume again, but this time he ignored it, fascinated by the half-sphere. Then he started to feel dizzy – no – not dizzy; the light was fading from green to amber.

'Do you like it?'

Kester leapt forward in fright onto the floor of the booth. It was soft and he stumbled as he turned around.

'Jesus, you nearly –' Kester checked himself.

Alexis Farrell was standing in the doorway of the booth, one hand on either side of the frame.

'I've never seen one before,' Kester confessed in his hurry. 'I didn't know what to expect.'

Farrell kicked her shoes into the booth, then slunk in after them. She moved like fine cloth.

'The lab,' she said. 'I meant the lab.' Her hair was pulled back tight and she had the same hard business face on that Kester remembered from the interview. Not at all like the other night in the bar.

'The lab.' Kester's mind flicked back to the lab, the suite, everything and he was filled with a bustling joy. 'The lab is perfect – I can't believe it – thank you so much.'

Mrs Farrell put a hand on his chest and pushed him backwards until the ledge at the rear of the room chopped the back of his knees. He sat involuntarily. She pressed a button on the vending machine, caught the capsule as it left the opening and slipped her hand up her skirt discreetly. Kester could see that she was still wearing his new virus. Her eyes were still golden, solar flashes. He could feel his trousers growing tight. His pulse was all in his crotch: all flow; no ebb.

'Next stop, the tailor,' Mrs Farrell said, hitching up her skirt and straddling Kester. She found a dip for each knee on either side of him.

'I don't have anything new for you,' Kester mumbled to his chest as he watched her unzip his trousers.

'I know. Think of this as a welcome.'

Farrell grabbed the handholds on the wall and pulled so that she lunged violently towards Kester, her hot bosom rising to his face. In moments, they were humping like teenagers. She held white-knuckled to the hand grips on the wall behind him. He was a fairground horse, spinning round, rising and falling surrounded by colour, like a fitting in the booth made for riding. Wrestling her shirt from the tight waistband of her skirt, he forced it up over her breasts, then bit and sucked her hard-working flesh. Who cares, he thought. Fuck it, who cares.

'Let's make it quick,' Mrs Farrell said through gritted teeth, without stopping. 'Gerald will be on his way back down.'

'Not a problem,' Kester said, the colour in his chest rising. He let out an involuntary cry as she upped her speed and their pubic bones clattered together like machine parts. 'After you,' he struggled out.

'No!' He felt her clench her muscles around him.

Her permission came just in time. On the word, Kester's eyes glazed, his jaw muscles clenched and twitched. He gripped her wiry body, pulling her tight down onto his lap, forcing her to stop her pounding. The room was moving.

They relaxed in each other's arms, Kester involuntarily, Farrell through control.

'Didn't think you'd ever use the booths, did you?' she asked, sitting up, still perched on top of him. She brushed a slight sweat from her forehead and smoothed her hair back.

'No,' Kester said, half-laughing. 'No.'

He leaned in to rest his forehead against her chest but she dismounted suddenly, letting him slump forward.

'Let's get cleaned up before Gerald gets here.'

Farrell reached back to the dispensing machine for a Dryvul. Kester looked away for a moment as seemed polite. Smoothing down her skirt, Farrell stepped towards the door, which opened onto the decon room without giving its usual greeting.

'Oh,' Kester said, hurriedly tucking himself back into his trousers. 'The room *was* moving.'

'Come on, step to it.' Farrell rushed him. She held her hands under the sanitiser by the door, then rubbed them briskly. 'I like to keep my comings and goings to myself,' she added with a smirk, 'if you get my meaning.'

'I do.' Kester walked to the door, his legs unstrung, a small pool of disappointment sloshing in his stomach.

'You're not bad looking you know,' Farrell said as he stepped through the door. She was scrubbing her hands in the decon room sink. 'Moody suits you.'

She said it as if she had only just considered him aesthetically.

Back in the lab, they had fallen into genuine work conversation by the time Gerald returned.

'Welcome...Gerald.'

'Mrs Farrell,' Gerald said. 'Is everything in order?'

'Yes.' She turned away from Kester's monitor. 'Most impressive. Doctor Lowe was just telling me what he'd like to get started on first.'

-o-

Kester's flat seemed even smaller and darker than it had that morning. He put his feet up on the table and flicked on his wall display. His Book rang. It was his mother, looking for some information to base her fancies on. Kester could imagine her sitting at the kitchen counter with her Book in one hand, watching the neighbours out of the front window as she spoke to him. She would take the information she gleaned from this conversation, add in some things she'd seen on the telly, times it all by five, turn it back to front and inside out and that's how it would get reported to the rest of the family. He put the wall on mute and answered.

'Hello, dear,' she said.

'Hello, Mum.' Kester just about managed to get the words out before she jumped on him.

'Well?'

'Well what?' Kester was suddenly anxious that it was an angry 'well'. A 'well, what on earth have you done to Delilah'.

'How did it go? Your first day in the big City!'

'Oh. It was...strange...great, it was great, but it was strange.'

'Strange. Strange how?'

'Just the way new work is.'

'I suppose they're all at it all the time,' his mother said, distaste in her voice. 'I've seen it on the web you know.'

'Mum! What sites have you been watching?' Kester asked, a little taken aback. He stared at the voiceless images on his wall, a magazine programme showing the inside of a LadySqueal.

'Just the news,' his mother replied.

The prim reporter was indicating the main contraption, which looked a bit like a pink motorbike with an excited seat. She pointed to the handles and leaned over to rev them in turn.

'They talk about it all the time,' Kester's mother continued.

One handle increased and decreased the size of the fitting, the other did something unseen.

'So and so from such and such getting arrested at the Pigs. All the big-shot companies defacing old monuments with sex cubicles.'

'Exchange booths they call them, Mum.'

Talking seriously about some aspect of design, the reporter stepped out of one LadySqueal booth and into the neighbouring one, which housed a variation on the same theme.

'Sex cubicles, knocking boxes, whatever you want to call them – it's disgusting. And all running around wearing VD like scarves. I mean really – whoever thought it could be a sign of success to have a dirty sex-disease? If my mother had lived to see this she'd have had a coronary. And your father, well I swear it was all this nonsense on the news that did him in.'

'The news doesn't kill people, Mum.' Kester laughed at her softly, flicking off his wall.

'Tell that to his grave.'

'Mum!'

'He was a strong man when he was young, Kester.'

'He had cancer, Mum.'

'Modern living; that's all I'm saying.'

There was a pause while she took a slurp of tea.

'You wouldn't believe the size of my lab, Mum. It fills up a whole floor of the building. I've got ranks and ranks of workbenches and testing rooms and I'm going to have a massive staff.' Kester giggled to himself.

'Kester! The smut in that place is rubbing off on you already.'

Kester giggled again.

'Good Lord boy. So what are you and your army of lab people supposed to be doing?'

'Well, there are in-house projects, of course.' Kester swiftly sidestepped the entire nature of his job. 'But the best bit is that I can use the lab for whatever I want in my spare time. I can start working on my new screens.'

'That's great, Son.' There was unexpected pity in her voice. 'But do you really think they'll let you do any good with it?'

'How do you mean?'

'Aren't V a pharma and therapies company too?'

'Yes.' Kester was surprised that his mother even remembered which company he'd moved to.

'And don't they make the drugs you have to take with your screens?'

'Yes. All pharma companies will soon – it's not under licence for much longer.'

'So…' She paused.

'Oh come on, Mum, you watch too many of those spookumentaries. We're not as much under their control as you think. And anyway, it's my own research time – whatever I do in my own time belongs to me. They don't have to know.'

'Well,' Kester's mother said in a warning tone and then switched subjects suddenly. 'How's Delilah?'

Kester paused. She would have said something if she knew, surely.

'She's fine,' he said.

'I haven't spoken to the dear for ages. She's never in these days. We used to have such nice chats.'

'It's a while since I've seen her too, to be honest.' Honest; the word dried out Kester's tongue. 'Betta reckons she's got herself a man, so she's busy I guess. I haven't been seeing her as much.'

'It won't last. Mark my words.'

'Mum.' Kester rolled his eyes.

'Some people just keep coming back to one another. I know you don't like to hear it but…'

'Mum, we were never together.' Kester felt himself turning into a teenager again.

'All I'm saying is, she's your oldest friend and your old friends are your true friends – you'll see. Once you're done having fun in the knocking boxes with all the pretty girls and boys in your office…'

'Mum!'

'…and you get to know all your new lab people, it's the old friends you'll end up back with.'

Kester let her finish and sighed.

'How are things with you?' he asked in an attempt to lead her off the subject.

'Oh, you know. The shop's doing well. People will always need underwear, as your father always said. Girls are going for bigger knickers again.'

'I'm glad to hear it.'

'Not inside the City, I don't imagine though. I shan't be sending you anything to give to the ladies – I expect it's all split-crotch, easy access fanny flaps with your lot.'

'Mother!' Kester shrieked, appalled, but blushing at the knowledge that there was a distinct shortage of underwear at V. 'You can't say that!'

'I'm a grown woman, Kester. I'll say what I want. Lord knows their dry cleaning bills must be astronomical with nothing between their mucky fu-fus and their fancy suits.'

'Please, Mum.' An explanation of how this was managed was involuntarily forming in his head. 'You're the last person I want to – can we not talk about this? How about you answer my question? How are you?'

'I'm fine, darling. I told you: business is good, I'm keeping well, the dog's picked up something nasty but I've got a special shampoo for it. Now there's a thing.' Finally, she had taken the bait. He should have asked after the dog earlier. 'They've been giving me medication for mange for two months…'

'You've got mange?' Kester let his head fall back and stared up at the ceiling; another new damp patch.

'Don't be silly dear, the dog does, and it wasn't working and it wasn't working and guess what?'

'What?'

'It's not mange at all! It's ringworm. Can you believe it? And I've had one hell of a time getting my money back. I said to them: my son's a doctor and I'll get him down here to sort you out. Here's my dog running around all falling to bits – he would have looked quite the thing in your office, no doubt, covered in scabs and tufts. Except I don't expect they eat their scabs.'

'Well,' Kester said doubtfully.

A shriek of high pitched laughter made the speaker on his Book rattle.

-o-

For the next few days, Alexis Farrell kept a dedicated display on her desk for the lab. It was a curious fisheye view from the corner of the lab above Kester's office door, its only blind spot the benches on the far side of the central hub.

To begin with, Kester worked alone in the centre of the lab. Farrell smiled whenever she saw him there – leading from within a non-existent team, setting a sterling example to the fixtures and fittings around him. He looked like a cartoon character with his messy just-out-of-bed hair and dishevelled labcoat, attractive in his disarray, more like a band member than a scientist. His complete lack of awareness of his cool was charming.

Farrell timed her visits for moments when he was starting to look distracted. By the time she returned to her crow's nest he was always back at the centre bench, working with renewed enthusiasm. These small ego boosts were working for him, fuelling his confidence and with it his ambition. She was going to make him a star and in return he would propel her to the heights of V Global; the more inspiration she could provide, the smoother the ride would be.

The fitters came and went from Kester's suite as he worked, customising it to his steadily multiplying wishes. Gerald began to appear on camera more and more frequently, coming and going between departments, at first alone and then, as they became useful, with others to introduce. The activity in the lab grew slowly outwards from Kester, its epicentre. Racks, vials and reports multiplied, spreading out across the lab. One by one people filled the chairs around him.

Two weeks in, Kester's work projection for the next six months landed in Farrell's inbox along with a request for additional test models. Three weeks in, his office and quarters were pretty much finished and the lab was comfortably full. He had stopped returning to his flat in the evenings.

Chapter 6

'Lady wants to see you, babe,' Tim said, leaning into the dressing room.

'Me?' Marlene called from behind the rail and inside a wool dress that was refusing to fit.

'No, darling – Cherry.' Tim shook his head. 'Come on,' he said, looking back to Cherry.

'What are you? My escort?'

'I thought I'd walk you along. You never know what dodgy characters are hanging around in those corridors.'

Cherry rolled her eyes. 'Let me get some shoes first.'

'Those red ones.'

'Not too much?'

'If you're going to the corner shop, maybe.'

Cherry had managed to bagsy the black and red dress again and the shoes would go well. She grabbed them and slipped them on.

As they walked through the corridor, Tim took Cherry's hand.

'You're my little sweetie, you know,' he said.

'You're acting weird,' Cherry said. 'Who's she got in there?'

Tim looked at his feet for a few paces before he answered.

'Some stiffs from the Real Church.'

'Is that all? So what are you worried about? What do you think she's going to do to me? Send me to a nunnery?' She laughed.

When they got to the narrow corridor that led down to Lady's rooms, Tim stopped.

'I just hope you haven't been poking your nose into anything you shouldn't have.' He ducked towards the wall as he thought he heard Lady's door opening. 'I'm supposed to be out already.'

'Run along then spooky.'

Tim pecked Cherry on the cheek, smacked her on the arse, then skipped off down the corridor. She watched him for a moment. He was like a little inverted comma, lithe and light, seeming to spend more of his time off the ground than on it. His tunic just skimmed his narrow hips. He was just bone and muscle underneath, sculpted. Cherry couldn't imagine him really doing anything with a client. Except perhaps standing in the corner of the room holding to his lips their chosen piece of fruit, posed like a statue, motion captured. That, she could see. He glanced back over his shoulder. People never let him walk away without watching him go and he knew it. She laughed and turned to walk to Lady's office.

It was twelve more paces to Lady's door. Just enough to get nervous. The Real Church? Cheerful face of Christian fundamentalism. What were they doing here? Had Tim been serious or was his imagination getting the better of him? What could they want with her? She stopped for a few long breaths before she knocked on the door. She could hear that there were two men in there talking to Lady, but she couldn't hear what about. She knocked.

'Come!' called Lady.

Cherry opened the door slowly, poking her head in first, body following after. There were two men seated on straight-backed wooden chairs opposite the sofa. They didn't look particularly clerical to her. At any rate they didn't look anything like the men who preached on the web. They weren't plastic enough. Lady was sitting neatly on a third chair alongside them, so that they made a semi-circle in front of the couch. It looked ominous to Cherry. It was set out like an interview, an interrogation maybe. Lady indicated the couch. Cherry walked over, sat down and gathered her dress neatly around her legs. She pressed her knees together and held them with her hands.

'I'm sorry, Lady, I haven't had time to do my hair and face.'

'Don't worry, Cherry dear, these gentlemen aren't clients,' Lady said.

A buzz rushed up the back of Cherry's neck. Not clients. She looked at the two men. One was tall and thin, one short and fat, like a straight man and his comedy sidekick, except that they both had stern, concerned faces. They were both dressed modestly in loose garb more befitting of monks than the showmen preachers she was used to – though the short man's clothes, obviously designed to be loose-fitting, stretched uncomfortably across his paunch. Their clothing was beige. The only things she could see that connected them to any church were the Real Church clockwork symbol pendants that hung round their necks.

Lady introduced them formally.

'Gentlemen, this is Cherry. Cherry, these are Ministers Clarke and Blotch.'

Clarke and Blotch. To Cherry it sounded like one of those ridiculous City firms.

'Ministers Clarke and Blotch are here to ask for co-operation from the Hospital. I wanted to introduce you to them as you have qualities that I believe they will be interested in.'

'My nanoscreen.'

'There are many things which mark you out from the other girls here, Cherry. Your nanoscreen is one of them, but in this case it's your looks and your trustworthiness that the gentlemen are interested in.' Lady spoke as if reading from an autocue.

Cherry gave a puzzled frown.

The tall man, Clarke, touched his pendant and took a long breath. The fat man, Blotch, was looking at the floor beside his chair.

'Cherry. A pleasure to meet you.' Clarke's voice was deep and thrilled Cherry unexpectedly, rattling her voice box. 'Thank you for agreeing to meet with us today. We know that you are...a busy woman. I wanted to tell you a little about our project. How much do you know about the Church?'

'Which church?' Cherry asked, holding a straight face.

The men looked pained, as if they had both caught wind of an unpleasant smell.

'The *Real* Church,' Clarke said, touching his necklet again. 'The only true church.'

'Of course,' Lady said, leaning towards him and smiling. Her hands began to wander and though she clasped them firmly on her lap they continued to strain and twitch against one another.

'Of course,' Cherry repeated, 'but you know how it is, all these organisations calling themselves churches.'

'Oh, we know.' Clarke shook his head sadly. The wrinkles on one side of his face and then the other deepened in turn with the movement of his head.

'Cherry,' Lady said, catching her eye.

Cherry closed her mouth and smiled, putting on her best

listening face.

'As you will no doubt know,' Clarke said, 'the Real Church is working to re-establish a presence in the City in order to help the poor fallen souls who live and work there.'

'Poor in the spiritual sense.' Blotch made his first contribution to the conversation, but continued to look at the floor.

'Yes. Thank you, Minister Blotch. We have made great inroads in the past but this year we are launching a more…aggressive approach to the problem.'

'Problem?' Cherry asked.

Lady shot her a sharp look.

'The problem of sin,' Clarke said.

Clarke was a kindly man, Cherry decided. He was more genuine than the shiny suits on the web.

'Sin abounds in the City and their sin affects us here on the Outside. It was their protected promiscuity that first saw the hideous diseases they wear emerging, their behaviour that has sparked the epidemic in STVs. Do you think you would be living in these conditions if it weren't for the City folk? Do you think the…' Clarke couldn't bring himself to say the word and touched his necklet. 'Your trade would be necessary if our land wasn't run by…' He looked to his portly compatriot to take up where he had left off.

'By a giant pen of filthy, sex-obsessed sinners.' Blotch burst into life, looking up. His eyes burned straight through Cherry's, focused on the hellfire he was visualising. 'By the fallen; by the worshippers of power, money and sin itself.' This sort of speech was a bit more familiar to Cherry. She could picture him in the lamé uniform of the web preachers, a bird all foiled up and cooking in its own rage.

'I see,' Cherry said.

Lady nodded and smiled approvingly.

'Have you heard, young lady, of designer viruses?' Blotch asked.

'I don't know. I suppose I might have heard something.'

'Have you heard, young lady, that the right hand of Satan himself is working in the City right now under the name Doctor Kester Lowe?' Blotch's voice and colour rose as he spat the word 'Doctor'.

'I don't think I did know that, no,' Cherry said, trying not to smile.

'Doctor Kester Lowe is a virus designer –' Clarke took over again, the move perhaps triggered by the obvious rise in his colleague's blood pressure, 'the designer chosen to head up V's new viral design department. Now, the department is currently recruiting for models.'

'Models?'

'Models to be used as test subjects for Doctor Lowe's new viruses and of course to eventually model the end result, presumably in some kind of photoshoot or public appearance – we don't yet know.'

'A fashion show,' Blotch conjectured, standing up. 'A show the likes of which has only ever been witnessed on the catwalks of hell!' White spittle flecks flew from the corners of his mouth as he spoke.

'I'll take it from here.' Clarke stood and laid a soft hand on Blotch's shoulder. 'Young lady, your kind benefactress has arranged for you to fill one of these modelling positions.'

'What?' Cherry glanced over at Lady in disbelief.

'The position will guarantee you City resident status for the duration of your employment with V, which Lady's contact has assured us will be lengthy, if not permanent in the contract sense. However, the position isn't without its responsibilities.' Clarke's brow furrowed. 'We would require you to pass regular reports to my colleague Blotch regarding the activities of the department and its employees.'

'Reports? You're asking me to spy on them for you?'

'That's rather an indelicate way of looking at it. We fear that V is straying into some unholy territory with their virus development and we just want a pair of eyes on the inside so that we can keep a handle on things.'

'Right…' Cherry drew out the word. She looked from Clarke to Blotch and back again.

'We know that this will be a big change for you but we'd ask that you consider our proposition seriously. It is, after all, an opportunity for absolution. It is a chance for you to leave behind your life of sin and start anew as an agent of the light.' Clarke took a breath and smiled. 'It was wonderful to meet you, Cherry.'

'I look forward to working with you,' said Blotch, 'should you choose to help us. And remember: if you do, yours will be the hand that saves every soul within those walls that can be saved.'

When they were gone, Cherry tucked one leg up underneath her, put her forehead down in her hand and thought hard. She took her

Book out of her pocket, switched it on and stared at the picture of her mother. It was the perfect opportunity for her. But it wasn't right. Outside, she could hear Lady's tones soothing the churchmen down the corridor and out of the side doors.

'Cherry?' Lady came back in to the room.

'You really think this is wise?' Cherry asked.

Lady walked to the window to check that the Church men were out of earshot. They were back at their van across the car park. She waved at them with a tight, polite smile.

'What do you mean?' she said.

'Spying. What they're talking about is spying. It's not exactly your classic clean slate they're offering here.'

'Cherry, if you've any brains you'll take the chance you've been given. If you want to find out about your mother, the City is the place to do it. You know my advice on the matter, but there it is. Don't get me wrong – this is no favour. They needed a girl and you fitted the bill – that's all. If she was taller and narrower and had a screen I'd as soon have sent your friend Marlene. Anyone in this place would jump at this opportunity and you have more reason to than most. Don't be a fool. Do it.'

'So I go in there and find her, but what? I tar myself with the same brush in the process. Like mother, like daughter. Is that why you suggested me? Do they know?'

'Cherry, you'd just be taking a job and keeping your eyes open. It's hardly on the same scale as terrorism.'

'Alleged terrorism. Do they know?'

'Of course they know. So there'd be no snooping around while you are working for the Church. Nothing – you understand? You wait until this is all done and dusted. If you're lucky, you get to stay on long enough to investigate. But if they find out you have been snooping around, putting their operations at risk, they wouldn't hesitate to drop you in it. You wouldn't last long once it got out – you working for V, with your pedigree? I don't think so.'

'And the fact that they'd sent a spy in there?'

'The word of a religious body against the prostitute daughter of a convicted terrorist?'

'Don't call her that,' Cherry said. *Convicted terrorist.* All she knew of her mother was archived headlines that began with those words.

'But you get my point,' Lady said. 'This is a church we're talking about – when it comes to controlling people, they wrote the book. Look, you are being asked to swap all this for a life inside the City, a legitimate job, fame even and all they want in return is for you to report back to them once in a while. What's wrong with you? You have to think about the long game.'

'What if it turns nasty? You're making these guys sound worse than the lootmaster generals. What are they up to? You say it's not terrorism, but who's to say?'

'You're a worrier, Cherry. You've always been a worrier since the day you came here. It's nearly cost you your job once or twice, you know? How can someone work harvesting disease when they are so paranoid? If you didn't have that screen you know you would have been out on your ear.'

'I'm not paranoid. What if my screen is just part of it? What if they want someone with terrorist "genes" to frame for something they're up to? You've just told me these guys could turn on me at the drop of a hat. I just want to know what I'm getting into. '

'I'll tell you what you're getting into. I've seen it before with countless Real Church schemes. They want to make a point. They want to make us think that the City is the seat of all woe and try to get permission to reopen a site there and they think sending you in to V might get them some juicy gossip to help them do that. If they managed it they'd be top of the religious pops and blow all the old churches out of the water.

'But they won't manage it. They'll cause a bit of a stir outside of the City, support will rally for a short time and then things will go back to normal. The City will issue a statement with some platitudes for the ears of us outside and they can say whatever they want because no-one inside the City will care. Nobody cares, Cherry. Even the people out here who think they care about who's in charge, what's going on in the City – all they really care about is whether they and their families are getting by. If they are, everything's fine. If they're not, they need something to rally round. This might be the latest thing to rally round, but it's not going to change the world.'

'And what's in it for you?'

Lady's neck began to grow red and blotchy.

'What do you think, Cherry? Money. Big money. Enough to make this place over good and proper: a new coat of paint, new tunics for all of you, a revamped wardrobe. Maybe even some blackmarket nanoscreens so that we can monitor things ourselves instead of giving a cut to those bloodsuckers at V. I could blow Franco out of the water with those kind of resources.'

'You really don't think they're going to do anything drastic? If it's worth such a lot to them, doesn't that mean they've got some master plan?'

'No!' Lady laughed. 'They may have a plan, but they're not going to get anywhere. We can help them out, do what they want, take the money and when it doesn't work, that's their lesson to learn. Lord knows they've never managed to figure it out before. Plus, V's new business model is a bigger threat to us than any harebrained scheme those two could hatch and anything they do that might stall V's progress can only be a good thing.'

'But what they're asking me to do, it's still...'

'You have a moral problem with it? A religious problem with it?' Lady raised an eyebrow.

'No, but...' Cherry thought for a moment. 'What's to say I have to do it anyway? Can't I just take the job and then wave them goodbye, wave it all goodbye? You ask for your money upfront – everyone's a winner.'

'Cherry,' Lady lowered her brows, 'I'll be getting paid a wage just like you. You cut yourself off, you cut us all off; your friends will never see the benefit. You get in there, do the job and keep your nose clean and you'll be fine.'

Cherry waited for a moment to check that Lady was finished. 'I see...well...' she said.

'Like I said, you'd just be doing a job and keeping your eyes open.'

'I need to think about it.'

'Go on then.' Lady indicated the door. 'Think.'

Cherry got up and walked to the door. Opening it slowly, she looked back over her shoulder.

'But Cherry,' Lady added, taking the handle and pulling the door back and forth a little, as if she was working up to slamming it, 'you've got a new job, or you've got no job.'

-o-

'Gerald, I've got to go,' Kester said. 'Mrs Farrell has set me up to talk with some other scientist. Sounds like she might be from a competitor, so I'm not sure how that'll play.'

Kester stood as if waiting for Gerald's permission to leave. He was sweating in all the wrong places – knees, eyelids.

'Don't worry about it,' Gerald said. 'She wouldn't send you if she didn't think you'd cope with it.'

In the lift, Kester started clicking out a rhythm with his fingers, quietly at first, then louder and faster until both arms were going, a sort of edgy syncopated rhythm; the frayed nerves rag. Then, realising what a weird thing it was to be doing, he stopped and put his hands in his pockets.

Two days previously he had spent the whole night with Farrell and he wasn't sure what to make of things. It was hell having no boundaries. The technicians in his lab freely used the exchange booths. He'd had a couple of hard-to-turn down invitations and one when the lab was quieter that had proved impossible to turn down. Farrell knew about these, presumably. She had made comments about the technicians in question and their 'ambitions' – seemed to see it as a mark of quality. And then there was Farrell herself. They had been together quite a few times, but always at her initiation. Should he be approaching her? Was that the right way to show his own ambition? He must act professionally. He felt he should have had etiquette training; it should have been included in his induction. His stomach fell heavy as the lift came to a halt.

-o-

Alexis was waiting for Kester in the lobby. She watched as he came out of the lift. He looked like he was lost. She smiled, turned and walked out of the front entrance. He would follow her, sure as a mongrel would follow a pedigree. She could hear his hurried footsteps behind her. About halfway across the square he caught up with her and appeared by her side, walking a deferential sideways walk, looking up at her. She kept her eyes on where she was going. Kester bumped into someone and fell out of her vision briefly, then popped back into sight, panting.

'Mrs Farrell,' he said.

'Call me Alexis.' He should call her by name. She wanted him to call her by name, but she felt uncomfortable saying it.

'OK, Alexis.'

'But not in front of anyone.' People would talk and she wasn't sure yet if that would be a good thing or not. She was walking like a machine, pistons driving. Kester fell out of view again and gave a little skip to catch her up.

'This meeting,' Kester said. 'Are you going to brief me? I didn't know if I should bring anything.'

'We're not going to a meeting.'

'Oh.'

'I thought I should show you round the PlayPen. You're not getting out enough.' Alexis strode on. She had been watching him on the lab cameras. He was always there. He didn't seem to go out with friends particularly, didn't seem to be having much fun with the booths. As she inhaled, she felt the breath draw into a satisfied sphere, rolling behind her nostrils. She snorted, dismissing the feeling. 'But we can't arrive back together.'

'Really?'

'You told your colleagues you were going to a meeting?'

'Yes.'

'Well let's stick to that truth shall we. I don't like to look partisan – people get restless if they think I have favourites.'

'Favourites?'

'I said if they *think* I have favourites. I don't, but people are paranoid.' Alexis looked round at Kester. She didn't want to give him the wrong idea. 'Don't you think?'

'I suppose so.' He shrugged. 'I'm not so in demand myself.'

'That's not what my spies tell me.' Alexis laughed.

Kester's reflection of her laugh was thin, wobbly, a hall of mirrors laugh.

'Have you been to the PlayPen before?' Alexis changed the subject. 'I assumed you hadn't.'

'Assume away. I've only seen pictures.'

'The Millennium Pen?'

'Nope.'

'Non-City workers can get passes you know.' Alexis knew that few of them bothered. Unless you were a rich tourist or a visiting worker who had an agent or department to sort out your pass for you it was a real pain.

'I know they can in theory, but have you seen the form you have to fill in to get one?'

Alexis felt a smile building behind her face, but didn't answer.

'And it's pretty expensive too.'

'They should build one for the Institute. Your academic friends appreciate good clean fun, don't they?'

They were almost at the north entrance.

'Yeah, but who's going to pay for it?'

'It's not always a case of paying. A little bit of sponsored research here and there would probably do it. PlayPen might even build one for free to give perceived strength to their own "scientific" claims. Who knows?'

As they rounded the corner, the PlayPen came into view and its sound hit them: a recording of a swimming pool slowed down, the squeals lower and longer, the laughter deeper, coming from City workers of all ages, but the unguarded joy the same. Alexis felt her body lightening. It was one of her favourite places. From her office in the V building she could see the hole it made in the City skyline. It was shorter than most of the surrounding buildings and looked like a shaft running down that might never stop, might continue on down even after it hit the ground. When she felt trapped she liked to imagine herself freefalling down through the buildings to reach it.

As they crossed the road, Alexis glanced over at Kester. He was gawping. She smiled, pleased at his reaction as if the PlayPen belonged to her. She followed his gaze back to the structure, looking at it properly for the first time in years. It stretched a quarter mile in both directions from where they had emerged and was enclosed by chicken wire fences like a gargantuan kids' play park, many stories high. She let her eyes fall up the twenty themed floors, from the more traditional lower ones with their slides, swings and roundabouts up past a jolly-roger flag, the leaves of jungle plants, the tip of a dinosaur's tail, each floor connected to the next by a network of ramps and ladders right up to the top where a glass, lozenge-shaped room appeared to float above the rest of the structure. At each corner, there was a circular lift shaft, taking the less energetic clients straight up to the floor of their choice.

Alexis looked back at Kester. He was trying to suppress an idiot grin. As she watched him he laughed out loud.

'They've extended and improved it a bit since you read about it, I expect,' she said.

Kester drifted away from her side towards the fence, his hands reaching to grab the chicken wire. She took hold of his arm.

'This way. We've got a corporate pass for north entrance.'

They entered through the wide quadruple doors, which were constantly greeting people with a squabble of different names. Alexis thought she heard the sharp kick of Kester's name amongst the rabble, but couldn't be sure. Just inside the door, the rush of clients were channelled into eight short corridors, divided by rails of orange boiler suits that were revolving at the same pace as the moving walkway below. There was a beep alongside each of their chests as they approached the rail queue.

'Sizing information,' Alexis whispered into Kester's ear from behind. 'See – the suit alongside you will be your size. It sometimes gets confused though – can't keep up. Don't be offended if it misjudges your girth.'

She giggled as she drew back to take her own suit off the rail, observing Kester's confusion as he realised that everyone was stripping down to their underwear, if they were wearing any. He did the same, wrestled his clothes onto the hanger and managed to clamber into his suit just as he was turfed off the walkway.

'It's a fine art,' said Alexis as they emerged onto the first level. She took his elbow and moved him out of the way of the stream of clients entering behind them. 'You didn't do badly for a first time.'

Alexis drew her hair back into a tight long plait with deft fingers and wound and rewound a band around it. She reached into the pocket of her suit, took out the mesh mask that was supplied with it and slipped it over her head. It was soft on her face and pretty much invisible, except when she turned her head and it ruched up. Kester would be able to see her eyes, the shape of her face, her lips moving behind the mesh, but from a couple of paces away she could be anyone.

'Anonymity,' she said. 'The only way to play.'

Would he realise this was an order? She watched as he looked in his own pocket, found his mask and put it on.

'Right,' Alexis said, nodding. 'There are rules. No funny business – this place is just for play.'

She saw him tense. Play was perhaps the wrong word to use. She would have to draw him in. She grabbed him by the hand and dragged him at a run up the first ramp.

'And not *that* kind of play.' She looked over her shoulder, hoping her grin was visible through her mask.

All around them were boiler-suited adults, frolicking like kids, shrieking and running, climbing, falling over and rolling on the ground, play fighting. Some faces were masked, others were uncovered and flushed with fun.

After climbing a few staircases they came to a floor which was filled with different coloured rubber hoops, some standing on end, some racked up the way to form ladders.

'OK. Rules are you have to take the same route as me. Catch me if you can – tag!'

Alexis punched Kester on the arm, then ducked through the first hoop. After two more hoops, she realised that he was just standing there.

'Have you forgotten how to play?' she asked.

She glanced around to see that no-one was watching and flashed a nipple at him through the poppered front of her suit. For a second there was no indication what effect it had had, and then he burst out laughing.

'Mrs Farrell,' he said in mock shock, then dropped to all fours and wriggled after her through the first of the hoops, grabbing at her bare feet.

'Lex.' Not Mrs Farrell, not Alexis, not in here. Mrs Farrell was hanging on a rail with several hundred other corporate identities in the basement of the building. 'Call me Lex.'

She squealed like a child and they were off. It should have been so inappropriate. But then that was half the fun. As Alexis grew breathless, she felt a familiar sensation in her chest. A high up ball of excitement – elation, the sort she hadn't felt for years, even here. A silly disconnected elation, the thrill of playing chase. Nothing mattered.

They soon sat in a panting, smiling heap at the side of the play area, backs to the fence. Alexis drew her feet up in front of her like a gangly child. She stared at Kester's gauze mask until she felt sure she was seeing all she could of his face.

'Where to next, cowboy?'

'I can't. I'm knackered!'

'You can, you can. Our meeting's scheduled for two hours.'

'Two hours?'

'You wondered how we all stayed so skinny, sitting in front of our ludicrous desks all day, didn't you?'

Kester laughed, then gazed into his lap for a few moments.

'How about...' He shook his head as if the choice was just too much for him. 'How about...'

'How about the space shuttle level?'

'Space? Yeah!'

They clambered and skidded their way up to the space level.

At the centre of the level was an orrery climbing frame, its arms rotating slowly, sweeping careless climbers from their planets, back to the padded floor. After a couple of goes trying to mount Mars, Kester gave up and staggered towards the chill-out area, where egg chairs styled as planets sprouted from the floor and spangly nets dangled from the night sky ceiling.

'You know, I'm surprised,' Kester said, lowering himself into the core of Mercury.

'Why?' Alexis asked.

'Surprised at how low-tech everything is. I mean there are lots of props and scenery and stuff and it's amazing...but it's all just stuff – there's no clever technology.'

Alexis relaxed and shrugged. She pulled herself up into a starnet, laid back and closed her eyes.

'You spend your working life surrounded by technology,' she said. 'Don't you feel like you want a break from it?'

'Yes. I wasn't complaining about it – I just – I'm surprised. It's nice, but I'm surprised by it.'

'Didn't expect it from City folk.'

'Didn't expect that I would go somewhere in the City that reminded me what good clean fun was like. Is that it? I don't know.'

She didn't speak, let him struggle it out.

'All the wearing and all the stupid behaviour that went before it – the sexual boasting, the drugs, the risk-taking – I don't get why all these people do it when from what you see here it looks like all they want to do is get away from it. Why do they do it?'

It was a good question. Alexis looked around her. People were having fun, but they weren't playing safe. To her right, a man –

probably a man – was standing on the top of a tall spaceship, right on the nose. Two of his mates were standing at the bottom, creasing up as he tried to keep his balance, one foot on the uncomfortably sharp-looking tip, the other slipping repeatedly down the cone of the nose. A few seconds later, he fell with a holler, clattered his back on the wing of the shuttle and landed on the matting below, an orange sack of painful angles. His mates' laughter reached a crescendo as he lay groaning on the floor.

'Testosterone,' Alexis said. The word sent her straight back eighteen years to her interview at V:

'Testosterone.'

It wasn't the usual 'what would you bring to the role' response. And from all of the interview candidates for the job, Gaunt probably hadn't expected this answer from Alexis: 28 years old, tall, slim, beautiful. At least it would get her remembered.

'I would have said balls, but that wouldn't be strictly true.' Alexis had already sniffed out Gaunt's liking for a bit of smut and innuendo. 'But I can confidently say that I have high testosterone levels. Aside from escalating my waxing bill it shapes my attitude and fuels my ambition.'

'Your ambition is plain,' the chief interviewer said.

Juno Chen was a handsome and petite Glaswegian of Chinese descent, not much older than Alexis.

'We've seen you in the proof pictures on several of the news sites. Some of the candidates haven't even made an effort to be seen. You, on the other hand, have been pictured engaged, shall we say, with my opposite at Stark Wellbury. An ambitious target indeed.'

Alexis permitted herself a smile. By sleeping with him she had put herself well into the right bracket for the job. If he judged her to be of the right calibre to take to bed, that was a pre-stamped seal of approval. And she had made sure she was pictured talking to him at length beforehand – made sure it wasn't interpreted as just an old man risking his reputation for the sake of a nice arse.

'I have been researching the company and I'm aware that relations with Stark Wellbury will be crucial to the success of your biggest new project. Supplying immunosuppressants for one patient group of screen users is one thing, but when they roll out the nanoscreen scheme to all the inner cities and keyworkers in the country – that's a big ramp-up in production.'

Chen stared at her for a moment. Alexis wondered what she was thinking. This was information she shouldn't have. It was a gamble using it. Gaunt looked round at Chen and she nodded.

'You're quite right, of course, my dear,' Gaunt said. 'You are aware though, that we aren't recruiting externally on that project.'

'I'm aware that good relations will be of ongoing importance and that it was sensible to put myself in a position where I already have contacts with your primary collaborators and clients.'

Some of her contemporaries still treated performing outrageous sex acts as an outlet for their frustrated risk-taking sensibilities, something to fill the hole that drug controls and protectionism had left in their worlds. For Alexis it was purely business. She had been one of the first to see how recruiters were treating the gossip pages – a Who's Who of the ambitious and desirable. It had been a trend she'd assured her fiancé wouldn't continue, but with the new nanotechnology being rolled out to everyone in the City people's sexual freedom would be complete. Why wouldn't they continue? Still, if she got the job at V, she wouldn't have to do it any more.

'You've been getting to know our clients too?' Chen asked.

'You could say that.'

Alexis looked down at Kester. So much had changed since she was new in the job like he was. So little had changed.

He was lying as if relaxed. She remembered the feeling of being constantly on guard, on display. It was harder for him. She had been up on the sexual politics of the City from the beginning of her career and had moved with it, managing to make it look effortless, but to Kester it was a whole new world.

'You like it here?' she asked. 'In the PlayPen I mean.'

'Yes.'

'But?' She sensed from his body language there was something more to come.

Kester looked up. There it was, a shadow at his brow. She could see it. He was a grown man with a bag over his head; like the rest of them he had to hide to reveal himself. No. She must stop him from thinking that way. She must help him lose himself once again before he slipped up and called her Mrs Farrell.

'Nothing,' he said, before she had time to say anything. 'Come on – pirates!'

-o-

Kester sat on his couch, eating noodles and inspecting his shins for bruises. He was sure he deserved at least two or three. His two-hour meeting at the PlayPen had completely knackered him, but he felt the most relaxed he had in months. The place was amazing. If it could bring out the fun in Farrell it could bring out the fun in anyone.

He took his Book out and put it on the seat beside him. *I've got corporate passes for the PlayPen*, he typed, *how about it?* The first five or six messages he had sent to Dee he had spent hours crafting. They had been long and full of explanation and apology. These hadn't worked. But this would – how could it not? It was just a really cool fun thing to do.

Kester flicked off his wall, slipped on his dressing gown and slippers and went to his desk, leaving the noodle box sitting on his couch. He removed the paper file he kept in his bottom drawer, picked up his Book and wandered out into the lab.

It was late and the lab was empty. On Kester's lead, most of the technicians were starting to work what he considered 'normal' hours. It freaked him a little bit when they did odd shifts. The thought that while he was sleeping there was someone through the wall filling test-tubes seemed sinister to him. Anything could be happening through there. The human testing models for the viruses lived on the same floor too, confined to the isolation suites. It was odd knowing that they were there, cut off, unseen, unheard.

Kester gravitated to the central desk where he had begun his work, sat down and unpacked the file.

The exploded diagram of the screen looked like a car advert to him, like an image of something massive made smaller and not vice versa. It was decorated with highlighter and notes, pointing out which technologies were patented and which were public, which bits might be of use to him in a new screen and which would not. The engineering side had taken him a while to get his head around and the thought of grinding through it had been keeping him away. Hard nanotech was not his strong point. He turned the page over and was calmed by the plain white of it. Taking a pen out of the file, he noted down the names of a few viruses and the basic functions he needed.

'Request *Advanced Virology, Seacombe and Witt*, Chapter IV,' he said to the ceiling.

The display on the desk in front of him popped up, sliding his papers forwards.

'OK,' he said, chewing on the end of his pen.

Chapter 7

'What do the models think? Are they all showing OK?' Kester asked as they walked along the beluga-white corridor to the lab. The first round of in vivo testing was underway under Gerald's supervision.

'Fine, sir,' Gerald said. 'Hera is finding things a bit itchy, but I'm pretty sure we can find a fix for that before it goes out.'

'I thought they were experienced wearers who could take adverse symptoms OK. I thought that was half the thing with these guys.'

'The more macho ones, yes, but remember, they're usually on serious painkillers. I just feel a little sorry for her. She's so dainty and she fidgets like a whippet when it's getting to her. She's not going to look good walking down the catwalk looking like she's running away from herself.'

'Fair point.'

Kester took a breath and puffed it out. This would be the first time he had seen his results first-hand and his stomach was wringing out. He held in his head the picture his graphic designer Helena had created. Would it live up to his vision, her vision?

It seemed to have come around quickly. The torso testing had been brief – twelve weeks perhaps – thanks to the fact that he had used a tried and tested carrier virus, but introducing non-viral matter and effects was risky. He was confident the torsos had screened out all the versions with less desirable side-effects. Now he got to see it working in practice. This was the fun part. All the more extreme projects he had worked on at the Institute had been taken off his hands for in vivo testing. The stuff he'd done was based only on interaction with human tissue – torso testing. Of course, in those cases the results in the relevant tissue were usually enough to tell you how things would play out in a whole human body. The aesthetics of the viruses hadn't been a particular concern, except where the customer wanted the visible symptoms to be minimised, so for the most part it wouldn't have been pleasant to be involved in that stage.

'I'm guessing your last lot of customers didn't care how much something itched,' Gerald said, smiling to himself.

'I was just thinking about that. About the aesthetic side of things. There were only a couple of times that anyone cared a jot about the visual symptoms of the virus and that was to conceal it.'

'Conceal it?'

'One was for private use. A self-administered treatment I suppose you would call it. Think about it – if you were self-medicating for something you wouldn't necessarily want it plastered all over you, would you?'

'I suppose not.' Gerald's interest was piqued, but they had reached the entrance to the lab. He shifted his weight on his feet for a moment as if he was about to ask something, then changed his mind. 'How are the minions doing?'

Along the ranks of benches, white-coated figures bent over test-tubes and terminals. Each movement made was controlled, focused. Even the breathing of the technicians was restrained. Every now and then, the silence was broken by the whirr of a machine, or the mechanical creak of apparatus unfolding from the ceiling above.

'As you know,' Gerald said, 'we tested a wide range of genoprofiles in the torso testing. In vivo, we're testing on six subjects with different racial origins. In an ideal world, we want the symptoms to be as close as possible in the different subjects.'

'Close,' Kester said as they zigzagged their way across the room between lab benches, 'but Farrell reckons variations are good. Every one is personalised.'

'But you need to know what they're wearing, right? What point's a designer label if it isn't hanging out?'

'Well,' Kester said, shrugging.

'We're keeping the subjects quarantined. You know what people are like. We don't want the virus getting out – being leaked, so to speak. And we don't want any other factors interfering with the outcomes, if you know what I mean.'

'Yes, I think I do.' Kester shook his head. They must recruit for oversexed individuals, he thought. He'd never seen anything like it.

'But we're testing males and females with both of course, so it's not like they're totally deprived.'

'Totally depraved, maybe,' Kester said, half to himself.

Gerald repeated Kester's comment and let out a burst of simian laughter.

'And they're coping OK with the quarantine?'

'They're coping so far and they've not got long to go. Here we are,' Gerald announced as they approached the locked sliding door to isolation suite 12. The door recognised him and hissed open, welcoming them both.

The isolation suites were fitted with infection locks, smaller versions of the lock at the lab entrance, making them suitable for any type of experiment Kester might want to do.

'If we find we need the infection lock, something's gone wrong, right?' Gerald asked.

'Yip.'

Kester followed Gerald through the secondary room.

'We'll think of more interesting names for them as we go. Not very catchy is it? KL02? Sounds like a virus for robots.' Gerald said it again, this time in an old fashioned robotic voice, 'K-L-0-2.'

Kester laughed. He was pleased that Gerald shared his enthusiasm, even if it manifested itself in peculiar ways sometimes. It was strange. He had appeared such a smooth character when they met.

'Here we go. KL02. K-L-0-2.' Gerald led Kester into the testing suite. 'It's...I won't tell you what to think. You can see for yourself.'

They entered the testing suite. The suites were more like hyper-modern hotel rooms than laboratory rooms, but then the models did have to live there while the experiments were running. The suite was the size of Kester's own and had a one-way wall that looked out onto the building opposite. The windows across the way had their blinds down.

A couple of the subjects were lounging on the white couches that sat along the walls. Two more seemed to be hard at work keeping up with the outside world at the terminals that had been provided. At the sound of the door closing, the remaining two appeared from behind the examination screen. Kester snorted quietly, noting their flushed faces. There was a dorm room through the way, but he guessed it didn't make such a good setting for playing doctor and nurse.

The whole place looked like a photoshoot. All the models were beautiful, fine-boned creatures. Many of them, Kester was aware, had come from long lines of models. He suspected they were more closely related to coat hangers than humans these days. They were masters of self-abuse, picking up and over-wearing any virus that surfaced, so they were the perfect candidates for testing.

'As you can see, all subjects are in good health.' Gerald checked the display projected on the back wall. 'No unexpected visible side-effects; no physical damage at this level of wear. And the best thing is it can be maintained at a wearable level for quite some time – perhaps indefinitely.'

'I'm still itching, Gerald,' one of the models said. She was short and blonde and looked like no-one had ever said *no* to her. 'I can't see how anyone would wear this ridiculous invisible itch. Look at me.' She held out her arms for inspection, turned her head about so that they could see her from all angles. 'Boring as hell!'

'Indefinitely.' Kester ignored the model and responded to Gerald's comments. 'Yes, because there are no other adverse symptoms.'

'You said it. Now, do you want to see it?'

'Yes.' Kester swallowed.

'Uh, hello? Itching,' the girl said. 'And Gerald, Rio's cleaned out the mini-bar again.'

'OK guys, drop 'em!' Gerald said.

The subjects stripped down to their plain white lab-issue underpants. They gathered in a loose group in the centre of the room as the back wall misted up behind them, a self-consciously cool perfume ad.

'Ready?' Gerald asked and hit the lighting control.

Kester could feel a smile coming up, right from the bottom of his gut. Here it was: the beauty.

In the place where the test subjects should have been erased by darkness stood six luminary beings. KL02, Luminescence. Their lymph nodes were glowing under their skin. The deeper the node, the softer the glow. The locations of the nodes mapped out their figures with an instinctively pleasing focus around the face and groin.

'Give us a twirl,' Gerald said and before their eyes the subjects rotated in the darkness, the glowing ovals mapping out their contours, appearing and disappearing as they turned.

'I never thought...' Kester's words tailed off. 'Buzz Alexis – buzz Farrell. Get her down here.'

While Gerald was waiting for Farrell to pick up, Kester stood staring at the figures.

'I love it,' one of them said out of the darkness, finally. It was a young man's voice, deep and smooth.

'Suck-ass,' came the nippy voice of the blonde model.

'I do – I really love it. Look at me, look at yourself.' The nodes around his jaw moved as he spoke. 'We're glowing – we're beautiful.'

'We were already beautiful.' The blonde model turned and slumped down on the couch.

'He's right,' one of the others said. 'You think you looked beautiful with those scabs all over your face when you came in?'

'You could see it.' She got up again and paced amongst her companions. 'And you know full well those weren't just scabs – that was Aiko's Revenge, direct from Bosch himself. It hasn't even hit the catwalk yet.'

One by one, they joined the discussion. All of them were impressed except the blonde girl.

'Doctor Lowe,' one of them said eventually.

'Yes?' Kester thought it was the same one who had spoken first, but they had been moving around the room so he couldn't be sure.

'Ignore her – I've never heard her happy with anything.'

There was a slapping noise and the shortest of the glowing figures rushed through the curtain into the dorm room.

'Thank you,' Kester said.

Suddenly the lights came up.

'Sorry,' Gerald said, 'I just want Mrs Farrell to get the full effect. Hera, get back in here.'

'It's got to be tough stuck in here together all the time,' Kester said.

Hera raised her eyebrows at him as she walked back into the room. 'Tell me about it.'

There was a whisper as the doors opened and Kester felt Alexis enter the room. He glanced round at her, smiling.

'Mrs Farrell.'

'Doctor Lowe; Gerald.' She greeted them each with a nod and stopped a few paces behind where Kester stood.

With Alexis standing next to him, Kester became more aware of

Hera's attention. She had been staring at him unnervingly since she walked back into the room and had ignored Alexis' arrival.

'Perhaps you could rescue me from here and take me for a private consultation,' Hera said, wandering towards Kester.

'Gerald,' Alexis said, 'you wanted to show me something?'

'I have a thing for white coats,' Hera continued.

Kester tried to breathe steadily. She was moving like a cat, posing her lithe body at every possible opportunity.

'Into position please, Hera,' Gerald said.

Hera held Kester's gaze steadily over her shoulder as she walked back to the group. Kester imagined her creamy flesh against his red throw, her blonde hair spread out like rays on his pillow. As she looked away to turn round, his eyes fell to her curvaceous buttocks. He looked away sharply at the ceiling, composed himself, and then looked round at Alexis again. He didn't see her face; as he turned his head, Gerald flicked the lights.

There was silence for a long time. Then Kester felt Alexis draw close behind him.

'It's...' Alexis paused. 'It's beautiful.'

'Just like the man promised.' Gerald's grin was practically visible in the dark. After they had watched the models for a few more moments, he asked, 'Enough?'

'No, wait,' Alexis said. 'A few more minutes.'

'OK. You forget when you've seen it a few times. Last Friday I had these poor guys standing in the dark in their pants for a full half hour.'

'Move around,' Alexis said.

They watched in silence as the models milled gracefully about one another. Kester started as he felt Alexis' hands on his cheeks. With deliberate stealth, she pulled his face round to meet hers, and kissed him like a teenager, as if she was tasting a toffee apple. Leaving him burning, she pulled away, her kiss lifting off from his lips like a bubble of syrup.

'OK – enough,' Farrell said. 'I want it.'

There was a moment of silence. Kester could see the models looking at one another.

'OK,' Gerald said, bringing the lights up. 'Kester?'

'Kester, I think you should have it too,' Alexis said, 'or you, Gerald. One of you. I want to show this at the next strategy meeting.'

'What good is a designer who won't wear his own clothes?' asked Gerald, smiling at Kester. 'I'd love to try it, but I really don't want to go to the strategy meeting.'

Kester was surprised by his forthrightness.

'Gerald has been burned by previous board level experience,' Alexis said. 'But don't worry. He's a coward. They don't bite.'

'They bite,' Gerald said in a stage whisper.

'Kester will be joining us at the next strategy meeting regardless,' Alexis said. 'What does the next stage of the trials involve?' she asked Gerald.

'Vector and virulence testing,' Kester replied before Gerald could, 'human-to-human transference and the rate of spread.'

'Perfect,' she said, stepping forwards with intent. 'We can get started.'

'Before I go,' Gerald said, turning his attention to the models, 'I need you all to record your non-disclosure statements before you go on shore leave. You'll be wiped at the weekend and you can go out as soon as the symptoms have cleared, but you won't be going anywhere if you haven't made your statements.' He turned back to Alexis. 'That's all.'

'Some privacy please, Gerald?' she said.

In a moment, the security cameras were retreating behind their shutters. Gerald left, a wry smile on his face, hitting the lights behind him.

'Long time no see, Rio.' Alexis spoke into the darkness.

Kester could hear the rustle of her clothing falling to the floor.

'You don't come to the Stud Farm any more,' said one of the male subjects.

Kester barely had time to be disgusted. Hera's mouth was on his, her lymph nodes glowing at the corners of his vision. Her hands were on his chest, unbuttoning his labcoat – no, they were at his belt – no, those were someone else's. When he escaped her kiss, there were three glowing bodies around him. Across the room, he could see a writhing mass of glowing nodes suspended in the air where the couch must be. Suddenly there was a hot mouth around his cock.

'Get off!' Hera exclaimed.

There was a mumble and then the velvet-voiced youth replied.

'You insult the man, then you expect him to let you serve him?'

The caressing continued.

Shocked, Kester tensed, but the overwhelming feeling of six hands and three mouths all at his service, of the surreal dark, dispelled any reservations. He was up in the air, suspended. They carried him to the couch, weightless, and laid him down like a treasure chest. He saw an insistent head pushing its way towards him. Hera was muscling past the others to climb on top of him. His eyes flicked over to the other couch. He couldn't see Alexis, except where the glow of a group of nodes lit her hip-bone, then her arched neck for a moment.

'Doctor Lowe.' Kester heard Alexis' voice through the muffle of kissing noise.

'Yes.' Kester pushed himself up on to his elbows, eliciting a shriek from Hera as he unsettled her. She righted herself and pulled her knees in close to his sides.

'Careful,' Hera growled in his ear, 'or I'll let Leon have his way. He may talk smooth, but he's rough.' She gave a little bark.

There was a soft growl and a giggle from the youth. The third mouth, belonging to another woman, though Kester had no idea which one, continued wordlessly to work its way down his right leg. Kester groaned as she bit the back of his ankle gently.

'You will be attending the next strategy meeting,' Alexis said.

'This is really –' Kester dodged Hera's mouth as she tried to get in the way of the conversation and her toothed kiss bumped off his jaw. 'Really not the time to be talking about this.'

'This is exactly the time.'

Distracted, Kester fell into self-focus, forgetting to wonder whose hands were whose, exactly what they were doing, only feeling heat, buzzing pleasure. He let his hands wander. He felt the four of them knot like a mural, a Celtic fertility charm, each beginning and ending inside another, snakes swallowing one another's tails. The ritual sensation lifted him.

'What's the infection rate like?' Alexis' voice invaded Kester's fantasy, snapping everything back into context.

'Should be 60, 70 per cent, higher for anal,' he said, this time his lips dodging an insistent nipple, 'if the models are right.'

'Mmm?' a voice came to attention.

'Not you,' Kester said, giggling. 'The statistical models.'

'You –' he heard Alexis say, 'let's up my chances.'

Kester couldn't help but look over. They were standing now and the girl was sitting on the sofa, watching, it seemed, from the angle of her head. Face to face, side on, the patterns of glowing nodes from the standing bodies were almost symmetrical. Alexis' form was lost in the middle, a dark no-man's land, every man's land. Kester lay watching. He imagined himself into one of their skins as Hera moved on top of him. He put out his hands and guided her hips so that she moved in time with the figures across the room.

When it was all over and the lights came up, everything looked hyper-real. The models were pottering about as if nothing out of the ordinary had happened. Perhaps it hadn't.

'How long?' Alexis asked, as she pulled her culottes up and knotted them beneath her navel.

'48 hours until full potency,' Kester said.

'Promise me you won't upload.' It was more of an order than a request.

'What is the "Stud Farm"?' Kester asked under his breath, straightening the pens in his labcoat pocket.

'Oh.' Alexis laughed. 'It's an old exchange venue down near Rimfords. We used to go there when I first joined the division. Rio was one of the only boys worth going for, but mine wasn't the only eye he caught. He's been modelling for five years now. Hasn't changed a bit.'

'Really.' Kester tried to sound disinterested, though Rio was back at a terminal, engrossed. He looked up at Alexis. 'Let's get into my office. I want to do some early indicator tests on you.'

Alexis smirked and then, seeing that his face was straight, swung on her jacket.

'OK,' she said, 'but I have a meeting at three and I want to shower.'

-o-

'That was an excuse about the Strategy meeting, right?' Kester asked once the doors to his suite were closed. 'We can take the subjects in.'

Alexis wandered across the room to the leather couch by the window and flung herself down, letting her legs swing up casually beside her. Her flushed cheeks made her look younger.

'I haven't decided yet.'

Kester was still wary of Alexis. She flicked like a machine between cold businessperson, shamelessly oversexed woman and playful child. He still had no idea who else she carried on like this with and, so far, he had been too afraid to ask. She might see it as him being too forward and back off. She might prefer that her sex toys play it cool. He remembered how after his interview he had been concerned about her, how he had treated her like a fragile goddess until the moment he left. But it seemed though she had everyone, she needed no-one. Even though it wasn't just sex any more – they talked, they went to the PlayPen – every encounter was at her instigation.

'Do you really have a meeting at three?' Kester asked.

'No,' Alexis replied after a few moments staring out of the window.

Kester walked to his fridge and opened the door.

'And later?' He poked around the shelves, peered about a bit. 'What are you doing later?'

'Working.'

'Is that all?' Kester asked, to no reply. 'All night?'

Alexis stayed still on the couch in her relaxed posture but she looked curiously stiff, like a posed mannequin. She didn't reply.

Jealousy, Kester thought. Should he have felt jealousy? Why did she insist on getting the virus from the models like that – to please him? To please herself? To annoy him? Had he said something stupid the last time he saw her? He had been drunk, he remembered, and had been surprised to hear her in the shower when he woke on the couch the next morning. He needed to grow some balls.

'Go back to your office, then come back up by the outside entrance at seven. Don't have any dinner,' Kester said.

He held his breath, staring into the fridge again, trying to stand in a relaxed way. Just how long could he stare into the fridge without becoming ridiculous? Soon his trousers would start to hoop around his waist, his nose would grow red, his shoes would become bulbous, and fat make-up tears would rise to the skin on his face.

'We'll see,' Alexis said.

-o-

Kester's apartment was bright, like his office, with floor to ceiling windows all down one side. Though the next building was only a few feet away, the angled mirrors that sat at the foot of the windows stole plenty light and sent it his way. The top third of the wall which faced onto his personal office could be demisted to let light through from the front of the building.

He'd had the room decked out to make it feel as little like the office as possible. The designers had managed to find him an old oak carved four-poster, which sat in the middle of one wall, draped ostentatiously in silk blankets and velvet throws. It was a nod to the creative in him, he liked to think.

The bathroom he had left as it was, though he was considering extending it and adding a sunken bath the next time he was allowed budget to redecorate, or when he saved up enough money. The wet room was wonderful, but he liked to soak and think once in a while.

To balance out the decadence of the bedroom side of his suite, he'd had the other side made super-modern, with long low apple-green Bauhaus couches in a c-shape and a projector facing onto the window. When he misted it out it made the perfect screen. At the foot of the window was a long low integral unit comprising his connect box and his airtricity transmitter.

He had been confident it was all cool until now. Alexis had been in there a few times during work conversations, but the prospect of entertaining her there was rather different.

Kester frantically got everything ready for seven, calling the cleaners, arranging dinner with catering, getting the lighting right, arranging the programmes casually on his big screen, making a playlist. Of course she wouldn't come at seven, but he needed to be ready. He booked dinner at nine to give them time for whatever, for her being late.

At eight o'clock, she arrived. He was lying on the couch, music blaring into his ears, when she came in.

'Oh,' he said, as she slunk across the room towards him, 'you came.'

'I got hungry,' she said.

Kester looked her up and down. He wasn't going to be afraid of her tonight. He was going to show a bit of what she would call 'ambition'. She had changed into the same red catsuit she'd had on that night in the champagne bar.

'Had to make an appearance at a champagne reception for the Science Ambassador for China,' she said. 'We were there representing the big business end of science in the British Isles.'

Perhaps it was an excuse. Perhaps she too had been reminded of the champagne bar and that was why it was the first word to her lips. She hadn't mentioned any reception earlier.

'Fair enough,' Kester said, 'but I wouldn't have minded if you'd dressed up just for me. Can I get you a drink?'

He pushed himself up and reached over to the cooler bucket at the end of the couch. She didn't bother to answer, so he poured her a glass of champagne and brought it over.

'Who needs to give an answer when the question is champagne?' She smiled, taking the glass from him.

Kester laughed.

'I've ordered dinner for nine,' he said. 'You didn't eat, did you?'

'Just canapés,' Alexis said. 'For nine? I thought it was just going to be the two of us.'

She took a seat on the couch opposite, looking pleased with her deliberate misunderstanding.

Kester had pulled the curtains down on his four-poster to conceal it and make the place look less like a bedsit. However, it just made the thing more solid, more present, and it was constantly in the corner of his eye. Its presence swallowed up her joke.

'What were you going to do with the food if I didn't show?' Alexis asked.

Kester shrugged – he hoped it looked as if he hadn't entertained the possibility, as if there had been no doubt that she would turn up, as if it wouldn't have mattered anyway. They sat in silence for a few minutes, then he put on some music, watching her face to see if she approved of his choice: his new favourite band, The Itch. She seemed to, or at least if she didn't like it, she didn't show it.

'I had some things I wanted to ask you,' Kester said.

'Here we go.' Alexis cast her eyes up, as if this was a familiar scenario.

'I see. I guess that answers a few of them.'

Kester took a sip of his champagne, then decided to continue. What difference would it make?

'You're married, right?'

'That's why they call me Mrs Farrell. I know it's a bit old fashioned, but it stops people from getting the wrong idea.'

'Does he know about what you do?'

'I take it you aren't asking about my job?' Alexis shifted in her seat. 'Yes, he knows. He knows how things work. We've both lived our professional lives in a world where sex is power. People might not always have worn, but even when I started work in the City we were openly trying to shag the right people to get where we wanted in our careers. He understands that to be seen to be successful I need to be seen to be desirable, and vice versa.'

'Doesn't he get jealous?'

'I suppose so. Not that it matters.'

Alexis took a slug of champagne and sat forward, slowly turning the band of metal on her ring finger.

'And he lives in the City too?'

'No – outside London. He took a job out there so that we could raise the children somewhere more "traditional".'

'And you do? I mean that's where you raise your children?'

'I can't have children, Kester. I overdid it with the viruses when I was younger – overwore, or whatever they're calling it now.'

'But that's not the end of it these days. There's personal organ regrowth – you can afford it.'

'Well, perhaps it's not that. Perhaps it's that I never leave the City any more. Perhaps it's that we have separate lives now. I'm past wanting children.'

She got up suddenly and poured herself another glass of champagne. Maybe she had been at a reception after all, Kester thought to himself, she did seem a bit tipsy. Ideal.

'How often do you see him?'

'Not often. Not for six months now.' Alexis laughed. The hand holding her glass looked stiff, bloodless, as if she had been standing out in the cold. 'If you ever repeat any of this you'll never work in this company again.'

'I know.'

'He runs a virus clinic out there, if you can believe it. I don't know what he makes of you.'

'But I don't see why he'd disapprove of what we're doing. We're making things better – making it safe, beautiful.'

'The whole idea of disease as a fashion statement...it doesn't go with what he does. He doesn't mind the sex, but he doesn't want to know about my wearing. I'd have to clean up completely if I wanted to go and see him again.'

Kester watched her. She rubbed her neck where the barest remains of the sores were still evident: small darker patches of scar tissue mottling her skin.

'You could tell him it was just something that was going round the office.'

'It was.' She laughed. 'And you. You must have a woman, a man, someone to get jealous.' It was almost a question, the closest she had come to showing an interest in who he was, but her tone was odd.

'No,' Kester said.

'No girl?'

'No. Not been too good at all that lately. The last person I slept with was an old friend I shouldn't have. And to make matters worse I infected her.'

'By mistake?'

'After the interview, by mistake. She's pretty pissed off about it.'

Alexis laughed. 'So what's the problem? She gets a freebie – two freebies from the UK's most desirable up-and-coming virus designer. She was expecting more?'

'No. She was expecting...less. She doesn't wear. She's an academic through and through.'

'Like you were?'

'No, not like me.' Kester stared at the wall as if there was a picture of Dee there. 'Cut her and she bleeds public money.'

Laughter again. Alexis was relaxing. She seemed satisfied that Dee was no threat.

'And the others?' Kester asked, reverting to his first line of questioning. 'There are others, right? Here at V?'

She pushed herself back onto the couch and got comfortable.

'This is the question – I knew you'd want to know. They all do.' She smiled to herself. 'There, I answered your question without answering the question. Do you see what I did there? Pretty good.'

'At the moment?'

'Mostly you.' She let her shoe fall off and pushed her big toe into the rug in front of her in an inappropriately coy gesture.

Kester laughed. 'Right.'

'Seriously. I go through phases. I have "favourites" just like the rumours say. Tactical favourites.'

'Tactical favourites.' Kester lifted the bottle from the cooler and moved over to the couch beside her. He filled both their glasses then lifted his in a toast. 'Well, here's to your new favourite.'

She lifted her glass and chinked it against his.

'Are you trying to romance me, Doctor Lowe?'

'What's the longest anyone has managed to stay your favourite?'

Alexis shrugged and a thin smile drew her closed lips tight.

'I'm going to discover the secret,' Kester said. 'I'm going to make sure I stay tactically favourable.'

'You are ambitious, Doctor. I wish you the best of luck,' Alexis said, taking a drink.

The door buzzer went.

'Hungry?' Kester asked.

'Always,' she replied.

Chapter 8

'I'll be gone a while,' Cherry said. 'A few weeks, maybe.'

She was sitting cross-legged in Tim's runk, waiting to talk to him while he rooted around in his locker. He was trying to avoid her, a feat impossible in such a small space. There were so few things in his locker that his rooting was becoming a bit of a farce.

'Have you lost something, darling?' she asked him.

'No.' Tim stopped and looked straight at her. 'You have. I'm looking for your loyalty. You had it last time you were here.'

'Tim –'

'I'm sorry. I just can't believe you're going.'

'I don't have any choice.'

'We always have a choice, Cherry. Once you realise that your life will leap forward.'

'Like yours has?'

Tim's shoulders fell and he looked down, closing his eyes as if in prayer.

'Sorry,' Cherry said. 'That sounded harsh. I didn't mean it.'

Tim kept his eyes closed and bowed his head further. As if he was willing it, his runk blossomed and became new to her. They were sitting in a jungle clearing. Roots, snakes, rodent tails and tendrils embraced vines and laid out a tangled geometry along the jungle floor. The vines climbed up, around and between tree trunks, into the grip of boxy creatures. Here, a monkey yanked the tail of a parrot as it snatched an insect from the tongue of a lizard; there a clutch of irregular-shaped eyes stared from behind the waxy backdrop of foliage. Cherry's eyes tripped along a branch until they reached the edge of the runk.

'I've been practising,' he said into his lap. 'Clive's door, Deepa's – Marlene's going to let me do hers too. I've been sending out planes – all different ones – look.'

Tim reached behind him and took out a paper plane. The

outside was crazed with intricate doodles. When he pulled its wings it opened up to reveal his runk number and a neat hand-written advert. Cherry swallowed. She had been sitting in the middle of his dream, his escape route, ignoring it, oblivious to the remarkable effort that he had put in. She felt sick. She'd always thought of the paintings as the product of boredom. They were amazing, but when you'd seen them so many times you just took them for granted. She didn't answer. She watched as he folded the plane back up and pushed it out into the air. He paused, arm extended, hand splayed, as if he had cast a spell.

'Here,' Tim said.

He turned and put a hand up to the top of the back wall of his runk. He eased his fingers over the top, then pulled forward. It wasn't the wall, Cherry realised, it was a large thin canvas. Tim tipped it towards him. The jungle clearing persisted beside and above them, but before them was a window to another time and place, another canvas, a work in progress. It was a stylised image of London painted as from above, a ring burning around it in place of the Green Belt, a symbolic representation of 2017, year of riots, year of London's fiery circumcision. Cherry opened her mouth and waited for words to fill it, but none came.

'One of my regulars owns a gallery,' Tim said, picking up another flyer and fiddling with it. 'He's invited me to exhibit next month.'

He held out a flyer to Cherry. It shouted, then whispered: CUT THE CITY'S ART OUT – *visions of near past and near future London.*

'Tim, that's amazing!'

Tim pushed the animal canvas back up so it became the wall again. His tunic was bright white against the jungle background. He looked distinct, looked sure.

'Espionage isn't the only way out,' he said, a smile creeping onto his face. Her earlier comment had snapped his elastic, but he was starting to spring again. 'But if you have to go, any chance you could do some flyering in the City?' He put on a New York accent. 'They got fat wallets in there!'

'Tim, you're not even supposed to know I'm going anywhere, never mind what I'm doing.'

'Is it really only for a few weeks?'

'No, probably not,' Cherry admitted, sighing. 'They said it would be long term, maybe permanent.'

'In that case, we should say goodbye properly.'

Cherry laughed and picked at the hem of her white tunic.

'Oh come on, babe,' Tim sprang back to full strength and reached across with his lean arms, whipping her tunic up over her face and shoulders.

Arms trapped above her head, slouched back, cross-legged, Cherry was completely exposed.

'Ooh, you're like a little peach salad,' Tim said to her with a blushing grin visible through the fabric of her tunic.

'Lay off it!' Cherry laughed, squiggling, and then squealed with surprise as he ducked down and licked her, quick as a hummingbird. 'You know this is why Marlene calls you Bonobo?'

'I've never heard her call me that.' He kissed her on the belly and let go of her tunic. 'I'll get you one day, little miss picky.'

Cherry snorted. 'I'll come around when I can afford to be picky. Right now I'd rather you weren't a member of the *I've banged Cherry* club.'

She put her hand out to touch one of the animals on Tim's frieze, then stopped.

'The minute I'm out of this place, you'll be the first, I promise – if I can't find someone my own age!'

Tim laughed into his lap.

'If you ever come back, you mean.'

Cherry stared out at the room full of runks. She let her eyes dry and blur until she was forced to blink.

'You know I do *want* to go,' she said.

'Of course you do. Your mother, I get it. You want to; you need to. Just don't get caught. And don't forget about us.'

-o-

Cherry dumped her small backpack on the path in front of her. Its seams were stretched and the stitches were showing. She took off her light jacket and threaded it through the handle at the top of her backpack. The sun was out, for now; best that her jacket was easy to get to. Turning, she looked back at where she'd come from.

The outer edge of the Green Belt was lined with residential

builds. Some had been built as part of the redevelopment effort and some independently by wealthy London commuters who'd had high hopes of the Green Belt. The former were showing their sixty years badly, both in terms of design and quality and some had already been bought up and flattened to make room for new projects. Beyond them, she could just make out the spires of the Hospital clock tower, lending an oddly venerable shape to the horizon.

Cherry turned back. Her eyes glanced across the width of the Green Belt, a long stretch of unkempt parkland curving into the distance, spoked with roads and footpaths all leading from the suburbs into London proper. At its inner edge lay the City. She walked.

The spaces between the outer City buildings had been bricked up, creating an ominous patchwork wall. Looking square at it, even from this distance, you could have been fooled into thinking it had no top, that there was no sky above it. The closer Cherry got to the wall, the fewer trees there were. Those that had survived further in were stunted and leaned in the direction of the prevailing wind. She paused and put on her jacket, turning up the collar. Just then, a backdraft ignited in her mind – the enormity of the riots, the sheer volume of City that had been razed – Tim's depiction of the flaming corridor.

At the end of the footpath was their local perimeter railway stop, B3, comprising the B3 City checkpoint. Cherry passed through and took a route under the City and out of the other side, riding the tube to Embankment. At Embankment station she bought a sandwich and then walked up onto the Hungerford Footbridge to get a better view.

The sun was setting and the familiar London landmarks were beginning to light up: St Paul's, the New Eye, the Shard, the Bloom, the Swiss Cheese. All were backdropped by the steeply rising scoop of the City, thousands of lit windows and hundreds of logos all fighting for attention with the cooling bulb of the sun. Halfway across the bridge Cherry found a plaque, rubbed almost clear of its cityscape and labels. She leaned on it, munching on her sandwich, and took out the instructions from her pack. They must be putting her up somewhere – a hotel? She got suddenly excited – she had never stayed in a hotel before. She checked the address:

Dempsey's
32 Lambeth Walk
Ring five times

Dempsey's Refuge for the Faithful was not far from the Embankment, on the south side of the river. It was a poorly executed stratification of a Victorian building; a stack of damp shoeboxes on a modest wedding cake. Cherry rang the bell five times as instructed. There was no answer at the intercom, but after a short pause she heard a faint buzz and the door pinged ajar. She pushed it wide cautiously and walked in.

The hallway was narrow and the paintwork bubbled with damp. Cherry pulled her shoulders in and headed for the stairs. On the top floor was an open section of landing with eight dejected looking doors leading off it. There was no-one to welcome her. All the doors had a number and a hook to one side. Door three had a key hanging on its hook. She lifted it gingerly. It was tagged with a parcel label which was thin and furry with repeated use. 'Woodlock', the label currently said in shaky pencilled capitals. Cherry looked up the corridor, then back down towards the stairwell. There was still nobody there, so she took the key and let herself in.

The room was basic but clean and, to Cherry's relief, had a large window that looked out onto the street below. Besides that there was a small double bed and a desk and teen-sized swivel chair. A few pieces of yellow foam were escaping the back of the chair pad.

Closing the door, she saw that a small wet-room with a flip-down sink and toilet had been built into the corner of the room. The two outer walls of the wet room were translucent plastic with a three-stripe pattern across the midriff area. It made the room look like it had had an old-fashioned shower cubicle installed in the corner. In fact, Cherry reflected, that's probably exactly what had been done, with the toilet facilities added later. A cosy arrangement.

Before putting anything down, Cherry opened the window, checked the desk drawers and smelled the bedclothes. She also ducked down and looked under the bed. She wasn't really certain why, but it seemed a good idea when she was checking everything else. Having locked the door from the inside, she unpacked. Everything from her bag was spread out on the bedclothes within minutes. It didn't take long to take stock: a change of clothes, her instructions, her dog-eared map, the vouchcard, her temporary V pass, and a bottle of water. She took a swig of water and sat down on the bed, feeling its spindly legs shift a little. This small room, its fragile partition walls; she could feel the enormity of the city outside pressing in on them.

'Holiday!' she said to herself in a cheerful tone.

The word disappeared into the powdery walls, its brightness absorbed, nothing reflected back. It was as if she had never said it, as if nothing had ever been said in this room. She reached into her pocket and brought out her Book. She switched it on and propped up the picture of her mother in front of her.

'We're in,' she said. 'But don't get too excited. You're going to have to wait until my job here is finished. On pain of crucifixion.'

-o-

At least it was a nice morning, Cherry told herself, squinting in the reflected sunlight. And at least she had managed to sleep a little.

After half an hour in the City, she was starting to feel nostalgic for the postcard London of the South Bank. There, only one in twenty people wore – perhaps even fewer. The rural tourists were obvious by their reactions to the wearers, giving them a wide berth and sometimes even trying to sneak photos. People even dressed normally, for the most part. But this morning, she hadn't seen a clean face since she got off the tube.

And people in London proper had time to stop and look around, chat to one another, do whatever. Here, when she so much as paused to look at something, people would deviate from their paths just enough to miss full collision, but not enough to stop their clothes from brushing against hers. They were too busy to step further aside, or they wanted her to know that they could bash into her if they wanted to, to realise she was inconveniencing them.

She looked at the faces as they moved past her. No, this was not conscious behaviour; they were on some kind of City autopilot, eyes fixed on their final destination, cutting through steel and glass, people and air, their brains silently computing the most efficient way to get there. They were unaware of her presence, probably unaware that they were even walking round anyone, their heads already in the meetings they were headed to. Cherry tried not to stare when they were wearing symptoms on their faces, though they wouldn't have noticed if she had done. Many of them had patchy hair, shaved short, and no eyebrows, she noticed. Was this the latest thing? She reminded herself that the diseases were only transmitted sexually, though it didn't stop her trying to curl her body away from anyone who looked particularly diseased.

Cherry entered the square on the south side and headed for the fountain at its centre. As she drew closer, she saw a door open at its base and two young men exited and went their separate ways. Bumping her way to the edge of the fountain, she saw that there were exchange booths all the way round. She checked the time. She was early. She climbed the stairs up the side of the fountain and dropped down to sit on its edge, where umpteen suits were eating pastries, legs dangling, occasionally knocked by the doors below. Moving her shoulders in a slow circle, feeling them crunch, she surveyed the square and enjoyed being still at the centre of it all.

She sat facing the famous V building. She had only seen it from the back and yet it was so familiar. Its violent façade was a universal symbol of big business. V, the giant with more pies than fingers. An image came into her mind: a chaotic room, a half-remembered half-constructed memory of a study, a large picture of the V building pinned to its wall, small notelets stuck all around it. A ghost from her half-remembered childhood. She was filled with a fondness for the building. Its symmetry and the rapier elegance of its lines pleased her. The V drew the eye down to what seemed like an impractically small entrance.

Out of the crowd two figures attracted Cherry's eye: a tall striking woman striding with purpose and a man who looked out of focus, less precise than the other figures. Cherry smiled as she watched him trying to keep up with the long-legged progress of his companion like a scruffy terrier running after a greyhound. She checked the time again. She wasn't supposed to start until ten, but judging by the size of the building, getting to the right floor might take some time. Hopping off the edge of the fountain, she made her way across the square to the front door.

The ground floor of the building was huge, almost empty. Cherry's eye was drawn by the back wall on which the image had just changed. It was showing a street scene. She paused and watched it for a moment. It wasn't London. The people were more tanned. The sunshine had a different quality. It was definitely a business district though: even at a distance she could see that the stars of the scene were wearing; they looked not quite right, set her teeth on edge. The clothes were ad-splattered just like they were in the square behind her, but they were even brasher, less concerned with fitting with the general look of the outfits.

'New York,' came a slightly tinny voice from behind the reception desk. 'The view from V Manhattan's front doors.'

Cherry looked over and smiled at the plastic receptionist. The scene changed again.

'Spain?' Cherry asked. In this scene the clothes fitted more neatly; the advertising was more discreet.

'Milan.' The image changed again. 'And that one's Glasgow.'

Looking back again, Cherry laughed. 'Of course.'

It was raining. The scene was all golf umbrellas and legs. Every second panel of each umbrella was given over to an ad or logo, one or two newer looking ones sporting moving ads on repeat. The man at the centre of the scene, his back turned, was twirling his umbrella over his shoulder, creating a hypnotic swirl of colour, a giant lollipop. It was like a sequence from a strange musical.

'Can I help you?' the receptionist asked.

'Yes, thank you.' Cherry turned back to her. 'It's my first day. I'm starting as a model for Doctor Lowe.'

'Lucky you,' the receptionist replied with a knowing smile. 'Just take a seat and I'll get someone to welcome you.' She indicated the silver cantilever swoosh in the middle of the tiled floor.

'That's a seat?' Cherry asked.

'Yes, a very expensive one.'

The receptionist raised an eyebrow at Cherry and then gave her a small smile.

'If you say so, but if I get thrown out for sitting on this thing…'

Leather soles clicked across the floor towards them.

'Gerald, I was just about to buzz you,' said the receptionist.

'I'm expecting someone,' said a man's voice, 'which means that you must be…'

Cherry turned to face the voice. It belonged to a man, youngish, good-looking, sort of. His hair was slicked back in too formal a way.

He looked like someone out of the movies. She could imagine him in a sharp old-fashioned button-up suit, her in her print dress on his arm as he led her into a bright building – a bar, a theatre. She had seen him before, she recalled, at the testing centre. His face had appealed to her, though she couldn't really say why.

'Cherry,' she said extending a hand. 'Cherry Woodlock.'

'I'm Gerald. Nice to finally meet you.'

'That was good timing. Your receptionist had just persuaded me to sit on this lovely piece of art.'

Cherry winked at the receptionist and Gerald laughed.

'This way, please.' He led her to a small booth by the central hub of the building. 'If you would step inside please and stand still for a moment. This will just scan your biometrics. By the time we get upstairs the building should recognise you.'

Cocooned inside the lift, Gerald launched into a welcome monologue.

'Yes, I'm so glad to meet you. I've been welcoming all the models personally at Doctor Lowe's request. Of course, the professional models expect special treatment but to be honest we haven't managed to recruit so many of them this time round – they're not such fans of the quarantine policy. Our original models are tied in though, which is great – we need a few high-profile faces. And of course it's important for us to launch a few new careers too.' Gerald smiled pointedly at Cherry. 'Here we are.'

Gerald's monologue continued as he led Cherry through a featureless white corridor into a decontamination chamber, equally white. Here, he apologised.

'I'm afraid it's standard-issue garb from here on in,' he said, tipping his head to one side as if addressing someone important. He stretched out an arm towards the bank of white lockers. 'This locker is yours. It should – ah!'

It popped open as Cherry stepped towards it.

'Yes, good – you are officially one of us now. But watch. You need to step away quickly once you're finished or it gets all excited and thinks you want in again.'

'I know some people like that.'

Gerald blushed and swept a hand across his slick hair. Cherry looked in the locker. Hanging up was a white kimono, draped over a square hanger that had a pair of white knickers and a white sports-bra stretched around its frame. Beneath these sat a pair of fluffy white slippers.

'White,' Cherry said, the feeling of her terry towelling tunic suddenly there on her skin.

'White suits everyone!' Gerald's blush was gone and there was a twinkle in his eye. 'If you wouldn't mind?' He indicated the clothes – a request – then turned his back politely.

Cherry smiled to herself. This was the biggest show of manners she had experience in a long time. She quickly disrobed and folded her own clothes into a neat pile in the corner of the locker.

'Right. Done,' she said as she tied her kimono.

'Beautiful,' Gerald said as he turned. 'Great, I mean. Let's get straight to the testing suite.'

Cherry took in as much as she could as they crossed the lab floor. She was supposed to be finding things out, she reminded herself. Nothing she looked at meant anything – vials were all labelled with numbers; all the fancy swoop-down monitors had privacy filters on so that to see them you would have to stand directly behind the user; all the workers looked neat and respectable in their matching white labcoats and there was little chat going on.

'Welcome…Gerald. Welcome…Ms Woodlock,' came a voice as they reached the doors for the testing suite.

Gerald led Cherry into the suite and directly into a side room. Once inside he sealed the door, took his Book out and tapped it a couple of times.

'OK,' he said. 'Have a seat.'

Cherry looked around the close white room. There was a small table, a bench and a swivel chair, all white. She sat down on the bench.

'This is the only place in the building we can talk safely,' Gerald said. He sat down on the swivel chair and pulled a flat, white case from under the table top. Setting it down on the table, he opened it up to reveal a selection of packaged swabs, syringes and sample tubes. 'If you don't mind I'll get your initial checks and tests underway.'

'No problem.' Cherry eyed the syringes.

So that was the reason for his ceaseless talk in the lift: stopping her from talking.

'Why are you doing this Gerald?' Cherry asked. 'I mean why did you help get me the job?'

'Why?'

'Are you a sympathiser?'

'Listen,' Gerald said. His tone was serious, but not unpleasant. 'I said this was a place we could talk but – and don't take this the wrong way – I don't know exactly why you're here and I don't want to know. I'm just in it to keep myself in dental bleach and Brylcreem.' He avoided eye contact as if the conversation wasn't happening. Swabbing her inner arm he took up a syringe. 'Look away if you're squeamish. In a second you'll feel a scratch. There. I'm assuming that Lady hasn't just gone all altruistic and paid me to take you on for your own good. Just be careful and keep my name out of whatever it is you're doing.'

'Of course.' Cherry waited to see if he had more to say, but that seemed to be it. 'So how will this all work? The testing I mean. I don't know too much.'

'I suppose you don't,' Gerald replied, looking up at her. 'I'll send a copy of the original job spec to your Book.'

'My Book is about three hundred years old – that'll probably explode it.'

'Oh. Then we'll have to sort you out with a new one.'

Easy as that.

'Where to start then?' Gerald said. 'We've got a few initial tests to run and a bit of training to go through, so you'll be able to come and go for the first week or two depending on Doctor Lowe's plans. After that, once he's assigned you a virus, you'll be quarantined for the testing period. Test periods vary, but it might be anything from a few weeks to a few months. It all depends on the virus and the techniques the Doctor is employing…but you don't need to know about that.'

'And access to the web and that sort of thing? Can I phone people?'

'For the duration of any quarantine periods you'll be cut off from the outside world completely. Well, not completely – we have web terminals in the suites so that you can keep up with the news and receive incoming messages etc, but there's no outgoing data of any kind.

'Once the quarantine is over, you'll have a break of a few weeks or whatever fits in with the schedule – contract minimum is one week – the virus will be wiped from your system and you'll be allowed home. Of course you'll have recorded a non-disclosure statement regarding the nature of the virus that has been tested on you and any others you have seen during your time here.'

'Right.'

Cherry was starting to feel a bit woozy. Looking down she saw that Gerald had taken three vials of blood and was waiting for a fourth to fill.

'Are you alright?' he asked.

'Fine,' she replied, pulling herself up a little.

'Last one. I'll get you a sugary snack and a drink when we're done. I should show you where the refectory is anyway. After that, we'll meet Doctor Lowe, if he's back from his meeting.'

Gerald pressed a small ball of cotton wool to Cherry's arm and indicated to her to hold it. She held it in place with a tight pincer grip and watched Gerald as he arranged his vials and tidied up his equipment. She had expected she might have some sort of ally or confidant in Gerald, but it looked like she was on her own. Shame, she reflected. His side-parted black hair was impossibly glossy. Again she was transported: this time she was holding his suited arm, giggling in a red-velveted cinema, silent movie music full of peril blaring out around them.

'You know you look the part,' Gerald said.

'Oh,' Cherry said, surprised. She looked down at her lab clothes. 'Lab rat chic, eh? Hard to carry off.'

'I didn't mean the clothes.' Gerald smiled at her then looked away.

'Thank you,' Cherry said.

-o-

Blotch looked both ways down the corridor before closing the door and returning to his desk. He opened up Cherry's first report, licking his lips.

I'm not sure how to put all this down. I've never written a report in my life so hopefully this will be OK. It's just a preliminary thing. Just wanted to check that it sent OK and whatnot. Have kept it short like you asked:

Met Doctor Lowe. Charming, though he doesn't know it. Scruffy. He doesn't spend much time in the booths but seems to want a reasonably close relationship with his test subjects, so that could be a way of getting close to him. Obviously some sort of thing going on between him and Alexis Farrell. She wears the trousers.

V building very secure and very white. All access to terminals is via biometrics so I won't be able to get in and look at anything, not that I'd know where to start anyway.

Will be quarantined for testing in two weeks' time for an unspecified amount of time. No outside contact possible during quarantine.

I'll be in contact again before I go into quarantine.

Blotch could feel his head getting hot. He read the last point again, then slammed his hand down on the desk.

Chapter 9

Wouldn't it be more fun just to stay in and play games, Kester thought, his gaze alighting on the PlayStation icon projected on the corner of the window. He took his Book out of his pocket and zapped it at the off icon in the corner of the display.

'Stop taunting me,' he said to it.

Dinner at John's would normally have been a no-brainer but this time Kester wasn't sure how welcome he would be. He'd seen John and Sienna since he started at V, but he hadn't seen anyone else and he'd skipped a few of their regular meets. Betta had been one of Dee's best friends for a long time and was too scared to face Dee's wrath if she got in touch with him, so after a few initial texts she had gone quiet. She and Dee had fallen out once before and it hadn't been pretty.

Kester walked back across the room to the long mirror by his bed and scrutinised his image. He was already dressing differently. That would make things weird too. During work hours you had to wear clothes by the corporate sponsor and theirs was also the only casual range covered by the allowance. He was still wearing jeans and a shirt, but they were heavily branded and had ads on the pockets. The ads were for cool stuff and they were nothing by general City standards but it still made him feel like a human billboard. He wondered what Dee and her new man would make of it. He wondered if Sienna's reports of a new man were right and, if so, if he was still on the scene.

Kester pulled at his top pocket to see if the ad, or maybe even the whole pocket would come off without ruining the shirt. A stitch, just loose enough to cut, revealed itself at the top corner. Kester walked quickly into the bathroom and started unpicking the pocket with his nail scissors. After a focused five minutes of lip biting and swearing, Kester dropped the pocket in the bin. Back at the mirror, he smoothed his shirt back down. The fabric underneath was a different colour, but it looked like it was supposed to be that way, sort of. He walked away and then sauntered back past the mirror, trying to catch his image unawares, to see what it might look like to other people. Satisfied, he checked the clock, then struggled quickly out of his jeans and started unpicking some more ads.

Ad-free and still too early, Kester sat on his apple-green couch, one leg jiggling. He looked at his Book. He could leave in ten minutes. He didn't want to be on time. But he should go. It would be his turn to host the dinner party next time round and he'd like to reunite with his Institute friends on familiar territory first. Maybe he'd even have a date to invite by the time they came to him. Perhaps Alexis. Finding himself wishing she was coming with him tonight, he laughed. Neither she, nor his friends would be comfortable with it. And as for Dee – the thought of the two of them meeting...the thought of seeing her himself was bad enough...

A weight grew in Kester's stomach, prequel to letting down a friend. He got out his Book, picked John from his favourites and tapped 'call'. It rang long enough that he thought it would go to answer-phone and then John picked up, surprising him.

'Hello, mate,' John said. 'You all set?'

'Oh, hi,' Kester replied, as if he hadn't expected to speak to John. 'Actually I'm just calling to say I can't –'

'You can't come,' John cut in and then paused before he continued. 'Typical. Dee's just cancelled on me too.'

'Oh, in that case...'

'Don't worry, I get it. Yes, you can still come. You guys are like children you know.'

'I know.' Kester laughed. 'But you know what she's like. Did you really want your dinner party to end in blood and snot?'

John laughed.

'I'll see you at seven.'

Kester looked at his watch again. He sat for five more minutes before he left, figuring that would make him just late enough.

Unfortunately, everyone else was late for real reasons – disorganisation, the tube – so Kester made a lonely entrance.

'Finally, a guest!' John said, smacking him on the back as he came through the door. 'I was beginning to think nobody was coming.'

'I brought some wine,' said Kester, passing a bottle to John, who added it to the row on the worktop.

'I got a bit overexcited in the wine aisle,' John said, shaking his head.

'I don't think it'll be a problem,' Kester said.

The door buzzer went and John rushed past him into the hall.

'Don't be mad!' John called as he pressed the button on the videocom.

'What?' Kester asked.

'Hiiiii!' Betta's voice screeched through the speaker.

'Nothing!' John called. 'Not talking to you!'

John opened the front door and then hovered in the hall, waiting for them to make their way up the stairs.

'So are things, you know…have you spoken to her?' John asked.

'To Dee?' Kester said. 'You must be kidding. She totally went off.'

'But she'll be OK though. I mean you guys were drunk – and you said the virus was nothing, really.'

Kester reached for the decanter close to him and helped himself to a glass of red. 'She doesn't quite see it that way.'

The hall was small with voices. Betta and Sienna bubbled past John into the kitchen.

'Kester!' Sienna rushed forward and gave him a hug.

'No men with you?' Kester asked.

'Nope,' said Sienna, 'we've given up on the men thing. Every one we invite to one of these stupid parties high-tails it quick sharp afterwards. It's our intimidatingly witty banter.'

'So we're each other's dates tonight,' Betta said, swinging an arm around Sienna's shoulders and kissing her on the cheek.

'Fair enough.' Kester laughed.

'No lady with you?' Betta asked.

'Touchy subject,' John said, pushing past to get to the wine. He filled two more glasses and handed them out.

'Ooh, lovely,' said Sienna. 'I was getting bored of cocktails.'

'Shh,' said Betta, blushing. 'We went for just a little one before we came round. Girl stuff, you know.'

'You don't say,' John said. 'I could smell the fumes through the intercom. Right, everyone go through, take a seat. Dinner's nearly ready.'

Kester counted the place settings as they sat down. There were six.

'Who else is coming, John?' he called through to the kitchen, where John was rummaging in cupboards.

'Just the old guard tonight,' came a muffled reply, 'but no Calvin. You know he's gone to the Max Planck in Freiburg?'

'Fancy!'

The buzzer went a second time.

'Don't be mad!' John called again.

Kester could hear him answering the intercom.

'Hello, darling – oh you brought him!' said John. A few moments later, as the flat door opened, he said again, 'Don't be mad!'

Kester could hear voices in the corridor. There was chattering for a moment and then silence. There was some hissed conversation, followed by clanking in the kitchen and then Dee came striding through the door. Kester started. Her eyes were golden. The effect was fading but was still there.

'Hello everyone!' she said.

She put her arms out, then dropped them and moved to a chair before anyone had a chance to get up and greet her. She was followed closely by a man that Kester didn't recognise. He had the air of a stag about him, chivalrous poise worn over a pungent masculinity. Kester noticed his suit – the fact that he was even wearing a suit, for starters. It was expensive, but not ostentatious, with colour-co-ordinated ads and looked more like it was made from a beige liquid than from fabric. He wasn't an academic.

The man's eyes darted between the three guests. Sienna grinned at him and Betta blushed and smiled. He swung his jacket from his shoulders to the back of his chair in one fluid movement, putting Kester in mind of a matador. As he sat down, Kester thought he could see the shadow of some marking through his shirt – a tattoo? Or was he wearing?

Dee introduced him. 'This is Sebastian.'

'Hello, everyone,' Sebastian said and then turned his attention to Kester. 'I won't pretend I haven't seen your picture here and there – nice to meet you, Doctor Lowe.'

'Please, Kester,' Kester said, standing slightly so he could lean across the table to shake hands. Sebastian's handshake was a little more firm than necessary, but the smile never left his face.

The conversation was stilted at first and was only just kept afloat by John as he drifted back and forth from the kitchen, bringing the starters and various extras he had forgotten to put on the table.

'Jesus, John, sit down,' Kester said eventually. 'There can't possibly be anything left to bring through.'

John grinned and sat down to begin the meal.

'Get stuck in everyone,' he said and snatched up his knife and fork.

After a few moments of clanking cutlery and appreciative noises, Sebastian sat back in his chair and picked up his glass. He looked like he owned the place, made it feel like there might be many rooms beyond this one, long halls, a sweeping staircase, a library.

'So, Kester, tell me about your viruses.'

Kester, in the middle of a mouthful, tried to swallow quickly so he could answer.

'Obviously I've seen what you did with Dee's eyes – it's most impressive.'

Dee cut in, 'I explained to Sebastian that you needed a test-case for your interview.'

'She's very brave to offer herself up as a guinea pig like that, don't you think?' Sebastian looked over at Dee.

'Yes.' Kester glanced between the two of them, trying and failing to read them.

'You say that,' Sienna said, waving her glass, 'but scientists are always experimenting on each other. I remember when Kester was developing a vaccine for some nasty and we'd run out of funding for human torsos. You remember John? Oh – you know what a torso is, Sebastian?'

'Yes. A person with no head, no consciousness – for testing on, right?'

'A person? Let's not get controversial,' Sienna said. 'They just call it a torso because of the obvious resemblance – it's just a bag of humanoid bits and pieces that acts like a body. Anyway, Kester's at the end of an important project, making this vaccine and he runs out of funding. His trials are stuck in the mud and he needs to do one more clinical test to get the numbers up to the required level before it can be licensed. So what does he do? He tests it on himself.'

'You make me sound like a mad scientist,' Kester said. 'We knew it was safe by then – it was just a matter of getting the admin right.'

Sebastian laughed. 'And it wouldn't be the first time a scientist who was sure of him or herself put themselves in the hot seat, right? It seems like quite a lot of pioneering scientists have been forced to test their own methods and theories on themselves. I've read a bit about it. It's pretty gripping stuff.'

'Yes.' Kester held Sebastian's eyes to see if he was genuinely interested but it was Dee's face that confirmed it. She was pissed off that they had something in common. Kester smiled. 'I read a book about smallpox when I was doing my general education. That's what got me started down this path.'

'Yes,' Dee said, 'you were quite the idealist when you started out.'

'Yes, yes, it's fascinating,' Sebastian said. 'Jenner, wasn't it, who first managed to prevent it – he made a vaccine out of cowpox.' He turned to Dee as he said this. Misreading her expression, he added, 'But of course, you already know that.'

'Jenner made the first vaccine,' Kester replied, 'but it was actually a woman called Lady Mary something – a noblewoman who'd had smallpox herself – she started the ball rolling in the West.'

'Really?'

'She travelled to Constantinople – her husband was an ambassador, I think – and she saw people being inoculated against smallpox there.'

'Inoculated?' Sebastian said, puzzled. 'Isn't that the same thing?'

'They were using smallpox scrapings,' Kester explained, to various disgusted noises. 'You put a little bit of infected material into a person's vein. It's enough to produce a small scale infection and resulting immunity, but not enough to kill the host, usually.'

'Usually!' Sebastian laughed.

'Quite – that's why Jenner developed the vaccination as a safer option. In layman's terms vaccination uses weakened or dead viral matter to provoke an immune response.' Kester took a sip of wine. 'Montagu, that was it, Lady Mary Wortley Montagu.'

'Wortley!' Sebastian laughed again. 'How fabulous.'

'I know. She was so sure of herself that she had her son inoculated to try and convince people of the effectiveness of it. And her daughter, I think.'

'Really?' Sebastian leaned forward. 'Did she ask them? Tell them what she was doing?'

'Smallpox,' said Dee. 'What charming dinner conversation.'

Kester ignored her.

'So what do you do, Sebastian?' he asked, sitting forward in his chair.

'I'm a fund manager,' Sebastian said.

Dee looked up at Kester, lifting her cutlery so that it rested upright in her clenched fists, pointing at the ceiling.

'Wow,' Kester said.

'You seem surprised,' Sebastian said.

'I am. You're not the sort of type that normally mixes in the scientific community.'

'That's mad,' said Sienna. 'Where on earth did she find you?'

'It was peculiar. We were both at an art exhibition launch. I'd had rather too much champagne and I commented on her eyes. We got talking. When she told me about her screens project I was fascinated.' He shrugged as if to say, 'and here we are'.

Kester raised his eyebrows. Her screens project.

'Her screens project. Yes,' Kester said, 'how is that going, Dee. Last thing I heard you couldn't get funding.'

'This latest application is different,' Dee said, lifting her nose in the air. 'They've fast-tracked it to the final round. Seems like I might be better off doing it on my own.'

Kester watched her closely. She was still strangling her cutlery, which must mean something: she was bluffing, she was angry, she was on the defensive.

'I can't believe you met at an art exhibition. How did you end up there?' Sienna asked.

'I'm a member of the gallery,' Dee replied. 'They send me free tickets to these things all the time.'

'You never take me!'

'You don't like art.'

'I like champagne.'

'Fund management,' Kester said. 'It's not the sort of thing I thought Dee would approve of. Not unless it's the kind of fund she could apply to.'

Sebastian looked surprised and Kester instantly regretted saying it.

'I was steaming when we met, you see.' Dee held Kester's eye as she said this.

'You were pretty drunk.' Sebastian laughed. 'You were mooning about some guy, I recall. She wasn't at all impressed by my job until I mentioned that I specialise in ethical funds.'

'Anyway.' Dee's smile was factory-made. 'We were both drunk. We slept together and guess what – top marks for compatibility.'

Sebastian's colour rose but he was too polite to say anything. He picked up his cutlery and started picking at the remains of his starter.

'You scanned him?' Kester asked, horrified.

'And you're telling us,' John said. 'How rude – really, Dee.'

'Everyone does it darling. Didn't you know that? Tell him Betta.'

Betta looked apologetic and held out for a few moments before crumbling under Dee's stare.

'I'm afraid so,' she said, nodding and giggling.

'Sienna?' Dee said.

'Always!' Sienna looked pleased with herself. 'Unless I already think I've made a mistake! No use finding out someone's super-compatible if you think they're a dog.'

'Or a moron,' Dee said.

'You scan everyone you sleep with?' Kester asked her. He took a long swig of wine.

'Sure. Everyone.'

Kester stared at her.

'Everyone,' she repeated.

'OK, you two.' John laughed a little too loud. 'I think we've covered that one. Who's ready for steak?'

Betta and Sienna reacted as if this was the best conversational gambit ever and launched into a discussion about the best steaks they'd ever had. Sebastian rose from his seat and offered help with serving. Kester and Dee sat opposite one another, Dee staring, Kester avoiding her stare until the main course arrived.

'So there's no Mrs Kester?' Sebastian said, attempting to revive some semblance of convivial conversation.

'No,' Kester said.

'What about your hot boss, Kester?' John said.

Everyone except Sebastian shot a glance at John, knives from every quadrant sharpened different ways.

'Yes, speaking of steak…didn't you say she had some share in a restaurant?' Sienna said.

'You're getting her confused with that woman from LayTech.' Betta picked up Sienna's cue and ran with it.

Kester ate in silence, letting the conversation garble on around him like a bad dream. Then, when Dee got up to go to the bathroom, he headed for the kitchen.

'More wine?' he asked John, picking up the two wide-mouthed decanters that lay within arm's reach.

'Yes – bring a white and a red will you?'

Kester swapped one of the decanters for a cooling jug, went to the kitchen, filled them and waited. As Dee walked past the doorway, back towards the dining room, Kester called her and reached out to catch her elbow. She followed him into the kitchen more freely than he had expected.

'What's wrong with you?' he asked.

'What's wrong with me? Asks the rogue scientist who sows the seed of his virus wherever he goes?' She had retreated behind blank, drunken eyes.

'You scanned me? Is that what that was all about?' Kester ignored her jibe.

'Kester,' she dropped her voice to a harsh whisper, 'you slept with that bitch at V, gave me a fucking virus and then dumped me. That's what this is about.'

'Dumped you? Dee, you kicked me out. And it was just one night. How can I have dumped you when –'

'You dumped me – dumped our dream.'

He looked again at the traces of gold still in her eyes.

'You liked them then?'

'What?'

'Your golden eyes. You only uploaded a few days ago. I can tell. It's been months.'

Dee slapped him. He didn't respond.

'You just disappeared into your new life. It was the only thing I had –'

'Dee!'

'– the only thing I had to remind me what a cunt you were. I didn't want to let myself forget too quickly,' she said, her face pale, two pinches of red on her cheeks.

With them both out of the room, laughter was flourishing next door.

'You scanned me,' Kester said.

'So? You don't have to ask permission you know.'

'Why would you do that after the fact?'

'For reassurance.'

'What?'

'For reassurance that you were bad news.' Dee backed away into the corner of the kitchen where the decanter and the jug sat.

'And?' Kester asked, the anger falling out of his voice.

Dee turned away and picked up the two wine vessels.

'And?' Kester repeated.

'Red or white?' Dee asked him, turning round with one in each hand.

'He wants one of each. Now will you tell me?'

'Red or white?'

Kester shrugged his shoulders – she was playing some game he didn't know.

'White,' he said, backed by a roar of hilarity from through the house.

'For fuck's sake, Kester,' Dee screamed, cutting off the laughter, colour flooding her face. She threw the white wine over the front of his shirt, clattering the mouth of the jug off his breastbone. 'You didn't even have the decency to say red.'

She smacked the jug down on the worktop and pushed past John who had appeared in the doorway.

'Oh god,' said John, 'what was I thinking?'

Kester pulled his sodden shirt away from his chest.

'You need to practise your whispering,' John said.

Kester groaned and then winced as the front door slammed. Through the open kitchen window they could hear angry voices below, followed by high heels and leather soles clattering off down the street in opposite directions.

'She scanned me, John,' Kester said, sliding down the kitchen unit to sit on the floor.

John lunged forward. 'Not there mate.' He grabbed Kester's arm and pulled him up. 'You'll have a wine-soaked arse too and I'm not lending you a whole outfit. Come on, I'll get you a fresh shirt.'

'She scanned me.'

'They all do it. You heard them. You remember when we were

in school they all played on that name-match compatibility site? Sarah loves Deter 76%? This is the real thing for them.'

Kester sighed. 'But why do it when you've already bust up with someone – when you haven't really even...'

'I don't know, mate. I don't know. But I'm not sure you should take it personally, either way. And for the record, that was bullshit about her funding proposal. She hasn't even finished it yet.' John looked a bit guilty for saying it. 'Do you want to stay here tonight?'

'No. No thanks. I'm going home. But first, we're going to get very, very drunk.'

-o-

As Dee unlocked the door to her flat, her Book beeped. It was a message from Sebastian saying, *Not sure what happened there. Will call you in the morning.* He was perfect, but she'd scanned him. He wasn't perfect. Infuriatingly, they were incompatible. Not a complete travesty, but a genetic mismatch nevertheless; there was high potential for a serious genetic condition in any offspring. She was stupid to have done it. To have scanned Kester too. Nature was perverse. Why not just make it if they were attractive to you, then they were right – if the body could do it with immune complement, why not with genetic compatibility?

Inside, Dee took a bottle of scotch into the kitchen and started to make herself a whisky sour. Unable to find any lemons, she gave up and drank it neat, standing at the worktop. She tried to call Betta but she was still at the party. Turning on her heel, Dee saw her laptop sitting on the kitchen table, half finished funding proposal open on the display. She lunged forward, slammed it shut and swept it off the table with an animal cry. It landed on a pile of A4 and went skidding into the kitchen doorway, sheets of paper fanning out behind it.

'Fuck,' she said, then stepped over her laptop through the doorway into the lounge, swiping the bottle from the counter as she went. As she entered she noticed the flashing voicemail icon on her wall display. She slumped down on the couch, reached out with a toe and touched the red icon. The room swilled around her.

'Hello, Delilah darling!' It was Kester's mum. Again. 'I just wanted to see how my favourite girl was doing. And wondered if you'd seen my wayward son recently. Tell him if he doesn't call me soon I'm going to get myself a pass and come and find him at his fancy new office. That'd embarrass him! Speak to you soon, darling.'

The message ended with a kissing noise.

Exasperated, Dee refilled her glass and fumbled around for her Book. She flicked over to movies and, grimacing, searched the chick flicks. There were hundreds to choose from but it seemed like she'd seen them all. The ads down the side of the display were all for helplines aimed at pathetic creatures like her, she thought. People who had come back late and drunk, in need of a soppy movie. Infuriated, she aimed her Book like a gun at the second ad and selected it. It didn't ring, but segued into a soothing welcome speech with calming visuals to match.

The Real Church. Here to help you when you need it. Here to listen. Tending the path to heaven for seventy-five years.

'I just want to rant at a real human! Is that too fucking much to ask?'

You may not always have been interested in the Church, but the Church has always been interested in you. Our mission is to bring religion back to humanity, and to put the humanity back into religion.

'What does it even *mean*?'

We believe that everything in the world is perfect, just as God intended – how could it not be? So why all the pain and suffering? Well, while things may be perfect, not everything is in the right order. Imagine the perfect human body. Now mix it up. Put the arms where the legs should be and already things are starting to look a little messy – here the voice gave a soft chuckle – *it's the same with the world. The Church specialises in getting things back in the right order: in the world, in your community, in your life.*

Dee was throwing stuff at the wall, now. This was more like it.

'You think you can get money out of me?' she roared. 'You think you can take advantage of people who are down on their luck and give them false hope. Fucking parasites!'

We're not claiming that we can work miracles…

A crackle interrupted the voice-over.

'No need to. I've seen you do miracles – turning despair into crystal buildings and gold lamé suits – you've got the fucking Midas touch alright.'

'Oh! Dear me!' said an elderly voice.

Dee jumped and jerked her Book up to her ear.

'Sorry, I think I've got…'

'Don't worry, dear, it's not a wrong number. And we get lots of angry people ringing up. It's OK to be angry.'

The voice belonged to an old woman. She sounded like a kindly grandmother.

'I'm so sorry I swore at you. It wasn't you,' Dee said, then made a face to herself and took a swig of scotch.

'No, no, don't you apologise at all, dear. I expect it's not me you're angry at.' The voice was so fragile, creased and soft with age.

'No, it wasn't you,' Dee said. 'I was just angry because the ad came up – I just wanted to watch a movie.'

'You sound lovely, dear,' said the old lady. 'You have such a lovely voice when you aren't swearing.'

Dee smiled despite herself.

'Yes, I'm sorry about that – it was nothing to do with you at all. A guy, that's all. I caught a stupid virus off some guy and…'

'Oh dear. You want to be more careful than that, dear. You're calling from London aren't you? Didn't you have your uploads set?'

'Yes, but – it's hard to explain. He's a scientist, you see. He was…he tested something out on me without my knowing.'

'That's awful, dear.' The old woman sounded appalled. 'Have you reported him to the police?'

'No, no, it's fine,' Dee insisted, keen not to upset the woman. 'Kester's a friend. I mean he was a friend. It was a mistake.'

There was a pause on the other end of the phone. Dee stood and looked at her image on the wall, face pale, ring of fading gold around her irises, whites of her eyes bloodshot from the drink. She downed her Scotch.

'Was it a mistake?' the voice asked softly.

Dee stared at herself.

'Was it a mistake?' the voice asked again.

'I was…' Dee started to talk and saw her face contort in the mirror. 'I was…' Tears escaped her eyes. In the blurred corner of her vision, her laptop. 'Why would he do this to me?' Her voice broke into sobs and she slumped down on the sofa, shuddering, rubbing her forehead violently with one palm.

-o-

Kester took the outside lift up to his apartment. Dawn was starting to glow through the part-misted wall. He walked straight across the room to the bathroom, chucked his wet shirt on the floor and fought the borrowed one off over his head. Leaning on the sink, he stared down the plughole. Why had he done it? It wasn't like he had slept with a colleague he was leaving behind. She had been part of his world since childhood, friends because they had always been friends; what had possessed him to think he wouldn't have to deal with the aftermath?

And what had made him think it was a good idea at all? He had seen how all her previous relationships had unfolded, disintegrated. He knew exactly how she felt about one-night stands. Everybody who knew Dee loved her, but they loved her in the way that you love an unpredictable cat; they knew better than to touch the wrong bit. Idiot. She had rolled onto her back, stretched luxuriously and he had put his hand straight into the trap. Double idiot.

'What happened to your shirt?' Alexis' voice startled him.

Kester groaned. He wobbled over to the couch, sat along from her and then let himself drop into her lap, not even bothering to wonder why she was there. She stiffened for a few seconds and then he felt her hand on his head.

'A woman?' she asked.

Kester mumbled.

'That woman you infected before?'

He mumbled again.

'She attacked you?'

Kester didn't reply.

'Do you want me to do something about her?'

Kester sat bolt upright and stared at Alexis. He couldn't quite focus on her face. He forgot why he had sat up – things had been steadier with his head in her lap. He lowered himself back down until he felt warm brushed cotton and the tolerance of flesh.

Chapter 10

Blotch was kneeling at his altar picking at the candle wax when he heard the knock on the door. He assumed the position of prayer and murmured, 'Come in.'

The door popped open as if caught by a breeze. Blotch looked over his shoulder and then pushed himself, huffing, to his feet. A small grey head peered round the door. An old woman. His first thought was *cake* but though she did resemble his grandmother, it was unlikely that she had come to bring him cake.

'Come in, come in,' Blotch said, squeezing his bulky form in behind his desk.

It was a small office but he had managed to fit in quite an elaborate altar, the surround of which came right to the edges of the wall. It was directly opposite his desk, so that whoever was sitting in front of him had their back to it. People generally hunched forward when sitting there, or checked over their shoulders now and again as if Jesus might reach out and grab them if they didn't keep an eye on him.

The little old lady shuffled in and sat herself down with the aspect of a pensioner skipping a bus queue. She must have been in her late eighties.

'I have some information for you, Minister,' she said.

'And you are…'

'Sorry, love, I forget myself. I'm Nan – I work the night shift on your helpline, so we don't see each other much. Desk 28.' She smiled and cocked her head like a bird.

Blotch couldn't help but smile back. The way she held her hands suggested knitting, though she wasn't carrying any with her.

'We've had a call I think might be of interest to you,' she said.

'Oh, yes?'

'And you know you said that any information on the sinning ways of the City folk that you could use would be rewarded.'

'Rewarded by the good Lord, I think is what I said.'

'Well, dear, I hear you have the password to the Good Lord's bank account,' Nan said, winking. 'I'm sure he'd approve a transfer for this.'

Blotch sat up straight in his chair and pulled down on his office vestments, forcing more chin up and over his collar.

'Continue,' he said.

'I spoke to a young girl last night. She was drunk and upset; you know the way. Her boyfriend had infected her with some virus without her knowing and she was mad as hell – oh, I do beg your pardon minister – she was mad as hell, because she doesn't engage in the practice of wearing and he knew that full well.'

'And?' Blotch had heard it all before.

'Here's the juicy bit.' Nan caught up the edges of her cardigan and wrapped them tight around her low bosom, folding her arms. 'He's a scientist. He made the virus himself. He was going for some job with a big firm from what I could make out, manufacturing fashion viruses for them to sell.'

'I'm sorry to disappoint you, Nan,' Blotch said, toying with a golden baby Jesus from the nativity on his desk, 'but we already have a contact inside the highest profile viral manufacturer of all and it looks like it's rather a dead end.' He glanced over at his monitor where Cherry's latest mail titled 'Little to report' was sitting unopened. He was beginning to think that he'd wasted a skipload of Church money just to set a prostitute up with a modelling career. To make matters worse she was in quarantine now, so she was essentially out of action for the next few weeks.

'Young man,' Nan said, her jowls shuddering, 'I'm not a fool. I have ears and I wasn't finished. This boyfriend worked at some Institute in London, creating military viruses for the government – the poor girl seemed to think that this was a much nobler calling than what he's doing now, but she told me about the sorts of things he'd been developing and I tell you, the red-top sites would have a field day with this stuff.'

'His name?'

'Lowe,' the woman said, checking her notes. 'Krister Lowe.'

'Kester Lowe!' Blotch cried out and smacked the desk. 'Bingo!'

-o-

Clarke was tall, angular, made out of deckchairs. Being in the room with him made Blotch feel wide. It seemed unfair to him that there was so much room for Clarke to clonk around in his office, when he had to breathe in to fit behind his desk.

'You think you can handle this, Blotch?' Clarke said. 'You think you can take this on?'

Blotch could feel his blood pressure rising. Did Clarke think that he couldn't?

'Of course, Your Reverence.'

'The timing is perfect,' Clarke said. 'If what the girl's reports say is true, V is setting Lowe up as a masthead for the whole wearing community. He's taking it all above board. For us that means two things. One, more people than ever are going to take up this filthy practice and its associated activities; two, it'll lose its hedonistic appeal – even if it does remain common practice, the more extreme elements will soon be looking for the next big thrill and then we'll have a new vice to battle.

'If we can show him for what he is – a bringer of pestilence – if something were to happen to show the people of the City that they are playing with hellfire, just give them a glimpse of the damage this sort of behaviour could bring upon the world, that would truly be God's work.'

'Yes, Your Reverence, I understand. It does seem the perfect moment.'

'Our previous experiences –'

'We have learned from our previous experiences, I assure you.'

'Given an opportunity like this, with God's blessing, it would be unthinkable that we should fail.' Clarke took a long breath. He lifted his Book and pointed it at the back wall of his office. The wall pivoted round like the doorway to a secret passage to reveal a lavish altar. 'I know you've been looking for promotion, Blotch.'

'Yes, Your Reverence. For some time now.'

'This is a career-maker.'

'Yes, Your Reverence. I have been thinking about how we can use the girl.'

It had taken him time to see how the pieces could fit together but now that he had figured it out it seemed so obvious to him. All he had to do was wait until Cherry was out of quarantine and persuade her that a little extension of her duties would be worth her while. Time would tell whether she could get him what he needed.

'You have a plan?'

'A plan is coming to me, but I would need Your Reverence's help.' Blotch paused for a moment. He found this bit of the process distasteful. 'Money, Your Reverence.' He stopped there; he knew that Clarke would rather not know the details.

'Of course. Send me an official request for the amount you need and I'll make sure the money's available to you.'

'Wonderful, Your Reverence.' This could be his moment. 'And you'll consider nominating me for the Centenary promotion?'

'Ah, the big one. Promotion is promotion is promotion, Blotch…though I suppose they don't all come with a gold necklet. If that's what you want, if you can pull this off and it helps me to get us back in, then yes, I'll find something palatable to nominate you for. Of course this is all between you, me and the Almighty.'

'Of course,' Blotch said, smiling.

'Shall we pray?'

-o-

The woman sitting at the head of the table was Juno Chen. Kester knew that much from the V portrait hall. She was a middle-aged woman, with Chinese heritage and a Glaswegian accent that she had remodelled with limited success. She was wearing some type of STV-yoked molluscum virus which had spread to her arms; they were dotted with bobbly blisters the size of aphids.

'We have a special guest with us today,' said Chen, addressing the room. 'You've probably heard his name bandied around the departments over the last few months – Doctor Kester Lowe.' Chen indicated Kester where he sat, at the bottom end of the table next to Farrell. 'He has joined us for the first part of our meeting today as the scientific foil to our business thoughts on the new commercial function in V Division V.' Chen nodded at Alexis. 'So for Doctor Lowe's benefit I will make some introductions before we begin today. I, as you will know, am Juno Chen. I'm Managing Director of VDV. On my left is our Sales and Marketing Director, Mr Roger Yule.'

Kester nodded at Roger Yule with what he hoped was a businesslike smile. They had met before, at Kester's interview. Yule was a man of unusual proportions; his form sloped down and outwards from his slightly pointed bald head and for all Kester could see, might have continued on outwards under the table, like an iceberg. His skin was the colour of putty. His electric blue eyes and the dazzling smile he returned Kester looked out of place. The dark circles he had been wearing when they first met had gone.

According to Alexis, Roger had always had alopecia and had once been a stunningly attractive young man who was always tanned all over. Since he had stopped dealing with clients he had been expanding at a rate almost visible to the naked eye. Her take on this was that he didn't consider it as important to impress his wife or his colleagues as it had been his clients and consequently had let himself go. He no longer had a wife and the rumour went that he had had a personal 'pig room' installed in the back of his office so that he could relieve himself and put on new viruses in privacy and comfort.

'Continuing clockwise round the table we have Mr Byron Gaunt. Byron handles the pharmacology and pharmaceuticals side of the business. He came to us ten years ago as an expert on chronic disease.'

'Long-term rot, dear boy.' Byron smiled his charming carnivorous smile. 'It's where the money is. And the longer we can keep them shuffling their god-forsaken carcasses around this mortal coil the more money they can pour gratefully into our benevolent hands.'

'Quite,' Chen said.

Byron, a tall man, gaunt in stature as in name, was grey as a wizard but lean and fit-looking for his age. The only thing that took away from this were the scabs at his collar, the same Kester had previously seen on Farrell. Gaunt's demeanour reminded Kester of his grandfather. He recalled how he would say the most horrific things to his dog in a soothing babying voice. As long as the tone was right, the dog just kept on wagging its tail and staring at him adoringly. Despite the rather unscrupulous introduction he had spun for himself, Kester got a good feeling from Gaunt.

'On Byron's left,' Chen continued, 'is our Acting Director of Strategy, Ingrid Jones. Ingrid has seen us through the past business year during our DS's illness.'

'Long-term rot,' Byron Gaunt said in his silky moneyed tones and winked at Kester.

'Quite,' Chen responded as before to Byron's comment.

'I'm keeping his coffin warm for him,' said Jones without a trace of humour.

Kester was unsure whether to laugh. Jones turned her Arctic eyes on Kester. She was stunning. Her hair was pure blonde, almost white, and she had a fine yet severe Scandinavian bone structure. She looked young to have taken on such a huge role. She wasn't wearing, or at any rate she wasn't wearing anything that was visible when clothed.

'You were an academic?' she demanded of Kester.

'Yes, I was.'

'I thought so. I can see it in your clothes. It will be good when you have a proper wardrobe consultation.'

'This is…' Kester started to reply, stroking his new tie, but she had flicked her cold eyes back to her meeting notes. Alexis put a hand on his arm to silence him.

Chen sighed heavily.

'Down your side of the table, to your left, we have Alexis Farrell who you already know, then to your right, my left, Felicity Agbabi, our Finance Director.'

'Nice to meet you,' said Felicity warmly.

Felicity was a comfortable-looking middle-aged woman with glowing skin the colour of caramel and she gave off a maternal impression. Kester was sure he smelled fresh baking when she spoke. Her eyes were kind and pleasant despite the styes. Their gaze melted the uncomfortable freeze Jones had laid on him.

'And that's everyone,' Chen said, 'except for Bradley Farmer who is absent this time.' She nodded to an empty chair at the foot of the table. 'Farmer is Director of Corporate Social Responsibility and Ethics.'

'You have a dedicated director for that?' Kester asked, surprised.

'We have a whole floor of the building,' Chen said, smiling in a way that made Kester feel uncomfortable for having asked. 'We're very serious about such things.'

'That's great…I mean –'

Feeling Alexis' hand on his arm again, Kester stopped. He sat up straight and clasped his hands on the table in front of him, trying to hold his nerves steady.

'Let's get started,' Chen said. 'There are many things we need to talk about that Doctor Lowe won't be interested in and we don't want to waste his precious time, so let's kick off with his presentation.'

Kester was unsure whether she was being sarcastic about his time being precious. The strange echoes of Scots in her accent influenced the emphasis she placed on words and phrases and sometimes made her tone ambiguous.

'OK,' Alexis said. She flicked on the display at the foot of the table. The HoloPoint logo swirled on the wall.

'HoloPoint.' A subsonic voice filled the room. 'For killer presentations.'

Alexis shook her head. She caught Gaunt's eye and set him off chuckling. Standing in front of the Board, she looked less tall than usual. Kester clenched and unclenched his hands. He recalled going to see a girlfriend perform in her first University Dramatic Society play.

'This morning I'm going to take you through a short summary of the latest wearing stats. I'll then hand over to Doctor Lowe who is going to talk more specifically about the viruses that he has been developing and their advantages over naturally harvested viruses.'

Behind her, a graph showed the increase in wearing for the previous ten years.

'What we're looking at here is the data from Yule's market study – it's by far the best data set ever collected in this area and it's been put together in conjunction with Stark Wellbury, using quantitative analysis of the interaction between individuals' screens and the Stark biological database. As you'll be aware, this bypasses a lot of the problems with the qualitative surveys that have been done in this area in the past.

'As you can see, the greatest increase in wearing is in young professionals and the celebrity arena – the existing target market for street mods and commissioned mods respectively.'

The image behind Alexis changed to a pie chart showing the

demographic breakdown of virus wearers.

Kester tuned out as she continued to talk through the figures. There were some things that just couldn't be improved on. The pie chart was undoubtedly his favourite type of chart.

Alexis didn't say much and she said it economically, so before he knew it Kester was standing before the Board, mouth biscuit-dry, legs mallow. When he began, Alexis had her eyes focused firmly on the table in front of her. As Kester spoke, taking the Board through a simplified version of the virus design and testing process, his legs grew steady. This was way easier than a conference talk – no experts or rivals waiting to take him down. As he grew in confidence, Alexis' head lifted slowly. By the time he was finished, she had her head held high and her golden eyes were fixed on him.

'Are you telling us that these viruses have no sequelae, Doctor Lowe? No long-term effects at all?' Chen asked.

Kester considered the question carefully, looking out of the window for a moment to help clarify his overheating brain.

'No,' Kester replied, to rumbles from the Board members, 'I'm not. But I can say with confidence that the risk of any serious long-term effects of wearing these viruses, my viruses, is considerably lower than that of wearing harvested viruses. And any sequelae are likely to be of a less serious nature.'

Chen stared at Kester for a moment.

'I like the way your brain works,' Chen said. She almost smiled at him.

Out of the corner of his eye, Kester caught Alexis' expression. She knew what was coming next.

'And that's not their main selling point, Director Chen,' Kester said, trying to suppress a smile. He flicked to the next slide. All it said on it was KL02. 'KL02 stands for Kester Lowe...02. We had to come up with a new convention for naming the V viruses – I hope you don't think this first attempt too conceited.' Kester smiled at Gaunt, setting off a chuckle which went around the table. 'Now KL01 you've already seen. You'll have noticed that neither,' Kester paused, swallowing Alexis' name, 'neither Mrs Farrell nor I appear to be wearing today.'

Alexis looked up at him. Had she expected him to really do this, he wondered? She had said it would reflect well on him to be wearing, but it was no show of virility like it would be with an exchanged virus and he had no need to show his ambition. This was pure theatrics.

'Lights please,' Kester said and the room went dark.

'My god!' Gaunt spoke first.

In the darkness, Kester removed his shirt so that they could see the effect more clearly. Alexis stood up and came over to him. She fumbled for his hand and squeezed it hard, as if she wanted to squeeze it gently, but couldn't bring herself to. Out of the corner of his eye he could see her glowing hands move to un-knot her wrap-around dress, open it wide to display to the Board. Kester glanced down to look at her body before realising that his glowing nodes would give him away.

'Brilliant!' Chen's voice came from through the darkness.

Alexis closed her dress and sat back down.

'Lights,' said Kester.

The command had been unexpected enough for him to catch the unguarded reactions of the Board members. Gaunt and Jones were whispering to one another, a little too close, Felicity Agbabi had a rosy glow rising through her dark cheeks and Roger Yule was grinning. He was already jotting down notes in his Book. Chen looked satisfied.

Kester realised his shirt was still unbuttoned. He buttoned it back up as he continued talking, trying not to seem too keen to cover up.

'That's a virus?' Gaunt asked.

'Absolutely,' Kester replied.

'An STV?' Yule asked.

'Yes.' Kester nodded, suppressing a smile as Yule massaged the scabs on the backs of his hands. 'We've twenty-two more viruses in development as I speak and we're gathering pace all the time.'

'Thank you, Doctor Lowe,' Chen said. 'Please, have a seat.'

There had been more to say but Kester was happy that the Board was convinced. He looked at Alexis, who nodded, and then returned to his seat.

'Excellent,' said Roger Yule. Tiny sweat beads were appearing on his forehead, forced out by fat thoughts of fresh revenue. He was still jotting. 'So where do we start?' he asked, then tapped his Book and swiped a finger towards each of them. 'This is an updated copy of the outline strategy I sent earlier in the week. Let's take a look and get your thoughts.'

A few moments of silence followed as the Board members flicked through the document. Nothing had appeared on Kester's Book, so he stared out of the window for a bit and felt pleased with himself.

'I had heard, Doctor Lowe,' Chen said after a few minutes had passed, 'that you never wore.'

'Quite right,' Kester said, relaxed now, 'and that, if I have my way, is the last time you will ever see me wear visible symptoms. This reputation has obviously gone before me and I'd like to keep it intact.'

Chen raised her eyebrows at Kester's apparent leap in confidence.

'Well, Doctor Lowe,' she said, 'your secret is safe with us.'

'Yes, that's just the sort of thing we need to encourage,' Yule said. 'And the image. We need to sort out your image. Not wearing is good, distinctive, but we need to make sure you have an image. We need to connect you with the fashion world if we're to market your viruses as a designer product – section eight.' He held up a hand as everyone started to flick through to the relevant section. 'But let's not get ahead of ourselves here. I'll go back to the beginning and talk you through.'

'We present him as a fashion designer.' Chen considered the idea, continuing to scan section eight of Yule's report. The rest of the room gave her time to go through her thoughts. 'Yes. This is the difference. V viruses are designed, created, fashioned to be beautiful.'

'Yes,' Kester said.

'We need to do more with this,' Chen continued.

'Quite,' Yule said, 'but shall we start at the beginning?'

'Big clients,' Alexis said. 'We need to make this exclusive.'

'Or we could go through this section now,' Yule said. 'Let's go through this section first and then we'll come back and put it in context.'

Kester watched Yule try to hide his annoyance. He wondered how many of the Board had read the plan before the meeting.

'We can't rely entirely on the big clients,' Agbabi said. 'They're fickle and we could be hit with a competitor any time, once someone clocks what we're doing and catches up with our research.

And once your product is out there they can start to extract the viruses and analyse how they work, make copycats – can't they?'

'Copyright,' Yule said. 'Paragraph 10.'

'There are ways of protecting the viruses,' Kester said, a little uneasily, unsure if he was supposed to be contributing.

'We'll talk later,' Yule said to him across the conversation.

'So you're proposing that we hit the high street with these things as well as the high end?' Alexis asked Yule.

'Exactly,' Yule replied. 'We license selected viruses to the Pigs – at a higher premium than the harvested range, obviously – perhaps only to a few upmarket outlets to keep it exclusive.'

'Right,' Alexis said.

'But we need to differentiate between the products we're providing to our high-end clients and our high street customers – paragraph 12. So we have exclusives – guaranteed originals sold to only a few high profile clients. We make these available to the high street after a certain amount of time – similar to the contracts you'd see for a commissioned mod at the moment. There'll be a grey area where people think if they buy it quickly enough they can pass it off as having been contracted from someone big, so we bring each one in at a high price and then drop it down to the normal rate once that period is over.'

'Yes,' Chen leant forward and pointed her pen at Yule. 'There'll be a rush, then market saturation, and then they'll be on to the next thing.'

Kester watched Alexis tracing a finger around the edge of her Book. She was mulling something over, looked pleased with herself. He watched as she noted something on the display and then nudged her Book towards him. *Fashion show?* it said *Gucci, Brinkov…Lowe…*

'It's just like designer clothes,' Yule said. 'Fashion doesn't move on as quickly on the high street as it does on the catwalk, so there'll still be a fairly lengthy period where you still get spread and purchase just because people like the look of it, or because so-and-so was seen wearing it.'

'Nice,' Gaunt said, licking his lips.

'But here's the catch – paragraph 18.' Yule was getting more excited as he spoke, his pale form jiggling like agitated panna cotta. 'The product is the same. The fashion world works on the principle of one-off designer items and lower-quality copies. Fair enough, you can make the one-offs, but they have to stay one-offs for good for them to retain their value. These viruses will never have retained value – they are ephemeral by nature.'

'So something has to be different about the designer items,' Kester said. His brain started to tick over. How could he make them different?

'Exactly,' Alexis said, shifting in her chair.

Kester could see her stockinged knees rubbing together through the glass table. He looked up. Chen had been watching him watching Alexis. There was a paper-thin smile on her lips.

'Exactly,' Alexis said again and slouched back in her chair, crossing her long legs.

'Mode of delivery,' Kester said, 'or certification, something like that. Or slight differences in the patterning.'

'Models,' said Gaunt, leaning forward on the table. 'Beautiful boys and girls. Don't worry, Yule, I've read your plan. We're going to give the initial buyers a package – they go to a day spa or something to be serviced by our expert team – if you get my meaning.'

'You're talking a high-class version of the Pigs?' Alexis asked.

'If that's how you like to think of it, my dear,' Gaunt smiled, toying with his fat pen, 'but it would be so much more than that. You really ought to read the plan.'

'But it's still the same virus – it's essentially the same service with the price bumped up,' Kester said. 'You end up with the same thing. Who's going to go for that?'

Chen was watching him again. He slid back in his chair and pulled his hands down into his lap. He would keep his mouth shut now.

'You need to think of it like flying,' Yule said, turning to Kester. 'There's a service that has no retained value. There are broadly three different classes on air services, yes?' Everyone turned to listen. Yule was onto his specialist subject. 'You can fly first class, business class or economy class. The secret is that the service is really very similar. Buy first class and what do you get extra?'

'A bigger seat?' Alexis said. 'Free champagne?'

'Better service?' Gaunt said the word 'service' slowly, with a sly smile, drawing a smirk from Alexis.

'And?' Yule asked.

Everyone looked around, shrugging.

'A big fat bill,' Agbabi said.

'Exactly!' Yule nodded. 'Nothing but a big fat bill. At the end of the flight you've made the same journey in the same amount of time – you arrive in the same place at the same time as everyone else.'

'You let them charge you ten times the price,' Agbabi said, 'for a comfortable seat and however much you can drink. But the seat takes up only four times the space of a normal one and the drink is bought on discount in bulk. They multiply their margins to a silly degree.'

'Six times the price for business,' Yule said and rested back in his chair, 'up to twenty times the price for first, and all provided by the same company on the same plane. No lasting value; just fleeting prestige and comfort – that, people are also willing to pay for.'

'It's all about 50,000 Euro a night service – disgraceful!' Gaunt smiled to himself. 'Delightful!'

'That's what this Vspa you're proposing provides,' Chen said, as she caught up with her reading.

'Right. And we keep the Pig customers happy by calling their service something that makes them feel good about it – not that "economy" really fits the bill here,' Yule said.

'Ugh,' Jones said, her first contribution, a look of distaste on her perfect features.

Gaunt laughed at her, drawing a sharp glance followed by what Kester thought was a fleeting smile.

'I'm open to suggestions here,' Yule said.

There was a long pause while the Board made their various thinking faces.

'*Express*,' said Alexis. 'It's not for people who can't afford the top price service – it's for people who are busy, pushed for time – they're too important to swan off for a day and get pampered.'

'Sounds a little bit TescMart,' Kester said. 'How about *Vector* – as in means of transfer. It sounds cool and modern…and it starts with a V.'

Alexis looked round at him, her golden eyes sending a shudder across his chest.

'*Vector*.' She took the word in her mouth and snapped it on her tongue like a cracker.

Kester tried desperately to visualise his calendar – where did he have to be after this? Somewhere he wouldn't be missed?

'Doctor Lowe.' Chen's voice made Kester start. 'I believe you have somewhere to be.'

'Yes.' Kester gave the only sensible answer.

'Good,' Chen said. 'Let's take a break.'

The other Board members filed out while Kester closed down the presentation file and put away his Book.

'We need to set up a meeting, Lowe,' said Roger Yule, holding out his hand to Kester.

Kester shook it, resisting the urge to withdraw his own hand when he felt the rough scabs on the back of Yule's.

'I need to talk to you about how we control this thing once it's out there,' Yule said. 'It'll affect how we market it and the price points and whatnot.'

'Of course,' Kester said. 'Call my office.' For the first time, it felt good saying this.

'*Vector*,' Gaunt said, slapping Kester on the back as he walked past him to the door. 'I like it.'

'Well done,' Farrell said to him under her breath once Yule had moved on. Only the two of them and Chen were left in the room.

'A moment, please?' Chen said, looking at Farrell.

Farrell turned and left them without replying. Chen approached Kester as he slid his Book into his pocket.

'Very impressive, Doctor Lowe,' she said. 'You don't disappoint. Or so it seems.'

'I like to think not,' Kester said, turning to face her.

She was standing a little too close. Her perfume was harsh, like the pleasant end of petrol. She wasn't as tall as he had expected. With her heels on, she only just came up to his height. Her small figure was complemented by her simple green tunic dress; it was tiny, but there was still enough room between the fabric and her skin for a pair of hands.

'I liked the look of KL02,' she said, looking straight into his eyes, searching for a reaction.

'Well, you own it Ms Chen,' Kester said, smiling, still pleased with himself.

Chen was nearly the same age as Farrell, but she was just as well-preserved, if not more so, and she was aware of the fact. Her Chinese features were less liable to betray age.

'And that means I can take it whenever I like,' Chen said, the Scottish undertones bringing an air of threat to her voice.

Did they teach the women at V to talk this way? Kester wondered. On some induction course, perhaps: *Discomfiting and Manipulating Male Members of Staff Using Just Your Tone of Voice.*

'Whenever you like, Ms Chen,' Kester said, unsure of what he was agreeing to.

'Hm,' she said, apparently satisfied. 'I look forward to watching your progress.' She indicated the door.

'Thank you, Ms Chen,' Kester said and walked past her.

She followed him, holding a palm to the small of his back as if guiding a child, so close he could feel it though she did not touch him.

-o-

Back at the lab, Gerald's smile was threatening to sever the top of his head.

'Sir! Sir, it's working,' Gerald said almost before Kester had entered the room. He had his hands spread out like he was about to sing a show-tune.

'It is?' Kester asked.

'Yes, it is.'

'What? What's working?'

'Keep with the programme, boss.' Gerald took Kester by the elbow and led him to the central bench. There was a rack of test-tubes sitting there, some marked with red, some with amber, and some with green stickers.

'These stickers all look very high-tech,' Kester said.

'One of your techniques, I believe, sir.'

'Yes. What am I looking at?'

'You are looking at the skin serum for KL03.'

'Serum? Do you mean the liquid catalyst?'

'Mrs Farrell's idea – makes it sound good for you. Serums are associated with health, glowing skin.'

'I see. Well, we've done glowing skin.' Kester lifted the pot and sniffed it.

'Doesn't smell, doesn't taste too bad, but we're not sure quite what ingesting too much of it would do to you so we'd best put some kind of warning on the label. Hera is primed and waiting when you're ready to give it a go. Her virus population has plateaued just like we expected, tropism's good, host tissue is reacting well, that is to say, not at all – it's ghosting. There's a greater differentiation between areas than we expected, but it shouldn't matter. It did take an extra day to reach optimum levels but that could be quite good, don't you think – delayed gratification and all that?'

'It's not something people are great at these days, but maybe...'

Gerald took the pot in one hand and put the other hand back on Kester's elbow, steering him towards the testing suites.

-o-

By the time Kester got back to his apartment, Farrell was already there. She was perched on his couch, shoes off, hair down, a glass of champagne in her hand. She reached over to the table next to her, picked up a second glass and held it out to him.

'They went for the fashion show.'

'They did?'

'Yule loved it. Believes it was his idea – it's the way to get him onside. Though he was half-way there already with his "designer" concept.'

'Wah!' Kester said, taking the glass. 'Good thing the models are actual models.'

'It was inevitable that they would be put on show at some point – though I wasn't counting on that being on the catwalk.' Alexis smiled to herself, knowingly.

She had been. He could see that now.

'You've got them all dancing to your tune, haven't you? You may have the Board fooled, but you don't fool me.'

Kester walked to the fridge, opened the door, stared into it for a moment or two, and then closed the door again. He took a long swig of champagne.

'Your mother called,' Alexis said.

He spat.

'Oh, fuck, sorry!' Kester grabbed a towel and threw it on the floor. 'My mother?'

'She's a nice lady.'

Kester groaned.

'She asked if you'd been getting any work done in between trips to the knocking boxes.' Alexis smirked. 'Speaking of which the Board, including myself, thinks it would be a good idea if you went to the Pigs – at least once – just to give you a better idea of who we're marketing to – what the experience is.'

'The Pigs?' Kester said, face contorted, snorting out the remembered smell. 'The Pigs? That's ridiculous. I don't need to know what they're like. It's not my job to know the market.'

'Jesus, I was just kidding.'

'God, it's just horrible.'

'Did you hear me? I was kidding?'

'I know, I just – guh.' Kester shuddered and laughed. 'You know why it's called "the Pigs", right? You do know?'

'Oh come on Kester, that's just an urban myth.'

'Oh yeah? Where do all those tons of bacon we eat in the City come from? Shipped in from the countryside? Unlikely. And you don't see pigs wandering free on the tops of buildings do you, so they must come from somewhere.'

'You don't see cows up there either but we manage to get our hands on milk. It's transported in, crazyface. Nobody goes to "the cows".' Alexis was openly laughing at him.

'Don't crazyface me. The Pigs, say no more. Don't have to.'

'You're mad, Kester. It's a story told by mothers to stop their teenage boys going there. Really, what kind of society do you think we live in? They're just latex holes in the wall – whatever you want on the display in front of you, but it's just a hole.'

'Yeah – a hole that every other fucker's fucked.'

Alexis raised her eyebrows and took a sip of her champagne.

'What would your mother say, Doctor Lowe, if she heard your filthy mouth?' She got up from the couch and stalked across the room towards him. 'And Chen? What would she say if she heard you bad-mouthing one of our potential clients like that? She wouldn't like it.'

Kester's laugh was dulled by the memory of Chen's hand at his back. He finished his glass, put it down and reached out to grab Alexis' waist as she came near. She hovered just out of reach for a moment and then drew in close.

'She'd spank me,' Kester said. 'She'd spank me with her manky little blistered hands.'

'I'd like to see her try,' Alexis said. She blinked slowly, a cartoon blink, calculated. 'I'm going to make you famous, Kester Lowe. They'll all want to spank you.' She put her lips to his ear. Behind her on the misted-out window a fashion show was running on mute, twice life-size, hips swinging with military verve between slicing cheekbones and precision footwork. 'Every filthy little one of them.'

Chapter 11

Blotch rubbed his hands together as he read through Cherry's report. It had been a long three weeks, but it was worth the wait.

...we don't know when the show will be yet – not sure a date has been set, but it's going to be like an actual fashion show, only the viruses are the clothes.

I won't be in the first show. My lot go back into quarantine next week for secondary testing – another three weeks. I heard Doctor Lowe say to Gerald that our virus probably won't be ready for another few months and might need another round of testing, so maybe that gives you an idea of timescales if we're not being included in the show.

So the rumours were true. They were planning a big showcase. It was the perfect opportunity, but he would have to work fast to make sure they were ready: it was time to make the call. He took his Book out and left his office, moving swiftly to the front doors of the building.

Walking along in front of the Real Church building, Blotch flicked his Book on and found the number he needed. As the line rang he stopped and swiveled slowly on his heel. There was more graffiti on the front wall. *The ONLY REAL Church is CofE.* Punchy. Blotch made a mental note to report it to the caretaker.

'Hello?' The voice that answered the phone was thin, watery. The woman sounded as if she was concentrating on something else.

'Doctor Delilah Campbell?'

'Speaking.'

'This may seem a bit out of the blue, but I'm calling because I've got a proposition for you.'

'Stop,' Doctor Campbell said. 'Whatever you're selling I'm not interested. This is my home number and your sorts of calls are supposed to be blocked.'

She was focused now and her voice bristled with spite. She was angry. Not angry at the phone call; just angry. Blotch could feel himself going automatically into call centre appeasement mode. But that wasn't right. He wanted the anger, wanted to direct it.

'This isn't a sales call, Doctor Campbell. I'm calling because I'm interested in funding your research.'

'My research?'

'Your research on screen development. My organisation was informed about your plans by another funding body which I believe rejected a past application.'

'Your organisation? What organisation?'

'My organisation would prefer to remain anonymous. We are a benevolent fund that prefers to remain under the radar.'

'Under the radar. Really.'

She was going to be a joy to deal with. Blotch was already annoyed with her tone. He was relieved he wouldn't have to meet with her.

'Yes. There would be some conditions attached to the funding, but I'll send a representative to talk these through with you.'

'I see.' There was confirmed disappointment in her voice. 'This all sounds a bit vague for my liking. What sort of funding are we talking about here?'

'Name it.'

'Name it? You mean an amount? On my current proposal I've suggested an initial budget of €250,000, but depending on your "conditions" it might have to be considerably more.'

'That's fine,' Blotch said.

There was a long pause on the line. She was trying to get rid of him with big numbers. She thought he was a time waster.

'What was your name again? This all sounds a bit weird to me. Why don't you send your details over and I'll apply to your fund in the normal way. I don't want to get into any trouble with the department.'

'My representative will come and speak to you this evening,' Blotch said. He had to ride out her doubts. A big enough transfer should do the job. 'I'm sure she'll be able to set your mind at rest. Can you be in your lab until seven?'

There was another long pause. Blotch could hear the whirr of a lab machine in the background.

'Yes.'

'That's settled then. I look forward to working with you, Doctor Campbell.'

'Let's not be too hasty,' she said, and the line went dead.

-o-

'This is fabulous,' Yule said.

Yule was sitting at Kester's desk, making it look small, while Kester pointed out the viruses from his board that had worked and would be ready in time for the show. He looked round to gauge Yule's reaction. Yule looked properly impressed by the last one on the list. It was in its final round of testing and was performing well. It caused a fine crest of hair to grow down the wearer's spine. A pregnant technician had named it 'Lanugo-go' after an early version's tropism selection had failed during torso testing, resulting in the torso growing hair all over.

'There will only be five,' Kester said. 'I know you were hoping for six.'

'No, no,' Yule said, his gaze still lingering on the concept of Lanugo-go. 'Kester Lowe's Big Five – that's absolutely fine. We've got enough going on around the edges to make the show substantial.' Yule hauled himself out of Kester's chair and shuffled over to the wall. 'This one really is fabulous.' He craned in closer to look at the notes that Kester had scrawled beside the illustrations.

'Unfortunately, I'm not sure if it would work on you, Roger, depending on the cause of your alopecia.'

'No. I expect not, I expect not. My hair follicles just don't work, so it's unlikely to.'

Kester watched Yule closely. He wished he was better at reading people.

'But it may,' Kester said after a few minutes. 'You could always give it a go and see.'

Yule laughed and returned to Kester's chair. Kester tried not to wince as its insectile frame creaked under Yule's weight.

'Don't worry, Kester, it's not a thing. It's just that when you've been bald all your life, hair holds a certain tactile fascination.'

'I understand. You might fancy a trip to testing suite seven then.' Kester winked.

'So we're free to focus on preparations for the show?' Yule said.

'That's why you've come up to see me?'

'Precisely. Didn't seem necessary to get everybody involved at this stage. There are a number of things we can just take decisions on and it'll be quicker without having to dodge traffic on the innuendo highway with Alexis and Gaunt.'

Kester laughed. It sounded like a show – tonight on *The Innuendo Highway with Alexis and Gaunt*.

'What's first?'

'Let's see.' Yule took out his Book and flicked to the right set of notes. 'OK. In order of urgency: image; photoshoot; interviews. Now, I'm not one to take fashion advice from, but don't worry – we've got you a stylist.'

'Did you say interviews?'

'Yes, interviews – talk shows, Night Daily, webcasts and that sort of thing.'

'Not Night Daily. I can just see them sneering about it as they miss the point and discuss over my head whether it's "art" or not.'

'Don't worry.' Yule placed a steady hand on the desk. 'We've got the best media coach in the business. Your coaching is nine until twelve every day this week.'

'They must think I really need it.'

'Our image team are going to have their way with you this afternoon, so you'd better start sewing all those labels back on. Photoshoot is Thursday, early morning. They want a couple of sunrise shots, so up to the studio at five and no carousing on Wednesday night.'

'Five?' Kester closed his eyes and sighed like a teenager.

'It's just a one-off. I've put all this in your diary with reminders.'

-o-

'Just left a bit…No – back to where you were and rotate to the left a bit…OK. Come on, relax and look at that beautiful sunrise. You're cool; you're sexy.'

Kester didn't feel cool and he didn't feel sexy. It was five-thirty in the morning and it was windy at the top of the V building. He felt puffy and a bit dizzy. He had never been up here before though it was one of the most famous bits of the building: a cantilever reinforced glass platform the length of the building and twenty feet deep that jutted out over the City boundary from the back of V's flat roof. The location was 'symbolic', Yule had assured him. He was inside the City; he was outside the City. Why that mattered, Kester wasn't quite sure. The view would have been phenomenal were the rising sun not leaving an ever-changing rash of blobs in his eyes.

'Right at the sun,' the photographer said again. 'Hands on hips, please. No, one hand on your hip – other hand. Relax. Widen your stance a little. Just stand naturally.'

The collar of Kester's brown fabric biker jacket was tickling his neck. He was beginning to doubt whether the corporate photographer was the best choice for the job. He folded the collar down again, trying to remodel it with a squeeze.

'OK. Now a few with your labcoat please, Doctor Lowe.'

A team of three stylists descended on him. One removed his jacket, the second slipped his labcoat on over his outstretched arms and a third ruffled his hair. As they retreated, Kester re-ruffled it. They returned and ruffled it again, and then paused for a moment to check he wasn't going to mess with it.

'Right, let's snap!'

Kester took a breath to cool the wooziness in his throat. He had avoided carousing the night before as instructed by Roger Yule, but he had stayed up late almost by accident. The lab was empty for the first time in a couple of weeks and he had decided to spend some solid time on his screen development. His in vitro tests were complete and he was ready to do some torso testing. He had commandeered one of the unused isolation suites and ordered a few extra torsos in.

Kester had injected three of the torsos late last night. The screens would be creating themselves now. He closed his eyes and thought himself into the system of one of the torsos. He let the sun-blobs become blood cells, allowed himself to be pushed through veins to the scene of his first screen's creation: the slithery shrunken phallus of the appendix. Here, prompted by the key virus, a cell mass was growing around a resource capsule of nanotransmitter materials, transforming the bored vestigial structure into a magnificent cathedral of immunity. Genetically modified host tissue bloomed, a froth of new growth creating an immunoglobulin factory, its benches hundreds of strands of virus-enabled cells. Rubbery tubes arose in a ridge along the length of the appendix and began birthing pods that carried transmitter packs and viral triggers, on their way to create network nodes throughout the body.

'Forward a bit.'

The photographer's voice shunted Kester onwards from the appendix out into the bloodstream where he was carried to a network node already under construction, spinning itself from native flesh near the subject's cervix, one of many blossoming across the torso at likely infection sites. Complete, its spongy structure began to shoot out cruisers, bruisers and antibodies like spores from a fungus.

'If you can just pull your coat back a little.'

The cruisers swilled past him, large and small. They were white, semi-translucent, and covered in protruding hallelujah-wide mouths, sirens singing for antigens to lure in and bind to. At the hearts of the large cruisers, confined to the bloodstream by their size, were the nanotransmitters, waiting for a binding to take place – an antigen to dock and reveal its nature, a smaller cruiser to latch on and report back from through the looking-glass of the body, a native antibody to pause and pass on information with a kiss. Bruisers rolled past, great wet tumbleweeds on patrol, reaching out tendrils, feeling for intruders, ready to help the body's macrophages where there was good eating to be had.

'Your coat – can you pull it back a little? Wardrobe?'

Kester grinned to himself as he flicked his coat back over one hip. He could see it, like a network of swirling laser beams: information from the cruisers and from other nearby screen users made a cat's cradle of straight green lines back to the nodes and to information central in the appendix. From there a great umbilical cord stretched out to Kester's central database. For a moment, the invisible corridors of the database were open to him. He sat in front of an endless, moon-high wall of microscopic compartments, each housing a biological menace terrifying in its own way – snarling mouth, strangling limbs, the calm pale open mouth of the reaper.

From here, as he watched from his white throne, he could see the database's reply to the threats, pulse after pulse in an endless wave of information streaming out to the screens. Each pulse was an upload package delivering response blueprints and mugshots of the latest antigens. Each would trigger near-instantaneous responses in all his subjects. Their nodes would start spitting out antibodies like rapid-fire weapons, maybe before an infection was even present, targeting the imposters and spreading the word amongst the body's own defences to multiply the effect.

Kester opened his eyes. He felt powerful. He drew himself up and took a deep breath.

'That's perfect,' the photographer said. 'If you can just widen that stance a bit – you're a sex god; you're a rock star.'

'I'm a scientist,' Kester corrected him.

-o-

Kester sat in his office, watching the activity on the lab benches outside. It would have taken him six months, a year to develop a virus at the Institute. Here he had a team of thirty people all working on researching, developing and testing. Within his first six months they had managed to get twenty-two different viruses into development, six of which were already undergoing torso trials, and another four human trials. It was incredible. It was brilliant, he told himself, without passion.

It was easy to feel inspired on a rooftop; less so behind a desk. Besides which it was nearly lunchtime and his early start was catching up with him. Status reports were stacking up on his wall display. Had he been into the nuts and bolts of development that wouldn't have been so bad but he hadn't touched a slide or a test tube on his V projects for weeks. He was living a double life: manager by day; scientist under cover of night. From day to day this fact took on different aspects: it was a good thing; it was a bad thing; it meant nothing.

He was neither, Farrell kept telling him. He was a designer, a proper designer, a visualiser. They were still his techniques and blueprints that were being used, and to develop viruses for which he had come up with the concepts. That was the fun part, coming up with the concepts from basics. But now, with so many already on the go, there was no reason to come up with more. Not for now, anyway. Kester's board wall was still covered in concept sketches and notes for the viruses already in development. There was no space for anything new. He would spend most of the week checking the work of others and managing the trials process. Still, the fashion show was coming up fast. It was already there in his mind like a memory or a dream, velvet curtains and Super Trooper lights at the end of the tunnel.

He swung round on his chair to look at the wall. It was beautiful. Each virus had its own area, drawn up on Kester's Book and 'pinned' to a segment on the plasma wall, hand-scrawled notes alongside it. Farrell had sent in an illustrator, Helena, to work up the concept drawings. They were less for Kester and more for the Board, but Kester found that they did help him and had been working quite closely with Helena until she unexpectedly handed in her notice.

'So.'

Kester jumped and shuffled his chair round to face the door. Alexis, unannounced as ever.

'Have you got anything new to show me?' Alexis said. She put her hands on his desk and leaned forward with a conspiratorial smile. 'I'm bored,' she stage-whispered.

'Maybe,' he said and smiled sweetly at her.

She hung back from the desk again and turned to see what he had been looking at.

'I see you still have Helena's drawings up.'

'The concept drawings?' It was bizarre – he could step into the exchange booths with many ambitious lab hands as he liked, but one pretty woman set foot in his office and Alexis' hackles raised. 'I want to see how the final product measures up.'

'Yes.'

Kester was beginning to suspect that Helena's sudden disappearance had less to do with her wanting to leave and become a 'proper' artist, as Alexis had suggested, and more to do with Alexis' peculiar brand of jealousy. He was still trying to puzzle out what the key ingredient was – not beauty. Her own absence, perhaps. The feeling that she was missing something or that something was going on out of her control.

'Come through.' Alexis indicated Kester's living quarters as if she were inviting him into her own rooms. He got up slowly and followed her.

'You're still wearing Corona.' Kester indicated her eyes. He thought she might have got rid of it by now.

'Yes, I'm hanging on to it. Come the fashion show I'm going to be wearing all of the Kester Lowe Big Five. It's important to mark one's territory.'

'I'm your territory?'

'This project is my territory, my baby. I want that to be plain. You'll be in the limelight, but I'll be standing right behind you, making all this possible.'

'The puppeteer.' Kester smiled.

'I beg your pardon?' Farrell pushed him backwards towards the bed.

'I said the puppeteer.'

'Say that one more time,' she pushed him a little further, 'and I'll have to beat you.'

'One more time?'

'One more time.' Farrell moved so close that Kester could barely keep his balance.

'I have got something to show you.' He stepped sideways and headed back towards the office. Anger flashed in Alexis' eyes.

'Good,' she said, composing herself. 'You know how I hate to punish you.'

Kester walked up to his plasma wall and looked at the drawings.

'Viruses three and four: Lanugo-go, Persona.' He pointed out two illustrations, one of a naked woman with a crest of hair down her spine and one of a man with a butterfly-shaped mask of colour on his face. 'In theory the mask should appear in different formations on everyone because it depends on the patterning of cell types in your facial skin.' His hand lingered over the second illustration. 'That's what happened with the chest skin in the torso testing anyway. But it should tend to one of two rough patterns depending on whether the wearer is male or female – because of facial hair distribution, you see.'

'Nice.'

'Pretty neat, eh? They're about to go into human trials – we've got our next lot of models in now, ready to load them up. I'll let you know when they present and we can join in the testing if you like, *in vivo*.' These last two words he said in his best sleazy voice.

'Starting to enjoy yourself, aren't you?' The look in Alexis' eyes was hard, as if she was measuring him against her expectations, studying him objectively.

'I started enjoying myself the minute I saw this lab...I'm starting to relax.'

'That's what it is, then. Yes, maybe.' Alexis took a long breath, and then her mood flicked to business. 'Come to my office.'

'Yes, Miss.' Kester held out both hands, one towards his office and one towards the outside exit of his apartment. 'Front door or back passage?'

'Front door today, Doctor Lowe.'

Kester followed her out and up to her office.

When they got there, Alexis misted up the office-side wall, blocking out the meerkat eyes of the desk workers. She walked to the window and held both hands up splayed against the glass.

'We're going to do it right here,' she said with a smirk, looking out onto the square below.

'Well, why break the habit of a lifetime,' Kester said, joining her at the window.

Standing, face close to the glass, the smell of Farrell all around him, Kester was transported back to his interview – his own pale, freckled forearms, Farrell's arms trapping him against the window, her desktop over her shoulder. He glanced over at the desk and felt an involuntary twitch.

'Down there.' She pointed at the V front doors below them and then out towards the centre of the square. 'The catwalk will run from the front of our building right out to the fountain.'

'And the models turn their heels over a box of shagging fans.'

'We had thought we'd shut off the exchange booths but, come to think of it, that might be nice.'

'This all sounds pretty grand.'

'There's not much point in doing it if we don't do it in style.'

'Welcome...Roger Yule,' said the doors.

'Hello, Roger,' Kester said.

He watched as Yule began his approach, and then he looked away. It was taking too long to be comfortable, looked like such hard work. It wasn't just a matter of moving his legs; Yule had to lift each side of his body alternately. It reminded Kester of a time when he'd had to move a free-standing fridge freezer. He imagined Yule gaining too much momentum, tripping on the way and bulldozing through the window in slow motion.

'Kester,' Yule panted a greeting, small beads of sweat gathering on his pale forehead.

'Alexis was just telling me about your plans for the square.'

'Ah, yes. I've had Helena on the case – she's done us some wonderful concept drawings. We've yet to see what the events management company can do with them.'

'Helena?' Kester raised one eyebrow at Alexis. 'I thought she had moved on.'

'You know there are people in this building I haven't seen for years,' Yule said, oblivious to the half-annoyed, half-flirtatious exchange that was going on beside him. 'So, Alexis, how far did you get?'

'Ask a personal question, Roger,' Alexis said, with a lewd smile.

'Welcome...Byron Gaunt,' said the doors.

'I'll ask you a personal question, my lovely,' Gaunt said, striding over to join them. 'When was the last time you put on a pair of knickers?'

'Just before I took them off again.' Alexis pecked Gaunt on both cheeks.

'Kester, my boy.' Gaunt laid a firm hand on Kester's shoulder.

'Gaunt. Nice to see you.' They shook hands.

'That looks good on you, boy.' Gaunt indicated Kester's outfit.

Kester had had a consultation with his stylist the day before. There was even less choice of what to wear now that he had a public image to consider, but he liked the way it was going. Rita, his stylist, wanted him to be 'in character' at all times, even under his labcoat. Kester's new outfits were a little retro – jeans and t-shirts carrying faded slogans, labels pre-removed. His clothes, to Alexis' annoyance, were not to be easy-access. As a part of his image as someone who didn't wear, he had to appear less attainable. Rita's theory was that with the exception of checking out people's shoes and what logos they were wearing, the first thing a person observed these days when considering another was how one might 'get at them'.

'I was down at wardrobe, the other day,' Gaunt said, 'and they tried to put me in some kind of all-in-one suit – like a pin-striped babygrow. I explained to Carlos that if he didn't come up with a sensible wardrobe for me soon I would have him deported for crimes against fashion and decency and that upon reaching his home country he would need surgery to remove said pinstriped babygrow from his anus.'

'Nice,' Kester said. 'Fortunately I don't object quite so strongly to my "new look". It's very much like my old look. And they're customising my clothes for me now.'

'Does cutting the labels off count as customisation?'

'Frankly, if it means I don't end up lacerating my hands with the nail scissors every time I want to wear something new, I don't give a shit.'

'That's my boy.' Gaunt chuckled. He turned to Yule. 'So this is where we will be worshipping the Great One come August.'

'Talk us through the rest of it, Roger,' Alexis said, growing tired of their banter.

'Well, the date's set now that the tickets are on sale,' Roger began. 'Five weeks from now – Saturday 5th August.'

'Five weeks?' Kester gawped. 'I know the viruses are ready, but will that give people enough time – I mean do you think –'

'Lines opened at 9:00 this morning,' Roger said with a smile. 'We had sold out by 9:02.'

–o–

The Department of Microbiology and Immunology was in an old building on a wide side street close to the Strand. The building was built in Victorian proportions and was several storeys high. Perhaps it was this and its proximity to some of London's more protected buildings that had enabled it to escape stratification. Cherry let her gaze drift upwards, her eyes pausing on lit windows as they might on eyes in a crowd. Though the shell of the building was intact, it looked like the Institute had restructured its insides. Floor divisions regularly appeared halfway up windows. In the bottom half of one window there were tops of heads working away busily, close to the ceiling; in the top half of the same, serving the room above, two sets of brogued feet loitered on the crossbars of stools, one set pressed together and pointing eagerly towards the other.

As Cherry entered the building, the warden smiled at her and said hello through his mouthful of sandwich. He tapped on the visitors' screen on the counter in front of him. She glanced across to the previous day's entries and copied a name. Once she had signed in, the warden pointed her towards the lifts.

The department was less high-tech than Cherry had imagined. Once inside, there was no security between the different labs that she could detect, despite numerous signs saying who was and wasn't allowed to go where. Some of the doors were sitting ajar. Through the small grill-glazed windows in the doors she could see the cluttered labs, equipment accrued from years of research. It could have been a technology design museum. The colours of the equipment, the lettering on their names and the names themselves were all clues to when the pieces had been purchased. Perhaps some of these things had never been bettered, or perhaps they were kept as curiosities.

As she walked along the corridor, she realised she hadn't thought past the door of the lab. What was she going to say to this Dee character? What if she called security the minute Cherry mentioned the Church's conditions?

She arrived at the door and, before she realised what she was doing, knocked on the glass. There was only one figure in the lab and she had her back turned. The sleek black hair matched the description, shining like lacquer beneath the daylight ceiling. Dee looked round a moment later, as if it had taken time for Cherry's knock to filter through into her consciousness. Cherry smiled and waved enthusiastically. This drew a puzzled look from Dee but she came and opened the door.

'Can I help you?' she asked, jade eyes interrogating Cherry's face and clothes.

'Yes.' Cherry maintained her smile. 'I hope so – you spoke to my employers earlier about an offer of funding. Can I come in?'

Dee drew her head back. She was expecting a man in a suit perhaps, someone older, more official. Would that make this harder or easier, Cherry wondered.

'Yes, come in,' Dee replied eventually. 'I'm just finishing something off here – do you want to grab a seat?' She indicated one of the tall stools at the other end of her work bench.

This lab was no exception when it came to clutter. All around the walls there were cabinets and pieces of equipment from different eras, even some paper storage. In the corner of the room, a display was flickering away to itself, showing a series of lines that wandered their way up and down – some sort of activity that needed to be monitored. The benches were rib-height, right for working when standing, or when perched on one of the high stools. They were an unpleasant grey colour. This was one of the floors with low level windows. Mucky orange light spilled in on the floor, competing with the yellowing glow from the daylight ceiling. Cherry had expected everything to be white and clean like the lab at V. It smelled unfamiliar, as if the whole place were steeped in formaldehyde.

'Sorry about the mess,' Dee said, drawing out the words as if speaking too quickly might upend something. She was staring intently through an eyepiece and tapping notes in to her Book with one hand, but she seemed to have sensed that Cherry was looking around the room. 'We've been a bit short-staffed lately. One of my colleagues got religion and left to join one of the big corporates.'

'Kester?' Cherry asked, after a short pause.

Dee's head ticked to one side with an urge to look round, but she continued and finished what she was doing before turning to face Cherry.

'Yes. Kester,' Dee said finally, folding her arms tightly beneath her chest.

There was a low noise in the lab that came and went, rising and falling, like a headache threatening to start; a near silence made up of numerous barely audible tickings, drippings, buzzings, static. Dee's face was chalk-pale. It made her cold green eyes stand out and her hair look absently black, sucking light from the room.

'You know him?' Dee asked.

'I know of him. I know you were planning to do some research together. I know that he let you down in more ways than one.'

'If you're from one of those worthless gossip sites I have no interest in talking to you. I've already told your colleagues I have nothing to say about the matter. We weren't doing any research on fashion viruses here before Kester left and we're not doing any now. He did it all in his spare time. I should have known – you don't look anything like –'

'Wait. Maybe I don't look the part but, believe me, my employers are for real. They've got money and they want to fund your screen research, so hear me out.'

Cherry swallowed and cast her eyes about as if there might be something in the room that could help her. Blotch had sent her the notes from Dee's call but, though she had read them, she hadn't planned anything she would say.

'OK,' Dee said, giving herself time before she continued. 'How can I know to trust you?'

There was something volatile about Dee's voice, something sub- or supersonic that was hard to identify, but which made Cherry uneasy. What if she flipped? Called the warden? Cherry imagined the scenes to come. Dee was going to go for some kind of panic button underneath the desk, or try to throw her out or call security. She would grab Dee by the wrist and spin her round. No, the hair – the hair would make a good hold. She would grab her by the hair and slam her pretty face onto the worktop. That chair in the corner was good. Something to tie her up with…

'Well?' Dee asked again.

'Take a look at your bank balance,' Cherry said, trying to suppress the twitching in her smile. Blotch had been confident, but it seemed so dodgy. It was so dodgy.

'My bank balance?' Dee lifted her Book and started tapping it on the bench.

'Just do it.'

Dee looked down at her Book and touched an icon. A flush rose and fell in her cheeks. When she looked back up at Cherry her eyes were intense, as if her pupils were trying against nature to narrow.

'What is this?'

'It's €100,000.'

Dee coughed, then laughed and looked at her Book again.

'I can see that.' She shrugged her shoulders and shook her head. 'I have to say this isn't normally the way it's done. For starters, the funding would be paid directly to the Institute. I'd say there's a good reason your employers want to stay anonymous and it's got something to do with the "conditions" they mentioned. So let's start with that.'

This was progress. She was at least engaging with the idea. Here came the hard part. There was no disguising that it was dodgy, no matter what Blotch said.

'I'm going to be straight with you and get to the point.' Cherry slid her hands under her thighs to stop them from shaking. 'Your colleague Doctor Lowe worked on a number of viruses before he left the Institute and my employer would like to get a hold of one or two for demonstrative purposes.'

'Demonstrative?'

'They want to get a hold of them.'

'You know that all the interesting stuff is done off-site, right? Secondments. Nothing is held here. You've seen the security – let me guess, he was eating a sandwich?'

Cherry nodded.

'For starters, all that stuff is protected. It would be illegal to give it to you. And on top of that, we just don't have it. I can't help you.'

'You worked with Doctor Lowe on a number of his papers.'

'Yes.'

'Do you think for the right price you could recreate some of his work?'

Dee took a deep breath, looking at Cherry as if she could see the rest of the conversation unfolding before her. Cherry saw an opportunity and jumped in before Dee could reply.

'I take it that's a "no". I mean you can't do it without him.'

'Of course I can.' Dee hopped down from her stool and paced a little before coming back to her bench. Cherry had hit the sweet spot.

'Then we can talk properly. You want the funding for your screen work?'

Dee ignored Cherry's question and stared at her.

'The money in your account; it's not part of the funding.'

Cherry watched as the expression on Dee's face changed. Under her pale mask emotions were fighting to get through and the realisation of the possibilities was dawning.

'It's –'

'I know what it is,' Dee snapped, as if she didn't want Cherry to say it out loud.

'Just so we're clear, the funding itself can be directed wherever you need – we don't care whether you want to take it through the Institute or if you want to use it to set up and do your research independently. Hell, you can spend it on shoes for all I care. You'll receive it in two payments, one after you deliver each virus.'

Cherry took a printout from her pocket and laid it on the bench next to Dee, text copied and pasted from Blotch's message.

'I'm not going to pretend to be an expert. These are the viruses we're looking at.'

Dee leaned forward and looked at the printout, reading it without touching the paper. Her brow tightened.

'How do you know about these?' Dee asked, her voice dilute.

Cherry looked at her. Blotch had told her not to mention the call. It was too close to the Church. But this woman was no fool. Cherry didn't have to mention it; she could see that. A memory was sliding its dark hand up over Dee's skull.

'I know how you feel about Doctor Lowe's activities. I know about the virus he passed on to you; I know how long you've relied on each other; I know he betrayed you personally, professionally. He's a common enemy. We don't wish anybody else any harm. We just want to show him for what he is and put an end to V's activities.'

Dee turned her back on Cherry.

'When you shared this information you set things in motion for us,' Cherry said.

'Sounds serious.' The emotion had dropped from Dee's voice. 'When you say you'll use the viruses for demonstrative purposes...what is your plan?'

'To bring him down.'

Chapter 12

Dee walked. She needed to make a decision soon. A door had opened right in front of her. Revenge. Revenge without getting her hands dirty. And for Kester – what? With V's reputation in tatters and his job lost, where would he be? Back on her doorstep, telling her how right she had been, begging her to name him as second author on her screens research. No damage, no real damage done. Just the righting of wrongs. She felt a small swell of triumph in her breast. Finding herself close to Trafalgar Square, she took a detour.

The square was packed full of people and there was an uneasy feeling in the air. The jostling was less impartial than normal. For the most part the movement was smooth, but now and again she was struck by what she felt was an aggravated elbow, or pushed by an angry shoulder. Some people were passing through, some had stopped to watch the big screen and some were looking up at the top of Nelson's Column. She followed their eyes upwards.

Nelson was boxed up, at first she thought for cleaning, but as she focused on the figure projected on the box, she realised it was not a standard 'we're refurbishing – here's a picture of what you came to see' box, but a promotion. Kester was projected on three of its sides. The fourth was advertising his show. What a distance to fall. She looked to the big screen. Text was scrolling across a fast-paced montage of fashion shows and attractive virus wearers. SATURDAY 5th: BEAUTY IS REDEFINED the text announced.

Up at the fourth plinth, a man in a trench coat was bellowing out across the crowd, a small number of whom had stopped to listen. Dee tuned in.

'...to our bodies. Abuse. Self-abuse. Abuse of nature. Perversion. These people think they are indestructible. We've been given these screens to protect us – whether or not you think they're a good thing – given them for free – and they're taking them for granted. The world was able to ignore this perverted counterculture until now but how harmless is it now? How harmless is it when the ones who make our screens are selling us viruses to wear like circus freaks?'

'Presumably much more harmless than wearing street viruses,' the girl next to Dee said to her friend. 'I thought that was the whole point.'

Dee walked on through the crowd, tuning in and out...*so cool...make them safe...like a rock star...freaks – freaks!...as well be safe if you're going to...not about the screens...fed the cat this morning...sexy, yeah smart.*

She stopped and looked up at the screen, which was coming to the end of its montage. Kester was standing silhouetted against the rising sun, hands in pockets. He stood in an uncomfortable casual pose at the edge of a glass platform, looking out over the Green Belt. BEAUTY IS NOT SKIN DEEP. The bright yellow words stopped scrolling, paused there for a minute, then vanished, leaving the lettering hanging in Dee's eyes, a cerise stamp on the dark canvas of the image.

'Skin deep,' she spat to herself.

'...wouldn't be allowed to happen.' The man was still talking.

Dee was surprised that people were stopping to listen. He wouldn't be there for long. It wasn't a designated protest area. He'd be relocated pretty smartish to somewhere less public where he would be able to protest all he wanted.

'And where are the politicians? Queuing up at the Pigs to get the first Kester Lowe? Spending the money we pay them to run the country to fuck a wall and get a designer rash? What about the...'

He was cut off by a loudspeaker screech.

This was big, Dee thought to herself. People were getting excited about it no matter which way you looked. Some were angry and some were ecstatic, but it was all passion. Kester's enemies had their timing just right. All they needed was for her to work quickly, get the first virus to them on time, say yes.

She took a deep breath and looked up again. The screen was now showing a heavily edited news report, slicing clips of Kester's recent media and red carpet appearances together like a pop video. Something about the style of the thing made Dee bristle. The ticker across the bottom reported news and rumours in a seamless stream. *Five brand new viruses to be revealed at fashion show. Special viral technologies episode of* Horizon *to air tonight. Lowe and Farrell reported to be touring Europe to promote show. Tickets for V fashion show sell out in under two minutes.* What a bubble to pop.

Dee stop-started her way back through the crowd towards the Strand, a bright tumbling feeling in her chest accelerating her gait. She passed the lion statue at the square's south-east corner. A group of young girls were riding it and standing round it, babbling. Two of them were wearing labcoats. All at once they shouted, 'We love you Kester!' then screamed in unison, rattling Dee's eardrums. She stopped and looked up at them in anger, her small rough scream swallowed by the clamour. She took out her Book.

-o-

Cherry fumbled in her pocket for her Book and checked again that it was on vibrate. Still no message from Doctor Campbell. She had expected a *yes* or a *no* by now. Blotch would burst a blood vessel if she didn't get an answer by the time she went into quarantine.

Taking a deep breath, she looked around the room. All the out-of-quarantine models had been gathered together in one of the empty testing suites. There were about forty of them sitting on white plastic chairs, facing the side of the room, where a small semi-circle had been kept empty bar two more chairs. The models looked like they were in uniform. They were in uniform, sort of. Wardrobe had been asked to assign them all several sets of the same casual outfit – the idea was that people would know who they were, particularly around the lab, but out on the street too, to get a buzz going. Each of them wore a fitted black high-collared tunic top with a broad panel down the front that sported a large metallic V. Tight fitting black trousers and a jaunty V-badged cap completed the look, though Cherry noticed that many of the hats had been ditched. Hers sat in her lap.

Cherry looked over her shoulder, smiling briefly at the man behind. On the back wall was projected a montage of all the testing suites. The models in each suite were also gathered to listen and had pulled their chairs round in broadly the same configuration; their white-kimonoed figures were ghost battalions, reinforcements in waiting. It must have been an audience of over a hundred all in. Cherry was surprised. She hadn't really thought of there being that many testing models involved, perhaps because they were always out of view.

'Welcome...Doctor Lowe. Welcome...Gerald.'

All the models looked to the doors at once.

'Hello,' Doctor Lowe said.

He looked surprised. All those eyes on him. You would think he would be getting used to it by now. Perhaps it was different when it was your own private army of models.

'How embarrassing,' he stage-whispered to Gerald, 'they're all wearing the same thing.'

Doctor Lowe made himself comfortable on one of the chairs at the side of the room and Gerald took the floor.

'Thank you all for coming,' Gerald said, then looked up to the camera that was transmitting their image back out to the suites, 'or for tuning in. I know some of you are supposed to be off-duty at the moment but it really made sense for us all to come together for this briefing, so thanks for that.

'You'll all know by now that the date for our first V fashion show has been set for the 5th of August, so about four weeks from now, give or take.' He gave them a sparkling smile. 'Hands up training team.'

Six models in the front row all put up their hands. Cherry recognised a short blonde model from a series of perfume adverts. The others, male and female, merged into a moodboard of cool: tall, thin, slicked-back hair, perfect skin of every shade. Blank canvases. Perhaps that was what was needed.

'For those of you who haven't met them, this is my crack crew of model trainers. I know that not all of you have modelled professionally before, but do not fear, we'll be sending these guys in to teach you everything they know.'

There were a couple of snorts from the back of the room.

'They'll teach you your routines for the big night,' Gerald continued. 'Now, especially if you're going to be appearing in the show on the 5th, we'll need you in peak physical condition, so get on those mini-gyms. We know it's tempting to veg out during quarantine, but we don't want to have to reinforce the catwalk.'

Silence. An apologetic look from Doctor Lowe. He reached up

and put a hand on Gerald's arm. Cherry smiled to herself. Gerald's lame jokes washed over her. She found them quite charming, especially given the huge smile which normally followed them, but she knew they grated on the nerves of some of her compatriots.

'Shall I?' Doctor Lowe asked.

'Yes, if you wish.' Gerald deferred to him and sat down. 'Thank you.'

'As you all know,' Doctor Lowe said, 'live viral exchange is covered in your contracts and the show is where this will really come into play.'

'We finally get some action, Doctor?' The short blonde model asked. The way she spoke made it sound like they were in the middle of a game of Doctor and Nurse.

Cherry looked over at her. She was slouched as if she was accustomed to sitting on a chaise, one arm over the back connecting her to the group, one leg pointed out towards Doctor Lowe. It was as decent an effort at lounging as could be made on a plastic chair.

'That's right, Hera. The way it will work is we'll have a VIP area at the front of the stage. Once you've finished your part of the show, you'll get to go down into this area and choose yourself a willing partner for exchange.'

Doctor Lowe paused and looked around the room, then up at the back wall, as if gauging the response to this suggestion. He ruffled his brown hair. Cherry looked round too. There were a few raised eyebrows; a few models were smiling and nodding as if this was what they had been waiting for; some were staring into space. She looked back at Doctor Lowe. He seemed a little stunned, as if he had expected some backlash.

'Doctor.' Cherry raised her hand. 'What infection rate are you expecting? They won't all pick up the viruses, will they, from a five minute bonk. So what about methods for optimum transfer – will the trainers cover that?'

Cherry raised her eyebrows at Doctor Lowe. If they weren't well versed, she might get herself in to the training team – perhaps an opportunity to work more closely with Gerald and Doctor Lowe.

'You've modelled before?' asked Hera, before Doctor Lowe could answer.

'No, but I've worked in the sex trade as a seeker.' Cherry tried to ignore the heat in her cheeks. This was good. She needed to lay this out there. 'Believe me it's worth knowing the pick-up tips – I know we're working the other way round, but you want to give your clients the best possible chance of infection.'

'You harvest Pig viruses?' Hera said. 'Ugh! How TopShop.'

'That's right, I'm a prostitute, if that's what you're getting at, but then aren't we all?'

Cherry glanced over at Gerald and caught him smiling, a nervous twinkle in his eye. Kester lifted his hands against the possibility of conflict.

'We prefer the term "models" here,' he said.

'How about "professional sextresses"?' Cherry replied.

Hera managed a little sideways smile. Cherry laughed to herself. There was a small sadness sitting just at the bottom of her gullet. She was suddenly very aware of the wall of white-clad men and women watching from the back of the room.

'You know what?' Doctor Lowe was smiling too. He held up his hands. 'Call yourselves whatever you want – I'm leaving the country for three weeks.' He looked suddenly pleased with himself as if he had just remembered. 'Gerald's point was that you'll be in the capable hands of our training team here, and...' Here he stepped forward and had a short exchange with Hera, ending in a nod from her. He stepped back again. 'And our newest member of the team, Viral Transfer Consultant Cherry Woodlock.' Turning to her he added, 'That alright with you? Extra remuneration on top of your basic.'

'Sure,' Cherry replied with a smile. He knew her name. He must know all their names. This surprised her.

When Doctor Lowe and Gerald had finished their presentation and gone through timetabling for the training, the models were dismissed. In the midst of all the chair-scraping, Cherry milled up to Doctor Lowe.

'Thanks for that, Doctor Lowe,' she said.

'Not at all – thank you,' he replied. 'You had a good point and it's great that you can help out. And please, call me Kester.'

'Kester, right.' Cherry smiled. 'So where are you going for three whole weeks, Kester? Sunning yourself while we get on with the hard work?'

'Hardly. I'm V's prize show pony. Farrell's taking me off round the world on a whistlestop tour to all the V offices. So don't worry –

I won't be having too much fun. Unless you think presenting to the boards of all the regional offices sounds like fun.'

'Hm.' Cherry couldn't think of anything worse. Hard to believe that this was what he was actually going to be doing, considering the massive smile that had come to his face earlier. There must be some perks to the trip. 'Well, good luck.'

'Thanks,' Doctor Lowe said with a smile. 'I guess I'll see you when I get back. Hope you get on well with this lot.' He nodded to the training team, who had arranged themselves in the corner, leaning at angles, heads tipped back, watching the room clear.

'Sure I will,' Cherry replied. She may as well chance her arm. 'You taking the show viruses with you, Doctor Lowe?' she asked. 'Letting the big dogs have first dibs?'

Doctor Lowe stepped backwards shaking his head and touching his nose with a smile.

'Top secret, I'm afraid!'

Cherry's Book buzzed. She took it half out of her pocket and glanced at it. It was an unknown number. This was it. *Yes*, was all the message said.

-o-

'They're not bothered at all!' Kester said as the door to his office closed behind them.

He touched his Book, misting up the walls and blocking out the vista of white-coated industry. Looking up, he caught Alexis smiling at him. She was pleased to have been right again.

'I told you so,' she said. 'We made clear in their contracts that commissioned exchange might be a possibility. And they don't see it as a paid part of their job anyway – it's a bonus shag with a celebrity once they've done their bit on the catwalk. You've got to remember that a lot of them are professional models, or aspiring ones – especially the first tranche – they do it all the time. Ever been to London Fashion Week?'

Kester made a face. Of course he hadn't been to London Fashion Week.

'No. God, what a relief!' He slumped down in his chair. A smile built up to a grin, which built up to a laugh. 'It'll be so good!'

'We've certainly worked our arses off to make sure everyone's excited about it.' Alexis grinned.

'Well, you know how passionate I am about raising the profile of science, darling.' Kester grinned back at her and stopped his capering.

Alexis drew a deep breath and walked over to the window.

'The show's going to be the event of the summer,' she said. 'While we're away Yule's team are going to be talking to some high profile wearers, setting interviews up. You packed for our little trip yet?'

Kester watched her as she looked down into the square below. He hadn't packed yet. He hated packing. The light from the window defined the silhouette of her body within her light tunic top and made her blonde hair glow. Smiling to himself, he reached under his desk and brought out what looked like a small tub of paint.

'Here.'

Alexis turned and looked to see what he had, then raised her eyebrows. 'What is it?'

'A pot of procrastination. Take your shirt off.'

'What?'

'Shy? Come through next door then. I've got something for you. You'll like it.'

Farrell walked ahead of Kester back through to his quarters.

'Take your shirt off,' he repeated in his best commanding voice. He had been practising this tone for a while now. He was convinced that she quite liked it. No-one ever told her what to do and it must be a relief to allow herself just to follow instructions for a change. Not that she would ever admit it. He wouldn't dare speak to her like that outside of their private quarters and the exchange booths.

'Yes, sir.' Alexis smirked. She whipped her tunic top up over her head and flicked open her bra.

'Did I say your bra?'

'You didn't have to, darling.' Alexis smiled saucily and squeezed one of her breasts, staring him right in the eye.

'It's unnecessary, but I won't say it's not a bonus.' Kester laughed to himself as he unscrewed the lid of the paint pot, set it down on his coffee table and started looking in his labcoat pocket for something. 'It gives me more to work with.'

'I like this.'

Alexis had found Kester's new recliner, made in the same apple-green leather as his Bauhaus suite. He'd had it specially made, having seen one in someone else's office. The colour made it look a little like a dentist's chair, but Kester kind of liked that. Alexis laid herself down on it. The waistband of her culottes tweaked the flesh of her midriff as she settled herself luxuriously, as if preparing to nap.

'Where do you want me, Kester.' She still kicked out his name like a spitting cat.

'Actually, that's ideal. Stay where you are.'

He had found what he was looking for: a long-handled paintbrush.

'I gave you a gift a few days ago,' Kester said.

'I don't remember.'

'No, that's because you weren't aware of it.'

'You slipped me one while I was sleeping?'

'Lex, I'm pretty sure even you couldn't sleep through that.' Kester glanced down at his crotch, failing to keep a straight face. 'Besides which, everybody knows you don't sleep.'

'Really? They know that?'

'No machine needs to sleep. Not even a sex machine.'

'Kester, that's dreadful.' Alexis rolled her eyes.

He couldn't be annoyed with her about Helena, he decided. Helena was sweet, but for some reason she had reminded him what it was like to be embarrassed about sex, ashamed even. With Alexis it could be businesslike, intimidating, fun, but never embarrassing.

'So this gift,' Alexis said.

Kester suddenly looked round at his bedside table.

'Wait,' he said and dashed over there, returning with a plain black blindfold in one hand. 'Now hold still.'

He pumped his foot repeatedly on the height control of the recliner, bringing the seat up to waist level. Alexis laughed as it jerked her higher into the air.

'Jesus, Kester, don't you have an electronic control on this thing.'

'No! I had it made this way. It's low-tech chic.'

'A little inappropriate, don't you think.'

'These are my private quarters.'

'And what you do with your private quarters is your own

business.'

'And what you do with my private quarters...'

Alexis cried out, off-guard, as Kester pushed the recline lever, sending her jerking backwards a notch, so that she was lying almost flat, breasts falling into soft ovals. He pulled over a tall bar stool, perched beside her like a dentist and proceeded to blindfold her.

'This isn't very scientific, Doctor Lowe.'

'This is all very important. Now shut up and stay still.'

A little smile on Alexis' lips showed Kester that he had judged her right today. Taking the slender brush in one hand and the pot in the other, he began.

-o-

Alexis allowed the darkness of the blindfold to become the room. She loved the feeling of complete darkness. It was like floating, like being dead. It made it impossible to think about the world; it wiped your mind clean. The seat shuddered as Kester leaned over her, the tail end of his breath and then, at regular intervals, the air-con sweeping over her bare chest. She felt a tingling twist at the centre of each breast as her nipples tightened with the cold. The first touch of the brush made her flinch and giggle uncharacteristically, a small cold tongue licking her. He was painting her. When the air-con came, the paint cooled again, as if fresh. She opened her mouth to ask again what he was doing and then changed her mind. No talking.

'No talking,' he said, as if he had read her mind. His voice was low and close and it gave her a tight feeling in her throat, a miniature thrill.

The more he painted, the more she could feel what the marks were – swirls, dots, long thin stems of cool slithering down her flanks – as if her sense of touch was focusing. Her culottes were softly undone, let fall away to the side, ceased to exist. The cold licks moved downwards, making her belly shudder. Everything was magnified. She became aware of her viruses. The gold in her eyes shone through her eyelids, through the blindfold, burned a glow-edged hole through the ceiling above, the floor above that, upwards, through more floors, more ceilings, melted through metal, glass, stone, out through the clouds, through the atmosphere, into the sun; the sun was her projection in the sky. And about her body, her glowing lymph nodes cast a blue-white light contrasting the gold, bathed the room outside her in light. She imagined Kester's hard-concentrating face made pale, cool.

The sound of footsteps receding flicked her out of her focus. When had the painting stopped? She couldn't say. Couldn't say how long she had been lying there. The footsteps came back towards her and then there was cool air pushing down on her, light fabric landing on her skin. Kester's hands pressed the gauze softly onto her body, palm over palm, moving methodically from neck down to waistline. He was mummifying her. Then, starting at the neck again, she felt the gauze peeling away – not mummifying; blotting.

'OK,' Kester said. 'Now you need to dry for ten minutes. I'm going to fix some drinks.'

Alexis listened to the clinking of ice and glass as she waited to dry. The wet scrape of a bottle-cap twisting open, soft glugging, scraping shut again. Now a deeper scrape, a different container. Then the soft pad of feet across the room, the crack and tumble of ice once, twice, three times, filling up a metal container. Feet padding again, pouring, then a sound she had never realised she loved so much: the sound of metal slotting together, ice and liquid being shaken. The sound of the ice was softened by the liquid as it hit the glasses. By the time the glass arrived on the table beside her she was dying for a drink, but didn't dare reach out for it.

'You can have that after your shower,' Kester said. 'Now stand up for me.'

His hand slipped carefully under hers. She grabbed it and pulled herself up, stiff, not wanting to let her body crease, though not really sure why, or what Kester had done to her.

'Shower is this way.'

His hands were on her shoulders, pointing her in the right direction, pushing her ahead of him. Then they fell away and she was walking blind on her own.

'Wait,' his voice came and she stopped.

There it was again, the cool lick, this time on her right buttock. She snickered to herself. Kester giggled back. The spell was breaking; she was coming back to reality. He pressed what felt like a square of gauze to her buttock and then peeled it away.

'Let me guess,' Alexis said. 'Ten more minutes.'

'Yes,' Kester said. 'Maybe a little less. I'll let you know.'

She reached up to her blindfold.

'Not yet,' Kester said and grabbed her wrist. 'I can keep you occupied for ten minutes I think.'

When her ten minutes were up, Alexis showered with the blindfold on, soaping up hard and pressing her fingers firmly across her flesh, trying to feel for something – what, she wasn't sure. Something was different. There was a roughness, a change.

'OK,' Kester said when she had rinsed off. He guided her to the full-length mirror and pulled off the blindfold.

It took a moment for Alexis' eyes to adjust to the light. She was covered in patterns, like a primitive warrior, growing outward from her navel.

'Paint,' she said.

'Virus. KL05.'

'Virus?' She felt sleepy, unable to reply fully.

'Better than a virus, in fact. A virus that you have to buy a pot of this with.' Kester indicated his unmarked paint pot. 'The virus induces sensitivity to the chemicals in the paint. It's a sort of biological tattoo.'

'And it heals.'

'It's a minute rash. And yes, it heals over the course of about twelve hours. You choose your own patterning.'

'Like makeup, body paint.'

'Better than makeup – it's textured, it won't run, it won't sweat off or smudge. Of course the best way to test whether it's the real thing or not is to make someone sweat. And did you enjoy that?'

Alexis turned and kissed him. She smiled, satisfied, and then turned to look at her back. On her buttock, where she had expected more of the same exotic motif, was a childish scrawl – *Kester is my favourite.*

'Kester!' she shrieked, hurled out of her trance, cold water thrown on her warm satisfaction. 'What if someone sees that?'

'I've got to mark my territory somehow.'

Alexis snorted a laugh and gave him a gentle slap. She wasn't sure whether she wanted it to hurt or not.

'Touché baby.'

'Touché.' Kester smiled and stroked the markings on her front.

Chapter 13

The plane banked subtly, as if trying to tip its passengers out onto the vast bed of cloud that stretched beneath them. Kester allowed the falling feeling to take him. The clouds were luminous white as if lit from inside, soft and solid at the same time, perfectly walk-on-able. They weren't flying high; they were flying low to an unformed, unpainted landscape.

Travelling on a private jet wasn't something that Kester had ever expected to do. Even during the planning for their trip he had imagined that he and Alexis would travel on a commercial service. In business class, perhaps, maybe even first, but this? He grinned and took it all in.

Classical music filled the cabin: Peer Gynt. Everything was shades of beige. Even the smell was beige – soft milky air-conditioned tannins. It was a calming environment for someone so used to being barraged with logos and ads. Past Kester's raised feet, about two metres in front of him, was the door to the pilot's cabin. On either side of the door, the wall was given over to screen space. His side currently showed a live feed from the nose of the plane with a large-scale map of their route superimposed. The plane was moving swiftly, intersecting the dotted lines of other services from time to time, skiffing across the North Sea and heading towards the south-west coast of Sweden. Alexis' side was on silent, but showed a montage of news channels.

Their two mesh fully-reclining chairs were the main fittings in the spacious cabin. Each was served with a decent sized swivelling table and by a central table that rose up out of the floor when required, allowing them to turn their chairs to face one another to eat or share papers. At the back of the cabin, a semi-circle of banquette seating was interrupted by the door to the kitchens and staff areas. The two unused seats between them and the back of the cabin were folded up to the side, creating extra space for…Kester wasn't sure what for. For dancing. He smirked to himself and glanced up at the ceiling to check that there wasn't a rack of disco lights. There wasn't. Still, with enough alcohol at high altitude, who needed lights to dance?

He and Alexis were the only passengers, but they were accompanied by a small staff: a hostess to take care of their safety and comfort needs, a chef, who was behind the scenes somewhere tidying away their lunch things, and a beauty therapist who was working on Alexis as they flew. Alexis looked asleep. Her chair was fully reclined. The beautician was performing a slow facial massage and Kester could see that Alexis' head was giving to every push and pull. Her arm was resting just on the edge of the seat, perilously close to falling and shattering her rest.

Kester reached out to his table and picked up his Book. Flicking it to widescreen he brought up their itinerary again. Flight times, destinations, hotel names, meeting times – boringly straightforward. He tried to see in the lines of times and names the colour and luxury and excitement that Alexis had promised him.

'Cabin crew: ten minutes to landing.' The Captain's voice was beige.

The beauty therapist stepped back from Alexis and the two chairs manoeuvred themselves into upright positions in synch. Alexis stirred. Kester looked away. Waking was such a personal moment. It was one thing watching it occur when you were in bed with the person; elsewhere it seemed like an intrusion. Out of the corner of his eye, he could see Alexis stretching her neck back and forth.

'There already?' she asked, eventually.

When Kester looked round the therapist had gone. Alexis was rooting in her bag for her makeup.

'Ten minutes,' he said.

By the time Alexis had touched up her makeup and smoothed her hair, they had landed. Her preening left Kester feeling unprepared. He checked his tie and ruffled his hair.

'OK?' he asked Alexis.

'Gorgeous,' she replied with a fresh blood smile, unclipping her seatbelt.

Picking up the small black case that sat next to her legs, she handed it to Kester. As she did so, there was a clank. Hanging down one side, clipped to the handle, was a pair of handcuffs.

'You're to carry this,' she said. 'Every arrival from now on. Cuff it to your wrist.'

Kester took it from her. It had a pleasing weight to it.

'What is it?'

'It's a little piece of theatre. Gaunt's idea. Give the press something to talk about. Let's go.'

Kester stood up and pulled his clothes back into order, then walked to the exit which had just been opened by the flight attendant. Stepping out onto the open-air staircase, Kester was hit with the cold. He pulled his collar up. Looking down, he was surprised to see just tarmac, a man in a yellow jacket, a small trailer onto which their bags were already being loaded. All the talk of the press had left him expecting a sea of cordoned-off fans, flashbulbs and trench coats. Of course security would never allow it. He laughed to himself. Waiting for Alexis at the bottom of the stairs, he offered her an arm in a gesture that made him think of Gerald. She reached over and grasped it with her far hand, slid the other up his back to squeeze his shoulder, then let it settle between his shoulder blades, propelling him forward towards the entrance to the gate. In seconds she transformed herself from his glamorous date into his security detail.

'Don't worry.' She leaned in close as they walked. 'They'll be waiting at arrivals.'

-o-

'This compensate for the meetings?' Alexis shouted.

Their engagement at V Stockholm had been short. A meet-and-greet affair as they'd been promised. The invitation to *Rysa* had come through a conversation at dinner later in the evening. Somebody knew somebody knew somebody – they always did. Alexis looked over at Kester. His form was picked out in shifting brightly coloured lights and disco-ball pinpricks, tiny diamonds shivering across his bare skin. He caught her eye. He had heard her speak, but showed no sign of understanding what she had said, just grinned. Laid back, propped up on both elbows by the side of the

Jacuzzi-sized lube pit, he looked like he was lounging by the pool. That would make Will, the young man working Kester's groin, an overenthusiastic pool boy. And the naked woman in the lube pit? Alexis smirked to herself.

She turned away and shuffled forward on her knees to the large two-way mirror that fronted the suite, allowing a private view of the scene unfolding on the dance floor below: self-conscious writhing and grinding, joyful bobbing, arms punching the air on and off beat, more flesh than cloth, all glistening with sweat. This was where the journey through *Rysa* ended. Customers sated their appetites in the sparse Michelin-starred restaurant on the first floor, loosened their bodies in the brown velveteen lounge bar on the ground floor, and then laid bare their intentions on the dance floor in the basement. But it was here, in the private exchange suites, that the real dance began.

Alexis put her forearms up against the cooled glass. The heat left her skin and then the flesh below. She forced herself to ride out the nip of the cold. The cooled blood from her wrists would flow on, ice crystals forming in a wake through her body as it branched on and out through her veins. Closing her eyes, she let the shifting lights become the aurora borealis and the warm air enveloping her body a fur.

Then, something that didn't fit: a golem hand slithering up her heel, grabbing round her ankle. Alexis looked round. It was the girl in the lube pit. She couldn't remember her name – some acquaintance of Will's. Alexis watched as the girl slid her hand up and down the back of her calf, focused on the insistent pressure and let its effect roll up through her body, dispelling the cool in her blood. The girl was beautiful – short slicked black hair, classic hour-glass figure, wasp waist. Alexis looked up at Kester. Will had come up for air and they were both watching the girl hungrily as Will pounded away at him with one hand. A sudden heat flushed up over Alexis' shoulders to the top of her head. She kicked out at the girl, just managing to hold back, make it playful, then turned and slid down into the pit with her. Leaning in close to the girl's ear she opened her mouth and bit the lobe, pressing until she felt the girl flinch.

'You in it to catch something?' Alexis said in her ear.

The girl leaned back from her and smiled a "yes" in a pathetically staged way, then looked over at Kester. How many times a night did she practise that in the mirror? Every time she visited the toilets to pop one for another desperate exchange. Alexis leaned in again.

'You cut yourself?' she asked, sitting back in time to see the girl's face spasm as if she had bitten a caper.

Alexis tried to smile, felt that she was snarling and laughed. She put a hand to the girl's chin and pulled her over towards Kester and Will. When they were close enough, she took control. So the little bitch wanted to catch something. Well, Alexis was the gatekeeper. Access to Kester for this tail-chaser was through her only.

Alexis performed the transfer with a savage impersonal smile. In her head she toyed with the reality of what she was doing, ignored the sensations she would normally revel in and turned it to pure transaction: extraction of fluids, preparation of infection site, application. She was porn flick, paper cup, hook, speculum and syringe: a one-woman service.

Transaction complete, she withdrew from the girl to kneel at the edge of the pit, knees wide, hands on hips, and watched as the girl recovered from her prone position, moving tentatively. Reaching forward, Alexis stroked a stray lock of the girl's hair back into place and gave her chin a little lift with the hook of her index finger. Then there were hands around her ankles again, strong this time. She found herself pulled backwards into the pit and into Kester's arms. She leaned her head backwards so it rested on his shoulder, her mouth close to his ear.

'I said does this compensate for the meetings?' she said again, watching the girl as she sat up on the edge of the pit opposite.

The girl's face was in conflict, trying to ease herself back into the mood. She was wondering perhaps if this was common in London, if she would catch something worthwhile, what the damage was.

'Just a scratch,' Alexis mouthed at her with a wink, running her hands along Kester's arms where they encircled her.

'Definitely,' Kester said.

His voice was hot. Alexis pressed her head against his. They would go back to the hotel soon, wash together, dry each other and feel skin properly – soft resistance, the tickle of a touch on near-invisible hair, friction and grip.

-o-

'Did you rip that girl?' Kester asked as he held out Alexis' coat for her. 'Did you ask her permission?'

Alexis raised her eyebrows. He hadn't shown any concern at the time. She smirked and shrugged. It wasn't something she had done before but the girl wasn't to know that – it was common enough in more extreme circles. And the girl didn't know they weren't carrying, so she needn't suspect Alexis' motives.

'More theatre?' Kester asked.

Alexis shrugged again. She thought for a minute.

'Word'll get around we've brought something interesting with us.'

'And when we've fucked the other half of Europe and nobody's caught anything?'

Alexis laughed. It was supposed to be an off-hand laugh, a *who cares, we're having fun* laugh. Its cruelty sent a shudder through her. She watched his eyes to see if he had heard it too.

'They won't care,' she said. 'And they'll be prime customers when we take the show on tour.'

'On tour?'

'Yule will want to do it.' Yule had already spoken to her about it. 'If not after the first show, after the second when we've got a good product range. Let's go.'

Their taxi was waiting outside. They stepped out of the front doors, should have frozen instantly. The air was cold, clean, blank. This was where air was made – breathe it and you would be clean again. Alexis drew a long slow breath through her nose, felt it cool her windpipe and swell her overworked lungs. She would carry it with her, this breath; use it when she needed to exercise control.

-o-

'Wow, that's so amazing. You know you should give a talk on this – here in New York. The wearing public would find it fascinating.'

The young man standing next to Kester drew in closer. He was wearing a dinner jacket and a white mesh shirt that showed the raised purplish patches on his pectorals. His tight formal trousers made his legs look like piping bags, green patent loafers squirting out of the bottom. The rest of the group drew closer too, not to be left out in the cold: two more young men in similar garb and two young women, twins, in superhero-style catsuits, one red, one yellow, eyes running and wearing thick coloured eyeliner to emphasise the effect.

'It is amazing,' Kester nodded. 'The human body is an amazing thing.'

He took a long swig of his champagne and laughed. They all laughed with him. He was laughing because he had been talking gibberish for the last five minutes and they were all still nodding along with him as if they understood and agreed. He was laughing because they didn't care about the science. They cared about standing close to him.

He wondered what the night would hold. Images from the parties they'd ended up at in Stockholm, Paris, Milan, wherever, crowded into Kester's mind: the Colgate sponsored smiles of their hosts – models, musicians, dignitaries; out-of-proportion cherubs on the arched ceiling of a bright restaurant; fifty, sixty tobacco pipes on the walls of a lamplit private bar; an underground club, ceiling supported by columns of flame and snow; beds – circular, water, four-poster; sunken baths full of slender arms and legs and bubbles; cars and the night passing by as they raced from party to party. All they had to do was arrive and wait for the invitations to flood Alexis' inbox. One party led to another.

Here, in New York, the company had laid on an official welcome function in a restaurant on Madison Avenue. They'd invited a heady mix of business leaders, officials and local celebrities. The building was luxurious, real art deco, brass and mirrors, with domed ceilings and thick carpeted floor in reds and greens. The mezzanine at the back of the room where they stood gave Kester a demigod's view of the swilling guests. When they had left for Stockholm the previous week, the attention had been embarrassing to him, but he was starting to enjoy it.

Alexis slithered into the space between the twins, hands sliding up over their shoulders. Kester winked and smiled at her. She had shown him how to enjoy it.

'Have you met Miff and Prunella?' Kester asked her, trying to keep his smile under control.

'No,' Alexis said smoothly, looking from one to the other, 'I don't believe I have.'

'They're friends of Franz, remember, who we met in Berlin?' Kester could see Alexis scanning through her blurred memories of Berlin. They had gone to five parties in one night and met at least three people called Franz.

'Franz with the...' Alexis said, waiting for a cue from Kester.

'Yes! That Franz,' he said with a broad smile. He had no idea which Franz they were talking about either, but it seemed that news of their antics had gone before them.

'Wow! What a coincidence,' Alexis replied.

'This is Mason, Jonathan and Bryce.' Kester indicated the three young men in the group. 'I'm sure you all recognise Alexis Farrell.'

'So, Alexis,' Mason began, shifting his weight in his green loafers. 'Can I call you Alexis?'

'You can call me whatever you like, darling,' she replied to a chorus of titters from the crowd.

'I'll stick with Alexis,' Mason said. 'We've been trying to winkle out of Kester just what he's been carrying around in that mysterious black case of his.'

Alexis smiled and shrugged.

'The press are saying it's an exclusive. Is it something we can get our hands on?' Mason said.

Again, she shrugged. Again, Kester laughed to himself. At each airport they had visited, Kester had alighted with his mysterious black case gripped tightly in his hand, cuffed to his wrist. The press loved it and he found it hilarious that they did. They questioned themselves in their articles. What's in his little black case? Why won't he check it in? Won't he trust anyone to carry it? And they'd all come to the conclusion that this was either a new top secret viral exclusive that was being transported to high profile wearers in advance of the show, or that it was a network-isolated laptop carrying details of all the viruses to be used at the event. They were so close to the end of his trip he was sorely tempted to admit to the subterfuge. Alexis opened her mouth to speak.

'And don't change the subject!' Mason said.

'I'm changing the subject.' Alexis raised her eyebrow and then looked at the twins again. 'I'm guessing you two are models? I recognise your faces – your face.'

'No,' Kester said, seeing the twins pass a smile between them. 'Miff is the new Marketing Director at V New York – you would have seen her picture on the appointments bulletin – and Prunella works at Lapetus Finance. Don't ask me to explain what she does. She tried to tell me and I've had to talk virology for half an hour just to make myself feel intelligent again.'

'My apologies,' Alexis said. 'A pleasure to meet you.'

'And you,' Miff said. Her voice was painfully high and nasal, as if it were being squeezed through a Barbie doll. 'And don't worry, Kester,' her whole face dimpled, 'I don't have a clue what Pru does either. Don't tell the boss, but she got the brains.' Everyone laughed. 'I am looking forward to your presentation tomorrow.' She smiled at Mason and narrowed her eyes.

Kester's tired brain jolted at the thought that he might have to do a presentation the next day, then he blinked long and calmed. Tomorrow's meeting would be fluff, the same as the others. Chen and Farrell were trusting no-one with details of the viruses and he didn't blame them; the models gossiping in the London bars while they were on their quarantine breaks was one thing, but a full-scale leak would not have been helpful. Kester's mind began to wander back to how they'd achieved their real brief – to be seen and talked about – whirlwinding together through the nightlife of the global wearing scene, teasing people with half-talk of plans for the show, charming and bedding the most desirable of their hosts and fellow party guests.

Kester finished off his champagne and found another glass placed in his hand almost directly. The waiter was gone before he had time to say thanks. He took a swig of the fresh glass and smiled. The room was shining, the features of his new disciples bobbing in front of him. The last thing to leave his head that night when he closed his eyes would be their bright white Cheshire grins.

Chapter 14

Kester left his apartment through the outside door and stood in the small square hall, trying to empty his head of what the apartment looked like. He walked back in as a guest, acting as if he'd never seen the place before. It was easier having been away for three weeks. What were they going to see? What were they going to think? He imagined the chattering voices of his friends coming out of the lift into the narrow white hall and spilling in through the doorway.

What would his friends see? An expanse of tiled floor, clean. A good start. A long wall covered with flock wallpaper, his outrageous carved four-poster. Should he have had a fold-down bed, he wondered, like Alexis' – one of the catalysts for the 'she never sleeps' rumour. No – this was a brilliant bed. He should defend it. He had called in the cleaner to make it up to hotel standards. No matter how carefully he did it himself it always looked like there had been an animal sleeping on it. Should he draw the curtains on it? No. He'd just end up pulling them back to show people.

He turned and looked at the half of the room behind him. At the left was the door he'd just come through at the end of a boxed-off corridor; to the right was his living area, centrepiece to which was his green three-piece suite. They'd like that. It was pretty cool, wasn't it? But not too flashy-looking. Nothing on the window – it was lightly misted, allowing light in but obscuring the view of the building across the alley. Should they see that, or would it be best to have some music up? Music, he decided. This was his home now and he wanted it to feel homely and lively when they came in. It would be getting dark too, by that stage. He should have the lights low to take the clinical edge off the tiling.

Of course, John would go straight for the PS controller anyway – he wouldn't see anything else. So it was just Betta and Sienna he had to worry about. He walked over to the couch that faced the window and looked up at the remaining walls. Both were floor-to-ceiling screens, so they could be changed to fit the occasion. Right now one looked like a normal wall, with a picture hanging on it. He took out his Book and changed the picture a few times, and then he changed the whole wall. Finally, he settled on plain white paint effect.

His cocktail bar was laid out neatly, but not too neatly, and next door his vast glass desk was set up as a dining table. Catering had brought in everything he needed. Had he warned his friends that he wouldn't actually be cooking for them? He was sure John knew that he didn't have a kitchen.

The catering order page was themed so that you could choose what impression you wanted to give your guests. Kester had chosen 'Casual Cool – you don't want them to think you've sweated over it, but you do want them to think you are pretty cool'. The only problem he'd had with catering was that they were a bit sniffy about removing the labels from the tableware, but when he suggested that the pre-fashion show dinner would use the same theme, they capitulated. As far as he knew, there was no pre-fashion show dinner planned, but who would have time to pull him up on it? They would have forgotten about it by then.

The table dressing was minimal. The expanse of white cotton was given completely to the tall slender glasses and plain, long-handled cutlery. Kester picked up a fork and eyed it. He had used this set at Alexis'. It was beautiful on the table but made you look like you were knitting when you started to eat. Too late. He put the fork back down and turned his attention to the lighting. He would have it set low in this room, with the window to the front of the building clear so that they could see the view. Or should he start with it misted and set it to slow reveal?

'Does it even matter?' he asked the empty room.

Standing there, considering the answer, he noticed the spare place-setting he had asked for, sitting on the covered side unit. He fumbled out his Book and checked the time. He had spent every spare moment over the last few days worrying over this dinner party and more specifically over whether he should bring a partner. Glancing down at the graze on his wrist he remembered Boston with a pleasurable shudder. He knew that the only person he could ask without Alexis getting wind of it and taking offence was Alexis herself, but he was holding back. The transition back to being a manager hadn't been easy for him, though their three weeks away had evaporated quickly. His attention kept wandering back to the parties, to early morning hotel rooms with strangers, to strong coffee breakfasts at street tables with Alexis, laughing and shading their eyes from the headache sunlight. He had been looking out for some sign that the same had been happening to Alexis, but he hadn't seen anything. It was stupid, he decided. What happened to those balls he'd been growing? He flicked to her name on his Book.

'Alexis,' he said as soon as he heard the click.

'Kester, I'm in the middle of –'

'Then you shouldn't have answered. I'll be quick. Come up for dinner tonight. I want you to meet my friends.'

'I'll call you back.'

For the next twenty minutes, Kester paced around the flat. She was going to say *no* – that's what it was – this was too personal. Fooling around for business purposes was one thing, but this wasn't business. He thought again of their trip and then of her laid on his dentist's chair, allowing him to paint her. He was afraid she'd say *no*. He was equally afraid she would say *yes*. None of them except for John knew about his relationship with Alexis and John's response to the revelation had been, 'Well, a hole's a hole.' Not entirely what Kester had been hoping for.

His Book buzzed.

'Yes,' he answered without even checking who it was.

'Kester, darling, are you never in?'

It was his mother.

'Mum, I told you there's no point in routeing the call through the apartment.'

'I got you this time, didn't I? Besides it's cheaper. And I'm always curious in case someone else answers. How is that Alex girl? She seemed very nice.'

'It's Alexis, Mum, and she's not a girl, she's my boss.'

'That's not how she introduced herself, dear. If you think she's just your boss, perhaps you should tell her that.'

'What? I suppose she announced herself as "the future Mrs Dr Kester Lowe"?'

'Oh dear, you are in a bad mood. No, she didn't, dear. She just said she was a friend.'

'A friend?'

'You sound surprised, darling – don't you have friends any more? You were friends with all the people you worked with at the Institute. Speaking of which –'

'I still am friends with them Mum. In fact they're coming round here for dinner tonight.'

'In your new apartment? That's what this grump is all about? Don't be such a silly sausage, Kester. They're your friends; they're happy you're successful. They'll enjoy all the toys, and seeing another way of living. And you're still you.'

'Yes. Yes, I suppose I am. You're right.'

'And this Alexis, are you having her along? I mean as a friend.'

Kester laughed and sighed. Wandering across the room to the front window, he leaned forward and put his forehead to the glass.

'Mum, I don't know. I just don't know how they'll mix. She's older and –'

'Nothing wrong with being a bit older. How much older?'

'She's in her mid forties. Mid-to-late forties.'

'So ten years.'

'A bit more than that thanks, Mum.'

'Kester, that's nothing when you get to this age.'

'She just seems much older.'

'You want to stop saying "older" son; she won't appreciate it.'

'Well, maybe not older – more mature.'

'I don't know, Kester. I can't tell you what to do, if that's what you're after. If you like this girl, then you should give her the benefit of the doubt. I'm sure she's fun and I'm sure she can handle herself at a dinner party for god's sake.'

Kester laughed at her calling Alexis a 'girl'.

'Thanks, Mum. Truly you are wise.'

'Yes. I am.'

'Mum, I have to go I'm afraid.'

'The dog's fine now, by the way. I know you were worried about him. I'll speak to you tomorrow then – see how everything went.'

'Sorry, Mum. I'll have more time to speak to you then. We can have a proper catch-up.'

'OK, darling, I'll speak to you then. Good luck.'

'OK, bye.'

'Bye, love.'

Kester hung up and dropped his Book back into his pocket.

-o-

'You're early,' Kester said with a fixed grin as he opened his apartment door. John, Betta and Sienna filled the doorway.

Kester took a deep breath. He had hoped that Alexis would arrive first so that he could brief her on what to expect from them. Though this way round had its advantages too.

'Come in, sit down.' Kester ushered them in. As they entered the apartment they exploded into a chorus of 'wow's and laughter.

'Kester, this is amazing!' Betta wheeled around, pointing at things with an open mouth.

'Good call, man,' John said. He had already found the couch and the PS controller.

'Glad you all like it. Can I get you a drink?' Kester ran across the room to his bar and stepped in behind it. 'A drink from my *bar*? The bar in my living room.'

'Calm down, mate,' John said, 'it's pretty cool but don't get above yourself – it's basically a bedsit, isn't it?'

'Is Dee coming?' Sienna said.

'Sienna,' Betta hissed.

'What?'

Kester tensed. Should he have asked Dee? Had he missed his chance? As far as he knew she still wasn't talking to him. John had been keeping him up to date. She had split with Sebastian but she was mostly hiding in her lab being bitter by all accounts.

'Dee wouldn't come if the main course was Kester's balls on a silver platter,' John said.

'Eeew, John.' Sienna made a face. 'You're disgusting.'

'Nice. Right everyone,' Kester said, concerned at the premature nosedive in the conversation. 'I've got a friend coming tonight.'

'He means a lov-errr,' John said.

'Her name is Alexis – you all met her at the bar the night of my leaving do –'

'Your boss?' Betta said. 'Kester, you beast!'

'So she's not seen you at your best. Just…' Kester was unsure what he was getting at – he wanted to say *be professional*, but it didn't make any sense. 'Be nice.'

The door buzzed. Kester rushed over, then paused and took a

deep breath before opening it.

The sight of Alexis warmed him. She was dressed as casually as he had ever seen her. Jeans and a spiral knit top, logo tags hanging round her neck. He recognised the top as one she'd bought in Paris. Her hair was tied loosely in a pony tail, the ends curling over one shoulder and down her back. Her makeup was subtle and flattering.

'Alexis.' Kester felt a stupid expression appearing on his face but he couldn't stop it.

'You were expecting...?' Alexis smiled and raised her eyebrows.

'You look great.' Aware he was setting himself up for a jibe, Kester said, 'I was worried you wouldn't be smart enough, you know.'

Alexis gave a soft laugh. She put her hand up to his neck and pulled him forward for a kiss. It was the first time she had greeted him like a lover. So that's who she was tonight.

'They're a bit hyper, I'm afraid,' Kester said, 'but there are only three of them so I think we'll be OK.' He led her into the room by one hand. 'Everyone, this is Alexis. Alexis: Betta, Sienna and John. You may remember them from a certain bar incident.'

'How could I forget?' Alexis said, shaking hands with Betta and Sienna. 'But I'd be surprised if this one remembers me.' She met John as he stood up from the couch and took him by the hand. 'Actually, I owe you thanks. I had been looking for an excuse to get rid of that Cameron character –'

'Davis, wasn't it?' Betta said.

'Yes, Davis that's it. Betta, you'd be so much better at this management stuff than me. Anyway, I'd wanted to get rid of him for ages.'

'Why?'

Alexis made a face that might have meant *I don't know, I just didn't like him*, anything. Betta laughed. Kester felt himself relaxing. The room, which had seemed too large with four of them, adjusted itself to the right size. Things started to match again, blend into the background, and he started to see normally.

'OK,' Kester said. 'Who's hungry?'

'Well, I am,' Betta said, 'but I notice that you don't seem to have a kitchen.'

John frowned and looked around.

'I don't.' Kester laughed. 'We've got a catering department that does special "home cooked" food as well as everyday stuff. I may not have cooked it but I decided what to ask somebody else to cook.'

'Even better,' Sienna said. 'I shouldn't have had that burger on the way over.'

'She's joking,' Betta said, too quickly.

'It's just you haven't hosted one of our parties for so bloody long that we thought you might have forgotten how to cook,' John said.

'I have forgotten.' Kester held his head high and then stooped in a long bow.

'He's worked very hard at it,' Alexis said.

She placed a hand on Kester's shoulder. It felt different to the usual Alexis power touch. He tried to give towards her hand, let her know what it meant to him.

They went through to Kester's office. Once they had stopped crowing about the view and mucking around pretending to fall through the windows, he called in the first course. Everyone sat ill at ease while the waiting staff appeared and served their scallop starter from a silver platter. Betta looked like she could barely contain her giggles. This was catering's idea of casual. Right.

'You've all heard of The Itch, I take it?' Alexis asked them collectively. Her relaxed manner brought the room back to life.

'Yes, I've got all their albums,' John said. 'The guitarist's hot.'

'Not my type.' Alexis wrinkled up her nose. 'That's great that you're a fan though – you'll get to see them at Kester's fashion show.'

Kester's eyes popped.

'What's wrong, darling?' Alexis asked.

'Nothing,' Kester said, not even noticing that she'd called him *darling*. 'But you're kidding, right?'

'Worried that it'll get out? I can tell your friends – they won't spill the beans, will they?' She looked around the table, puckering her lips. 'Will you?' As if blackmailing children with the prospect of sweets, she added, 'You won't get tickets if you do.'

'Tickets,' John said. 'Awesome.'

'You're serious?' Kester asked.

Betta and Sienna laughed in unison.

'I've been dying to see The Itch,' Sienna said. 'It'll be amazing!'

'And it'll be brilliant to actually see your viruses,' Betta said.

'There's a real buzz amongst the student wearers.'

'I saw this little punk the other day,' Sienna said. 'He was wearing tartan trousers with a see-though crotch. You could see all the sores on his thingy – it was disgusting.' She made a face and took a swig of wine.

'The Itch. Wow.' Kester said, daunted.

Alexis was starting to look disappointed at his reaction. Angry disappointed. She knew they were his favourite band. It must have been hard to get them. He should be leaping about, punching the air.

Kester pushed his plate away. 'Are you guys finished with your starters?'

He got up to a chorus of nods and walked through to the other room to call the caterers up with the mains. He leaned on the bar for a moment. He shouldn't have had a drink before they arrived. He already felt steaming.

'Any more drinks?' he heard Alexis saying.

She arrived in his living room just as he finished the call.

'The Itch?' he said, chucking his Book aside.

'We got them,' she said, skipping over, looking younger than ever, cheeks flushed from the wine. Her complexion was as clean and healthy-looking as he had ever seen it. 'I hope you're pleased. It's going to be incredible.'

'Yes, I know – I just can't imagine it,' Kester said. 'They're so…cool.'

'Look at yourself Kester,' Alexis said, staring straight into his eyes. '*You're* so cool. Everybody wants a piece of you. Have you forgotten what it was like in Paris, Milan, New York? Listen to your friends – they're chattering about it through there like teenagers – you're like a rock star. You've seen this, right?'

Alexis took out her Book and held it up to him. At first he thought he was looking at an album cover, or a film poster. Slowly it dawned on Kester that it was him, an image from his photoshoot. There he was, standing feet apart on the glass shelf, gazing out over the sunrise, a giant on top of the world, chilling out, not giving a shit. Looking cool. He looked cool.

'Tell me that doesn't make you feel good. Tell me you're not cool enough for The Itch to play at your show.'

Kester broke into a smile. She was so convincing. He picked her up and hugged her tightly. It felt strange. It felt friendly in a way their physical contact never had before. Their time together on tour had changed something. She slid back down out of his arms, laughing.

'You're right,' he said, 'it's going to be amazing. I love it. I'm sorry, I'm such a tool. I love it, I love you. You're too good to me.'

'I'm having a special catsuit made,' she said, pushing away from him, eyelids suddenly low; her predatory look. 'It has a panel down the front that I can take off to show Touché once the models have been on.' She traced a V with her fingertips, from her shoulders down to two inches below her belly button.

'Sounds good,' Kester said, reaching out for her hips and pulling her back towards him.

'Get a room,' John said, striding through the doors from Kester's office. 'Oh, sorry, this is your room. Well, get on the bed and at least pull the curtains will you?'

Alexis wiggled her way out of Kester's arms, smiling as coyly as was possible for her and reached under the bar. She picked up a bottle of red and one of white and rushed on tiptoe back through to the other room.

'Well, well,' John said.

'Well what?' Kester asked.

'She's not quite how I remember. The fire-breathing woman from the bar.'

'John, can you even remember the bar?'

'I remember arriving.'

'You see where I'm going with this?'

'I mean it in a good way. I like her. I like her sense of humour. I like her, eh –'

'Good.' Kester leaned back against the bar. 'I'm glad...I'm relieved.'

'And there's obviously a bit of, you know. I mean it's not just like, you know how you said everyone sleeps with everyone.'

'Who knows?'

'And frankly, who cares? She's getting The Itch to play for you at your own personal fashion show, man – that's so fucking cool I can't even tell you. You'd better get me tickets. I'll be getting myself a new chastity belt if I have to stand in a crowd of diseased City loons, but there's no way I'm missing your show. Now why did I come through?'

'Toilet?' Kester asked.

'Good call! That could have been unfortunate. Back in a mo.'

John walked across the room into the bathroom and started laughing to himself, presumably at the arse-height shelf.

-o-

Over the main course of venison, Kester sat back and let the conversation free-wheel without him. He watched Alexis. She looked natural, unaffected, a different Alexis to the business Alexis. Not Mrs Farrell and not Alexis the samurai-edged seductress, more like the little girl she became in the PlayPen. There was a soft-shouldered laugh that he had only ever seen before in that orange playsuit. He was drawn to her in a new way, a natural way. This was very unlike the push-and-pull of their usual relationship with its tricksy boundaries. Yes, she was Lex from the PlayPen, he decided. He couldn't handle there being four of her.

After the main course they rested, leaning back in their chairs to make room for their bellies, relaxed by conversation and wine. While the catering staff cleared the table, they talked nonsense, planning out the different levels of the imagined *PlayPen Scientifica*, and offering Kester helpful ideas for new viruses.

'I think its main fault is that you'd have to buy a whole new set of shoes,' Betta said.

'But that's the whole point of YetiFoot!' John banged his hand on the table. 'You wouldn't have to wear shoes! You guys. You've got no vision. Am I right, Kester?'

'John, are you ever wrong?'

'OK. Forget it. What's for dessert?'

'I didn't think you'd want any,' Kester said.

Betta sat bolt upright and John looked like he'd been slapped.

'Just kidding,' Kester said. 'It's chocolate mousse though – nothing fancy.'

The chocolate mousses arrived. They were served in small heavy cut-crystal bowls, perched on the top of fluted silver stems the length of forearms. Each was decorated with chocolate filigree and gold leaf.

'I like it,' John said. 'Nice and simple, like you said.'

'I think I might have to stand up to eat this,' Betta said, peering over her bowl, which came almost up to the height of her eyes.

They picked up their spoons and began eating.

'Setting aside YetiFoot, how's your personal research going, Kester?' Sienna asked, picking some of the lacework off her mousse and biting into it. It fell to pieces.

'My...' Kester's face blanched.

'Yeah,' John said, too soon for Kester to intervene, 'your new screens – did you get them working? I think you were torso testing...' John looked up and stopped when he saw Kester's face.

Kester looked round at Alexis.

'Yes, Kester,' she said. A barrier had gone up around her. 'Do tell us how you are getting on.'

How to explain? Kester imagined himself battering against her shield like a bird against glass, desperate to reach her, injuring himself with each shambolic attempt. He had been meaning to tell her. He knew it would have to come out sometime, somehow, but his plan had been to stall until he decided what he was going to do with it.

'My research?' Kester decided to brazen it out. 'Yes. I don't think I've told you about my private research, have I, Lex?'

Alexis shook her head, a forced smile on her lips. Kester's friends glanced at one another, spoons still suspended halfway to bowls, halfway to mouths. The room was quiet. Kester realised that the music had stopped.

'I've been working on a new type of screen. One that doesn't rely on drugs to work. It's based almost purely on viral technology – soft nanotech rather than the sort of hard nanotech that the old one uses, though there's still a bit of that of course. It works with the body and you don't need to take drugs to use it.'

'I still think this is awesome,' Betta said. 'This is what you were made for. I mean don't get me wrong, the fashion stuff is cool, but this is what you'll be remembered for.'

Out of the corner of his eye, Kester could see the colour rising in Alexis' cheeks.

'It's in the torso testing stage now,' he said.

'You've got it working?' John asked. 'That's amazing – woohoo!'

Kester couldn't help but look excited by this. He looked straight at Alexis.

'I'm sorry I didn't tell you, Lex. I thought it was safer that you didn't know for now. I didn't want you to get in trouble with Chen. But the company could really –'

'This is a real thing?' Alexis asked. 'You've got it working?'

Kester nodded. She looked conflicted. Was she angry, impressed, what? She took a slow sip of wine, eyes focused somewhere out on the City skyline.

'We agreed I could work on my own projects in my own time.' Kester started to defend himself.

'John's right,' Alexis said, looking up at Kester. 'That is amazing.' She stood up. 'Come on, then – take me to the lab – show me. I'll call security and get these guys on a group tour pass – they're on the system anyway. It'll take seconds. You can show us all.'

Alexis started tapping on her Book.

'But…dinner…' Kester said. Was she serious? What was she going to do to him? He cast a distressed look at John.

'Watch out, Kester, she's going to steal it for the company!' John said and made a comic suspicious face at Alexis.

'Come on – it's mousse, it's cold, it'll keep – the lab is right here,' she said, walking towards the door. 'Don't you want to show us?'

'The lab is right here?' John asked.

'Come on – can we see your lab?' Betta said.

'You live in your lab?' Sienna asked.

Before he knew it they were all standing at the door with Alexis, clutching their drinks.

–o–

'You know I'm angry,' Alexis said as she lay in Kester's arms.

'I know,' he said, slurring a little. 'You know I'm sorry.'

'I know.'

'Are you going to tell on me?'

'Kester, this is too big to even think about right now.' Alexis sat up and looked down at him.

'I'm aware of that,' he said sleazily, propping himself up on his elbows, 'but what about the screens?'

'Seriously.' Alexis suppressed a smirk. 'We need to focus on the show. Keep a lid on it. Carry on, but keep a lid on it.'

'It's our little secret, right?' Kester said happily and sunk back down into his pillows. He let the wine envelop him and was asleep by the time her answer came.

Chapter 15

'How was quarantine?' Dee said.

'That's it?' Cherry asked, looking at the Clarks' shoebox in front of her. It looked out of place amongst the technical equipment on the Institute lab bench.

'Yes,' Dee said.

'That's all they wanted?'

'That's all they need. Small things, viruses. And they have this handy habit of reproducing at quite a rate.' Dee was clearly comfortable in her role as expert and Cherry's uncertainty was feeding her confidence.

Cherry leaned in and examined the box more closely. On the label was a picture of a woman's brogue, the size 5 and the name *Broadway*.

'My size,' she said with a little smile and glanced down at Dee's feet to see if she was wearing the shoes. She wasn't.

'Not my box,' Dee said.

As Cherry reached to remove the lid, Dee put out her own hands quickly and took the lid off for her.

'There's an envirobox inside – pretty neat fit. It should keep the vials safe. It's all padded and sealed, so don't worry about it too much. On the other hand, I wouldn't play football with it either.'

'What if a vial were to break?' Cherry was suddenly aware she would be carrying a shoebox full of disease through central London.

'Don't worry. As I said, it's sealed. Plus, in the small amounts you're carrying the virus wouldn't last in open air for more than a few minutes, depending on the conditions. I'm not saying I would lick it up if it spilled, but you know, don't sweat it.' She replaced the lid on the shoebox.

Cherry unzipped her backpack and slipped the shoebox inside.

'OK,' she said. 'Once this gets to where it's going your money will be transferred across. I'm back in quarantine until a few weeks after the fashion show so you won't be hearing from me for about a month. You know what you're doing with the second virus?'

'It'll be ready for you when you need it. Now, if you'll excuse me I have some clearing up to do.'

'Of course.' Cherry walked to the door.

Outside, the weather was lacklustre. It didn't want to go either way and just stayed a light grey all afternoon. This was fine for Cherry – good weather for walking. It would take her a good few hours to get across London, but she didn't want to risk travelling on public transport in case of incident. She had no idea what the scanners on the underground could pick up, and anyway there were always spot checks and just generally too much jostling for comfort. On foot there was much less that could go wrong. She would walk up towards the Kilburn Green Belt train stop, avoiding the City and its checkpoints altogether, and then take the train round to City B3. Then it was only a short walk back to the Hospital.

Cherry headed for St James's Park. No point in walking all the way through concrete when she could go through the parks. It was worth the slight detour. She threaded up through St James's Park, Green Park, Hyde Park, checking her Book now and again. In Hyde Park she allowed herself to wander off course, heading down towards the Kensington Gardens end. The name Bayswater had caught her eye on the map. It was familiar, as were many of the street names in the area. Instinct told her she might know the place if she passed through. She crossed Bayswater Road and headed up Palace Court.

As Cherry walked, unexpected things slotted into place in her memory: the pattern on a cast iron railing, the shape of a tree in a private green, the positions of lamp posts. She paused by a small pre-school nursery, a normal town house with pictures in the window and a happy handmade sign. Sellotape, sunshine filtered through tissue paper, the chalky texture of drying paint. Was it her nursery? Unlikely, she decided, but the memory was real. This was the right area. She had lived here somewhere, or visited here. It was a place to come back to when she had the time. Checking her Book again, Cherry pulled herself back on course, back along Westbourne Grove, then up and under the Westway and on towards Kilburn.

To the east was Maida Vale. It must have stayed reasonably static during the building boom, as there was little stratification, particularly on the older buildings. Beyond it somewhere was Regent's Park past which the scoop of the City banked steeply upwards. Ahead, towards Kilburn, Cherry was faced with ranks of office buildings. The character of the more recent structures was different to those in the City, less slick, more uniform and, if anything, more oppressive. She felt as if she were walking towards the outer edge of a walled city. She stopped and looked back the way she had come. Bizarre that facing in towards the centre of London should give her the greatest sense of freedom.

The train ride from Kilburn and the walk across the Green Belt seemed short in the context of Cherry's journey. Too short. Though the wind was picking up and the weather was still grey, she felt herself start to work up a sweat as she drew close to her old stomping ground.

The Hospital looked small. Its grandeur was small-town grandeur, suburban grandeur. Despite the walk down the High Street with its long line of low level kebab shops and chemists, Cherry's brain was still working on central London scale. As she entered the front doors, the shabbiness of the building hit her. The paintwork was marked and peeling. The strip of veneer from the front of the reception desk had curled away and had been removed, revealing the desk's chipboard interior. A pair of court-shoed feet was up on the desk, crossed, one shoe hanging by the toes. Their owner was slumped in a swivel chair reading a magazine.

'Boo!' Cherry said.

'Cherry!' Frieda, the receptionist, jerked her feet down, sat up and closed her magazine.

'Hi, Frieda,' Cherry said. 'Just popping by to see Lady.'

'Lovely,' Frieda said. 'I think she's in her rooms at the moment, so you'll probably catch her there. Don't let the girls see you in that dress,' she added as Cherry walked on into the corridor. 'They'll be mad you took it with you.'

Cherry looked down at the dress. There had been smarter, newer clothes in Lady's collection, but this had always been a favourite. It seemed drab to her now.

It wasn't far to Lady's rooms. Cherry passed no-one on the way and was relieved for it. She was feeling something akin to embarrassment at being there, a discomfort she couldn't put her finger on; pity maybe. She knocked on the door to Lady's living room. There was a scuffling from behind the door and then, a few seconds later, Lady's voice sounded, slightly more high-pitched than normal.

'Come!'

Cherry opened the door and peered in. There was a gentleman picking up his coat and hat from the stand. He nodded to her briskly. As he passed her to leave the room, Cherry noticed his hand dart to and from his flies, an automatic check. Lady was standing at the window, smoothing back her hair.

'Is it a bad time?' Cherry asked. 'I can come back later.'

'Not at all,' Lady said. 'Our meeting had just finished.'

Things must be tight if Lady was starting to see clients again. She hadn't done for years as far as Cherry knew. Perhaps this was some special case. Perhaps he wasn't even a client. She decided not to pry.

'So,' Lady said. She turned to face Cherry and indicated the couch.

Cherry pulled out one of the chairs at the table and swung her bag down in front of her. She removed the shoebox. Lady opened the lid and nodded. She was obviously familiar with the envirobox.

'You've spoken to Blotch?' Cherry asked.

'I have. The Pigs are being careless. They're taking on as many new viruses as they can get their hands on ahead of the show and there's no time to try before they buy – loads of them are doing specials and presumably they're expecting a big rise in business. Your friend Marlene did a wonderful job posing as a German blackmarket dealer – I listened in to one or two of the calls. All the City branches are in fierce competition so once she got one to take it, they mostly followed suit.'

'Not to be outdone.'

'Quite. Anyway, they won't trace it back to us. And they won't want to admit where it came from anyway or they'll be in trouble for blackmarket trading.'

'Good. Doctor Campbell says you can sell it as whatever you want. Customers will just assume that it hasn't worked and with a bit of luck will go back for something else before the virus sets in – that should confuse the trail too.'

It felt like Lady was reporting to Cherry in an odd role reversal.

'Do you know what it does?' Lady asked, an offhand frown on her face.

'Didn't ask. I think it's best we don't know. But Blotch assured me it wasn't a horrible disease or anything like that. He seems to be a man of his word.'

Lady raised her eyebrows.

'Call it what you want,' Cherry continued. 'The vials aren't labelled yet.'

'Fine. I'll make the labels up myself. They'll be out for delivery by this evening.'

'Good.' Cherry zipped up her bag. That was it. 'I'll report back to Blotch tonight when I get back.' It seemed too easy.

'Thank you, Cherry,' Lady said.

She sounded genuinely thankful. It wasn't a tone Cherry had ever heard in her voice before. Then her face turned hard.

'With any luck that fat bastard will pay me now.' She replaced the lid on the shoebox carefully. 'Are you going to stop by the runk room?'

'No.' Cherry glanced down at her dress in search of a reason not to. 'No, I think I'd better get back. Good luck,' she added and headed to the door.

-o-

Kester lay on his dentist's chair staring at the ceiling, the phone to his ear, half listening to his mother, half trying to visualise what the show would be like. Only one day to go and he would find out. The build-up had been bizarre but enjoyable. The web appearances, his many personae: Doctor Lowe the scientist, Kester Lowe the designer, Kester the sex symbol, Kes, best buddy of The Itch, if the way they had behaved on their *Friday's House* slot was anything to believe. He had been on quiz shows, current affairs shows, lifestyle shows; he had launched products, attended photoshoots for designer gear (with the labels picked off); he had opened a gallery exhibition about the history of body art. He was knackered. He had stopped concentrating when his mother started telling him some story about the next door neighbour's dog. He didn't know the next door neighbour, never mind their dog.

'Kester? Are you still there?'

The change in her tone snapped him back to attention.

'I asked if they're looking after you alright.'

'Yes, yes they are. It's ridiculous really. You wouldn't believe it – they're employing a team to pick all the ads off my clothes, poor bastards.'

'Language, Kester! A whole team? Goodness me, you must be important. And I suppose they come and dress you in the morning too.'

'Not far off it, actually. They choose all my clothes and have them sent up to me.'

'Good god.'

'If I'm going out or on telly I mean. And I get to choose from a selection...and I've briefed them on the sorts of things I will and won't wear. I had an image consultation when I first started – you know we have to wear labels that are affiliated with the company – but this was all a bit more full-on. And they sent me for a haircut.'

'I should think so too, if you're going to be on telly.'

'Yes, the show.' Kester felt uneasy. He remembered coming home as a teenager and seeing that his mother had cleaned his room.

'Yes, dear. We're all very excited about the show – I'm having a party!'

For a moment, Kester was thrown. He didn't see the connection.

'A party – it's quite the thing. Lots of people are doing it – those that don't object too much and like a good show anyway.'

'A party to watch it?'

'Yes, darling, with drinks and canapés! Marvellous, don't you think. I'm asking people to bring friends of friends and I'll have some stock from the shop – all that shenanigans might get people in the mood to buy some nice undies, don't you think?'

'I don't know...I suppose...'

'It's going to be great! The dog gets excited every time he sees your picture in the trailers. Now, speaking of the panty party, I've been meaning to ask you if you could do me a favour. I've sent a box of panties for you to sign.'

'Mum!' Kester's cheeks burned.

'It's a bit late notice, but Justine in the shop only just thought of it yesterday. It should arrive this afternoon and I thought you could get one of your lab-monkeys to courier it back, in time for the show tomorrow.'

'Of course I will, Mum.' He closed his eyes and shook his head.

'I hope you can identify it in amongst all your other post – I bet you're getting sent loads of panties now you're famous!'

'Hundreds a day.' Kester looked up at the ceiling. 'Listen, how is the dog?'

'He's excited!' his mother replied. 'Just like the rest of us. Now you must have lots to do and I know I do – I'm making some spotty cupcakes for the party.'

'OK, Mum,' Kester said. 'I hope you sell lots of stuff tomorrow.'

'Me too!' She was close to bursting. 'I love you, darling. Bye!'

'Bye, Mum.'

'Bye.'

Kester put down the phone and flicked his wall to web. He had been avoiding the build-up, but maybe it was worth knowing what was being said.

'…and business at the Pigs is up by 50%, five - zero, because lots of people want to be wearing the latest viruses for the show.'

'But these are not Kester Lowe viruses?'

'That's right, they're not Kester Lowe viruses and indeed I've spoken to some young lawyers here today who have "cleaned up", as they put it, so that they can be blank canvases in the hope of getting their hands on a Kester Lowe original tomorrow night.'

'That's Doctor Lowe to you,' Kester said, changing the channel.

'Crowds are already gathering in the square outside V, trying to get a good spot for the show tomorrow night. If you look behind me here you can see some of the extent of what everyone is now calling "Kestermania".'

Kester's eyes widened. He looked across to the door of his office, as if he might be able to see the crowd from his seat, but he didn't get up. They'd been gathering since lunchtime and the pictures on the news showed hundreds of people already.

'If I could get across the square to show you, there is also a queue right down in the direction of the PlayPen of literally hundreds of fans hoping to get their hands on some of the on-the-night tickets. And it's not just the fans that are getting ready. You can see above me that the police and ambulance services are setting up their zip-wires across the square. Up here there's an officer testing out his harness – you can see him whizzing across above my head now.'

That, Kester could see. It had taken a few days to set up and by chance the zip wires and paramedic platforms were at the same level as the floor the lab was on. Kester was already on waving terms with one or two of the set-up crew. He changed the channel again. An angry man was being interviewed.

'…is just rubbish. You can't make it safe and even if you could, making it safe doesn't make it moral. But that's not what gets me most – what gets me most is that one of our top scientists is working on fashion accessories for bloated rich folk when he could be making viruses that are – viruses for medical use, to help all those people out there who have diseases they can't just switch off.'

Kester flicked again quickly.

'Commentators are starting to agree that a non-harmful form of virus wearing might not be such a bad thing. But one question that we haven't looked at yet tonight is perhaps, for our viewers, the most burning issue. Doctor Kester Lowe's spokesperson and V are claiming that they are, quote, "redefining fashion", that these viruses are going to be, quote, "beautiful", but let me ask our studio guests – even if a virus is beautiful – is it Art? Colin.'

Kester guffawed and flicked through a few more channels in turn. It was bizarre, amusing. He understood the build-up to the show, the excitement around seeing the new viruses for the first time, but the amount of discussion surrounding it was ludicrous. It was as if the press genuinely didn't have anything else to talk about.

'Me…me…me…me,' he said as he flicked. 'Me me me me me.'

He snorted, zapped the "off" icon and pushed himself up from the couch in the direction of the fridge.

-o-

'…and in the City itself: Old Broad Street, Cock Lane, St Mary Axe, Cheapside –'

'Marvellous!' Clarke interrupted Blotch. 'Marvellous.'

'The list goes on,' Blotch said. 'Almost all of the City branches have taken the virus.'

'Marvellous,' Clarke repeated.

'They were sold by a pseudonymous German blackmarket dealer and most of the houses have taken on new stock from quite a few places in the last few days as well – they're all getting new viruses in for the show.'

'An added bonus…'

'Quite,' Blotch said. He stood in Clarke's office feeling taller than usual. It was all coming off perfectly.

'Minister Blotch, this calls for a celebration!' Clarke said, clapping his hands together.

Blotch licked his lips. It was only eleven o'clock, but he could quite handle a little tipple. He felt giddy with success and it seemed a shame to waste it. Clarke reached under his desk. Blotch smiled at him conspiratorially. Just then, a soft buzzing sounded at the back of the room: Clarke's wall was revolving slowly to reveal his fabulous altar. His hand came up empty.

'Remote control,' Clarke said, waggling his fingers with a smile. 'Rather good, no?'

Blotch gave what he hoped was an impressed laugh and tried to hide his disappointment.

'Let us pray,' Clarke said.

Chapter 16

The square was illuminated as if by stained glass and sunlight. Opposite the V building glowed the alternating hellish red and pulsating green of the Stark Wellbury scaffolding, a reproduction of the frontage of their building, carrying on as normal and setting the colour scheme for the whole square.

The buildings that flanked the square had been decked with silk panels, transformed into two block-sized screens, facing off against one another. One depicted a magnified microscope image of KL01, Corona, at work invading a cell. The image had been enhanced so that it glowed the colours of a baroque theatre – gold, blood red, forest green – to complement the Stark Wellbury display. The other was devoted to ad-space for the show sponsors, clients and associates of V Division V.

The ad space alternated between a collage of logos and giant versions of individual logos. They came up so large that you couldn't really see them, but the more established ones were so engrained in the people's consciousness that they would recognise them from just a corner, the turn of a ribbon or swirl, from two colours set one against the other. Occasionally, where the company identifier was the building itself, this led to one building being projected onto another, life-sized, pictured against a blue sky on a clear day, a view which could never really be had of any building in its entirety. This created the illusion that the square opened onto a desert containing only the sponsor's building, inducing a vertiginous feeling which heightened the excitement of the audience.

The fourth side of the square was the V building itself. In front of it was the stage, split into three sections. A catwalk stretched from the central podium right to the middle of the square and ended in a circular platform above the fountain-come-exchange hub. The backdrop to the stage was a giant screen flanked by velvet swathes, in reality a high-definition image of velvet grain projected onto more silk panels.

The images on the screen shifted, alternating pictures of the audience, close-ups of celebrities in the VIP strips, stills of the models and, every now and again, a shadowy image of Kester. There he stood, legs wide, hands in pockets, on V's glass outcrop, the dying streetlamps of the suburbs stretching out a net of glowing nodes before him, the sun a bubble of molten glass swelling and spilling light at the horizon.

Watching the display on his dressing room display, Kester felt a buzz in his throat, pressure at the base of his skull. It was about to begin.

'There you are, Kester,' said Alexis, as his picture appeared on the big screen.

She draped her long arms around his neck and rested her chin on his shoulder. He could see her face reflected in the mirror portion of the display: feline satisfaction.

Kester's chest swelled. Yes, there he was. There he was, standing on top of the tallest building in the City. There he was, pictured as a dark hero, rock star to the rock stars, creator.

'The man who made destruction creative. We've done it. You've done it, Kester. You've recreated fashion.'

'Will they go for it?'

'Kester, look at the crowd. Those people out there are rock stars, politicians, top lawyers, sports heroes. They are standing there, waiting to see you. They've already gone for it. They're hungry because they've been kept waiting. Believe me Kester, they're wet as teenagers.'

'To see what the viruses can do.'

'To see you in the flesh. This is going to be big. They're going to want to touch you. They'll want to have you. They'll want the personal treatment.'

Alexis' grip on his shoulders loosened and she stood up. Kester could no longer see her face in the mirror.

'You think?'

'I know. That list I showed you earlier. Hot prospects for the business.'

'What about them?'

'Like I said, they're going to want you.'

Alexis was drawing away from him. Her limp arms dragged back across his shoulders until only her hands were touching him. Then, lightly, they lifted as if she had dissolved. He watched her in the mirror as she walked to the stand behind him and started rummaging through a jewellery box.

'And I guess I'm expected to give them what they want. For the good of the business?'

'If you don't like it, you're welcome to speak to Chen.'

It wasn't entirely unexpected. Kester had known for a while that the models would be exchanging with the VIPs. He had supposed that he should be as OK with it as they were, if it came to the crunch. But he wasn't.

'It's a one-off. It'll be worth your while to suck it up for this one show, maybe the next one.'

'I don't even wear. I'm not even supposed to wear. Talk to my image consultant.'

'You're wearing now,' Alexis said.

Kester frowned. She had asked him to put on Touché the week before because she wanted to paint him – she had agreed to do it in private and all below the neckline. Her designs had since faded, but she had persuaded him to keep the virus in his system. And here was the real reason.

'That was different, Alexis. That was just for you.'

'Well now it's for one VIP of your choosing.' Alexis finally found a pair of earrings she was satisfied with and pinned them through her ears with liquid precision. 'Just one – exclusivity is the key. That way you stay more...less...attainable. It's just a routine exchange.'

'Routine,' Kester said, half to himself.

He stood and turned so he was facing her, watched as she swivelled side-to-side, posing for him. She had said her gown was like a pair of chaps and now he saw what she meant. From small shoulder seams, it clung down her body in two parallel red velvet strips, mirroring the curtains in the setup outside. The gap between them was a long V, the two strips only coming together just above the bikini-shaped bottoms. The legs were slit right up the sides, in her distinctive style. It had been designed with her in mind, for sure, and for the viruses she was wearing. She had her hair slicked on either side of her head and shaped on top into a Spartan crest. The gown was backless, revealing how the spine of blonde hair continued down her back. The designs Kester had painted on her body were centred and framed by the V cut front which stopped below her navel.

The sight of Alexis garbed in his viruses made Kester feel strong, made him pulse all over. She fastened a chiffon collar round her neck and tucked in the panels of fabric that hung front and back. Then she turned to face him. She was wearing Persona too – he could see it shining subtly through her thick stage makeup, only noticeable if you knew what you were looking for.

'I wanted to be the first to wear all of them together,' she said, putting a hand over the chiffon. 'I want to wear them all first from now on.'

Kester laughed and looked down at his chest. 'You'd better keep it quiet. My boss is a monster. She'd have my balls if she thought I'd put my mistress before the client.'

'Mistress?' Alexis smirked at the old-fashioned term. 'They're playing your song.' She drew in close and looked over his shoulder at the display.

The music started. *Fashion*. First, in came the bass, steady as a heartbeat, a measured catwalk footstep, then the siren horns.

Kester pushed a kiss onto Alexis' lips, his heart racketing in his chest. With a triumphant smile, she slid past him and strode out into the corridor, her dress flowing after her, fawning over her body. He took one last look in the mirror and then followed her.

Backstage, Kester watched on the monitor as Alexis walked onto the catwalk. She was a cartoon character, the lights swimming green and red across her skin. The roar of the crowd came in squalls, each wave of excitement threatening to spill into violence, collapsing, and then building anew. Trapped in the square by glass and metal, the cacophony churned in on itself, a maelstrom of noise, vibrating the air. Kester imagined Alexis ripping off her cravat, overcome with excitement, but she stopped and stood still as a mannequin at the end of the catwalk, above the exchange booths. Her stillness and focus bled into the crowd until all eyes were on her and the noise had fallen to a steady hubbub.

'This, ladies and gentlemen...' she said, stamping her stilettoed foot three times on the platform that covered the fountain. 'This, ladies and gentlemen...' The noise fell to a tense mumble as she cast her steel gaze across the audience, turning smoothly on her heel.

'This...' she pointed above her head at the storeys-high image of Kester. 'This is why we are here tonight.' The audience screamed. She crouched and smiled, waiting for the noise to fall again. 'So you've come to see the future of viruses?' The crowd cheered. She came up until she was half standing, arms out towards them. 'You've come to see the future of fashion?' A louder roar. She stood straight and pointed at them. 'You've come to see the future of sex?' It seemed they couldn't get any louder. 'Well, ladies and gentlemen, let's not get too excited. Every man should be judged by his works, should he not?' She turned and walked back down the catwalk. 'I give you...' she said, halfway down, ratcheting up the cheers with her arms. 'I give you...' again, to louder cheers. 'I give you...' she was shouting now. 'I give you KL01 – Corona!'

Alexis disappeared backstage. The music stopped. The square fell dark. The crowd was silent, waiting. The celebrities down the sides of the catwalk and around the fountain squirmed in their seats. Across the square, the sea of close-packed faces glistened in the ambient light, softened with sweat. Just as their eyes were starting to adjust to the darkness, all the spotlights in the square hit the catwalk entrance full beam. Five models were standing there, as still as cut-outs, swathed in black, only their eyes visible through the slits in their black hoods. Still silence.

As the first model's foot hit the catwalk, the music blared out – *Fashion* again, this time a brilliantly unhinged live version played by The Itch. The crowd was bedlam as they tried to figure out what they were looking at. Then, when the first model stopped at the end of the catwalk, her face appeared on the big screens and on both sides of the square, stories high. And there they were, eyes encircled with gold. The crowd roared as she blinked. Four other pairs of eyes bobbed down the catwalk behind her, then posed in formation, each a different metallic hue: silver, livid rust, ruby, acid green.

Kester watched as one-by-one the models did their two runs of the catwalk, paused, milked the crowd, and then disappeared down onto the VIP strip. The models walked up and down the side of the catwalk, flirting with the celebrities. Then one of them took someone by the hand – Bo Omotoye, the heavyweight champion. The crowd watched the big screen above as she led him down towards the front edge of the catwalk and into an exchange booth. Its door lit up red to indicate that it was engaged. The crowd erupted. One by one the other models found themselves partners and disappeared into the remaining booths. Sweaty noises filled the square for a moment, the sounds from the miked-up booths mixed together, booming out. The crowd fizzed.

When the doors were all engaged, it was time for The Itch to do their part. The curtain rose on their stage to the side of the catwalk. Their price had been high. They had resisted 'selling out' at first but now that they had acquiesced, they were doing it in style. There was no fabric to the three members' outfits except the ads, each of them a ragged commercial collage. Gregor was sweating attractively in a full suit, while his female guitarist Zelda wore a bikini of logos. All that was visible of the drummer was his naked shoulders, but his bass drum was plastered with bastardised logos. All three wore a variation on Gregor's blue tidal wave Mohawk. While the exchanges were taking place, they blasted the excited crowd with their latest release.

When the song ended, the lights fell again. The lit doors of the exchange booths switched off as their occupants left and returned to their seats. One by one, the models glided up the VIP strip and disappeared backstage.

Kester found himself on the edge of his seat. He knew that each virus set would follow the same format, but somehow it was tense. Next up was Lanugo-go, then Persona, featuring a guest appearance from Latin Rap Superstar Pera Pera. Kester felt the evening slipping past him and snatched at the details with his senses, snapshots to remember. He felt as though he were running fast through a fairground.

Already it was time for Luminescence. Alexis announced it, wove nimbly through the backstage staff to where Kester sat and perched next to him. She didn't say anything, just stared wide-eyed at the monitor.

'You're doing great,' Kester said and her lips twitched.

This time, the lights stayed low, with the exception of a thin line of muted LEDs down either side of the catwalk. The models were in place, their nodes glowing dimly through their shrouds. The audience started to mumble amongst themselves, pointing and straining in the dark. Then, as the band started up again, five stage hands whipped off the shrouds and they were off, Hera first, Kester guessed from the height. The sound of the band disappeared into the crowd's hysteria. Kester and Alexis watched together as the luminous bodies hip-swinged their way up and down the catwalk, and ultimately into the VIP pit.

'Wait,' Kester said. 'Look – Hera.'

'What?'

'There – she's up on the barrier.' The camera had zoomed in on her, standing like a glowing goddess on the security barrier at the front of the pit. 'Is this part of it?'

Kester grabbed Alexis' wrist as Hera plunged forward in a crowd-dive, sailed across the dark sea of hands for about ten metres and then was engulfed. There was a dip in the darkness of the crowd, a vortex, as the crowd tried to get at her.

'What the fuck?' Kester said, then looked around, as if to get help.

'Wait,' Alexis said.

The frenzy lasted a few minutes, then there was a crack and a bright, pale flare fizzed into life in the centre of the struggle. The circle of people pulled back like water from an oil droplet, save for two frozen in the act. The two audience members crowded Hera's legs and hips like beggars, filthy with clothes, faces turned up to the light, mouths slack as gaping pockets. From their grubbing pile thrust Hera's torso, naked flesh marble white in the harsh light, blonde hair wild as a maenad's, her whole form focused upwards to where she held the flare above her head.

'Yes!' Alexis said. 'Go on, Hera! You didn't think I'd send her in there without some kind of protection did you?'

'You sent her…'

'Now watch this.' Alexis pointed at the top of the monitor.

From up above, one of the line police lowered down and picked Hera up from the ground, lifting her onto his lap where she pretended to hump him as they ascended to the safety wire.

'OK,' said Alexis, 'that wasn't part of the plan but she does like to improvise.'

The light went off on the two of them but it was clear some kind of wrestling was going on. Then Hera's form began to move in a familiar rhythm. The crowd were pointing and yelling.

'That's my girl.' Alexis punched the palm of her hand.

'She's crazy.'

'Complete looney tunes. It was her idea.'

The carnage below continued until all of the remaining models had disappeared into the booths. The Itch were once more in the spotlight.

In minutes, the song was over and Alexis was back at the side of the stage, announcing the finale: Touché. The models were congregating backstage. When Kester saw them, an involuntary laugh escaped his chest. They were all done up in labcoats. They had their hair scraped back in pony tails, or slicked back if it was short, and they wore safety goggles over their made-up eyes.

The labcoats drew a laugh from the audience too and either the models were too professional to react, or they really didn't see the funny side of it, which made it even funnier. Again, the music started with the first foot down. The models took up position evenly down the stage, facing alternate directions. On cue, they began a slow strip-tease, aimed partly at the VIPs, and partly at the rest of the crowd via to-camera winks and pouts. Considering they didn't have very much to strip out of, they did an amazing job, ending up in the modest white knickers they wore in the lab. By the time Alexis joined Kester again, he was in kinks. He hadn't known about the labcoats.

'Thought you might appreciate this,' she said into his ear, laying an arm across his shoulders and kissing him firmly on the cheek. 'You have no idea how much training it took to get catwalk models to act like that.'

When they had stripped down to their knickers, they still looked completely clean. Kester had been doubtful about the timings, but Alexis had been adamant it would work. They had done three trial runs and they seemed stable.

There it was: slowly but surely the Touché patterns were appearing on the models, drawing staggered bouts of cheering and whistling from the crowd as they realised what was happening.

'You've calmed down,' Kester hollered over the noise.

'We're almost there. But you're up next, baby.'

Kester had almost forgotten that he was a part of it. Alexis dragged him to his feet and took him over to wardrobe check, where a team of stylists ruffled his hair carefully and adjusted his clothes to make sure they were hanging right. He was wearing broken-down jeans, a yellow t-shirt with a faded logo for some B-movie that no-one had ever heard of – 'Pandemic!' Alexis handed him his labcoat to finish the outfit.

'They're really sending me out there in my labcoat?' he asked as he put it on.

'Kester, you look hot,' she replied with her spitting K and walked off towards the stage, hips swinging.

Kester walked to the wings where he could see her geeing up the crowd one last time. As she exited, she put her lips to his ear.

'You're theirs for tonight,' she said, then pushed him forward to stand at the catwalk entrance, ready for his cue.

When the lights came up, Kester couldn't see. They had warned him against the urge to lift his arm to shield his eyes, but he forgot all his coaching and did it anyway. He walked out in exactly the way the show director had told him not to, as if he was walking out of a spaceship that had landed on another planet.

The crowd went wild. He *was* from another planet – why shouldn't he act this way? As he worked his way down the catwalk, he began to enjoy himself and ceased fighting the adrenaline. He gave a few small bows and waves, then he laughed, buoyed up by the crowd's energy. He looked at the faces. He was on stage at a rock concert. Thousands of pairs of eyes were on him, wishing him well. Voices were calling out his name, clamouring into one big swell of excited shouts. Arms reached up amongst the smiles; hands flexed, desperate to get inches closer to him. The smiles filled him with a frantic energy – he grabbed the edges of his labcoat, held it out like a cape and did a lap of honour up and down the catwalk to a cacophony of screams. At the end he jumped right to the edge of the fountain platform, whisked off his labcoat and whirled it off out across the VIPs and into the crowd. He laughed, waving and bowing again, as it was ripped to pieces.

After a few moments lapping it all up, Kester lost his momentum and paced back and forth a couple of times above the booths. This was when he was supposed to go down into the VIP pit. His nerves rushed back in.

'Fuck it, Alexis, where are you when I need you.'

He turned on his heel and ran up the catwalk. She was already coming out to push him back in the other direction when he reached the top.

'What the fuck are you doing?'

Kester saw the words form on her lips. She had already taken off her makeup in preparation for the after-party. He grabbed her hand and pulled her at a half-run down the catwalk. Once she stopped resisting, he lifted her arm and presented her to the crowd. As they reached the circular platform he let her go. Then he grabbed her collar and, to rapturous cheers, ripped off the chiffon panel to reveal his handiwork all over the front of her body.

Alexis turned, laughing now. She shimmied her shoulders to draw attention to her golden-haired spine, then put her head down and pinched out her brown contact lenses to reveal her golden eyes. Kester took her hand again and turned her in a circle, then pulled her in and kissed her on the lips. He looked at her, amazed: she was a beautiful alien, he was Captain Kirk. Their chests were heaving. He had felt this before. The Stark Wellbury wall glowed opposite, a hallucinated memory. He squeezed her hand and glanced down at the pit.

'Go – go!' Alexis said, pulling her hand away.

She pushed him towards the steps to the left-hand VIP strip. Kester watched as she walked to the top of the stairs opposite, her grin still hanging in front of his eyes like the ghost of a bright light. At the top of the stairs she turned and mouthed something. Kester gave a small jump of triumph and dashed to the stairs.

Chapter 17

Kester stared at Farrell across the board room table. Farrell stared at the table, refusing to meet his eyes. She had been avoiding him since the after-party. Something had happened at the show. He had done something.

'Let me start by saying that the show was an unprecedented success,' said Chen.

She looked around at all involved and nodded, as if she had done her duty in praising them. This was as much as they could expect from her.

'So what now?' she asked.

'It was wonderful, wasn't it?' Gaunt said, with a dreamy, leery look in his eye, avoiding the question. 'Did you see that young model – what's her name again, Kester?'

'Hera?'

'Yes, Hera.' Gaunt smiled as if he had a mouth full of razor-sharp teeth. 'What a wonderful performer. In every sense.' He jabbed Alexis in the ribs. 'Oh Lord, woman, close your eyes before you hurt someone else – you've cut me quite open.'

Alexis ignored him.

Chen gave him his space as usual, and then repeated her question. 'What now?'

'With all due respect,' Roger Yule said, 'we've put a strategy in place, so we know what's next: following up the show with the campaign and getting these viruses into all the branches of the Pigs.'

'Yes.' Chen nodded. 'That was the plan, but we have to be flexible, Roger. You know better than anyone that a strategy is a living thing which needs to respond to the circumstances. And the majority of the Pig chains and large independents have already signed up.'

'Yes.' Roger squeezed his hands together, then placed them on the table either side of his Book. 'You're right. You're quite right.

Head's still a bit fuzzy from the event.'

'Dear boy,' Gaunt said, 'after three days? You need some of my special medicine.'

'You want to talk through your addictions?' Ingrid Jones said. 'I have a number for that. Now are we not here on business?'

Roger leaned over to Kester and whispered in his ear, 'She's never had a night's fun in her life. She wouldn't know what the aftermath –'

'Roger.' Ingrid smiled. 'Even if I couldn't hear everything you're saying your body language would incriminate you.'

Chen, who had been scrolling through something on her Book, turned her attention back to the room.

'What did we learn from Saturday, Roger?' Chen asked.

'Firstly, that we've created pretty substantial demand for another show. Since the event I've had agents calling on behalf of various celebrities trying to secure VIP seats for the next event.'

'As many as we expected?' Chen asked.

'More,' Alexis said.

Kester looked over at her. There was something about her eyes, something different. He couldn't figure it out. They hadn't seen each other since the show. By the time Kester's VIP had been done with him he was ready to drop. Even so, the dose that Gaunt's man had given him didn't wear off fully until lunchtime the next day. He had left a message in the morning suggesting she come round and take advantage of the situation – even though he didn't feel like it, he had wanted to see her – but she hadn't replied. She had been busy, he imagined, but now it looked like he had offended her. Was that what that look was? It wasn't a good look, whatever it meant.

'Yes, more than we expected,' Yule said, 'so a second event is a must.'

'And this time we should get the plebs involved,' Gaunt said. 'That should give the hype a helping hand and give the high street end of things a boost.'

'Involved how?' Alexis asked.

'You know how they love to be a part of things. We allow them to become a part of it. Literally. Run a contest to find the new models for the show.'

'A competition for people who want to prostitute themselves?' Kester asked.

'Come off it, Kester,' Gaunt said, pulling one of his best charming smiles, 'you're the biggest whore here. They'll love it. The chance to fuck all those celebrities they've only dreamed of getting close to. Most of the public may not wear day to day, or climb the shag-ladder like we do in the City but believe me, they'll spread their legs quicker than 25-year-old virgins for a film star, a Premiership footballer, any of our clients. The red-top sites prove that.'

'I like it,' Yule said. 'I think it could really work. We're looking for women and men beautiful enough to do justice to the next release of Kester Lowes.'

'Inside and outside,' Gaunt said.

'I'm sorry?' Yule looked confused, along with the rest of the room. Kester, too, assumed he had missed some innuendo.

'The City,' Gaunt said. 'We run the competition inside and outside the City, outside London even, internationally. More entries.'

'But winners from outside wouldn't be allowed in here,' Jones said.

'Come, come. Surely that's a little thing to overcome for the possibility of millions more entries – we'd make money for every submission. Besides, Alexis,' Gaunt turned to Alexis and winked at her, 'you have friends in high places at the City Population Monitor, no? We've already made an exception for one model.'

'Yes,' Alexis said.

'That's settled then. Get on to it, the three of you,' Chen said, making eye contact with Gaunt, Alexis and Yule. 'And the Vspa?'

'The Vspa, absolutely,' Yule said, running a finger around the collar of his shirt and casting a glance a Kester. 'Absolutely, yes. It's going to be a great success. We've secured the top level of the PlayPen and we've got our design and construction teams working on creating the facilities now.'

'Gaunt,' Chen said, 'do you want to lay out our plans for Doctor Lowe?'

'Well, Roger's the expert,' Gaunt said, waving a hand about his head, then rubbing his eye.

Chen stared at Gaunt, and then at Yule. There was a short silence. Kester had an odd feeling. It reminded him of the uncomfortable pause which preceded criticism. He shifted in his seat.

Looking around and observing the scene, Jones raised her eyebrows.

'Well,' she said, 'I will lay out the new strategy briefly for Doctor Lowe.'

Chen nodded at Jones and she continued.

'The Vspa will continue as planned. We will use the existing models who are working for us. We've also signed up some up-and-coming models who need a bit of publicity.'

'Up and coming,' Gaunt repeated and smirked, seemingly unaware that he had spoken.

'The Vspa will open one week before our second event, which will take place in just under six weeks' time. Kester, we will need two more viruses ready for the event. We can reuse the rest, but there needs to be something extra for the attendees. We need to look like we're growing our portfolio.'

'No problem,' said Kester, his mind starting to tick through where they were with the different viruses. 'Not a problem. We should have three to choose from, maybe four.'

'Roger, Felicity and I have a meeting booked to go over the pricing, but we think we've got a pretty good model. We've got our economists running it through the modelling systems trying to break it as we speak. The Vspa facilities are under construction here at V and we will transport everything in and set it up in four weeks' time.'

'Still tomorrow for our meeting?' Felicity asked.

Jones nodded.

'Get to the point!' Alexis said, clattering her coffee cup into its saucer.

'The next step,' Jones said, 'as we've got the facilities from two weeks prior to the second show, is to set up some appointments for pre-launch promotion. We'll spend the first week doing snagging and getting everything set up and the appointments will start one week before the show.' She turned her pale eyes on Kester.

'Sounds great,' Kester said. He felt he had to say something because she was looking at him.

'We'd like you to participate,' she said.

'You mean…' Kester stopped and thought about what he was about to say.

'She means they want to pimp you out, dear boy,' Gaunt said, winking at him. 'Alexis has come good. She said she'd fix you to the firmament and she has. You're the hottest new toy on the market – everybody wants to play with you.'

'I…' Kester laughed and then turned to Alexis. 'You said it was a one-off, just at the show – two shows at the most. Is that what you meant when you said I was "going to be busy"?'

'It was,' Alexis said, taking up his stare, sending a shudder through him. 'You didn't complain about putting out on our little World Tour. What's the problem now?'

'That was – what are you talking about?' Something was tightening in Kester's chest. 'That was for fun – that was sleeping with who I want to, something that normal people do, if any of you remember what it's like to be normal.'

'The first show was a one-off freebie,' Chen said. 'From now on, people will be paying handsomely for the pleasure.'

Kester opened his mouth to answer but found he could only shake his head. Paying for it. She thought that was a good thing? That was supposed to make it OK?

'That's why you're here today,' Chen said. 'We thought it would be only polite to let you hear the business plan, since you're such a large part of it.'

Kester was suddenly very aware of his penis, still tender from overuse at the show.

'So I'm supposed to sleep with anyone who's willing to pay for it?' he asked. His voice caught in his throat.

'Believe me, Kester,' Jones said, unblinking, 'if it made good business sense to keep you to ourselves, I'm sure we would.'

Jones held Kester's gaze. Alexis shifted in her chair.

'You're loving this aren't you?' Kester said.

'I'm Director of Strategy,' Jones said. 'Of course I love it. I wouldn't have gone for this job if I didn't. New opportunities like this don't just fall out of the sky.'

'So you're going to pimp me out?' Kester got up out of his chair and walked to the window.

'Byron's words,' Chen said. 'Not a good choice.'

'If they wanted to pimp *me* out, dear boy,' Gaunt said with a louche smile, 'I'd be more than happy to oblige, but for some reason the clients don't want my emanations the way they want yours. I have no idea why. Being paid to copulate is rather my dream career, though these days I might need strong pharmaceutical assistance in the matter.'

'You want to prostitute me to our clients.' Kester stared out of the window without blinking until the scoop of the city began to wobble before his eyes. It was sunny, but patches of cloud cast parts of the city into shadow, dark seams in a quarry of bright metal. He thought of his mother, proudly hanging signed "Kester Lowe" knickers in the absently clean window of her boutique.

'Don't think of it like that, Kester,' Yule said. 'We're just providing them with a service.'

'You employed me as a scientist, not a semen dispenser!' Kester couldn't look at him. 'You already had a building full of those.'

'That's right, Doctor Lowe,' Chen said. 'We did employ you. For a moment I suspected that you had forgotten. Give us the room please, everyone.'

Kester clenched his jaw repeatedly as the Board filed out, mumbling to one another. He listened for Alexis' voice but couldn't hear it.

'OK, Kester.' Chen joined him at the window. 'Let me make it easier for you. Alexis doesn't like the idea any more than you do, but she knows what her job's worth. You two teenagers need to snap out of it. I don't know what happened on that tour, but you need to remember how things work around here. I've told Alexis not to interfere, so if you don't want her to end up explaining herself to me, don't goad her. And don't goad me. Make no mistake about it, Doctor Lowe, I keep your reputation right next to the shredder and I can bring you down faster than she took you on. I can make sure you never work again, here or anywhere. I can destroy you – I can do worse than destroy you: I can make you disappear.'

Kester felt Chen's hand hovering behind his neck, only just touching the downy fluff at his hairline. Then she placed it firmly onto his skin, gripping his neck as if she might pick him up by the scruff like a kitten. She had always stopped short of touching him before.

'You can make us a fortune. You can make yourself a fortune. Alexis has made you into a star almost overnight and you have the top celebrities in the UK, in Europe, in the world lining up to take you to bed.' Chen's accent was getting more and more Glaswegian the more forcefully she talked. It clicked into place with the husk in her voice. 'Rock stars, sports stars, politicians, royalty – everybody you ever wanted. They aren't paying to use you; they are paying you to use them. They aren't paying for you the way they would pay for a prostitute; they're paying for your personal services the way they might pay for La Fey's personal services in fitting the dress he has made for them. In this world, everyone's serving someone. It's all a matter of what you get for it.'

'It's sex slavery.'

'It's only slavery if you don't get paid for it.'

'And what do I get for it?' Kester's own voice sounded distant to him.

Chen slid her hand down to his shoulder and turned him towards her. She leaned in until her lips were almost touching his ear. He could feel her warm breath on his skin.

'You get to play fuck bingo with the global A-list.'

-o-

It was Thursday, which was reason enough in itself for Kester's malaise. Alexis had continued to avoid him after their meeting on Monday. He knew for a fact that Chen had set her the task of lining up his appointments. They were running a private auction for the first spot. The auction would take place in four weeks' time on the Thursday and the appointment the next day, one week before the second show. Kester suspected that she was involved with setting this up too. He sat slouched at his desk, his Book in front of him, doodling, watching his swirls appear on the wall beside him.

The new viruses he had promised Yule were tested and ready to go, everything was under control, but despite the building full of people, there was no-one to share his success with. Kester's mind wandered back to his own private test torsos, sitting in the back isolation suite, being bombarded with viruses. Something would be going wrong right now. He daren't look at the data. And anyway, who would put their health in the hands of a prostitute, even a high-class one.

'I have Roger Yule here for you, sir.'

Gerald's voice gave Kester a start. He flicked off his design board and turned to the door. Yule had only visited him in his office once before. He preferred that people come to him.

'OK. Send him in please, Gerald.'

'Kester.' Yule started talking before the door had even slid fully open. 'I need to...'

'Welcome...Roger Yule.'

Yule flapped a hand at the door and huffed.

'Roger, take a seat.' Kester drew out the chair on the door side of his desk for Yule to sit. 'What's wrong?'

'Welcome...Roger Yule.' Yule's slow movement confused the door sensors.

They both stopped talking while Yule made his way across the room. Kester made a show of tidying some files that were on his display to take up some time, then sat down.

'Kester, I've got a problem with my screen. I wanted one of your guys to take a look at it.'

'A problem how?'

Yule sneezed and cursed. He hunched as though a bird had dive-bombed him. Holding one hand up to cover his nose, he rummaged in his pocket and took out a handkerchief.

'Guh! I can't see them coming!' he said, cleaning up his face.

'I see your problem. They haven't put out an upload yet?'

Kester glanced at his inbox. It wasn't normal for something as simple as a flu virus or cold infection to present – normally new mutations would be identified and uploads issued before the person even had a tickly throat. They would feel woozy at worst and then it would be over. This must be something different.

'No, no!' Yule was still panting a little from his journey across the room. 'It's my screen. It's stopped working. I've got the flu, for god's sake. Bog standard bastarding flu.'

'Your screen? Have the technicians at Stark Wellbury been in touch?'

'I had to contact them. They had no idea. Christ. Never felt so bloody in my whole life. Must have caught it from that damned Franklin or whatever her name was, came in on a day pass to do some marketing consultancy for us.'

'That's...irregular.'

'She comes in all the time.'

'I mean the screen.'

Kester stood up and walked to the window.

'What is it?' Yule asked.

Kester thought for a moment. This was bad. If the screen had stopped working Stark Wellbury would know all about it, which they didn't. If it hadn't stopped working then it was being blocked somehow and there was only one way Kester was aware of that this could be done. He watched the workers below, moving with insectile purpose across the face of the square, never crashing into one another, diverting from their courses only for physical objects, factoring the central fountain into their routes as if it wasn't there, working around its familiarity.

'Kester.' Yule's voice was gaining in depth and edge. 'Can your guys fix it? Stark Wellbury are putting me off.'

'That's...' Kester turned back to Yule and took his seat again, '...a question. But I think there may be another more important question.'

'Well?'

'Why has it stopped working in the first place? I'm going to need to get someone on this straight away. We'll take you into one of the testing suites so you'll be isolated from any other infections. No sex. Come to think of it, we'll need to see a log of your encounters for the last few days – when did the symptoms start to present?'

'I've been sneezing and snotting like this since yesterday lunchtime, but I've felt ropey since Saturday night.'

'For the last seven days, then – do you think you can manage that?'

'Kester.' Yule was leaning forward as far as his bulk would allow.

Kester waited. Yule lifted a hand to his face. What Kester could see of it was turning red. His breathing was laboured.

'I can give you that list.' Yule's voice was breaking.

'Roger, are you alright? Can I get you something?' Kester asked, hoping that Yule wouldn't have a heart attack in his office, then feeling guilty for having thought it.

'Fine, just...give me a minute, Kester.'

Yule took out a clean handkerchief and mopped down his face and neck with it. When Yule leaned back in his seat, Kester noticed that his eyes were red. He was calm for a moment, but when he started to talk again, tears welled up in his eyes.

'You don't need a list, Kester. Look at me. Nobody's this ambitious. The only sex I ever have is with that fucking hole in the back of my office.'

'Lisa? Lisa's a nice –'

'The Pig Port! I'd crush that little girl if I even stepped too close to her. And she'd never...'

'Roger, that's no big deal.'

'Not to you, Kester. I lost my wife because of these stupid power games we play – having to look like you've slept with so-and-so, or that you're so desirable you have a different virus every time someone meets you. My marriage couldn't take it. That's why I had the port installed in the first place – so I wouldn't have to cheat on her to keep up appearances, but she wouldn't buy it, didn't believe me.' He was sobbing now.

'Roger...'

Kester felt the urge to go over to Yule, but stayed stuck to his seat. He realised he was gripping the edge of the desk and tried to let go casually. His mind wandered back to his interview again and his assumption that Yule had paid for the virus he was wearing.

'She'd believe me if she saw me now, huh?' Yule looked up. His eyes were wounds in his pale, bald skin.

'Stay put,' Kester said. 'I'll fix you a drink and we'll sort this out.'

Through in the other room, Kester took his time over finding the scotch, the ice, everything. This was bad, he thought again. Worse. There was only one thing that could block nanoscreens without raising the alarm as far as he was aware. It was a virus called Trojan12. He had designed it on secondment to the Government a few years previously. The virus had been designed for premilitary use – knock out the enemy's screens and a whole world of bio-weaponry opened up for you, bio-weapons that your own troops were immune to. You could wipe out whole cities while you stood unscathed in the middle of it all. You could walk through a crowd and kill one man by laying a hand on him, a bad Jesus.

Of course it was all purely speculative stuff – the US Army were the only other force fitted with nanoscreens and in any case the use of the virus would have been illegal under the Beijing Convention. The project had been mothballed and the client had retained all files and samples. This could only have come from the MoD. He and Dee had talked about using some of the technology in their screen development project if it ever happened, but they'd stopped just short of recreating it. If this was out there for real, it had to be the

MoD – he knew for a fact they had live samples sitting in an envirobox somewhere. Some arse had probably put it in a skip or left it on a bus.

'Roger.' Kester handed Yule a large scotch. 'I'm going to look into this myself. Let's take you along to the testing suite and I'll get Gerald to take a blood sample. You can take your drink.'

'OK.' Yule took a deep breath. 'Sorry about…all that,' he said. 'Are my eyes red?'

'A little,' Kester said. 'We'll walk quickly.'

Yule stared at him.

-o-

Blotch strode down the corridor to the media suite. As his mouth rattled through the long Real Church Prayer his mind galloped forward to the broadcast ahead of him. He went to put a hand to his Real Church pendant then restrained himself. No smudges or fingerprints for his broadcast. He must be clean as clean, an example for his congregation. He entered the suite and smiled at the broadcast technician.

Clarke must be serious about promotion if he was letting him finally have a broadcast. Though Blotch's final draft had very little to do with his first, it was still his. Clarke's comments had helped to tone down, clarify. His passion was a blessing, Clarke had told him, but it sometimes got in the way of what he was really trying to say.

The Church's research centre had jumped on the news of the viral attack immediately, before it even hit the big news sites. The timing was perfect. It had worked – it was his and it had worked – and this would be the beginning of the end for Doctor Kester Lowe, for wearing, for V. Maybe even for the exclusivity of screen technology. And more than anything, it would be the beginning of his new career. The gold necklet was practically his. He would soon be a Minister to Mary, a Minister to Jesus, eventually – no, that was too far off. The girl could have whatever she wanted. She'd come through. They may not even need to use the second virus.

The microphone was enormous. Blotch stood on the stage, sweating. When he had seen his fellow Ministers' broadcasts, he had always imagined that the stage stood at the head of a massive stadium full of devoted congregation members. In reality all the broadcasts were recorded in this small room and the stage took up most of the floor space. The rest of the space was taken up with lighting and camera equipment. The only shouts of hallelujah were to come from a set of ten speakers, set around the room. Hard to get yourself worked up for.

'Don't worry,' the technician said to him in a kind voice. 'When we put the lights on it'll feel different.'

It did feel different. The lights were so bright that Blotch could barely see past the edge of his parapet. On the back wall, the projected scene of a mass audience came to life and the roars of the virtual crowd rattled round the room.

'This isn't a recording,' the technician said. 'This is the sound of all your online supporters. The ones that have headsets anyway.'

The noise suddenly meant something – these were live people cheering and shouting for his address to start.

'And we're ready to go when you are,' the technician said.

Blotch nodded and watched him count down on his fingers. The light on the edge of the primary camera flashed faster and faster until it went solid and the technician dropped his hand. Blotch looked up at his audience. He heard a swell in the cheers, which then dropped in anticipation of his words. He drew himself up tall, placed his hands firmly on the front of the parapet and began.

'Today, God weeps. Today we weep with him. We weep for joy, because twenty-five years after our expulsion from the City our necessity will finally become clear to our lost brothers and sisters. And we weep in sadness, because the lens which has provided this clarity has taken the form of a devastating terrorist attack.

'The nanoscreen scheme was sold to us as a way of protecting the key workers in our population-dense Government and financial centre from the proliferation of infection. Today they stand defenceless against nature's battery, diminished by drug use, unable to defend themselves as God intended. But it is God who, in their new condition – stripped, wracked with disease – reaches out a hand and says to them, "Come with me. I will show you the error of your ways. I will make you clean."

'Today, let us set aside questions of whether screen technology is right or wrong, issues of fairness and access, because today God opens his hands to us and speaks not of the wisdom of the gift, but of the abuse of the gift. After all, a gift from man is a gift from God and to abuse a gift from God is a sin of the highest order.

'Abuse. Abuse of technology, abuse of the body, abuse of the soul...'

-o-

'This is ridiculous,' Gaunt said, adjusting the gauze mask over his face. 'We look like a bunch of bloody terrorists.'

The Viral Development Board members, with the exception of Agbabi and Farmer, were seated around a giant mushroom table on one of the less popular levels of the PlayPen. Alexis looked around the table. Gaunt was right.

'I'll second that,' Yule said. Despite his face being covered, it was clear that he was suffering. The outsized boiler suit was tight on his landslide form and large sweat patches had already formed on the bright orange fabric around his armpits.

'Look, it is stupid, but let's get it over with,' Chen said. 'This is the safest place we could meet.'

'Who's minuting this?' Jones asked.

Chen's head snapped towards her, then back to centre.

'First thing's first,' Chen said, 'we need to shut down our less cautious operations.'

'You mean any XC transactions?' Gaunt asked.

'Transactions, buildings access, everything.'

'I've already briefed Gerald,' Alexis said.

Gerald had conducted their extra-City dealings with impeccable delicacy. If anyone could dismantle things without drawing attention, it was him.

'Do you think we might be overreacting a little?' Jones asked.

She looked tiny on her toadstool, pinched in around the boiler suit waist, managing to look good in it, resembling an annoyingly good child with her doll-like posture.

'Extra-City operations are extremely lucrative,' she added.

'We have a new revenue stream to protect,' Alexis said. 'That's why I've got Kester out there now being interviewed, and after that going over security protocols with representatives from the various Pig operators.'

She gazed at the covered faces around the table. It was the most sinister meeting she had ever attended. The masks were acting as windows into people's personalities, allowing their true faces to reveal in the ghostly hoods.

'We've got to protect this,' she said. 'It's potentially our largest revenue stream and it's a legitimate one.'

'Our newest, certainly; our largest, perhaps;' Jones said, 'but it is definitely our most unstable – we have no idea how long this craze will last.'

'Jones, we're way ahead of the game with this,' Alexis said. 'Other companies are on it, but the stuff they've been turning out is frankly unwearable – it's not pretty and it's too similar to the muck you can pick up from the Pigs – people aren't going to want that when there's a better alternative.'

'It's true,' Yule said. 'We're just getting started, but we've already recouped our outlay for everything – the lab, Kester's salary for the next five years, the fashion show.'

'The V Spa?' Jones asked. 'The competition?'

'The competition is making us money,' Gaunt said.

'We'd be fools not to continue,' said Yule. 'We're only just tapping into this. We're getting interest from people who would never even have considered wearing before – people who couldn't see the beauty in the expressions of natural viruses. The media coverage is being kind to us and that's a hell of a lot more than they've granted us in the past.'

'They're being kind to Kester,' Jones said.

'And Kester is ours,' Alexis said.

'Speak for yourself.'

Alexis snarled. It was as well they all had masks on.

'The point is that as long as the public can only see so far,' Gaunt said, 'and as long as they are creaming their panties over Kester, we're OK. As for our clients, they wouldn't know a moral dilemma if they woke up in bed with one.'

'This is all very good,' Chen said, 'but I didn't come here to debate our options.'

'Gerald and his team have always been discreet – I don't see any reason why we can't –'

'I said I didn't come here for a debate, Jones,' Chen raised her voice. She glanced over her shoulder. 'We need to talk about how we're going to wind things down without attracting too much attention. We're not leaving here until we have a detailed plan and one that leaves us on dry land by the end of the month. Gaunt, I want you to brief Agbabi and Farmer.'

Chapter 18

'It's on,' Alexis said. 'You're famous. Even more famous.'

She squeezed Kester's leg as he sat down beside her on the edge of his bed. She was lying on her front, arms hanging over the end of the bed like a teenager. Kester grunted.

'We're under attack,' he said, dropping his head back and staring at the ceiling.

The four days since Yule's screen broke down had been hell. First had come the statements from the various Churches declaring the attack 'devastating' and describing the 'uncontrolled' spread of the virus. Some showed real religious compassion, offering to help care for those affected by the attack, but others were thinly veiled condemnations of City culture. The Church broadcasts were followed in short order by the press with pandemic specials, technology specials, casualty projections and doomsday predictions. Whatever the source, the effect was the same: panic.

Fortunately, the panic had been short-lived. People's pupils had barely dilated when V released a statement, backed up by the MoD, that the virus was under control and could be easily treated. Roger Yule had been by far the worst physical casualty. From the outside, Vs containment of the situation looked easy; inside the building the air was sweat and swears as they figured out the best way to identify all those affected and negotiated with the health clinics to put out the anti-virus. Kester looked down at Alexis. At least their latest crisis had speeded her return to his bed.

'It could have been much worse,' Alexis said. 'Much worse. If anything we've come out of it looking like the good guys – this was no mistake of V's after all, or yours – it was a terrorist attack and we stepped in to sort it out. We've not lost trust, we've not lost face – all your appointments are filled – and we still have a room full of A-listers prepared to bid to bed you first.'

Alexis seemed to be making peace with their situation. Perhaps everything seemed brighter in the face of averted disaster. Perhaps she had enjoyed securing the highest price possible for her champion's services.

'It's nice that you want to pimp me out personally. It's not so bad that way.'

Alexis turned up the sound. There he was, looking bedraggled in front of the cameras, smiling politely as the interviewer asked a multi-claused question.

'They always choose somewhere windy. Why do they do that? I look a mess.'

'You look sexy – your collar turned up like a private detective.'

'*I've never designed a bespoke virus without considering how it could be stopped,*' windswept Kester said to the interviewer, eye-contact steady, hands visible and open. '*Ethical and safety considerations such as this are priorities for the Institute when agreeing contracts. It's one of the reasons that the Institute has such a trusted reputation.*'

'You did well,' Alexis said. 'I like the word "bespoke" – says less "weaponised" and more "small boutique affair".'

'But let's see what they did with it. Whose side are they on?'

The interview cut back to studio.

'So,' the studio presenter said, 'viral designer and heartthrob Kester Lowe saves the day. The MoD has issued the following statement: *Without Doctor Lowe's vigilance and quick-thinking, a serious situation may have ensued. While the MoD and the Government as a whole do not share all of the views put forward in Doctor Lowe's statement and do not condone viral wearing, we are grateful for his professional handling of the matter. A full investigation into the attack is underway and we will make sure that those responsible are brought to justice swiftly.*

'In the second half of this special edition we talk to top scientists from around the globe about our dependency on Stark Wellbury nanoscreen technology and the complementary immunosuppressant therapy provided by Doctor Lowe's employers V. Are we too reliant on this one safety net? How has our health ended up in the hands of these two technopharmaceutical giants and is there any way out?'

Kester raised his eyebrows at Alexis.

'But before that, we go live to Bond Street to speak to some Pig-users and get their opinions. Will they stop using the Pigs now security has shown to be compromised so easily or is a quick response like this enough to keep the public's confidence? Does it bother them that the Pigs are apparently happy to trade on the German viral blackmarket? And what do people say to the rumours that this was a religious attack originating here in the UK? We take a closer look at some of the Church broadcasts.'

Alexis flicked off her display and flipped over onto her back.

'What are you looking so smug about? They're going to rip us apart in that second segment,' Kester said.

'They've been squabbling over that stuff for years,' Alexis said with a wave of her hand. 'That's not us; that's a whole different department. Besides, what do you care? If they burned us to the ground would you not emerge renewed from the flames as Kester Lowe Enterprises, clutching your new screen in your hand?'

'You'd have difficulty clutching it in your hand,' Kester said, then scratched his neck, considering the suggestion. With the rush of the show and the fallout of the attack Kester's private work had taken a back seat, but he needed to figure out what to do about it. No doubt Alexis already had a plan. 'You know that is something we need to talk about. I don't know what to do about it. Do I take it to Chen? Do you think it's something the company might be interested in?'

'You know they're re-running your fashion show on eight channels tonight?'

Kester couldn't help looking impressed.

'And you get to meet your new models in a few days,' Alexis said. 'The contest is closed but we've managed an impressive number of entries.'

Kester looked down at her. She was smirking. Entries; dear god. Kester's Book rang.

'Hi, Mum,' he said, making a face at Alexis.

She slapped him on the knee and mouthed *be nice to your mother*.

'Kester, I was just watching you on the news!' his mother said. 'You looked so handsome!'

'I told you,' Alexis said.

'You can hear this?' Kester said to Alexis. 'Mum, you're shrieking – people can hear you.'

'People – sorry darling, are you in the middle of something?'

'No, Mum, just watching the news too.'

'With…'

'With Alexis.'

'Oh, lovely, I'm so glad it's going well for you two. I know she's a career woman, but don't let that put you off. Your father thought I had my head in the clouds when I wanted to start up my own business, but look at me now – self-sufficient and not even a bitch.'

'Mum.' Kester was painfully aware that his mother was still audible. He fumbled with his Book to turn her down while Alexis sniggered to herself.

'What? I'm just saying you shouldn't be intimidated by powerful women.'

'Mum, I'm not,' Kester said, 'but it's hardly the same, running an underwear store.'

'A *lingerie boutique*, Kester.'

'Whatever. Anyway, how are you, Mum – how's the dog?'

'The dog? What's the dog got to do with it? He's fine. I'm sending out invitations today for our next panty party. Everyone had such a fabulous time. Will you sign some more panties for me darling? They sold ever so well.'

You're blushing, Alexis mouthed.

Kester half expected the conversation to end right there with the dog doing something interesting to distract his mother.

'I'm glad, Mum. To tell the truth I was a bit worried you'd be…I was a little embarrassed by the whole thing, you know?'

'Embarrassed? You never need to be embarrassed about who you are, Kester. Look at what you just did – saved the whole City from catastrophe. A lot of people out here will be saying it just goes to show how lucky we are not to have those screens foisted on us, but believe you me, you did a good thing, Kester. A good thing. It doesn't matter who's in trouble – you should help them if you can. I'm proud of you, Kester.'

Kester covered the mouthpiece on his Book.

'I love the PR department,' he said to Alexis, smiling.

-o-

Blotch's hands sweated as he lifted the telephone. Jesus was looking at him from the front of his extravagant altar. The varnished enamel gave a watery look to the eyes, a look of infinite suffering and sadness. He wished his altar retracted into the wall like Clarke's did. He pressed a button on his phone to call Clarke and then swung on his chair to face towards the back corner of the room.

'Are you watching all this?' he asked as Clarke answered. 'Their blasted PR department! This is all going...tits up.' Blotch struggled with the words. 'They discover the thing within days and by Monday morning everything's hunky-dory and Doctor Deviant is a hero. The whole City is supposed to be in meltdown right now – disease spiralling out of control – this was supposed to be bigger than the Black Death!' He was shouting now, showering the handset with foamy spittle. 'And we look like idiots! *God's way of telling us to stop* – what did I say – I went out live on television saying it was God's will, calling it a major terrorist attack, and now Kester bloody Lowe has sorted it all out. We –'

'Calm down, Minister,' Clarke said in a too-even tone. 'We must not blame ourselves for this. You did well. You've got people talking. Not everyone is praising Doctor Lowe. And besides, you assured me that there was a phase two to your plan.'

Blotch breathed heavily through his nose for a few moments before answering. 'There is. It's already underway.'

On the display in the corner, the ticker was announcing that Kester Lowe was to help the Pigs tighten up their security protocols. Blotch gritted his teeth.

'Good. Then I expect you to go and get a coffee and a pastry and crack on. Don't lose your nerve now. You're making good progress.'

Blotch put down the phone. There was a phase two, but it was a poor one, primarily because the same thing wouldn't work twice. Stupid. He flicked channels on the display, up and up in an attempt to find something that wasn't Kester Lowe. Finally he found the boxing. It was a montage of Bo Omotoye's recent fights, the warm-up for a big fight later in the day, no doubt. Blotch turned the volume back on. The programme cut to a live pre-fight press conference. The two fighters were snarling at each other over the heads of their promoters. The camera zoomed in on Omotoye as he turned back to face the press. His eyes were surrounded with a shimmering chemical-green ring that shone against his dark pupils. He looked like a werewolf.

Blotch looked down at his desk. He leafed through a few bits of paper and finally found his scrawled spider diagram. He looked up at his Jesus, who was regarding him calmly.

'Thank you,' he said.

This was the last piece of the puzzle. He had the perfect mode of delivery for the next attack and he hadn't even realised it. He looked at the names on his diagram: Cherry, Kester, Dee, Farrell, Gerald. Then he lifted his pen and drew multiple lines out from Cherry's node, ending each with a scribbly dot. *Celebrities!* he wrote beside them. The speech was already writing itself in his head.

-o-

'It is to our great sadness that the Real Church today is compelled to make another statement to our congregation and to the broader population. This morning it was announced that a second so-called 'fashion show' is being planned at V. It seems the slim escape from the peril of last month's terrorist attack was not slim enough to lift the blindness with which our City brothers and sisters have been afflicted. The City has chosen over its true hero, Jesus, the agent of the evil that has been wrought upon it: Doctor Kester Lowe. We hear reports that it was his quick thinking that saved the city, that it was his innovation that allowed the quick treatment of the virus, but was it not he who first created the virus?

'As Real Christians, given to forgiveness by the will of Jesus and His Heavenly Father, we could forgive, even celebrate, the bomber who in a moment of clarity and repentance defuses his own bomb and in so doing saves the day. But if that bomber were to build another bomb? What then? Would we place him on a pedestal? Would we allow him to take from us our trust, our time, our bodies, our lives? No.

'And yet today we see that the man on the pedestal, Doctor Kester Lowe, still stands. He is insensible to the fact that he is opening the doors to a second attack. This atheist, on his pedestal, believes he stands the highest being in the known Universe. And believing himself the highest point, the greatest creator and controller, he looks down. He looks down on you, seeing only your faces looking up at him. But should he look harder, beneath you he will see the ground and beneath the ground the threat of hellfire. For he and his colleagues are planning another show. For he is building another bomb.

'In the absence of any clear perpetrator for this unlikely attack we must ask ourselves, could it be the will of God? Whether metaphorically or actually an act of God, God's point is made. And even if perpetrated by a sick soul who wishes nothing but harm on his fellow humans, by a lost individual seeking revenge for some private wrong, we cannot deny that any act perpetrated under the eyes of God, as all acts are, must be His will. God is a paradox. That He may use agents of evil even for His own powers of healing is testament to His all-powerful nature.

'Are you one of the ones looking up at Kester Lowe on his pedestal now? If you are, I ask you to look past him, look past your bomber hero to the sky above him and see your true hero, Jesus, expansive as the Universe, opening His arms to forgive all below him.

'And seeing His open arms, let us not mistake His forgiveness. Our merciful God is not shy of punishment when that punishment is the conduit for change and enlightenment, when the absence of punishment may allow widespread folly to cement its grip on our erstwhile congregation. Let us strive to understand what God's purpose is and join in bringing his plans to fruition. What now for those souls He sought to educate?

'Yes, it is in His nature to forgive the greatest of sins, but does this mean we should let sin run amuck? Of course not. We are His children and we are educated by His word. We know right and wrong and we can choose to expunge the wrongdoing that is happening before our eyes. We must understand that sometimes punishment is the vehicle of His forgiveness. And so, should it be necessary, we must expect punishment. Nay, children, we should welcome punishment in the glorious knowledge that where the Father punishes, the Son will always forgive.

'And should it be necessary? That is up to each of you. Without the sin, there need be no punishment.

'Now is the time to take the hand of the Real Church and repent. Now, on the eve of the Real Church's expulsion from the City, let us reconsider the perceived absence of religion in the City's rotting heart. Let us say loud and clear to our politicians, our leaders: we need a guide. We need a guide here and now, not just without but within those walls, a guide to protect us all and to bring us all to the right path, to lead us away from abuse and degradation, away from the worship of false idols. To lead us home to Jesus.'

Blotch stepped back from the parapet, blobs of light obscuring his vision, as if he were looking through a giant microscope slide. He felt larger than himself, powerful. God had surely spoken through him. And God would surely see good to move his promotion along. He picked up his notes from the parapet. It was right to take out the Son/Father, good cop/bad cop analogy, he thought. He was getting the hang of this.

'Not bad at all, Blotch.' Clarke was standing just inside the door.

'Thank you, Your Reverence,' Blotch said, allowing himself to sound pleased.

'Rather good in fact.'

Blotch watched as Clarke came across the room towards him, parts of his body erased by the light blobs, nightmarish.

'I've just put in a second request to the City authorities for a meeting with the Mayor. Hopefully it should come across the Mayor's desk while your words are still fresh in his head. We'll get back in there yet.'

-o-

Dee sat in the bar with John and Betta, trying her best to shake the dark mood that hung over her. It was hard when all they would talk about was bloody Kester and his fashion shows. And even harder were the pitying and apologetic looks they shot her every time they said something they thought might get to her.

'I'm so excited,' Betta said. 'It's going to be brilliant! Sorry Dee.'

'It's going to be pretty similar to the last one,' John said, taking a sip of his pint.

John was fine to be with. He wouldn't apologise for anything.

'No, no,' Betta said, 'it'll be totally different – different viruses, different band, different models.'

'I don't know why you're so excited about meeting the models,' John said. 'They were just plebs two weeks ago. Two weeks of model training won't have changed them. They're not rich or anything.'

Dee smirked.

'You're such a spoilsport, John,' Betta said. 'You loved the last one. Don't pretend you didn't.'

'It was pretty cool,' John said. 'But then that guy punched me.'

'John, there's always some guy who punches you – you need to get less drunk at these things or get over it.'

'What's he getting over?' Sienna asked, sliding into the booth beside Betta.

'Hi,' said John. 'Getting punched when I'm drunk.'

'Fair enough,' Sienna said.

The barman turned up the sound on the display and most of the people in the bar stopped what they were doing to watch, assuming something interesting must be on. It was another Real Church broadcast being reported on the news.

'God,' said Dee, 'you can't get away from them. When will they give it a rest?'

'Not until they've got whatever it is they want,' John said.

'So not until they bring down the City culture – they'll be at it for a while then,' Betta said. 'Hey, do you think they did it, like all the sites are saying?'

Dee watched her. It was hard to believe that she was really interested in all this stuff. Dee had chosen to believe in the past that Betta's bimboid exterior was cover for a serious scientific intelligence, but she was beginning to doubt it. The more time she spent with Betta, particularly with Sienna around, the more she was annoyed by her.

'You mean did they release the virus?' John asked.

'Yeah, why not?' Betta said.

'Because they're a bunch of fundamentalist incompetents?' Dee said. She felt her heart rate rising and concentrated on holding her glass in a relaxed fashion. Was it that obvious it was them?

'Like you say,' Betta said, 'the attack didn't work. They're incompetent. Clearly planned and executed by morons. Super-quick to come out with a sermon weren't they? But here's the worrying thing – me and Sienna were talking about it – the only place the virus could have come from is the department –'

'The MoD you mean,' Dee said. 'Kester was on secondment

when he made the virus. Why would there be anything at the department?'

Dee had been dreading this moment since she saw the first news report about the attack. But everything was clean. There was no evidence. And they couldn't see her desires – to see Kester's viruses ripping across the City, to see him strung up by an angry mob in the square outside V. Desires she hadn't seen fulfilled this time, but the second virus…she swallowed back a sick excitement, was momentarily repulsed by herself.

'True, there shouldn't be anything at the department, but whose security is more lax?' Betta raised her eyebrows.

'Betta, you've got some Scooby-Doo complex going on,' John said, 'I swear it. People are copying viral technologies all the time – it's not rocket science. If you ask me it's probably come from the Chinese. They're masters at copying military technologies. Who wants a drink?'

A chorus of 'me's rang out from the table, and one or two from further afield.

'Alright, don't pen me in then,' John said. 'Come on, move your arse.'

'So what does this new announcement mean?' Sienna egged Betta on. 'They made an announcement just *after* the attack. Does this mean another attack has already happened and we don't know about it yet? Or that one is going to happen at the next fashion show? Didn't it sound a little bit like an ultimatum to you?' She put on a New York accent. 'It would be a shame if something bad were to happen to your precious Ciddy – maybe if you were to, eh, let us back in we might be able to mitigate that risk for you boys.'

'I've been keeping a good eye on the sites and the general consensus is that even if they were planning it, they could never pull it off. They've got lucky once, but the first attack came through the Pigs and there's no way they'll get past the screening twice. John was just telling me that V have loaned Kester out as a consultant to the Pig consortium to advise them on any possible threats. He's redesigning their screening process to account for any methods he knows about for wrapping malicious viruses in with their product.'

'So that's the end of it then?' Dee said. 'And Kester's the big hero.' The word caught in her throat. She hoped the disappointment hadn't come through in her voice.

'That's our boy,' John said, putting down a large G&T in front of each of them.

'John,' Betta said, 'you didn't even ask us what we wanted.'

'I know what every lady wants,' John said.

'Get off.' Betta shoved him as he sat back down deliberately close to her.

Sienna stared up at the television for a moment. 'Of course, if they've got another virus, who knows – they might manage to sell it on to someone who does have the wherewithal to effect some kind of attack,' she said.

'Oh please,' John said. 'I'm with Dee on this – if it is the Real Church they're incompetent, they got lucky. And they didn't even get that lucky – it came to nothing in the end. They may not even have another virus. We don't know until someone finds out how they got the first one.'

'But it could be bad news if it turns out it's from us,' Betta said.

'It's not from us,' Dee said, then shook her head. They couldn't get suspicious.

'And how do you know?' Betta said. 'You keep saying it's not but how can you be sure?'

'We don't have any record of the project. It was black-coded – short of destroying Kester's brain it couldn't be any more secure.'

'Oh.' Betta's face fell. 'I suppose.'

'Plus,' Dee said, 'whoever did it would be unlikely to have the knowhow and equipment to manufacture the thing from scratch themselves – the Church almost certainly doesn't.' She paused for a moment. 'So they must have got a live sample from somewhere. And when I say somewhere I mean the MoD – another Government cock-up – what a surprise.'

'Don't be dull,' Betta said, pouting.

'Sorry, mate.' John put an arm around Betta. 'I know you sorely wanted us to be involved in a terrorist conspiracy to overthrow my best friend's employers.'

'So there's someone big involved,' Sienna said. Her eyes misted over as she retreated back into thoughts of conspiracy. 'They might attack again after all.'

'Maybe,' Dee said, throwing the rest of her drink down her throat. 'V's second big event is coming up – it's good timing.'

Betta and Sienna looked at Dee, then back at each other and

huddled into the corner, continuing their discussion. John rolled his eyes at the ceiling and gazed at Dee for a minute.

'I can't believe you're encouraging them.'

She laughed without emotion and shrugged. Why was she? She wasn't sure. Did she really want it to succeed? Suddenly all their Books beeped at once. Betta and Sienna started rummaging in their bags. Betta got there first.

'Oh what?' she said. 'The Director's sent round an interview schedule from the Met – we're all on it.'

John shook his head. He and Dee ignored their Books.

'You know it is pretty cool though, isn't it?' John said. 'How Kester came to the rescue like that? You know he's working on some pretty cool stuff at the moment – you remember how –'

'John.' Dee stared at John with sharks' eyes, her white face hardening further. No, even John was becoming insufferable. He wanted her and Kester to talk again, if only to repair his own social scene. No doubt Kester claimed to be working on his screens. 'I don't want to know.'

'No, it's exciting – listen, he's –'

'John.' Dee stood up to leave. 'I'd rather listen to brown noise.'

-o-

Cherry nursed her small glass of white port, taking pleasure in the thick slick of spirit that slid down the glass after each sip. A second glass sat next to it. It struck her as a late-night drink, a drink to be had in the bar of an old hotel, possibly with an old gentleman, but in the darkness of the wine bar it seemed allowable, even at this early hour. The place was half full and she enjoyed the unspoken pact she had taken with the rest of the clientele to make the bar another time and place, to make it midnight, winter, two hundred years ago.

On the way over, everything had been Kester Lowe. It looked like the Church's plan had backfired in style, which brought a smile to Cherry's lips. She had stopped to watch one of the news clips on the street – Kester being made to look more like a hero than anything, talking like an idealist and a true scientist. He was quite a good-looking guy, she had decided. When she had first arrived at V this hadn't struck her, but his lack of self-regard was charming and the more she saw his face, the more she liked it. Though his clothes were chosen for him, she liked the way he picked off all the advertisements and logos – in his own quiet way he was nobody's man. Whether that was really him or whether it was the V image department, of course, was anyone's guess.

'What a gentleman,' Dee said, sliding onto the low stool opposite Cherry. 'You've bought me a drink.'

Cherry slid the second glass of port across to Dee and watched as she removed her coat, shrugging it off her shoulders so it fell inside out onto the back of the chair.

'Drinking alone at this time of day is not to my taste,' Cherry said and raised her glass. 'Besides, we are celebrating are we not?'

'Celebrating what?'

'The success of phase one.'

'Success? You call that success?'

'You've got the first half of your funding and neither of us have been caught – I call that success. Whether the Church's stupid plan works is neither here nor there to me.' It felt untrue to her. It was untrue.

'To you...' Dee said, then stopped. 'Let's get the rest of this out of the way. The stuff is in the box, like before. Just one this time though, as per the new instructions. And this one is for infecting the people at V, right?'

'Right. What can you tell me about this one? How does it work when the person's wearing it?'

'Wearing isn't really the right term in this case. It's the nature of this particular virus – it has no real visible symptoms, aside from the possibility of moderate weeping of the tear ducts. Standard Mexodrol eyedrops will control that.'

'Moderate weeping of the tear ducts?'

'That's how Kester described it in the literature.'

'Runny eyes?'

'Yes.'

'OK, runny eyes. But what would it do to the people who got it, this virus?'

'Technically this isn't a virus. It's based on an obligate intracellular parasite. It's paired with a specially designed virus which controls and then eliminates the parasite once its job is done so that it can't be passed on.'

'Blah blah blah, when its job is done. What is its job?'

'It makes women infertile.'

'What?'

'It makes women infertile.' Dee held her hands out a little.

'But...' No wonder Blotch had been cagey about this part. 'He seriously expects me to infect myself with this thing?'

'Oh.' Dee sat back a little. 'You're the conduit.'

Cherry stared at Dee. She wasn't sure what else to say. A smile played on Dee's lips and Cherry realised she was being toyed with.

'No problem. I've included a direct-acting version of the control virus. Once you've infected enough people but before you are sterilised you administer the virus – cheerio bacterium – and it'll be as if you never had it. That's how it's designed to work, although obviously the control virus normally performs its deletion once the damage is done – it's a population control device, biological spaying. Of course it's designed to be used by people who know they are using it and self-quarantine at a private clinic, or those who are state quarantined. Used a lot in China. There are instructions included, in English.'

'But won't it show up on everyone's screens as an unidentified infection? They'd spot it straight away.'

'No. It's a controlled substance – it's already on the Stark database and flagged as an approved medical therapeutic. The screens will think they are supposed to ignore it – they don't know the infected people aren't in quarantine. Wear it for less than a week and you should be safe.'

'Right, that's...That's OK for me, I guess.'

'Yes.' Dee took a sip of her port, put it down, and then lifted it for another sip. Still staring into her glass she asked, 'You're infecting the models presumably, for the next show?'

'Yes.' Cherry's nerves were fizzing. She felt as if the box could infect her from where it sat on the floor between them, as if the infection were crawling up her inside leg like a line of ants.

'And Kester?'

'What?' Cherry's attention was shredded.

'You'll infect Kester? And that bitch, Farrell?'

'I don't know,' Cherry said, taken aback by the sudden venom in

Dee's voice. 'He...the two of them spent some time with the models before the last show, I know that much, but they're pretty busy...and it's not in the brief – Blotch's targets are the VIPs.' This didn't feel right. 'Won't they trace it back to me?'

'No. Not with the amount of shagging that goes on in that place. By the time they realise it's out there, so many people will have it that it could have come from anywhere. And by that point you'll be clean. Getting cold feet?'

'No.'

'Your fabulous new life depends on it right?'

Dee looked like a doll from a horror movie, dead-eyed and painted. Cherry looked down at the table. She could feel Dee's presence growing, as if she were standing up in front of her, shadow stretching across the ceiling of the archway.

'My funding depends on it too,' Dee said, 'so you'd better not get jittery.'

Cherry wasn't used to being faced down. She forced herself to look up to make eye-contact, but Dee had already turned away.

-o-

Dee walked away from the table. Kester Lowe. The walls seemed to bulge as she walked through the bar, the room fishbowling as if she was seeing everything through a spyhole. The dark wood should buckle, bending like that, the whole place splinter around her. She swiftened her pace, heading for the staircase that led up to ground level. Doctor Kester Lowe.

Outside, the sky was clear and the air warm. She tried to let it in, let it wash him out of her, wash out the darkness. The sun was already low on the horizon, but its heat was everywhere, leeching from tarmac, bricks, paving slabs. In the City the air would already be cold. The sun wouldn't have lain on the surfaces for long enough to leave any of itself behind. Dee walked with purpose. Her apartment was south of the river, a forty-minute walk from the bar near the Strand. She felt as if there was a thick layer of silicone between her feet and the pavement, as if she were walking slightly raised, trailing behind, above herself, as if she might detach at any minute, be left hanging like a puff of smoke above the pavement as her body walked on without her.

'Kester.'

The name jumped out at her from a passing conversation, shocked her. Two giggling students. She stared at them as they disappeared behind her into the crowded slope of Villiers Street. She took a few deep breaths, blowing out deliberately each time, and felt calmer again as she mounted the steps to the Hungerford Bridge. As she walked across the bridge she tried to clear her mind, letting the early evening scene lift her – the lights of London bringing the skyline to life, picking out landmarks and lighting the river in carnival colours.

Her gaze alighted on the bright images flitting across the walls of the Royal Festival Hall. As she walked closer, they slowly came into focus. A band playing, models striding, Farrell, Kester. They were playing footage of the fashion show right across the walls of the building. How could he get away with it? She looked down, swallowing hard, and walked on as if there were a mugger at her back.

Crossing under the arch of the bridges on the other side, she was faced with him again, in billboard form. She moved close to the river and walked on, keeping her eyes on the slow-moving water all the way along the embankment to Vauxhall. It didn't work. He was there too. He should have been destroyed. Why wasn't he in pieces? She could be saying it to him right now – *I told you so Kester.* This ludicrous fame should be his undoing. He should be crawling back to her, ready to finish what they'd started. Worse still, she wasn't the only one who could see through his fraudulent claim to being a hero. The Real Church saw it too and that infuriated her further. They had the perfect opportunity to attack Kester and Farrell personally and they were going to pass it up. He was going to escape again.

She crossed the road and ducked through the back street to Pleasure Garden Mews. It wasn't a real mews. They had hardly finished building the neat low complex of houses when they started building flats on top. She took the lift.

Back in her apartment, Dee took out her Book, flicked on her messages and went straight to the kettle. She did everything with artificial calm, with detached precision. Everything was normal. Yes, everything was fine. Someone should make him pay. Kester's nickname for the second virus popped into her head: Ladies' Choice.

'Hello, dear, it's just me.' Kester's mum's voice came through the house, high and concerned. 'Just wanted to see how you were.' She was a saccharine cartoon bird, cocking its head. Dee folded her arms for a second to stop her hands from shaking, then finished filling the kettle and strode quickly through the flat. 'And I wanted to talk to you about Kester and this Alexis girl – find out what she's like.' Dee picked up pace. 'You know boys – you can't get anything out of them. I wish you two would see each other a bit more, dear.' She hit the delete icon on the wall with her fist. 'He does miss you so.' She slapped it with her palm. It stopped.

Dee sat down in the middle of her couch and put her hands to her mouth.

Chapter 19

'You must just love your job, sir,' Gerald said, clasping his hands behind his back and rocking forward onto the balls of his feet.

Gerald seemed impressed with the competition results. Either that or he was keen to meet the new models. The pictures were compelling.

'I get to choose six from this shortlist?' Kester asked.

'Yes,' Gerald said. 'And they'll wear the headline virus along with a couple of our existing models.'

'Right. And who chose the shortlist?'

'Chen, Gaunt and Yule. I sat in on their deliberations to make sure they kept the balance right.'

'Not Farrell?'

'I think there was a feeling that Farrell may have a conflict of interests, if you know what I mean, sir.'

'And you're here to make sure I don't cause an imbalance in the final line-up I guess?'

'Something like that.'

Kester had the full length photos spread out on his desk before him. There were 18 on the shortlist, nine men and nine women.

'It feels wrong, Gerald, judging people solely on their looks.' Kester cast his eyes across the photos once again. 'I mean on first impressions – I don't like his or her face or whatever.'

'Only way to do it though. These people have put themselves forward to be judged in that capacity, so what are you going to do?'

'But they're all so much better looking than normal. It's hard to choose.'

'OK. This is why I'm here. We need a decision pronto. Let's split it down to make it easier. We need even numbers of male and female models, so you get to choose three out of nine for each sex. Not so hard. Plus, we only have three of each sex who come from outside London and Chen wants at least three overall to go through, so that narrows it down too.'

'Right.' Kester watched as Gerald shuffled the pack of pouts, rearranging the photos into their groupings – male, female and extra-London. He focused on the smallest group first. The extra-Londons. 'You know next time we should get this made into a show and have the public choose.'

'We would have done it this time, sir, if we'd had time.'

'You're calling me "sir" again, Gerald. OK – get rid of spreadeagle and fake-titty lady. Is this one a man or a woman?'

Gerald slid the two rejects from the table and picked up his notes.

'Man.'

Kester made a small surprised noise and continued to stare at the four remaining pictures in the group.

Forty-five minutes later, Kester had only two male models to eliminate.

'I just don't know, Gerald. It feels weird choosing one guy over another.'

'Can I help you with that?' Alexis said as the door slid shut behind her. 'I want to make sure there's something in there that takes my fancy too.'

'I'll leave you two to it,' Gerald said. 'Excuse me.'

'Keep this one.' Alexis pointed to a young Chinese man. 'And definitely this one.'

'Mrs Farrell,' Kester said with a cautious grin, 'we aren't choosing for ourselves but for our clients. I'm looking with the eyes of a sex-crazed celebrity, not with my own.'

Farrell laughed and pulled Kester's chair out from the desk, sitting down on his knee. Her flesh was only two thin layers of fabric away.

'I'm bored of this. Get rid of two of those men for me, will you?' Kester nodded at the photos.

'And what's in it for me?'

Alexis stood up in front of him and leaned over the photos in an exaggerated pose. The fabric of her trousers stretched tight over her buttocks, inches from Kester's face.

'I was thinking,' Kester said as he stood up and bent over her, placing a hand on top of each of hers on the desk, 'we should go to the PlayPen and break the rules.'

'Well, it might be tough choosing between the rest of these models. Perhaps I could take some of these delicious images with me.'

Kester looked down at the table over her shoulder. He saw her point. Eight pairs of beautiful eyes fixed on him like searchlights as he slipped a hand round and down the glide of her hip.

The buzzer on Kester's desk went and he growled.

'It's Gerald, sir. I have a message from Byron Gaunt saying he's sent over your "pimping rota" – said you'd know what that meant – along with an update on the pre-show auction clients.'

'Thanks, Gerald.'

Pimping rota. He tensed. Alexis slid out from underneath his arms and walked to the window. He followed her with his eyes. Had they been calling it that? Joking about it? He could feel his form filling up with repressed energy, his body tightening. By the time Alexis spoke he was buzzing with rage.

'Kester –'

'No, Alexis,' Kester said. He spoke as if to a dog, surprising himself.

'No?' Alexis' head snapped round. Her face was hard. 'Gaunt's just goading us.'

'Goading us.' Kester's voice sounded unfamiliar to him, shaky, as if his throat were constricted. He sat silent for a long time.

'Kester…'

'I won't do it.'

'Won't do what?'

'I won't be Chen's whore.'

Kester's anger was many-edged, directed not just at Alexis, but at everything in the room, the building, himself. Kester suppressed a snarl. He had thought she didn't like the idea of the "pimping rota" any more than he did, but they had been joking about it behind his back. And she had set up all the appointments, the auction, everything – hadn't had any problems with that.

'It's just for one week. Then we'll talk to the Board. They won't pull this stunt again.'

'Won't they?'

Alexis turned back to the window and folded her arms. Perhaps it did bother her. She hadn't dismissed his question as she normally would have.

'How can we stop them?' If he didn't push her, this would be the end of it. 'You've met Chen, right?'

Alexis rocked her body from side to side a little. She was struggling with something. Eventually she turned back to him.

'We'll make it worth their while not to.'

Kester sighed. This was the start. She was going to talk him round again. He would leave the room quite happy and wouldn't realise what had happened until he was servicing some honking millionaire.

'Your screen is ready for in vivo testing. It works, doesn't it? It's going to work.'

'What?' For a second Kester failed to see the connection. 'Are you serious?' He scrutinised her face. She couldn't joke with him about this.

'That's your bargaining chip. Take it to the Board. Chen's got the brains and the balls to take it on. I didn't want to suggest taking it to her before the first show because, to be honest, I didn't want it eclipsing my big moment – your big moment. But now...perhaps it's the right time.'

'And Stark?' Kester checked himself – why was he the one objecting?

'Come on, Kester, screw Stark. The drugs we make here are only under licence until the end of March, then what happens? Stark Wellbury keeps its half of the pie and everyone else rushes in to take a bite of ours. And once it's properly proven that the long-term users' immune systems are shot and they don't even need the drugs any more the market's going to shrink even further. We'll be screwed. Chen not only needs this, she's been actively searching for it – for something this big. The viruses are big, but they're not big enough to fill the hole left by the drugs.'

'But what about Farmer? The ethics department? Farmer's a shareholder at Stark Wellbury isn't he? And he sits on the London Board of Health. We'll never get a licence to produce the things.'

'So what was the point in developing them, Kester? Did you think you'd magically get a licence on your own, make your fortune?'

'I'm not an idiot, Alexis. I know –'

'Or you'd give the plans to the people – let them build their own? Come off it. We'll just do it. You make the things, we get it all planned out and we release the details pending licence. They won't be able to stop us then.'

'What?'

'Release the details pending licence – I've seen it done before. You want to influence Government so you make sure everybody knows you've created something "good" and something that they want. Put the Government in the position where they can only say yes, where they're under pressure to give it the go-ahead.'

'But with what proof it works? How do we get together a trial of that size without alerting anyone?'

'Staff – everybody at V – how many employees do we have? Even for drug development you only need a few hundred test subjects minimum for phase one and two development – we're well above that. We could have a whole building full of people living, working, using these things – no-one's going to be able to ignore that.'

'Alexis…' Kester felt a smile building.

'You know this is the only chance you'll ever get to make these things – actually make them and release them. We've got the infrastructure, the test subjects, the money – things you just didn't have at the Institute – you were never going to get funding from anywhere legitimate to develop rival screen technology – Stark is everywhere. Sure you could just rock up, whop it out and wait for the highest bidder, but it looks like you've got problems with that.'

Kester snorted.

'We've already got everything you need here, Kester. Let's do it.'

Kester felt light in his chair. He reached out to his Book and tapped an icon, looked up at his wall to see the streams of data coming in from the torso testing. It could happen. It could finally happen and he was objecting. He laughed.

'You'll talk to Chen?' he asked.

His Book beeped.

'Who is it?'

'Just Gerald.'

'I'll talk to Chen. Don't worry about it. She'll go for it. I guarantee it. I'll be over later.'

Once Alexis had closed the door, Kester walked into his living quarters, clutching his Book close. He looked again. Couldn't be. It was a message from Dee. *Can I come and see you?* He went straight to his bar and took a beer from the fridge. Another beep. Gerald. *We need a final decision.* Kester held the beer to his forehead for a few seconds, then walked back into his office. Later came and went. Alexis didn't come.

The competition winners' pictures were released the next day, Saturday, around the time that Kester got another message from Dee. *Let's meet up.* He deleted it.

On Sunday her message interrupted his appointment to view the Vspa plans. *Can I see you?* He waited a few hours, then deleted it.

Just after lunch on Monday, as he was calling Alexis to ask her if she had spoken to Chen, another arrived. *Shall we get together this week?* Alexis hadn't spoken to Chen. He spent forty minutes examining the wording of the message, then archived it.

On Tuesday, Kester was inspecting how the two new viruses had presented on their last test subjects when the message arrived. *I need to see you.* He archived it. Later, back in his living quarters, he took to his bed with a glass of red wine, opened up the two archived messages and compared them until he had finished the glass.

Wednesday's arrived late at night, just when Kester had stopped expecting it and had retreated to his private isolation suite to check on his torsos. He was flicking through pages of splendid data on his Book. It was working. It was working and there was nobody here to share it with. Alexis had declined his invitation to come up, perhaps aware that she couldn't be in the room without admitting that she hadn't yet spoken to Chen. He held the edge of his Book to his forehead and pressed until it hurt, gritting his teeth. Beep. *I need to see you.* Kester sat at his desk, the message open on his Book beside him and went over the data again. He talked as if Dee were there. He told her how well it was all working, how it worked and what the potential pitfalls were. Then he took to his bed with a bottle of wine, opened all the messages up and compared them until he had finished the bottle.

And, already, it was Thursday. Tomorrow the competition winners arrived and from then on in it was going to be hectic. Even more hectic. Two weeks until the show. This week entailed sorting the models out, training them, preparing for the auction, the auction itself and finally Kester's first appointment. Everyone was in perpetual motion, moving between offices, talking and walking in the corridors, never still. Kester found himself at the centre of it all, sitting at his desk, the eye of the storm. He was ready for the models. All the viruses were ready and allocated. Until the models arrived there wasn't much to do. His outfits were all chosen, his photoshoots done. The next slew of interviews didn't start until next week. But he knew that his feeling of calm was misplaced.

He looked through the glass wall that faced on to the lab. White-coated, white-masked lab technicians, bench upon bench of them, filled the room, test tubes in a rack. All working on new viruses – viruses that he would be expected to present to the Board before long. But he couldn't bring himself to care about them just yet. Shutting them out was the way to do it, he reflected as the window misted up before him, becoming a solid wall. What was he going to say to Alexis? He wouldn't know until he heard her voice.

'What?' Alexis' voice slammed down the line.

'We need to talk,' Kester said. It wasn't a great start.

'I don't have time.'

'Have you spoken to Chen yet?'

'No.'

'You said you would.'

Silence.

'If it's going to work, if we're going to bargain with this, we need to get her agreement before the appointments start.' Kester could hear himself turning teenage. He could feel how annoying he was being.

'Look. I'm on top of it, but right now you're a commodity I'm trying to sell. I can't think about anything else. I'm pleased for you that you have time on your hands to ponder your future, but I don't so if you're short of something to do go and fuck one of the models or something. Keep your mind off it.'

'On top of it? So what? You've spoken to her? You've set up a meeting? How are you on top of it?'

'Kester, drop it. When I've got something to tell you I'll let you know.'

'Oh piss off, you're not going to do it, are you?' Kester said, but she was already gone.

What an idiot. She had him dancing to her tune just like everyone else. The screens were just a convenient tool. Why would she take the screens to Chen? There was nothing in it for her. All she wanted him to be was her little celebrity puppet. She didn't want him to steal her fire with real science, for her triumphant fashion parade to be put in the corner by his screens. She had said as much herself. And why wouldn't she want him to sleep his way up the A-list? It all reflected well on her; he was hers to lend. She would never take it to Chen, even if it meant pimping him out every day of the week. How dare she use his screens to control him.

Beep. Kester's screen.

I need to see you. Come on Kester, can we just meet up?

Kester leaned forward on his desk and pressed his forehead onto the heels of his hands. He read Dee's message again. *I need to see you. Come on Kester, can we just meet up?* He picked up his Book and flicked to his appointments. *I need to see you. Come on Kester, can we just meet up?* His day was completely empty. *I need to see you. Come on Kester, can we just meet up?* He could see it sitting there in each half hour segment of his calendar: call Dee, call Dee, call Dee.

How about now? he typed. He hit send and waited.

Dee's reply was preternaturally quick. With one hand Kester messaged her to tell her which entrance to go to; with the other he started tidying his apartment. He hadn't thought this through. Chucking his Book on the bed, he straightened the covers and went to check the bathroom. By the time the door buzzer went, the place was reasonably tidy by his standards. Though it would look a mess to her. He should have called for an emergency clean.

-o-

Dee gave Kester a brief smile when he opened the door, then crossed the threshold and slipped past him before he had a chance to say anything. He let her wander around his living quarters, busying himself with the drinks machine, unsure how to begin. Having passed her a coffee he leaned against the side wall of his apartment by the bar, watching while she chose her seat with apparent care.

'So,' Dee said, finally, 'I saw you on the news.'

'You did?'

She had made herself small on the couch, hands cupped around her mug. The room seemed to bend around her. Her face was colder and paler than usual. Kester tried to read her, but she seemed as if she had risen above expression. It was as if this was what her face had always been working towards and she had finally perfected it.

'I saw the fashion show. Just bits of it.'

Kester nodded and took a sip of his tea. She had cut her hair so that it swung just free of her shoulders. It was still glossy, straight, black, but the free swing of gravity made it look heavier and thicker.

'It was pretty wild.' She breathed in, expanding, then breathed out again, becoming smaller even than before.

'Are you cold?'

'No, no…a little.'

Kester got up and touched his Book, adjusting the thermostat. His heating came to life with a small rumble.

'Did you choose all this yourself?' Dee put a hand out to the apple-green leather and stroked it as she looked around the room. Her eyes rested on the carved oak four-poster and stayed there.

'Yes,' Kester said.

'Is that real?'

'A real bed? No, that one's just for show. I have bunk beds round the back.'

Dee looked confused for a second and then laughed.

'Kester,' she said. Her smile didn't last, but it left an impression on her face, a warm hand pressed on frost. 'Still not taking things too seriously then?'

'It's hard to in this place. I should show you…'

He stopped himself. No he shouldn't. He should not show her the exchange booths on the eighteenth floor, with their rack of cartoon character sex-toys. That would be an extraordinarily bad idea. What he should show her was his private lab, his screens, but not yet. He wasn't sure how she would react. It had been her idea too. He should wait until he knew how fully he was forgiven.

'Show me what?' There was a smile again, but this time a suspicious one.

'Oh, just, there's loads of crazy stuff. You've heard of the PlayPen right?'

'Heard of it – you know I've heard of it. You said you have a pass.' Dee looked eagerly to the window, though it was frosted over. 'Is it far from here?'

It was the first time she looked real. She knew he had a pass. So she had been reading his messages, even if she hadn't been replying.

'No, it's really close. Walking distance. I've missed you, you know.'

The last words took him by surprise. He wasn't even sure they were true. It was like they were programmed in, the natural response of a man to an estranged lover who has come back to him, if they could ever have been called lovers. Had she been expecting it? he wondered. She didn't react straight away. Then she looked like she was making a decision, changing her mind about something, changing it back, an angel, a devil, flitting across her features.

'With all that excitement going on? I doubt you have,' she said, her smile confined to her lips. 'Like I said, I saw the fashion show. It all looked amazing. Those women. And the guys – foof!' She blew a breath up from her mouth, catching her fringe and sending it spraying up for a moment like a crest. It landed out of place and she shook her head until it settled as it should.

'Tell me about it. The models are crazy though. Trust me – you wouldn't want to if you could.'

'I don't know – that tall guy with the black hair, the one wearing the face-paint virus.'

Kester's body suddenly remembered soft suction, the low vibrations of a male voice transmitted through flesh. He shifted in his chair.

'I can introduce you.' He laughed nervously.

'This is horrible,' Dee said. 'Shall we get drunk?' She nodded. 'Let's get drunk.'

'Drunk? It's just gone midday!'

'I thought you kept whatever hours you liked out here in the City,' Dee said, putting her mug aside. She sprung to her feet, invigorated by having a purpose. 'Besides, this is just all too weird. I need a drink.'

'Fair enough.'

Dee had already located the bar and had picked up his ornamental glass Bond's cocktail shaker.

'Nice. Hey I know some tricks –'

She pretended to throw it, then laughed harshly at Kester's reaction. He laughed uneasily. Perhaps it was a good idea to get drunk. He wasn't sure what was happening, but it was bound to be easier with a few down him.

-o-

'Stop laughing,' Dee said, pressing her lips together in a serious face, then corpsing.

'I'm not laughing,' Kester said. 'Anyway, you're allowed to laugh.'

'But you're not allowed to be drunk!'

'Shh!' Kester said loudly, drawing sharp glances from the other people queuing for the PlayPen. 'Good thing we're not drunk then.' He smiled and nodded at a man in the next queue across, who was still staring.

At the front booth Kester grinned at the operator. 'Morning,' he said.

'Afternoon, sir,' the operator replied.

'Yes, afternoon. Listen, if I slip a couple of hundred onto your card do you think you could get us the top floor?' Kester winked. 'For private use. My company's fitting it out for –'

'Doctor Lowe, that won't be necessary. It will be cleared by the time you get there.'

Kester giggled. The operator knew who he was. He had hardly been out in public since the last show, had thought the myriad strange looks from passersby figments of his conscience.

'Are there, eh, cameras up there?'

'Not for private...functions.' The operator smiled.

'Brilliant! That's awesome, thanks.'

The top floor of the PlayPen was a perfect glass lozenge. There was nothing up there yet, just a large round padded platform in the centre. The furnishings for the show were being put together off-site and weren't due to be brought in until Monday. The previous occupants had just vacated the space – until recently it had housed a special play installation designed by a well known East London artist. Though it was shorter than the surrounding buildings, it offered a perfect view of their top floors. A block away, the towering Stark Wellbury building was just visible as it began its decon cycle, the red intensifying second on second.

Dee walked unsteadily to the wall and pressed her hands up against it, staring out at the spectacle.

'Do you remember?' she asked.

'I remember.'

Kester looked at the controller the operator had given him for the lighting and swiped a finger across the colour pad. The glass faded up to a transparent green and Kester watched as Dee's skin took on the otherworldly glow from his memory. He walked over to join her, turning and leaning beside her, his back to the glass wall. She stepped over and put her arms clumsily around his neck, leaning in against his chest. After a moment she lifted her face to his. It was a seeming invitation, but her body was stiff in his arms. Here he was again, trapped against glass. He thought of Farrell. Was this what he had intended, he wondered. He kissed her tentatively. Why take her to the top floor if not?

'Is this OK?' he asked.

She nodded, avoiding eye-contact. He looked down at the controller. He flicked it to black and they were enveloped in a solid room of dark. He reached out his hands and felt her form.

'Better?' he mumbled, as he slipped his hands under her jacket.

She kissed him in reply, putting a hand to the back of his head and gripping his hair until it burned at its roots.

The air was warm, body temperature, and the darkness thick around them, making their movements slow wrestling. They might have been wrapped in a dense velvet blanket. Every hand she laid on him felt as if it would curl up any moment into a fist. Her caresses were heavy, unfamiliar, anonymous. Her nails pressed into him frequently. They made their way pushing and pulling and turning across the floor, trusting with each step it would still be there, until they reached the edge of the platform, very nearly passing it by completely. They climbed on separately, then she found him with a firm hand around his wrist and pulled him over. She was ready for him, or had turned up ready. He dismissed the notion – that was only done by wearers who couldn't afford the luxury of endless foreplay. Then he thought of nothing, just felt, retreated low into his body, wordless, absent and there was only sex.

Kester lay eyes open on the platform, revelling in his blindness. The profound darkness was calming. It made it impossible to think of anything. He might have been alone, completely alone, non-existent.

Beep. The light from his Book shone through the fabric of his jacket, dissolving the illusion. He left it in his pocket, but its rectangle of light had opened a portal for everything else to come rushing back in.

Kester's head was beginning to hurt. He had drunk too much, not enough. He closed his eyes. Dee had forgiven him, then, but something wasn't quite right. This wasn't the sort of forgiveness he needed. Things were complicated again, still. There was Farrell. The thought of her brought a gush of defiance.

'My screens are working,' he said, half to himself, a consolation.

'Screens?' Dee's voice came. He was not alone, was not on his bed with his eyes shut. He wished it was Alexis by his side and not Dee. She didn't fit.

'John told you about them?' Kester asked.

'No.' It was a small no, scared of itself.

'Viral screens. No drugs. Like we always talked about. It works. They work. I'm torso testing them now.' His answer was tired. He couldn't be bothered explaining more. It was the wrong time.

'The company –'

'I've done it in my own time. *I* did it.'

For a long time, Dee didn't reply. The dark was shaking.

'Kester, that's…' She had moved, was sitting up. 'That's amazing.'

She was upset. Kester closed his eyes. What had he done now? She was pissed off because they were supposed to have built the screens together. Or maybe it was too soon. He breathed slowly for a few minutes. He wished again he was in his own bed, was close to his shower.

Beep.

Swearing, Kester sat up and took his Book out.

I'm in your office. Where are you? You'll want to hear this.

'Fuck,' Kester said. She had done it. She'd talked to Chen.

'Work?'

'Yeah, look…'

Kester wasn't sure how to continue. He felt he had just walked into his apartment to find it had been burgled. Everything was inside out, upside down. The mess went on beyond his field of vision and was just starting to come into focus.

'I know, Kester. I'm busy too. I think maybe we should just – I don't know. Maybe this wasn't such a good idea. Maybe I could see you after the show. Sober. As friends.'

Kester searched around for the controller and flicked the lights on to a low grey, an overcast sunrise. Dee was already dressed and sitting on the edge of the platform.

'You know what...' Kester said, shrugging and shaking his head. 'Yeah. I guess.' He stood up and started to pull his clothes on. 'I'll walk you to the tube.'

'It's OK.'

He watched as Dee padded to the glass staircase that descended through the floor to the lift. She tiptoed down it, as if trying not to disturb someone.

-o-

Alexis was in Kester's office when he got back. Still in his office? In his office again? He wasn't sure. He watched her from his living quarters and paced back and forth for a few minutes, then he took his jacket off and stood still. He must stop sweating, must be sober. His head was still throbbing and he felt a lingering drunken ineptitude. He went into the bathroom, did his teeth and put on some deodorant. He would want to hear this, she had said. It must be Chen. She must have spoken to Chen. There was nothing else he wanted to hear right now.

'Alexis,' he said as he entered his office, still a little out of breath, 'I got your message – sorry about that, I was at the PlayPen. You were right, I had too much time on my hands, had to get out.'

Alexis surveyed him, eyes narrow, judging perhaps whether he looked like he had been at the PlayPen.

'What did you want to tell me?' he asked.

'I thought you'd like to know.' She looked less excited than Kester had hoped. Maybe it was bad news. 'We've confirmed your Saturday night appointment. It's Pera Pera.'

'What? Oh.'

'Pera Pera – Latin raptress superstar?'

'Yes. I know who you mean.'

'Then what? She's not big enough for you?'

'Yeah, sure. Just, you know...did I have to be here to hear this?' Kester threw himself down on the couch and flicked on his display.

'I thought you might want to celebrate.' The suggestion would normally have come with a slathering of sleaze. Now it came as an accusation.

'OK, watch me – woo-hoo! Well done. Pera Pera. She's a pretty big deal.' Kester kept his eyes on the display, flicking channels. 'And for you – is she worth sharing me with? Is she rich and famous enough for your super-elite shag club?'

Alexis came closer. Kester glanced up in time to catch her nostrils flaring a little, an involuntary tightening of the muscles beneath her eyes.

'Are you drunk?' she asked.

'Yes.' Kester shrugged. 'A bit.'

Alexis took a deep breath and gave him a reproachful look.

'She meets my standards just fine, Kester. I had hoped I might make this as painless as possible for you. For both of us.' She paused. 'And don't get pissy with me. I've organised a meeting with Chen for Monday, if that's what you wanted to hear.'

Kester jerked his head up, unable to contain his shock. Was it really happening? Relaxing again, he became suspicious; she had organised a meeting, hadn't actually spoken to Chen. He needn't feel guilty just yet.

'You just need to show willing for the weekend's appointments. Make it clear that you'll hold up your end if she agrees. We need Chen in the best mood possible. Agreed? I don't want her to feel she's being blackmailed.'

'Agreed.' Kester couldn't argue there.

'Were you really at the PlayPen?' Alexis asked, eyes narrowing again.

'Yes.'

'Not out on the shag somewhere?'

'No.'

'Who were you with?'

'Dee.' There was no reason to hide it from her. 'From the department.'

Alexis sneered a little and stepped back from him. 'The bitch who threw wine on you? You made up then?'

'Sort of.'

'Good. The fewer enemies you have right now the better. Give her a ticket to the show if she wants one. Give her two. And you're free to take your friends to the PlayPen, but don't go there drunk again. You know we're liable to lose our company licence.'

'They didn't seem to care,' Kester said, laughing a little. He relaxed for a moment, long enough for the drink to talk. 'It's me, Doctor Kester Lowe.'

'Sober up, Kester.' Alexis turned and walked to the door.

Chapter 20

Cherry banged a fist on the wall above her desk. She had a new neighbour at Dempsey's who liked to listen to banging ratchet techno at breakfast to get himself keyed up for the day. The noise lowered. It would be back to the same level or higher within a few minutes – he seemed to think he might be able to sneak it up on her without her noticing – but any respite was better than none. She would ask Gerald if it was alright to stay in the lab for a few nights if it got too much. Some of the suites were empty and he would be a gentleman about it. Her second pay was through and her funds were starting to build up, so she could start to look for somewhere decent to stay soon.

She unfolded the sheet of instructions that Dee had included in the shoebox and flattened them out on her desk. They were printed with a hand-scrawled note at the bottom. They were mostly to the point, but here and there Dee's snide tone crept in enough to get Cherry's hackles up.

Lay off it until four days before the show, then put on the virus and infect whoever you like – the more the merrier as far as I'm concerned. I'm sure your employer would agree.

Once the virus has worked, not normally before six days or so, the control virus will kick in and female subjects may start to experience symptoms – you don't want this happening before the models get their chance to spread it to the clients and you don't want the symptoms presenting until after the show and after you're clear of infection so it can't be traced.

When you're done, use your control virus – remember you have to use this after your four days are up or you risk damaging yourself.

I've included some eyedrops that will control the weeping should you be lucky enough to experience it.

Cherry looked in the shoebox again. The viral applicator was like a long fat syringe. The hand-written postscript assured her that this was the best way to establish an infection quickly and at the necessary levels. Though it made some sense, she felt Dee might be having a laugh on her. She clenched her pelvic floor involuntarily and shuddered. It was all a bit farmyard for her liking.

She unclipped the lid of the envirobox. The liquid inside the vial looked innocuous enough. She imagined injecting herself, imagined a scuttling army of microscopic snapping mouths making its way into her reproductive system and chowing down. Putting a hand to her stomach, she closed the envirobox lid and put it back in the shoebox.

Her Book beeped. It was Gerald passing on an order from Farrell to go and see Doctor Lowe about "maximum spread". She assumed he meant the consultancy work she had been doing on boosting infection rates amongst clients. *Two pm OK?* she messaged back, *I'm at home.* He hadn't said anything about having to do it today, but it was a good reason to go back to the office and escape the encroaching techno.

Cherry rummaged in her rucksack. There was something she meant to take with her last time and had forgotten. When she found it she would remember what it was. As she rooted in the various pockets, a folded piece of paper came to hand. Was this it? No, it was a flyer for Tim's show. She didn't remember packing it; he must have sneaked it in there in the hope of persuading her to tell some people about the show. A sick feeling started to creep up from her stomach until she noticed the dates – the first week-long show had passed, but the second was opening tonight. She could still make it. Rooting again with renewed vigour, Cherry found what she had been looking for – lip balm. Was that it? How mundane. Still, it did annoy her when she didn't have any. She tucked it in her pocket, shoved the rucksack back under her bed and pulled on her coat.

-o-

'I should warn you that while I respect your input and everything…' Kester started to explain himself then looked up at Cherry and tailed off.

'I know,' Cherry said. 'Farrell set it up. Don't worry – I'll tell you enough to cover you if she asks. I've done you a crib sheet.'

'Oh.'

Kester sounded surprised that she was so organised. Cherry was unsure whether to be offended or pleased.

'I want to get away sharp anyway.'

'Hot date?' Kester grinned.

'A friend's gallery opening. I say opening – the show was already on for one week a couple of months ago, so it's a reopening really. Still, free champagne is free champagne, right?'

'Right.' Kester chuckled. 'Wish I was coming with you.'

He sighed and looked up at the wall of reports beside him. Cherry wavered on the spot for a moment. She was supposed to be getting close to him, found herself wanting to get close to him.

'You could come if you wanted to,' she said, trying to strike a balance between encouragement and nonchalance.

Kester looked her in the eye. He seemed so clean. It was nice to look at a face that didn't have either expressed symptoms or their remnants. She held his gaze and raised her eyebrows. His shoulders fell and he glanced guiltily back up at the board.

'I really wish I could. But I've got actual important science stuff to do that I won't be able to finish off once I'm out on the meat cart servicing our clients. Apart from anything else it's Alexis' birthday on Sunday and I haven't got her anything – this would have been a good opportunity. Her apartment is as bare as a prison cell.' He stared up at the ceiling for a moment. 'What sort of stuff does your friend paint?'

Cherry dug in her pocket and took out the flyer.

'There's not anything of his on here. But this is how the show is billed.'

'Near past and near future? Interesting. Maybe you could send me some pictures if there's anything you think she'd like.'

Cherry gave an involuntary laugh. The idea that she might know what Alexis Farrell would like was farfetched. They were both women, but as far as Cherry was concerned that was where the similarities ended.

'Point taken,' Kester said. 'I'm thinking something dramatic – something fiery, dark, but not too...you know.' He shrugged his shoulders and gave a clueless smirk. 'Just if you see anything.'

'Actually, I think I have just the thing in mind. I'll send you a picture.' Cherry pulled up a chair and sat opposite Kester. 'Now, let's go through this briefing sheet.'

-o-

John was late arriving at the bar. Kester ordered lunch for them both, then sat in the booth and fiddled with his Book. He looked again at the painting Cherry had found for him at her friend's show. It was perfect: London enclosed in a ring of fire, the riots that created London as they knew it, Alexis' London. Not just a birthday gift, he thought, a gift to assuage his guilt. He shouldn't doubt her. She said she had arranged the meeting. Though he was more comfortable doubting her somehow. He didn't want to jinx things by assuming the best.

Yawning, he rubbed his forehead. He had finished everything he needed to last night and early this morning, and now it was time to face up to his next task. He switched to calendar and flipped through his appointments. Friday night was the auction winner, Saturday Pera Pera, then during the week Tamsin Holloway, oil tycoon's daughter and professional vacuous zombie, and fat cat Basil Black. Kester shuddered. It wasn't a thing, he told himself. So he was a big guy. Not a thing. He just hadn't got round to swinging in that direction completely and it would have been nice to lose his other virginity with someone attractive. Was that shallow? He imagined Basil Black. He was sitting somewhere eating ribs with his bare hands, grease dribbling down his chin.

Kester started flicking faster and faster through his calendar, through days and days, well past any appointments, past the end of this year, the next year, on and on.

'Kester!'

Finally, John. Kester got up, smiled and hugged him.

'You alright, mate?' John said. 'You're crushing my ribs.'

'Not really.' Kester released his hold and sat back down. 'I start my new career as a high-class hooker tonight.'

'Really? Wait 'til Dee hears. Now there's selling out and there's selling out. Still, at least you haven't sold your soul.'

'You know I don't believe in the soul.' Kester took a sip of his drink and frowned. 'So how are things at the Institute? I hear they're still investigating the department – as if the virus could have come from there. You don't even keep live samples.'

'That's it really,' John said. 'It's dragging on, you know. They'll be out of our hair soon. And you know, gardening leave in September – shouldn't complain really. Word is they know it's come from them. They're tearing themselves apart with an internal investigation but I guess they need it to look like it was us.'

'Yeah,' Kester tried to sound like he cared. He knew he had failed, but there was no recovering it. 'Sorry, John. I do care.'

John looked at Kester's glass, went to the bar and returned with two more of the same.

'So tell me about it. Why the article rejection face. Who's your first client? Someone loathsome?'

'I don't know yet – whoever wins the auction. It's all happening behind closed doors and dark glasses. I won't know until I get there. Same time as the press. Not that they don't trust me. Then tomorrow night it's Pera Pera.'

'What?' John spilled a bit of his pint. 'Pera Pera? Are you fucking kidding me? I'll spot for you. Seriously, what's wrong with you? Then who?'

'Then Tamsin Holloway, then Basil Black.'

'Hold on. Black Senior or Junior? Junior I presume? Betta's going to explode with jealousy if it's BB Junior. Christ man, I know you don't normally take pickle but –'

'Junior?' Kester looked up.

'What's wrong with you, man? Don't you follow the gossip any more?'

'I'm kind of busy.'

'Black – just look him up will you. I want your job. You know you need to make the most of all this while it's yours.'

'You know if I could let you spot for me I'd be glad to,' Kester said, idly searching on Basil Black. A picture of a handsome, sleek young man appeared. He had the bone structure, and in a couple of cover shots the wardrobe, of a seventeenth-century poet.

'How's your sexy boss?' John asked, trying to change the subject. 'Are you going to bring her to our next little gathering? I hope you do.'

'I hope so too. She's promised to take the screens to Chen.' Saying it out loud, Kester was shocked by the lack of conviction in his voice.

'She will,' John said.

Kester looked up at him. It was nice of him to say, but why would he say it at all if he didn't doubt it?

'If she does, when she does, would you come and work for us?' Kester asked. He may as well cheer himself up.

'Magic! Of course I would. We all would. It'd be just like old times!' An apologetic look swept across his features. 'Well, it might not be *just* like old times without Dee.'

'You know I think even Dee might be up for it. Making the screens was her dream, our dream, so why wouldn't she be? I think she would.'

'If she didn't still want to chop your balls off.'

'What? Is she mad again? Christ, I knew something –'

'Mad again?' John leaned in, confused. 'No, I just assumed she was still building her Kester Lowe Death Machine.'

'You haven't spoken to her? We made up.'

'You made up?'

'Sort of. She came to see me.'

'You didn't do anything stupid did you?'

'No,' Kester replied too quickly. He wasn't going to admit to sleeping with her, but he had to give John something. 'We got drunk and I took her to the PlayPen.'

John sat back in his seat, shaking his head.

'At least you didn't, you know…'

John was waiting for him to admit it. He wasn't going to.

'Yeah,' Kester said, staring into his glass. 'I just get this feeling.'

'What feeling?'

Kester took a long slurp of his beer and stared up at the display on the back wall of the bar. There was a show update running. The camera was on a window on the top floor of the V building where the auction was about to take place.

'Do you think I'm being stupid, John?'

'Yes, mate. But I can't be any more specific about it than that.'

'Great. Thanks.'

'Just…make the most of it. When are you and Pera Pera making the naughty?'

'Tomorrow night, during her show.' Kester lifted his glass and looked through the beer at John.

'Tomorrow night?' John clapped his hands and rubbed them together. 'You should be at home scrubbing your sack. I want updates. Text me updates. And if you can get a picture of her –'

'John – I think she might have security with her.'

'What, in the room?'

'Well, you know…I don't know. Yule hasn't briefed me yet.'

'Hm,' John said, calming down a bit and sitting back. 'I can see why you're nervous.'

-o-

'Come on, Lex,' Kester said, 'just tell me who won the auction.'

Kester was due to arrive with his first client at ten. It was six o'clock and he had shaken off his lunchtime beers. Alexis had inspected him after his shower and had supervised as he got dressed. It had to be someone important. He was trying his best to take John's advice and get excited about it.

'Let's you and I not call it an auction, Kester,' Farrell said. 'You're making yourself sound like a slave.'

Kester raised an eyebrow at her.

'Why won't you tell me? It's a man isn't it?'

'No, it's not a man. Can you just –' Alexis bit her lip. 'Stop.'

Kester took in her expression. It was complicated, many expressions fighting one another, resulting in nothing understandable. He didn't like seeing it on Alexis' normally straightforward face, her lewd smirking beautiful face. It made her look weak. It didn't suit her.

'So is it a woman?' He would try to joke her out of it.

'What? No. I'm not telling you. Just calm down, Kester. You need to be a good boy.' Alexis narrowed her eyes. 'Shut up and put out. Keep Chen happy, remember?'

'Yes, Miss!' Kester said.

Keep Chen happy. Lex was really going to take the screens to Chen? She was? She was – why mention it like that when she didn't have to. Buoyed up, his excitement became real.

Kester acknowledged Gaunt's presence in the doorway. 'But just...if you were supposed to be sleeping with someone in an hour's time, wouldn't you want to know who it was?'

'Kester, she never knows who she'll be sleeping with in an hour's time – you know that,' Gaunt said. 'I'll give you a clue, young prince: your fairytale ascendency will be complete.'

Kester shook his head at Gaunt, drew a blank. Whoever it was, it sounded promising. He felt a little twinge of excitement.

'Come on boy, what would any fairytale be incomplete without?'

Alexis looked from Gaunt to Kester and gave a small sigh.

'I'll see you at the helipad in 30 minutes,' she said. 'We're taking the chopper.'

'We have a helipad?' Kester asked. Now he was excited.

'Just underneath that bloody great X on the roof where we did your photoshoot,' said Gaunt, nodding to Alexis as she left the room. 'Now come on, you didn't get it yet. What would a fairytale be incomplete without?'

Kester paused. What sort of a question was that? A dragon? He thought. A happy ending? Yes, that could be it. He looked at Gaunt, bemused.

'A happy ending?'

'Close enough.' Gaunt smirked. He handed Kester a set of dog tags. 'Keep these on. There's a panic button in the centre of each, just in case. Now, if you come up with me I'll introduce you to Terrence. He'll be your bodyguard for all external visits.'

-o-

Kester nodded off in the helicopter. When he woke they were landing on a stretch of baize-perfect grass. It was getting dark, but the grass was well lit. A football pitch? was his first thought. Could it be a footballer? A footballer's spouse? He lifted his head and looked out of one window then the other. He nearly choked.

'It's fucking Buckingham Palace!' he shouted to Alexis, who was sitting across from him, cold pride on her face. She snapped back to attention and smiled.

'Well spotted,' she said into her mouthpiece. 'You don't need to shout.'

'You knew we were coming here?'

'Of course. Why did you think I was coming along for the ride? It's not every day you get to come here on business.'

There were six internal security guards on the lawn to meet them. Four of them flanked Kester and two Alexis as they walked up the lawn towards the palace. Kester glanced over his shoulder anxiously every now and again, wishing the guards would let them walk together. Kester's bodyguard Terrence brought up the rear, a beast of a man, a bear crossed with a fridge, radio constantly to his chin, eyes darting back and forth.

Inside, they were taken up some back stairs to an exquisite waiting room. This was the real deal. Kester thought of his mock baroque bedroom. It was pathetic compared to this. Royalty would laugh if they could see his room – his half a room – if they knew how proud he was of it and how much it had made him feel like royalty until now. The guards seated Kester on a love seat with thick red and gold stripes woven into the fabric. Alexis and Terrence flanked him officially until the guards had left the room. They all heard the key turn in the lock.

Alexis sat down next to Kester on the love seat. She was about to start talking when a bell rang and the tall gold doors before them began to open with ostentatious reserve. Alexis shot back to her feet and retook her position at his left hand side. Kester smoothed the collar of his labcoat and planted a hand on each knee to stop himself from fidgeting. He felt ludicrous, as if he had turned up at a fancy dress party wearing the wrong theme, but Yule had assured him that the client would like it if he looked like he'd just walked out of the lab.

Two footmen, wigged and dressed in white, appeared from behind the doors. The doors had opened slowly because they were so heavy, Kester realised. This could be tolerable. The footmen stepped out in perfect time, stopped at the threshold of the door and nodded simultaneously to Kester, who found himself on his feet and walking towards them. This could be OK. They guided him into the room. This could even be good. He was at the top of a rollercoaster, about to tip over into gravity's clutches. He couldn't help the excitement.

'The Princess will be with you momentarily,' one of the footmen said. 'Please make ready.'

The footmen stepped out of the room in time, pulling the doors behind them, shutting out Alexis' face, skin pale, eyes burning.

The Princess. A rush of adrenaline sent a shudder up Kester's neck. He looked at the sweeping marks the doors had left on the thick-pile carpet. *Make ready*. He looked up and took in the room. It was a large bedroom, decorated like a Viennese music box in gold and scrollwork. The curtains were drawn and the room was lit by soft lamplight which emphasised the luxurious finishes of the rose-coloured textiles. Kester walked over to the bed and slid a hand up one of its barley-twist poles. He thought of his own four-poster and laughed. It would fit inside this one twice over. The bed was curtained with heavy silk which was gathered in a pleated canopy up at the level of the chandelier. The chandelier; it looked oddly understated.

Make ready. The Princess wasn't one for messing about then. Kester looked around for somewhere to put his clothes, humming himself a dramatic theme. There was a chair by the bed, presumably for this purpose. He started to strip off, fingers jittering over buttons and zips. He didn't want to be still undressing when she came in. He piled his clothes on the chair and folded his labcoat on top. Or should he be wearing it? No, that would look too porno, he decided. His heart was racing now. Where should he be? Standing? Lying on the bed? He tittered. On the bed, under the covers – best to be demure.

Kester could hear someone coming. He leapt onto the bed and wrestled the hotel-tight covers loose enough to slip underneath. Their weight – the gold spun through them must be real. It would be disrespectful to look like he was lounging. He sat up, covers to the waist, and ruffled a hand through his hair. With each heartbeat his dog tags gave a small clink and he became more ready. The door was opening. This was it.

The Princess walked through the door between the bed and the window, just a few feet away. She continued across the room without looking over at Kester. She wore a tailored old-gold coloured lace jumpsuit, with elegantly flared legs – no logos. So, he would have the pleasure of undressing her himself. Her dark hair was straight and neat as a dressage mare's. It was rude to speak first; Kester waited to be addressed. The Princess turned.

Her expression was a punch in the stomach. Horror, disgust. Kester panicked. He had made a mistake. She wasn't expecting him to be in the bed.

'They said to ready myself,' he said. 'I'm Doctor Lowe.'

She stared at him open-mouthed. Of course this wasn't what they had meant. She started to back away towards the dressing table, her expression less of shock now than disbelief. Kester caught sight of his reflection in the dressing table mirror behind her – pale, scruffy-looking against the elegant backdrop of silk damask, an intruder. Then she snorted. She snorted as if she had come in and found a pig in her bed, and she began to laugh cruelly, covering her mouth with her manicured hand.

'I know who you are, Doctor Lowe. I bought you, after all.' Her face was harsh. She was talking to a staff member who had got out of line. 'But let's get one thing absolutely clear: I am not going to sleep with you.'

Kester felt naked in a bad way, naked in a recurring nightmare way.

'But you won the auction,' Kester said. There was no point in putting on airs and graces now. His words sounded small in the big room, his voice common. 'Your majesty,' he added.

'Of course I won it. I wanted to have your virus first.'

'But I'm here to infect you...that's what you bought at the auction...not the virus, you bought me.'

That cruel laugh again. This was not Alexis-style cruelty, this was centuries of inbreeding and class segregation cruelty, this was cruelty handed down through generations of royals; this was guillotine.

'You seriously think I would sleep with you? You think I would *pay* to sleep with you. I'm sorry, my darling. You may be a high-class shag to the other bidders, those...celebrities,' she said the word with distaste, 'but I just want the virus. I don't want to have to touch you, or anybody else for that matter.'

'But why...' Kester pulled the sheets higher up his chest. 'Why bring me here?'

'They need to think I've screwed you. I want them to think that I got what they couldn't afford. I may see that you're just V's jumped-up little rent boy, but the public will go all frog-prince over it, the celebrities will be jealous and I get a lovely slice of homepage headlines for the next week.

'But I don't need to explain myself to you. All you need to know is that you are to give no details of our appointment to the press. You will remain here for three hours and then you will return to V. You are permitted to exhibit a knowing and satisfied smile when questioned by the press, friends and colleagues, but I draw the line at smugness. I want to inject the virus myself. Send over a package for me as soon as you get back to V. And it needs to be fast-acting. I don't want that dog-woman showing up wearing her virus before me.'

Kester felt skinny, dirty, small. He wanted to say that the virus would present when it presented, he couldn't make it work any faster than normal, wanted to tell her that only royalty would be vain enough to think that nature would make an exception for them. He glanced over desperately at his clothes. The Princess was standing there staring at him, examining him. She looked simultaneously amused and nauseated by his presence. After what seemed like an age, she flicked her eyes away from him and strode back towards the door.

'I'd hoped to have this conversation in a civilised fashion,' she said as she walked, 'but it makes no difference. I trust you have embarrassed yourself enough never to speak of this.' It wasn't a question. 'That will be all, Doctor Lowe.'

She opened the door, a skill Kester was surprised she had mastered.

'Princess, I'm a scientist...' Kester began, but he couldn't think how to continue.

She ignored him and exited the room, closing the door behind her.

Kester drew his knees up in front of him and rested his forehead on their bony plinth. The back of his neck felt exposed, as if waiting for the blade to fall. Three hours. He lifted his head again, avoiding his own eye in the mirror, shuffled to the edge of the bed and began to dress. What an idiot. He looked around the room. It was a great golden sneer. Three hours. What was he supposed to do in here, alone, for three hours?

-o-

'Well?' Farrell said. She was standing in Kester's apartment, fixing herself what looked like her third or fourth drink. 'How was it?'

She was plainly dressed, no logos, nothing, hair tied back in an impossibly smooth pony tail. Her skin was clear, makeup-less. It looked almost translucent. She wasn't wearing. The way the pinched waist of her green dress held her body should have aroused a pang of want in Kester, but he was numb.

'How was what?'

'Your royal opening.'

'You didn't wait for me.'

'You were taking your time. I had other things to attend to. So, did you enjoy it?'

Kester sighed and closed his eyes. He flopped down on the couch. This was one of those questions – one he could get so immensely wrong. The truth would crack him open. He wasn't good enough for the Princess; it would enrage Alexis, would make her doubt his worth. He would make a fantasy for her.

'What's better? What would make you happier – if I did enjoy it or I didn't?'

Alexis ignored his question and added a couple of ice cubes to her drink.

'This is what you wanted for me, isn't it?' he asked her. 'Superstardom? I thought it would make you happy.'

'Me too. But this isn't quite what I had in mind.'

Alexis took up her drink and perched on the edge of the dentist's chair. Kester's mind flashed a flick-book of images of her on the chair, tied up, tied down, blindfolded, painted. She hadn't asked to wear his next set of viruses. Not yet.

'Well?' Alexis probed again.

'She's a princess – you saw the setting – it was like being in a Mills and Boon, sort of. That was enjoyable, to start with. Who wouldn't enjoy that on some level?' His fantasy was faltering. He changed the subject. 'It's not like I haven't done it before. It was just like being in a bigger booth. One with gold fittings.'

'That was different. Things are different now.'

'It didn't feel that different,' Kester lied. 'I mean it wasn't like she handed me a wad of grubby tenners. Like you said, it's only a week, then I'm off the menu.' He tried to sound convinced.

'It felt different to me.' Alexis took a gulp of her drink, then clattered the glass down on the side table next to her.

Kester pushed himself up off the couch and walked over to where she sat. *The Princess didn't want me. She thinks I'm a dirty little prostitute.* What would he normally do? He put a hand to her cheek. She pushed it away. Kester took her shoulders in his hands and laid her back on the chair. He took a long look at her body, revealed by the liquid fabric of her v-neck dress, willed it to arouse him, reached in and put a hand to her breast. She slapped him in the face. He squeezed and she slapped him again. He put his other hand on her waist. Slap. Slid it down between her legs. Slap.

'You've got to be gentle with me, Lex,' he said, leaning in and biting her neck. As he came back up – slap. 'I'm expensive goods.' He unzipped the front of her dress fully and put his face down to her belly, breathing in the familiar scent of her skin. He wanted to just lie there, cry.

'Wash,' Alexis said, eventually.

'I washed already.'

'Wash again.' There was the glimmer of a smile on her lips.

Kester undressed and got in the shower, leaving Alexis in his living room. He stood there, fingers pruning, until his door monitor beeped. He wished there was something for Alexis to slam on her way out, to close the scene properly. He closed his eyes. There was no way he could rise to the occasion tonight.

–o–

Saturday night came thundering around like a pack of wild animals in heat. Kester started to cry. He couldn't stop himself. His penis was sore. The nurse who had injected him before the show seemed to have limited experience handling a syringe. It didn't feel erect; it felt as if it was swollen, hard with infection, like it was wrapped in nettle leaves. He wondered if she had got the dosage right. Gaunt hadn't said anything about the injection causing him pain – just that it would solve his little problem. Kester prayed for his pain killers to kick in.

Pera Pera was barking through her latest hit in front of the curtain and here he was behind it, ready to play his part. She would sing the song, Kester would appear on stage then disappear behind a curtain with her. Silhouettes were all the audience would see; Yule had been clear about it. Yet here Kester was, naked, on all fours, gagged and chained up in a giant Perspex box. They'd tied him up without him really realising what was going on, distracted by the pain in his penis and by Pera Pera's explanation that there had been a change of plan and he was to play the part of a character from her new video. Before he knew it he was gagged and stripped and by the time he'd remembered about his dog tags, he was unable to reach them. This wasn't part of the agreement.

Kester shuddered. The music had stopped and Pera Pera's voice was honking away front of stage, no doubt giving him an unfit introduction. In a minute he was going to have to look like he was enjoying this. He would have to brazen it out. He surveyed the rack of sex toys on the wall of the box, then closed his eyes. It was only one song, he reminded himself. Nobody really wanted to watch the two of them at it for any longer than one song. And he was playing a part – it was just acting. People would appreciate that. How bad could it be?

-o-

Alexis' head was thumping, pulsing from the inside out. She kept going over what Yule had told her: it was fine, the fans loved it, they could ride out all the other stuff. He was right, no doubt, but that didn't stop her feeling sick. Kester wasn't built for this. Kester the superstar was a cardboard cut-out, would blow over too easily in the storm. She needed to keep him with her so that she could prop him up, but she knew he would be mad at her, or worse. She had done the deals with the clients, set up the appointments. It had all happened at her hand. If she had grown a pair, spoken to Chen already...

'Happy Birthday, Lex.'

Kester's voice made Farrell start; it was quiet, accusatory. She looked up from her desk to see him walking slowly through her door, tense, as if he might break if he moved too sharply. Her seat was suddenly uncomfortable. The room was hot. Her glass desk misted up beneath where her hand was sitting.

'Kester, I'm busy.' She avoided his stare. If she looked at him his pain would be her pain too.

'What are we going to do about this?' He was holding out his Book, one of the news sites loaded with the Sunday headlines.

Farrell stood and turned to the window. She didn't want to look at him. It was all wrong. This wasn't how it was supposed to be. She had thought she could take a week of it – the reward would be great enough at the end – but this was brutal. Pera Pera was nuts. But what was done was done.

'What's done is done.' She gazed out over the City, looking up at the sky and inviting its cool emptiness in.

'Have you seen the headlines?'

Farrell heard the slap of his Book on her desk. Of course she had seen the headlines. BRITAIN'S TOP SCIENTIST? – a picture of him in the box, being tortured by Pera Pera, vitals blurred out. KESTER HITS NEW LOWE – him being pulled back and forth by her carnivorous labcoated dancers, his naked body smeared in luminous paint. The images were imprinted on her brain. She felt as if it had all been aimed at her, that Pera Pera, staring straight out at the camera was looking at her with a big *fuck you* in her eyes.

'Everybody is laughing at me,' Kester said. 'My reputation…'

The tension in Farrell's throat spread upwards, tightening her soft palate, and down and out across her shoulders as if her arms were making ready to lash out.

'The rest of the appointments are in private,' she said, trying to batten down her anger, sound confident. 'This will all pass.'

'Not even you will look at me! I'm a laughing stock! I've got fucking whip lashes on my back – my dick is a disaster area and I've only got two bloody days to recover before the next appointment.'

'You'll go through with them?'

'Alexis. If both our careers didn't depend on this I wouldn't be doing it at all.' Kester drew a visible breath. 'If Chen doesn't go for our deal –'

'We need Yule,' Alexis said. She couldn't talk about Chen now. If they didn't focus and get themselves out of the shit now, there would be no conversation to be had with Chen tomorrow. 'Yule can read the public mood.'

She braced herself and turned to look at Kester. He was paler than usual, his hair messier than usual. He looked small. What could she do? She wouldn't pity him. Who could love a man they pitied? She tapped her Book.

'Yule, are you free? Kester and I are coming up.'

Farrell drew a deep breath and focused on her chest rising and falling, stretched herself out into her extremities. She became aware of the cloth on her skin, the cool breath of the air con, the soft pull of her tied-back hair as she moved her head. Smoothing one hand over the skin of her inner forearm, she felt more like herself.

'Don't panic,' she said to Kester with a smile, approaching him with measured strides. 'I'll organise for a team to meet us up at the PlayPen this afternoon. Masseuse, physio, doctor, acupuncture, whatever you want. Get some hands on you.' Stretching an arm out as she reached him, she slid her hand to the back of his neck and drew him in for a kiss. When he turned his head away, avoiding her lips, she rubbed her cheek across his like a cat. 'We'll get you back in shape. I'll see to it personally.'

They walked in silence to Yule's office. Kester followed Alexis three paces behind, but she could feel the weight of his presence, a pressure at her back.

Yule greeted them with a pitying look. Farrell gave him a tight smile. No pity. She wouldn't have Kester pitied. He was a superstar.

'Don't worry, Kester, we'll sort this out,' Yule said.

A news report was running in the background on his wall. Alexis glanced up at it and an adrenalin pulse hit her crown. Kester couldn't see this. If he hadn't seen it already it would tip him over the edge. She signalled to Yule to switch it off.

'Wait,' Kester said, as Yule reached for his Book, 'that's the Institute – that's the Institute Director – what are they doing there?'

'Just...probably...' Yule said, fumbling with his Book. He looked to Farrell for help.

'Kester, let's just focus –'

'Put the sound on.' Kester pointed at Yule.

Yule looked apologetically at Farrell and turned the sound on.

'Coming just a day after the news that Kester Lowe's former place of employment, the world renowned London Institute of

Immunology and Viral Medicine is to have all funding and activity suspended indefinitely –'

'What?' Kester said.

'– many people are asking, "Just what was he thinking?" Last month, the Institute, one of the Government's largest scientific contractors and world leading research facility, suffered a suspected breach of security leading to a dangerous virus being released into the Pigs' supply chain and infecting hundreds of City residents. While the MoD investigators here at the Institute have turned up nothing so far, they say that this is almost certainly where the breach occurred. All funding to the Institute's work has been suspended until further notice and the Director here says that continued employment for the organisation's 200 staff cannot be guaranteed. We spoke earlier with the Director.'

Farrell glanced at Kester. He sat down abruptly on the closest chair and stared at the display, unblinking. The report cut to a clip of the longer interview Farrell had seen earlier.

'This is a gross public humiliation. Doctor Lowe's actions are crude and callous. The fact that he would go through with such a stunt when we may have just had the biggest blow to scientific progress this century just goes to show how out of touch with reality Doctor Lowe really is. His actions degrade the whole scientific community.' The Director's face was grim. The whole scene was grey: his suit, his skin, the building, the sky. The report cut back to studio.

'The Director went on to talk about the danger of removing a centre of scientific excellence from the country's capital and the possibility that the Institute would revoke Kester Lowe's doctorate as a punishment for the insult he has caused.'

'Off!' Farrell said. She snatched Yule's Book from his hand and the wall fell blank.

She looked round at Kester. His head was in his hands. He didn't speak for a long time. Farrell could feel the anger emanating from him. It was extreme, the kind of rage that shatters your bones, renders you unable to stand, to function; dream rage that leaves you punching through syrup-thick air, unable to defend yourself, all your blows misaimed or useless.

'When did they announce the freeze?' Kester asked, barely audible.

'Friday afternoon, just after four.' Farrell braced herself for the next question.

'Did you know?'

'Kester,' Yule stepped in to defend her, 'you had more important things to think about. We couldn't risk any distractions. We knew how hard it was going to be for you.'

'More important things?' Kester raised his eyes, his head still low, threatening, like a cornered dog. 'More important than my friends losing their jobs? More important than embarrassing the Institute? More important than losing my doctorate?' He sprung to his feet. 'Oh, that's right, I had more important things to do – performing as a royal rent boy, getting my arse ruined by a twisted egomaniac rapper.'

Farrell stepped back to give him room. She had never seen him properly angry before. This was not his face. She didn't like it.

'Chen –' she started to explain, holding her hands out in front of her in a protective gesture.

'I know, I know,' Kester spoke over her, his voice rising. 'Chen wouldn't let me – Chen Chen Chen. You swagger around like Mrs Billy Big Bollocks the whole time – Alexis Farrell, she's nobody's bitch – but the minute Chen calls your name you go yapping to her like a horrible little bitey dog and sit in her fucking lap.'

He was panting, looked fevered. Farrell closed her lips tight and tried to hold it down. He was angry. She wasn't the one under attack here. She stared at the wall for a few seconds, breathing through her nose, before replying.

'The MoD are bluffing. They're still investigating internally. I have it on good authority that they're tearing themselves apart behind closed doors. When they find the culprit this will all blow over.'

'It's fine, it's fine, it'll all blow over,' Kester parroted her in an unhinged high-pitched voice. 'It'll be fine after you do the VIP pit – it'll be fine when we book the appointments – it'll be fine, just get in the box and let her fuck you.' He paced around wildly for a moment. 'No! Enough!'

Farrell stepped back again, giving Kester a clear path to the doors. He stopped just before he reached them.

'It's – not – fine.' He pinned each word to the air with a jabbing finger. Turning to leave, he caught the doors by surprise. He slapped his hands against them as they started to slide open.

'Kester, I'm sorry,' Farrell said. It was worth a try. He didn't look back.

'Goodbye...Doctor Lowe.'

Kester swung a wild punch at one of the doors as it retreated into the wall, catching it a glancing blow on the edge, then tore towards the lifts, gripping his injured fist tightly in his other hand.

'That didn't go as well as I'd hoped,' Yule said. 'I have to tell you the public mood is surprisingly positive – his fans just don't care.'

Farrell shot a glare at Yule, said nothing, folded her anger in on itself. She watched the doors as they slid shut, a small splatter of Kester's blood sealing them like a ruby clasp.

Chapter 21

This was no Sunday. Sunday had no right to be this way.

Kester walked fast away from the V building, across the square. It was like any other morning in the City: swarms of people in logoed work clothes, branded lunatics going to and coming from pointless meetings. He put his head down and ignored the *heyhey!s* and *whohoo!s* that rang out every few minutes. Were they jeering him? Congratulating him? Autumn was playing around the edges of the September breeze, making the hairs on his arms rise despite the mellow sunshine. He should have brought a jacket.

He would go down to the Institute, see who he could find, apologise, do something. Kester headed down towards the Underground. As he looked up to navigate through the crowds, the scene before him became a spyhole. People were drawing in towards him, looming as they passed, grinning and leering like guests at a nightmare masked ball. Once, the stream of scabs, sores and rashes was interrupted by a clean face sporting a small stencilled letter like a beauty spot: L for Luminescence. The owner winked at him and pushed her face in front of him as she passed to make sure he reacted. Further on, the unmistakeable butterfly patterning of Persona bobbed past above a smug smile. His viruses were out there, starting to make it through the ranks. All those desperate fuckers fucking. He sneered.

Rounding the corner he was faced with a billboard of himself standing on the V shelf, looking like a tool. Cringing, he crossed the road. A large wall display was running the news, a group of angry Institute workers spitting words at an interviewer. Dee was there in the background, ignoring it all, staring right through the camera as if she knew he would be watching: emotionless, accusing, a psychotic shop dummy. At the next corner, he turned again. He would go back to V, confront Alexis properly. This was V's mess; they had to sort it out.

'Hoho!' a voice came at Kester and stuck with him at his shoulder, a thick European accent. 'That Pera Pera! What a crazy woman! You OK man? What a beast she is, but I'd take your place any day.'

Kester sped up as the man patted him on the back in congratulations.

'Hey, I come to your next show, get some myself!' the voice said, then became lost in the crowd behind him.

So, this side of the checkpoints he was some kind of sex-hero; the other side he was a deviant betrayer. Between them they would pull him apart. Kester looked up to see where he was. He was nearly back at the square. Changing his plan, he turned off again. Back at V they would be busy telling each other that it was all alright and they would try to tell him that too. Alexis would be planning his next degradation instead of speaking to Chen like she had promised.

It wasn't long until Kester found a bar. *Brass* was a popular City haunt, but was unusually quiet. The main bar was mostly standing room with a sweep of shelved pillars looping out from one end of the bar and ending at the other. Further back, small round tables with padded banquette seating were set back into the scalloped semi-circular wall. Everything was money. The Perspex pillars were inset with old paper notes, arrested in gentle floating motion. Kester smoothed one hand over the bar as if to spread out and count the thousands of brown one and two pence coins that sat below the surface. The place was a monument to traditional City values. The owners hadn't caved and rebranded in the face of wearing culture. They had understood that whatever the fad, money would still underpin everything.

'Will it stay like this?' Kester asked the barwoman.

'Doctor Lowe! What brings you to our humble establishment on a Sunday morning?'

Kester didn't reply.

'What can I get you?'

'Vodka.'

The barwoman took a glass from the rack above her head.

'A bottle, please. I'd rather not have to come back to the bar. It'll get busy right?'

'We'll be busy by lunchtime.'

'I'll pay double if you promise not to let anyone know I'm here.'

'Right.'

The barwoman's movements turned slow, like a bank clerk considering pressing the alarm button. She sensed something was wrong, but her disease-addled City brain couldn't make sense of it, even though there was footage of the Institute running on the news, even though she would have watched last night's debacle with the rest of the world. She produced a bottle and an ice bucket. She held out her pad and Kester swiped his Book for the amount, then went to swipe it again. The barwoman withdrew the pad quickly.

'Don't worry about it, hon,' she said with a wink, 'your secret's safe with me.' She handed him a card. 'Scan this and you can make your orders from the table. Had breakfast? You look a bit pale. You might want a bacon roll with that.'

Kester forced a smile, clutched the bottle and the glass and found the table furthest from the bar. The tabletop was the same design as the bar, a scree of loose change, this time copper and silver. He filled his glass.

Kester drank steadily as the noise in the bar behind him rose. Every ten minutes or so his Book beeped. He ignored it. What a fool. If he'd gone with his instincts and had the balls to say no to Chen and Alexis, none of this would be happening. Well, except for the Institute part, but he could be down there, supporting them instead of being strung up as a target for their anger. It wasn't his fault they had been shut down. He tried to figure out how it had all become about him.

The screens, he had decided by the time he was a quarter of the way down the bottle. The screens were the thing. But nobody wanted to see them developed besides him and Dee. He toyed with the idea of messaging her, telling her what he had achieved, then remembered the terrifying expression she had had on the news report. She would strangle him with his own innards. No: he was alone.

V wouldn't touch the screens despite what Alexis had said. If she really thought they would, she would already have taken it to Chen. She had been playing her pretty pipe and he had been dancing merrily along behind her towards the gaping mountain of her ambition. And why should she want to see the screens made? He was her creation – Kester Lowe the superstar viral designer – why would she be happy to have *her* Kester upstaged by Kester the serious scientist? But then the scientific community, despite their high and mighty act, were no better. For how many years had they been in thrall to the whims of the funding bodies? How could they have a clear conscience having blocked his proposals so many times in the past? He couldn't believe that still being with them would be any better.

Halfway down the bottle, Kester got up. He stood, wobbling, for a bit.

'Ha ha!' he shouted, as if he had just discovered something.

The people at the tables either side looked round at him.

'Hey,' said a pretty young woman with curly ginger hair. 'Doctor Lowe! The one and only!'

'Hey, it is him,' her male companion said. 'It is you. You still wearing your virus from the weekend? Any chance of a sneaky exchange?'

'You mistake me, sir!' Kester announced, lifting a heavy arm. 'I am not Kester Lowe, V's little shag-puppet; I am Doctor Kester Lowe, the scientist. Sci-en-tist – you know what that is?' Their faces went all indecipherable. They were impressed, he decided. 'The Kester Lowe you are looking for died suddenly in a bizarre sex accident involving taking the wrong job and a young lady who calls herself Dog Dog.' Watching their faces, Kester recognised laughter creeping into their eyes. He had their approval. It spurred him on. He stepped out from his booth and steadied himself. The room was full and he now had a captive audience. 'Dead, I tell you!' He became aware that he was talking in an outrageous English accent of the sort that normally came with a shooting stick and pack of hounds. This wasn't the way to go. He needed to be serious – look serious, look sober. He picked up the half-empty bottle and shouldered his way through the surprised drinkers to the bar.

'Oh,' the barwoman said, surprised to see him.

'Oi,' said the angry voice of the large man he had pushed aside.

As Kester turned, he felt the steam-iron impact of a fist against his face. The room toppled over. He curled up on the floor, his whole body a cradle for his throbbing, flattened nose. Large hands were pawing at him, trying to prise open his protective hedgehog curl. Voices were shouting at him, loud and muddled.

'Sorry sorry sorry,' eventually the voice came through, 'I didn't know it was you.'

Kester looked out from himself tentatively. A ceiling of saucer mouths stretched and swooned above him.

'Sorry, Doctor Lowe,' the man said again, 'I didn't know it was you. That was totally out of order.'

'Lance!' The barwoman appeared at the edge of Kester's vision, leaning over the bar top. 'That's two strikes. And that should count for two – it's not even four o'clock. One more and you're barred.'

As Lance and the barwoman withdrew into their own conversation, Kester pushed himself onto his hands and knees. Helped into a sitting position by the hands around him, he inspected his blood-splattered shirt front and put a hand back to his nose. The bleeding had been furious but had stopped as suddenly as it had started. He could already feel the blood drying into a crusty red snout, felt it crack as he flared his nostrils. They had him on his feet.

'Lance,' he said, tapping the man on the arm. 'I'm sorry. I pushed in. I shouldn't have. I had a bad morning.'

'Bad morning,' Lance said, 'but a badass weekend! Man you are crazed.'

Kester swayed. The bar was made of eyes, all tumbled in together like the coins in the tabletop. Things were still a bit twinkly round the edges.

'Here, I caught your bottle,' said an enthusiastic, androgynous youth, pressing the vodka back into Kester's hand.

'Thanks,' he said, still puzzling over Lance's comment. 'No, no,' he said eventually, having turned around a few times on the spot. 'You didn't hear me – that wasn't me.'

'What?' Lance asked.

'I said – I was telling these people…' Kester knew they were out there somewhere in the bar. He pointed in a couple of different directions, squinting, looking for red hair. 'I was telling them…'

This was no good. They couldn't hear him. They needed to hear the end of his explanation. He needed to get things straight with the redhead. Kester plonked his bottle down on the bar and clambered up after it, sliding up onto his belly. He grabbed the neck of the bottle and used it to push himself up on to his knees, then his feet. The lighting in the bar was strange, like a monitor on the blink, the colours slightly wrong, a scrolling lag pulling the picture up and up. He took a slug of vodka from the bottle and surveyed the crowd.

Seeing a shock of red hair, Kester pointed and smiled.

'You're there!' he cried out. 'There you are! Now...' He moved his feet further apart and stopped smiling. This required seriousness. This needed to be said and said now. 'Everybody, Lance, red haired lady, you – barperson – listen. Let me tell you.'

-o-

Blotch just couldn't stop laughing. He knew it was wrong to laugh at someone else's ills but he just couldn't help it. This was the best Monday in living history. He wiped a tear away from his eye and looked back at his display. Doctor Kester Lowe was on the front page of every site. He had thought it was good when he saw the Pera Pera pictures, but this was priceless. There was the City's precious hero, pictured standing on top of a bar, clutching a bottle, stains down his corporate front and blood encrusting his nostrils. His face was captured in mid-shout, distorted, his frowning brows sending horned shadows up his forehead. DR NO! the headline read.

Blotch clicked a link and his fallen nemesis came to life before him. The sound wasn't great and Lowe's voice was struggling over the drunken whoops of his audience but the message was clear – he was denouncing his employers, making lurid claims about his scientific ambitions and abilities – he had completely lost it. Blotch allowed a wild laugh to escape his shuddering form and clicked again to stop the clip. He mustn't revel in it.

This was unexpected to say the least. All the effort they had put in to get Cherry in place and here V was tearing itself apart from the inside thanks to its degenerate practices. The Doctor might even turn out to be an asset. Blotch took a few deep breaths to calm himself, flicked off his display and set off to brief Clarke.

-o-

Kester lifted his head from his arms and buzzed for another coffee.

Sunday's revelations had been brutal, but right now Monday was his worst enemy. He was poisoned. His head was solid pain, and his internal organs were tenderized and swollen with the after-effects of drink. His previous night's binge in the City was already homepage news: details of what he drank, the two fights, one with a stranger and one with a bollard, the slurred lecture he had given whilst standing on the bar in *Brass* clutching a bottle of vodka. It had made him feel better at the time. He chose not to read any of the reports; he didn't want to know what he had said.

When he had set out the night before he had been spoiling for a fight and had been determined that he was going to leave V. By the end of the night he was going to find a way to trace the first virus, go back to the Institute and save the day. This morning he was too delicate to make any decisions. Large portions of the night were blurred or missing and he felt guilty in a way he hadn't felt since fresher's week at Uni.

Everyone was leaving him well alone, communicating with him only via messages to his Book and only if they had to. There was no word from Yule since a message late the day before, after their aborted meeting. He had seemed adamant that the news about the Institute wasn't a big deal, that Kester's fans didn't care, that it was all good hype. But he seemed to have missed the point that all of Kester's friends were being put out of jobs. This morning presumably saw him mopping Kester's sick off the homepages. No doubt he would think this was great publicity too – a distraction from the previous day's stories.

There was no word from Alexis either. But Alexis had said she was sorry. What more could she say? And she needn't be sorry. It was Kester's own fault. He dropped his head back onto his arms as sober guilt piled on drunken guilt. If he hadn't taken funding to develop the viruses in the first place it couldn't have happened; if he hadn't come here and let Alexis make a stupid celebrity out of him he would never have become a target. Never mind that some bad people had taken it upon themselves to launch the attack – he had made it all possible for them.

And what now? He looked up again, wincing. His Book was beeping, reminding him that he had appointments with the models. They had been separated into their groups and assigned their viruses. He could leave some of the checks to Gerald, but he needed to check out the competition winners himself – it was part of their prize to be poked and prodded by the fabulous Doctor Lowe. He may as well see them all.

Images from the weekend kept slicing into his brain: the whip; the box; the hyena audience. Pointless. The second show wouldn't go ahead, surely. He couldn't imagine existing that long. He couldn't imagine remaining in employment for that long. But he'd made enough of a fool of himself for one week. He would get on with things and think it through properly.

'OK,' Kester said to himself. His voice sounded heavy and deep. He needed something before he could think about getting started.

A slight youth from catering appeared in the doorway.

'Your coffee, Doctor Lowe,' the boy said. 'Do you want me to send someone up to look at your machine?'

'Thank you so much,' Kester said, rising like an old man and meeting the boy halfway across the room. 'No, it's fine, it's working fine I just couldn't. I need this. I really need it. Thank you.'

He followed the boy back out into the lab and shambled over to the isolation suites. Gerald saw him across the lab and stood there for a moment with a grim but encouraging smile on his face. Gerald knew when not to talk. Kester felt a sudden warmth towards his right-hand man. He didn't appreciate him enough.

'All alright, sir?' Gerald asked. 'I wasn't sure you'd be coming. How are you feeling?'

'I feel used, Gerald,' Kester replied, his honesty bringing a lump to his throat. 'Tired and used.' He made a face and groaned to try to make light of it.

'Don't worry, sir,' Gerald said, 'it'll all be over soon.' He laughed a little too gaily for Kester's liking and proceeded through the doors.

'Morning, Doctor Lowe,' said one of the models as Kester and Gerald emerged from the decon room.

'Morning,' Kester said, without registering who had spoken.

His six competition winners had turned out to be excellent choices. All six were attractive, of course, but they all seemed to be reasonably sane as well. They also represented a nice slice of society. Three from outside London, three from within; three male, three female; banker, office junior, trainee beautician, fashion student, hydroponics technician and aspiring musician. Their conversations were quite something to listen in to. They were all pleasant, all eager to be there. Hera and Cherry seemed to have managed to make them feel welcome. Probably more Cherry's doing than Hera's.

Kester took the models one by one into the anteroom to check their charts and look at the presentation of the virus. He feigned deep concentration to keep conversation to a minimum, and saved his energy for one or two broad smiles and winks at the start and end of appointments. He saw Hera and Cherry last.

Hera was acting strangely, switching between smirking at him and looking concerned. Kester ignored her questions about his weekend and got on with the business of doing his checks. If he gave her a way in to rib him about his hangover she would rip him to pieces.

Cherry was easier to engage with, though she seemed withdrawn. She wasn't slobbering to gain approval or battling anyone for favour. He could be hungover with her. He started by dimming the light and passing his UV tube over her skin. She looked different to the other models – because of her skin tone, more of her was glowing in the UV light. The virus concentrated in cells with higher levels of melanin, creating patterns, making cheeks, shoulders, and forearms glow with freckles and moles.

'How are you finding it,' Kester asked her, 'being back to a plain old model after your consultancy stint?'

'Me?' Cherry asked, as if there were others in the room. 'It's fine I guess. The new models have been OK. A bit gossipy. I notice the suite is extra-nice though. You'll have trouble putting Hera back in a standard one.'

Kester felt a little sad at this. The accommodation, flash and modern as it was, seemed to him cramped for six people. The communal areas were nicer than the other suites, it was true, but they still all shared a bunk room. He turned the lights back up and laid his tube aside.

'So the company's OK?' Kester smiled up from the chart he was reading, knowingly.

'It's interesting.' Cherry clocked his expression. 'No, really. It's interesting to hear about what they all do. Some more than others, perhaps. The constant meaningless sex is a bit wearing when you can hear it through the walls though, if you can believe that coming from me.' She lifted her feet and swung her legs free under the bench she was sitting on. 'How are you finding it?'

'Me?' Kester looked up. The quick movement sent a jolt of pain to his crown.

'You had your first appointments over the weekend?'

'Yes. It was...it was OK. Fine, I suppose.' Kester hurried to finish his checks. She can't have seen the news. 'Well this all looks fine.' He felt as if his smile would break him.

'I know it must be hard for you,' Cherry said, with less kindness than seemed appropriate to the phrase. Or Kester couldn't hear it properly any more. It sounded wrong when it wasn't an innuendo. 'Just...if you need to talk...'

'Thanks,' Kester was unsure what else to say. He stepped to the door and nodded to her as she left the anteroom.

Back at his desk, Kester sat slouched in his chair. He felt like a dead body propped up, eyes pinned open; a sick joke. He deconstructed his lunch well enough to convince himself he had eaten some of it, and then turned to sugar for assistance. He took a sip of coffee and put a biscuit whole into his mouth. As he chewed he flicked his intercom on and off. Eventually Gerald's voice appeared on the other end.

'Sir, is there something I can do for you?'

Kester looked at the intercom suspiciously.

'Sir, there's a click every time you switch off. And munching whenever you switch on.'

'Oh, sorry. There is something. I was just mulling it over. Could you arrange for me to speak to Cherry Woodlock alone please? Perhaps in one of the other isolation suites.'

There was a pause. 'Yes, sir. Is this a social visit?'

'I just want to talk to her, Gerald.'

'Very well, sir. They're in the middle of a briefing session with the models right now, but I'll let you know when she's ready.'

When Kester entered the isolation suite, Cherry was standing next to one of the two couches, leaning with her back against the wall.

'Hi,' Kester said, wiggling his hands in the pockets of his labcoat.

'You wanted to see me again?'

'Yes.'

'Take a seat,' Cherry said.

Kester felt suddenly undermined. She was treating this like her territory. He wavered for a moment and then indicated the couch next to her.

'After you,' he said.

Cherry sat down in the middle of the couch. Kester watched her. He could see how slender she was even through the bulk of her kimono. Its luminous white made her golden brown skin darker in contrast. Her hair was wet, combed straight back over her skull. Her whole person exuded a defensive strength.

'So,' she said, when Kester had settled opposite her, 'what did you want to talk about?'

What didn't he want to talk about? Moments flashed through his head. The Princess staring at him, disgusted; Pera Pera approaching the box, strap-on flashing; the image of the Institute on the news, rain-dark dribbles streaking down from each windowsill; Alexis, an empty promise falling from her lips; the back of Dee's head as she left the PlayPen. She didn't care about any of that. Perhaps he could pay her to care. From prostitute to model to consultant to shrink all in a few months. Not bad going.

'You asked me how I was finding it.'

'Yes.'

'I'm finding it hard – I'm not being funny. I'm finding it hard work.'

Cherry laughed.

'It worries me –'

'Keeping it up?'

'No – not just physically. Psychologically. I just feel – I don't know. You were a sex worker, right?'

'Right. People keep on reminding me. You'd think I'd fit in perfectly here. You'd think nobody would care.'

'I'm sorry they're treating you like that.'

Cherry looked down into her lap. 'It got easier for me, if that's what you're wondering. Physically, mentally, morally. That doesn't mean it will for you. And it's the same, but – it's sort of the same, but…'

'No,' Kester picked up where she'd left off. 'It's not the same is it? I've got a fabulous apartment, a great job. Everything is paid for. I don't know what I thought you could offer me. A different perspective maybe. I'm sorry – you don't want to know all about my self-pity.'

Cherry ignored his apology. 'It is different here,' she said. 'No offense, but everybody is at it all the time. I'm finding it hard to know whether people are trying to bed me because they think I'm easy or they are just acting normally – if they're like that with everybody. It's not normal to me that every conversation should hold the possibility of sex – it makes me feel like I'm being judged. But I've seen the way they operate in here. If there's a power difference, the assumption is that you're going to screw. That's probably the assumption now.'

'No.'

'But it's a possibility in the back of your mind. It must be.'

Kester dodged the point. 'It's not normal for me either – it wasn't. I suppose I'm getting used to it. I haven't been here that long and it doesn't really work like that outside the City. Some people wear in the rest of London, but it's a real subculture and it's just about being seen to be sexually active – it doesn't have the same connotations of ambition and power as it does in here.'

'But you have got used to it.'

'I can remember being really weirded out by it at first but you know, I'm a guy...a guy who didn't really get much before.' He gazed at Cherry for a moment or two. 'But isn't it a bit like that in your line of work, I mean every conversation maybe being the start of sex?'

'Only when you're getting paid. I wouldn't be a very good seeker if I had sex with anyone I spoke to. Besides, it rather numbs the appetite for recreational sex.'

'Hm.' Kester felt vaguely embarrassed. 'I think I know what you mean. But it's not – I mean normally – it's not purely recreational here.' Why was he trying to justify this to her? 'It's a power thing. You don't get anywhere if you're not seen to be virile – to have ambition. That's why people wear – to show that they are getting around enough to have caught something. And to show their vigour as well I suppose, to show that they can take it. Or that used to be why anyway. Now, with my viruses, I don't know.'

Kester looked down into his lap. It sounded a bit silly. It was silly. He didn't want to talk about it. His situation was a constant drain on his attention, filling his head like tinnitus.

'Are you going to tell me next that sleeping with you is going to further my career?' Cherry asked. 'You know I'm doing pretty well without –'

'No! That's not what I'm about at all.'

'It's not?' Cherry looked around the room as if she could see through the walls, into every room in V, as if she could see what was going on there – the viruses being developed, the couples in the exchange booths, the employees further down the chain wringing their hands over who they needed to sleep with next to get ahead. 'You could have fooled me.'

'The truth is I'm a mess,' Kester admitted. He felt himself crack right down the middle, spill out, couldn't control it, let go. 'I've been taken in. I just – I feel like I'm giving it all away, like I'm losing it, losing everything. They're treating me like I'm just a prostitute – sorry, no offense – like a prostitute, but I'm a scientist. I was a scientist. And I...my friends. All my friends have just lost their jobs because of the first attack – I've been publicly berated by the Director of the Institute...' He glanced up at Cherry. She had a look on her face he hadn't seen for a long time. Not quite pity, more like empathy, she understood. He could tell her. 'I've got things I want to achieve. I see what the press are thinking – the press that Yule hasn't got back onside – they think this is it for me. They think I've peaked and this is me on my way down, but this was all stupid play for me. It was mostly for the money. The fame just...it was for Farrell. I won't say I wasn't starting to enjoy it...but that's not the point. This isn't what I'm here for. I've got things I want to achieve.'

'Like what?'

Kester looked up at Cherry. Her shoulders were drawn in as if she were cold. She folded her arms.

'I'm developing a new screen.' Why was he telling her this? 'A screen that anyone can use – a screen that won't make people dependent on our drugs, or destroy their immune systems. There's no complicated procedure, so it'll be affordable.'

'You can really do it? But why would the company pay you to undermine their cartel?'

'They wouldn't. They aren't. They don't know about it yet. I'm doing it on my own time, but the company – it's complicated – the market for the drugs is dwindling. The number of people who need the drugs is getting smaller and smaller as the existing population's immune systems die off, plus the drugs are going to be deregulated soon. The company needs something new. Farrell promised to take it to Chen but now...' Whenever he thought about it he felt a weight in his chest; it was the weight of future failure, of a promise he knew could only be broken. 'It was going to be our bargaining chip – it was going to get us out of this mess. Fuck, my head hurts.'

'Your binge, right. The others were talking about it. We were sort of surprised to see you this morning to be honest. I mean I don't know much about it, I haven't read the reports, but it sounds like you made things pretty clear last night.'

'I did?' A fuzzy memory lurched into view – the sea of faces at *Brass*. What had he said?

'But you can really make these things – we all thought it was just the vodka talking. That's great. You've got something you can go and do. You don't need to worry about all this any more.' She sounded like a mother scraping the burnt tops off a child's fairy cakes, assuring him they would taste fine.

Kester looked up. Cherry was staring at him. Her dark eyes were hard to read. She was looking straight into him, digging around, doing something.

'Never mind,' Cherry said. 'You know it seems like you've cleared up one mess by making another. Maybe you need to jump before you're pushed. Just leave. Take your stuff with you. Do it yourself.'

They sat on their separate couches. She made it sound so simple. So obvious. He let the suggestion ring true in his mind for a moment, pushing out all doubts about funding, politics, the consequences, and let his problems be solved. Cherry was beautiful, Kester reflected. An exotic fruit. Velvet flesh, rich colours, a hard core that could cross oceans unscathed. He wished he wasn't so sore, wished they weren't sitting on separate couches, wished they weren't having this conversation.

'I wish it were that easy. If it were, an old friend and I would have done it years ago.'

'An old friend? An ex-friend?'

'A reinstated friend. She was really pissed off at me when I joined the company. We didn't speak for months. It got quite nasty. But we've made up, I think.'

'Why was she so pissed off?'

'Because she thinks I'm wasting my talents working for big business.'

'That's all?'

Kester looked up at Cherry. She wasn't convinced. Her expression couldn't have been plainer.

'It was...' Kester rolled back through the year in his mind. There was Dee with golden eyes; there was Dee with bleeding eyes. 'It was more to do with the fact I infected her with one of my viruses. She didn't know about it. I mean it was a pretty one and curable. She did wear it for a while in the end, but...' It wasn't making much sense to Kester any more.

'That's what she was pissed off about? Why would she care about one little virus when everyone does it here? And why would she wear it if she hated the idea so much? That's really what she was pissed off about? I mean she was *really* pissed off at you.' The sudden certainty in Cherry's voice spooked Kester. She knew. She had seen into his memories. 'Wasn't she?'

Shrinks were supposed to just listen, weren't they, not question you constantly?

'Yes. She was.'

'And you stopped sleeping together then.'

'We only slept together that once, when I gave her the virus.'

This opening-up business was seeming less and less of a good idea to Kester. He felt like she was interrogating him, like she was on Dee's side. It was getting out of control.

'Right.' Cherry sounded as if she had sussed him out, but he wasn't sure what there was to suss. 'Why were you wearing a virus anyway?' More questions. 'I thought the famous Doctor Lowe didn't wear.'

'No.'

She was accusing him of something. The room was drifting out of focus. He had been wearing the virus for Farrell. A gift for Farrell. There was Dee's face in his memory again: black and white, blood in her eyes, red flushes on her cheeks, stylised, a picture from a graphic novel. Her mouth was moving in slow motion – *you slept with her.*

'Whatever.' Cherry's voice brought him back to the room. 'It's none of my business.'

Kester felt heavy. He didn't need all this brought back to him now. Dee's rage had nothing to do with his present avalanche of woes. But as its white roar tumbled closer, threatening to engulf him, he thought he could see a little girl at the top of the mountain, smiling, her tiny hands freshly sprung apart from a single clap. No. He wouldn't feel guilty any more. They had come past that. They had made up.

'We made up.'

'You said that. You surprise me.'

'Why are you here?' Kester asked. He needed respite from her questioning, to hear her talk for a while, to hear about something other than his own mess. 'How did you end up working for us?'

Cherry frowned briefly. Her expression hardly changed, but the shadows on her face seemed to deepen.

'Why am I here?' She stared, unblinking. 'I was a sex worker...and I got the chance to come and work as a model. Isn't it obvious why I'm here?'

'You wanted to get out? Or to get in? To get into the City, I mean.'

Kester looked at her encouragingly as she sorted her thoughts.

'If you're a high-flying banker, or a lawyer, or even a scientist,' she indicated him, 'you can get a pass to come and live and work in the City. I could never have got back in – there's no head-hunting for Britain's top prostitutes. At least until now.' She gave a short laugh. 'You hardly need them in here. Those who want sex have each other, or the Pigs or whatever.'

'Back in? You lived here before?'

'When I was a child. It's complicated.'

'But why do you want to be in here? I mean it's perfectly nice outside the City, outside London.'

Cherry raised her eyebrows.

'My mother lives outside,' Kester said. 'I grew up outside. I know there are the less salubrious areas, but mostly it's just the same. Maybe not the same as the *City*. But you know, not that different from London. It's not like we've got all the candy hoarded up in here. You could have got a modelling job outside.'

'You flatter me. No. It had to be here.' She paused for a moment. She was a lid teetering on the balance of its hinges; any second she would fall open, or fall shut. 'My mother was tried and convicted in here on terrorism charges. I can't find out the truth about what she did from out there, what happened in the trial, anything. I was placed by a dodgy foster agency into the hands of a madam when she was convicted – if she even was convicted. I have a few things I'd like to sort out.'

'Right.' Kester felt a blush rising to his cheeks. 'I see. Yes, I can see how you might want to...you really can't find out about her from outside?'

'Look, the one thing I know is that I didn't do anything wrong, so there's no reason that I should have been got rid of in the manner I was. I've tried to find out the whole story through the archives, but it's impossible. The coverage just fizzles out. It doesn't even give way to conspiracy theories – it just stops, like nobody cared. I need to get into the official court records and I can only do that here in the City.' Cherry sighed and dropped her forehead into her hand for a moment, before looking back up. 'Doctor Lowe, it may look dodgy me being here, but even if I wanted to follow in my mother's footsteps I wouldn't know where to start.'

'Cherry – I didn't mean that. Nobody thinks that. Not at all. I just...'

Just what? Kester thought for a moment. He needed to get back to his desk before he was sick. He stood up and his hangover lurched. His whole body was scrambled. He felt weak. But he could do something good here maybe, though it was just a small thing. Cherry stood up in response and Kester found himself standing too close to her.

'You know if there's any way I can help,' he said. 'Alexis knows people at the Population Monitor and the records office too. Perhaps I could set something up after the show. If there is a show.'

Cherry looked as if she was puzzling through something.

'OK. Thanks,' she said. She put out a hand to touch him on the arm. 'Thank you. That's really good of you.'

Before his mind could stop it, Kester's body had replied to her touch in the way it had become accustomed, sending his shaking hand to her waist.

'That's OK.' He stiffened, aware that the gesture was not what it should be, an acknowledgement of her thanks.

'Are we going to?' Cherry screwed up her face.

'I'm sorry. I didn't mean to – it's just automatic.'

'Yes.' Cherry let out a breathy laugh. 'After all, who would pay who?'

Kester walked to the doors, then turned and attempted a smile. 'Thank you,' he said.

Kester returned to his office and slouched down into his desk chair. How could it still be Monday? He picked up his Book. It was only two o'clock. His hands were shaking. He needed it to be bedtime. He groaned as he noticed the message icon.

'Kester...darling,' Kester sat staring at his Book as the message played. His mother sounded as if she was struggling to call him darling. 'Son, I just wanted to call to say.' Her voice was breaking. 'I just wanted to say that I've seen all the news stories. I've seen...' She gave a small sob. 'Sorry, I've seen the pictures. I just wanted to. I'm...'

Her voice trailed off for a moment into thick snuffly silence. Kester's sore brain filled in the words: appalled, disgusted, hurt, embarrassed, inconsolable.

'I wanted to tell you I'm not angry, I just...'

Another pause: hate you, can't believe you did those things, can't believe you did that to your friends.

'I'm just a little surprised, Kester. I know...'

Tears welled up in Kester's eyes, making the room wobble. He let them settle there and fatten, staring, unblinking.

'...I know you're having a hard time of it. I just...' Another snuffle released a torrent of words. '...I just wanted you to know that I love you and I don't care what silly things you've done – I don't want you to worry about me, I just want you to be OK and just talk to me or talk to one of your friends or...just, I am proud of you, darling. It was so brave of you to make that speech, never mind that you were drunk. It was true, everything you said and if they won't make your screens, then I'm sure there's someone who will. And if you need somewhere to stay you know you can always come home. It'll all be right.' The dog barked in the background, calling out an involuntary teary laugh. The message ended there.

Kester's mind was full of holes. That guilty feeling was back. He put a hand to his head. Why would his mother be proud of him for some drunken speech? What made her bring up his screens again? He needed to find out what he'd said. Cringing, he picked up his Book. Fortunately, some kind soul had filmed the entire thing and it was available on every site imaginable.

As Kester listened back to his speech, punctuated with gulps and drunken roars from his audience, the pieces of his guilty puzzle fell into place.

...that those bastards at Stark don't want you to have screens that work properly. They want to keep you dependent on their stupid technodge...technology. Stupid – that's right – stupid. They think they can sweep aside millions of years of evolution and there not be a comeback. Darwin would...Darwin's fucking rolling in his grave right now, poor bastard. Stupid – we're chucking it all away, all our defences and you know what? If this thing fails, if it really fails we're all fucked. All of us. And the really stupid thing is it doesn't even need to be that way. I mean come ON! You can make screens that work fine with the body. You can do it. It can be done – I've done it. That's right – yeeees! I've made them and I'm going to make sure everyone can have one. Not just you City fuckers either – everyone – EVERYONE! Everyone and their dogs too. That's right Mum, if you're out there, their dogs too...

Kester was shivering. He felt light, empty, like he might pop. He watched the grainy image of himself, standing at an angle on the bar, clutching a bottle as he went on to denounce V and Stark Wellbury's cartel and went into a long nostalgic monologue about the Golden Age of science. Enough.

The smile Gerald had given him. It was a 'what are you doing here' smile. The looks the models had been giving him, the surprised 'hello's from his lab staff, it all made sense. When Gerald had said it would 'all be over soon'...

Kester glanced over towards his apartment and saw Alexis' birthday present, a six foot by four foot elastoplast, wrapped in brown paper, still sitting waiting to be stuck on. There was no apologising for this. His eye flicked up and across the grid of model portraits that catalogued the viral presentations. There was Cherry. The look on her face was defiance, rebellion, focused anger. *Jump before you're pushed.* He picked up his Book and tapped it on the bed a few times, then called John.

With John on his way, Kester took his Book over to his bar and got started organising things. When the door buzzer went he was all set.

'It's not your fault, man,' John said, stepping through Kester's doorway and punching him on the top of the arm. His smile was hard. 'I liked your speech by the way. Thanks for the honourable mention.'

'OK, this is what I've got,' Kester said, turning his attention to the bar. Phase one of his plan. He started to name the drinks he had lined up, filling the surface, four bottles deep. 'Vodka, cider,

Quicksilver, dark rum, white rum –'

'Kester, what are we doing here? Killing ourselves?'

Kester's mind flashed to the shelf at the top of the building, to his tiny body falling, labcoat wound around him, tumbled by the air, plummeting like a wounded chick. He shook his head rapidly to dispel the unpleasant thrill.

'Enjoying it while it lasts,' Kester said, watching for a reaction. 'And don't worry – we don't have to finish it all, we're just doing a tasting.'

John shrugged. Kester grabbed him by the arm and dragged him through to his desk.

'Tah dah!'

Kester surveyed the catering display. Crazed automatons – they had sent up everything he had asked for and stacked it high as instructed: roast suckling pig, beef, chicken, turkey, tongue, trotter, kebabs, soup, mousses, cake, broccoli, trifle, crackers, a vat of dhal, fresh halved coconuts, boiled potatoes, mashed potatoes, roast potatoes, a cheese board so large it looked like a scale model of a town.

'Man,' John said, his voice full of awe, and he walked slowly around the table. 'International buffet.' He dipped his finger in a silver bowl of humous and licked it clean. 'You've really lost it, man.'

Kester looked at him, forced a smile and nodded. He couldn't do this alone. It would be no fun at all.

'Let's get stuck in,' John said, finally, with a tentative laugh.

Kester whooped and ran through to the bar. He grabbed at the first bottle he saw. It was a blue liqueur he didn't recognise. He poured two shots and ran back through, crying out as it sloshed out onto his hands.

'OK!' he said. 'What goes with blue?'

Chapter 22

Kester didn't hear the doors to his office open. The music was too loud. He didn't see them open. He was wearing a large silver cloche as a hat. He felt a sudden ringing. The lid was a bell and he was the clapper. John had bashed him on the head.

Kester lashed out with his French stick, hitting John in the stomach, and then watched as John's feet staggered about the table in front of him, demolishing whole platters of food. One of John's feet jammed in a chicken carcass. He continued stamping around a bit, coating the chicken in broken meringue and gravy, then he turned and collapsed, his face appearing on the table between Kester's feet.

'Kester!'

Kester could see that John was shouting to him. The music cut off mid-verse.

'Kester!'

'What?' Kester shouted back to the quiet room.

'Kester!' John rolled from side to side, then started to waggle his arms up and down, making a food angel in the mess of the table.

'What?' Kester laughed.

'There's someone at the door!'

'What?'

Kester jumped. He spun around, feet slipping in the food, and lifted the cloche up over his eyes. Panic drained his drunkenness for a moment and he stopped moving. Everything was silent. Kester was out of body, hovering above the tableau: himself standing in the middle of his desk in his labcoat and pants, peeking out from under his polished hat, smothered in food, a limp French loaf hanging from one hand; John lying at his feet, still flapping his arms, shunting piles of destroyed food onto the floor; the sea of opened, tasted and discarded bottles, and the slick of brown muddied drink that covered the floor around them.

Alexis was standing in the doorway with Chen at her side, beyond them, a lab full of staring eyes, open mouths, an audience of surprised sex-dolls. They all stood frozen. Kester responded in kind and stayed still, as if he might be able to stop time until he thought of a clever way out. It was all very bright, like leaving the cinema in daytime.

'Doctor Lowe,' the chirpy voice of the wardrobe assistant rang out. She was looking down at her clipboard as she drew level with the doors. 'I hope we were quick enough. We pulled out all the stops and...' her voice trailed off as she looked up.

'Saffron, thanks. Excellent work!' Kester said, standing up straight and brushing off his labcoat. 'Just leave them there would you?'

'Em, yes, sir.' The assistant smothered a giggle with her hand, tried her best to nod deferentially to Farrell and Chen, then waved at her helpers to hurry up. The racks of pre-unpicked clothes kept coming until there were eight lined up behind Farrell and Chen, at which point Saffron bowed politely and herded her helpers back to the lift.

Kester looked down behind him. John was asleep or passed out. What would John do? Brazen it out.

'I know what you're thinking.' Kester walked to the front edge of his desk. He went to remove his hat, then changed his mind and left it propped back on his forehead. Don't defer to them. Your office; your rules. 'I know what you're –'

'I doubt you do, Doctor Lowe,' Chen said.

Kester tried to read them. Chen looked astounded. She hadn't decided to believe it yet. Kester remembered his old head teacher opening the door on their unattended art class. The look on Alexis' face was changing. She might almost have been impressed, but it was a dark sort of impressed; the sort of impressed you might be as you looked over the edge of a landmark cliff before sliding a body off its lip. He waited for a moment longer. If they wanted to, they could walk away now and pretend they had never seen it. He gave them the opportunity – it was only fair.

They didn't take their chance. Kester took a deep breath and felt a sudden lightness. He wouldn't be pushed. Stick to the plan. So this hadn't technically been part of the plan, but he needed to think on his feet. He would skip to the end.

'Thank you for coming!' He held out his arms to them. 'I wanted to talk to you both. I'm not happy with the way things are going.

'Chen, you've abused your position of authority. I am not your rent boy. You've degraded me and you've degraded the whole company. I'm not sleeping with any more of your dirty little celebrities. Screw your stupid job.

'Alexis…' This was harder. He felt his drunkenness rushing back in, his shoulders rounding, his posture collapsing. 'You…you should have…' He felt his face contorting, closed his eyes and fought it. 'I gave up a good career for this. And you did what you promised – you made me a star. So…well done, I guess. But…' The rest of Kester's speech left him. He looked around the room, looked down at his hands, but the words weren't anywhere. They were lost in the mulch of food and drink. 'It's all gone to shit, Alexis!' Kester put his hands out, as if his situation had taken physical form there around them. 'Look at this mess. My friends are all going to lose their jobs, I've been ostracised by the entire scientific community.' He staggered a little and looked round at John. 'Except for John. My reputation is in tatters; I've embarrassed my own mother beyond all belief; I've got fucking stitches in my arse…I mean do I need to go on? This whole thing is a fucking disaster area. Alexis, I'm sorry I wasn't the perfect star you wanted. And Chen, actually I do know what you're thinking, fuck you very much. You've come here to get rid of me. Well don't worry. I'm going to save you the trouble and quit.' He slithered down off the table, strode over to where John lay and started rummaging in his pockets. 'My associate has got the letter right here.' He turned and held the crumpled piece of jam-covered paper out to Chen.

'That would seem rather rash,' Chen said.

Alexis looked at Chen. They were conversing without words. Kester couldn't figure out what they were saying. Alexis raised her eyebrows. Chen responded in kind and shrugged. Alexis cocked her head forward. Chen nodded.

'Kester – in here.' Alexis grabbed Kester by the arm and ushered him into his living quarters. Kester watched her warily as she walked over to the bar. She poured a large scotch.

'Thanks,' Kester slurred.

'This is for me, Kester, you fuckwit,' she said, bringing over a glass of water and handing it to him.

'Oh.'

Alexis looked at Kester long and hard. He struggled to look back at her. Her face was fluttering in front of his eyes like a broken film reel.

'I'm going to try and forget what I just saw,' she said, 'though it might take some doing.'

Kester swallowed. It felt like he had a knot of old boot leather in his gullet.

'And take that fucking thing off your head,' she added, without humour.

Kester had forgotten about his helmet. He reached up and lifted the cloche off his head. He held it in front of him for a moment, then realised it looked like he was clutching a bowler hat and put it down gently on the ground beside him. He could still feel its weight on the crown of his head.

'I thought about what you said.' Alexis turned away from him. 'You were right. And your stupid speech was right too. Yule's going to have your guts for garters but that's not important right now.'

Kester had no idea what was going on. He tried to stay very still. She seemed to be apologising to him, but that was ridiculous. Yes, best to stay still and keep his mouth shut.

'Chen wants to see the screens.'

Nausea. Elation. Nausea again.

'Oh fuck,' Kester stepped to one side and took hold of the bar.

'Kester, she's excited. She's livid that you'd presume to do the research in the first place and the way it came out...perhaps that's my fault...and as for whatever just happened – but forget that. She exploded, but when I told her that everything you said about the screens was true she put all that on hold. I've told her the basics but she wants to see it for herself. We need some good publicity badly, really badly and now, before the show. It may be your fault that we need it, but if you provide the solution as well as the problem this could end well for all of us.'

Kester's heart raced. She wanted to see the screens. He momentarily forgot his predicament and whooped. 'Lex, that's brilliant, but...' An image of his jam-smeared letter popped into his head.

'You know what this means, Kester?'

Kester's mind was going through a mangle. He was quitting. He was disgraced. His mother hated him. His mother was proud of him. He was a prostitute. He was a scientist. He was really, really drunk.

'Well...' Kester stopped almost before he had begun. No. He didn't know what it meant.

'Chen's gone for the deal. No more pimping.' She came towards him and curled her hands around his triceps. 'And if this doesn't mend your reputation with the scientific community...'

Kester laughed. The laugh hung in the air, a wisp of relief. Alexis smiled in return. Kester took in her poise, her angles, her eyes and the mind he saw projected through them, sure as a branding iron. She was beautiful. She could save him.

'Thank you. Thank you so much,' Kester said. He broke out of her hold and hugged her hard, held on as if it would all fall apart again if he let go.

'Kester,' she said, as he clung to her, 'you feel...heavy...just how much have you had to drink?'

He stepped back in as controlled a fashion as he could and thought about it for a second or two. Her exact question had left him already, but the jist of it was still within reach so he answered as best he could.

'Yes,' he said, 'but a few hours ago and I'm feeling much better now.'

'Okay...' she said slowly, walking to the coffee machine. 'I think you should get in the shower. Now.'

'I'm sorry, I was angry,' Kester said. He was a teenager who had trashed the house. 'I just needed to let loose for a few hours, that's all. The speech was a mistake.' He gave her a sheepish look that he hoped would prove endearing and removed his labcoat ineptly. He still needed to explain. Everything was muddled. 'I thought it was all over. I failed everyone. I needed to, I don't know. I thought it was all over...um...I got you a present.'

'Kester – just get in the shower.'

By the time Kester got out of the shower, the cleanup team was leaving. John was tucked up neatly in Kester's bed and Chen had gone.

'Are you ready?' Alexis asked.

Kester shook his head and picked up the coffee she had poured for him. He walked into his office and looked around. On his desk, beside a small smear of gravy that had been missed, sat his degree certificate, framed. Beside it lay his Book, a picture message from his mother sitting open – the dog sporting a pair of signed Kester Lowe knickers. Over the back of his chair hung a freshly laundered labcoat. Through the door he could just see the top of his best friend's head, tousled hair sticking out from under the duvet.

He flicked an icon on his Book and a stream of data covered the wall behind him. His torsos. They had been left to themselves. He surveyed the data, squinting against his encroaching headache and the possibility of bad news. Gradually, he admitted a smile to his lips. He took a deep breath and examined his state: legs functioning again, still drunk, but steadily sobering up. His mind felt hyperclear, his body light. Better now than with a hangover. Alexis appeared in the doorway.

'Yes,' Kester said. 'I think I'm ready.'

Alexis led the way through the lab. Kester cast out some embarrassed smiles as he passed the rows of workbenches and was repaid with friendly giggles and a couple of winks. Chen had just exited the lifts and was walking towards the isolation suites. Kester overtook Alexis and rushed to meet Chen with a hearty handshake. He ignored what had gone before, as coached by Alexis.

'Talk me through it, Doctor Lowe,' Chen said as they entered the suite. 'This had better be as good as she says it is.' Kester saw her shoot a warning glance at Alexis. 'I still have your letter.'

'It is,' Kester said as they stood in the decontamination lock. 'This is just a precaution,' he added. 'Cross-infection wouldn't really be a problem.'

They entered the suite. The torsos were laid out in two rows of five in the middle of the room, each in a transparent life-support box. Kester walked over to the work bench at the side of the room and called up a large display on the wall above it. It was divided into eleven sections – two rows of five boxes across the top, one monitoring each torso, and a main summary below.

'Meet the Baldwins.' Kester waved a hand across the torsos. 'They've been wearing my new screen for more than two months now and none of them have shown any signs of damage from infection. If you tap the log icon at the bottom of the screen you can see the viruses I've tested with. I've done airborne, blood borne, water borne; I've done mucal membrane infection, wound infection, ingestion, you name it.' As he spoke, Chen walked round the boxes, regarding each of the torsos, as if she could somehow judge the screens' effectiveness by simply looking at them. 'And now we're onto new viruses.'

'And that works how?' Chen asked.

'OK,' Kester took a breath. 'The screen itself is biological, yes? I don't know how much Lex has told you. It's built by a set of viruses and the only pieces of hard nanotech I've kept in there are nanotransmitters, which we need for obvious reasons. Its real power is that it can talk to the body and vice versa; its components are built by the body's own cells and this allows each to recognise the other's immunological responses and act in tandem, multiplying the effect. No messy implant to provide the raw materials. No immunosuppressant drugs.

'The first virus is programmed, if you like, with the structure of the screen. It gets the host tissue to build the screen bed. You might be aware that in the Stark Wellbury screen, the nanotech particles create the screen bed themselves. Of course it can't be coated with its diamond cloak until after it's assembled, so it effectively introduces visible foreign tissue, which is just the start of the problems the body has with it. Our screen is built in-house by the host body – problem solved.

'The second virus infects the newly engineered tissue, providing a set of factory cells – viruses are perfect factories but they normally make copies of themselves. Some of the factory cells make what I'm calling "cruisers" and "bruisers" – cells that identify and chomp on baddies respectively. Some of them make antibodies. These factory cells…' Kester fast-forwarded past some detail in his head '…will make copies of whatever we send them the blueprints for.

'You could think of it as the virus being on pause until we send it a set of blueprints. Once it receives its blueprints, it operates like a normal virus – reproduces until the cell bursts, sending the new viruses or in this case, antibodies out into the bloodstream. As you've probably realised, this means that the tissue needs a perpetually regenerating set of factory viruses. That bit was tricky.'

'OK,' Chen waved her hand. 'I think I can trust you on the details. How are they responding to the new viruses?'

'Exactly as planned. The cruisers and bruisers act like super-components of the existing immune system. When an antigen is identified, the body starts to produce antibodies using both its own processes and the new tools we've given it. The transmitter sends details of everything that is produced back to the central database, which includes the new blueprints in the next upload transmission. I've used a different set of new viruses on each torso and then cross-infected them to see how well it works. *And* the transmitters also pick up blueprints from other screen users in the local population, preparing the host for any likely infection that's doing the rounds, which is fucking amazing by the way.' Kester checked himself. Be sober. Be sober.

'And how well does it work?'

'It works well. Very well. There are two torsos you'll be particularly interested in.' Kester led Chen to the two boxes at the back of the room. 'These guys – Daniel and William. William has an old Stark screen and Daniel has no immune system.' Chen walked around the boxes as Kester explained. 'We successfully shut William's old screen down, using a variant of our old friend Trojan12 incidentally, and there has been no interference. And with Daniel, the screen was able to produce enough antibodies without the support of the immune system to protect it as completely as the old screen.'

Chen had stopped circling and was leaning against a workbench at the side of the room, a pensive smile on her face.

'Doctor Lowe. You have been busy.'

'In my own time – my own time. And remember, Alexis and I brought this to you.'

Chen stared at Kester for a moment, then looked away to the side, breathed in and nodded.

'I'm going to make this easy for you, Kester.' She looked back at him. 'Alexis has told me what you want. If this wasn't so big, I'd be furious. And as for recent events – well, this has been a hard week for all of us. I think some mutual forgiveness may be in order.' She nodded again, as if satisfied that this part of the issue was dealt with. 'Is it feasible to test this in-house like Alexis suggested? We don't need to worry about Farmer any more, not now this is out, and I'm willing to do some rearranging if he looks like causing trouble. Having said that, if we could keep the testing in-house for phase one that would be ideal – speed things up.'

'Absolutely. We've more than enough staff to do feasible trials, although we might need some externals to make sure the demographic representation is right.'

'And how long is this going to take? As long as a drugs trial?'

'Nowhere near. A year, 18 months maybe.'

Chen snorted as if this was nothing and then smiled. 'I think you have yourself a deal, young man.'

Kester looked over at Alexis, then back at Chen.

'Really?' he asked, like a child given permission to draw on the walls.

'Really. You'll want this in writing. Come by my office this afternoon.'

Kester couldn't conceal a nervy twitch. To go by someone's office at V so often implied more than it expressed.

'No funny business. You have my word.'

'Thank you.'

'And this is to remain top secret, you understand?'

'I'll treat it as if it's still my private work. You have my word.'

'One other thing,' Chen added. 'I've set up an appointment for you with our counsellor and put a freeze on your alcohol account.'

'Right,' Kester said. 'Fair enough.'

-o-

The week was accelerating. It was all unreal. Kester had believed it would all stop, that none of this would happen. Instead, V had acknowledged his research and had put out a statement telling the world that they were developing a rival nanoscreen to Stark Wellbury's: a screen that would be affordable and available to everyone; a screen that would work with the body, not against it. The rumours in the press were that Kester would make an announcement about it at the show – an official announcement this time – perhaps even do a presentation. While Chen hadn't asked him to prepare anything he was sure that the rumours had originated from V itself. It had to be a teaser to keep the show on track. Of course there was the embarrassment of the post-binge interviews, but Kester suspected that these were easier for him than for Chen, who had to appear with him as the reformed, philanthropic face of VDV.

On a high, Kester had agreed to go through with the remaining pre-show appointments under strict condition that the clients were briefed on appropriate behaviours and the consequences of overstepping the boundaries. To the public it must look like things were continuing smoothly.

The remaining appointments were at the Vspa in the top of the PlayPen. They seemed less of a big deal armed with the knowledge that this really was a one-off and that his screens would soon be in production. Kester was almost looking forward to them.

The Vspa was a blissful retreat after the sensory overload of the palace and the raucous confusion of Pera Pera's phantasmagorical stage show.

The walls, with their City view, were whited out so that all the clients could see was the sky. The large circular bed was set up in the centre of the main space along with a freestanding hot tub to one side. Round the sides of the room a sauna, a steam room, a wet room and a play room had been set up. The play room had walls which could be misted or coloured out. It had a soft floor and was decked out with cushions and furs. A discreet toy cabinet was nestled in the corner and the curved side of the room housed a large display on a default setting of open log fire. Finally, there was a treatment room which could be used by the clients before, during or after their appointment with Kester.

It was unimaginative in a way and Kester had his doubts about it being set up the same way for each client – wouldn't they all want a different experience? But his concerns were unfounded. Each client brought with them their own experiences and preferences, their own fantasies and fetishes. Each made it their own.

On Tuesday, with Basil Black Junior, the room became a log cabin in the wilderness. Kester, still hung over, was thankful for this. Black touched him as if they were the only two humans for thousands of miles and the feeling of isolation suited Kester. It was the first time he had experienced full sex with a man and the fantasy of this romance at the ends of the earth helped him to relax, allowed him to be taken in, wooed and brought around to the idea.

On Wednesday, with Tamsin Holloway, a creature of limited imagination, the room had remained a spa where her naughty masseur took advantage of her in every conceivable way.

Thursday was a confusing day. Kester spent it with the anonymous wife of a reclusive American billionaire who called herself simply 'Joan'. Her fantasies were unfocused, as if she wanted everything at once. Kester felt he was running around after her, a naked clown, always one step behind her desires. He was glad for Gaunt's 'medicine'. However, he was repaid fully for his efforts when, towards the end of the appointment, they spent half an hour worshipping each others' feet with caresses and kisses until he finally felt for the first time that day that he wanted and was able to please her.

When Kester finally got back to his apartment, he was completely spent. He was relieved to find that Alexis was still in her office, working on the last-minute arrangements for the following night. It was past midnight when she finally appeared. Kester woke when she slipped into bed beside him. He flicked his bedside light on.

'Sorry,' she said, 'I didn't mean to wake you. Gaunt told me about your vigorous session with "Joan".' She rubbed at her eyes.

'He did?' Kester replied sleepily. 'Yes…she was…tiring.'

'At least that's it now, apart from the show.'

'Apart from the show.' Kester waited for the brightness from his lamp to calm, for the room to come into focus. 'But that's just ten minutes of madness, one night, just like the last one. And it won't just be me. There'll be an army of models. And you.'

'And me. Yes, I suppose I had better.'

Alexis had been working hard this week, Kester reminded himself, taking in her face. She looked drawn, colourless. Her eyes were raw. In the dim lamp light she looked like a sexy vampire from an old movie, silken hair tumbling back from a face lost to life.

'Your eyes are red,' he said, putting a hand to her cheek.

'I know. I'm just tired is all.' She blinked a few times and wiped at them with her fingers. 'I'll be fine in the morning.'

'You should have a lie-in tomorrow.'

A laugh died in her throat. 'I'll be up early and it won't be early enough.'

'Anything I can help with?'

'No. I wish there were. I probably won't see you until the curtains go up.'

'Try to.'

'I'll try to.'

Kester kissed her, flicked the lamp off, closed his eyes, opened his eyes and it was morning. He felt like an old alarm clock, switched off at the wall, then switched on again, digits flashing in panic, unsure what time it was. He felt cheated, like he hadn't slept at all. He put out a hand. Alexis was already gone but her side of the bed was still warm. He rolled over and snuggled down into her scent.

-o-

Alexis cursed at her reflection. The bulbs around the edge of her mirror lit her eyes with tiny windows. She remembered the first virus Kester had given her, the room distorting as she contained her panic. Her eyes were still red and were starting to run. She had believed it was tiredness and that a coffee would banish it. Might it be an irritant? Had she touched anything, used anything unusual? She picked up her makeup bag and rummaged through it. That new mascara? But she'd worn it before and she had been fine.

'This had better be a side effect of your next wonderful surprise, my love.'

She flicked the light switch. The bulbs sputtered out and she stood listening for the twanging of the filaments as they cooled. She wiped a thick tear from the corner of her eye, then walked back through her office and out of the door, pulling her jacket from the back of her chair as she went.

Gerald was doing zigzag laps of the lab when Alexis arrived, stopping here and there to peer over shoulders and point at things. As he walked, he kept his hands gripped tightly at the small of his back. She moved to intercept him as he approached the end of a row of workbenches.

'Last minute preparations for the show,' he said without prompting as she strode towards him.

Her strides were wider than the tolerance of her skirt and with each step she felt it hug her lean thighs.

'Where's Kester?' Alexis demanded. 'I need to talk to him.'

'Alexis,' Gerald said, surprised, 'your eyes are weeping – here.'

He took a handkerchief from his pocket and handed it to her. Such a gentleman, even under pressure. She took it and dabbed at her eyes.

'Thank you, Gerald,' she said. 'Now where is he?'

'He's not here,' Gerald said, steering her into his office. 'He's already into his pre-show interviews. What is it? Can I help you?'

'It's my eyes. They've been running since mid morning. I don't know what's causing it – presumably one of his bloody viruses – and I can't get them to stop. I'm going to look a fucking mess tonight.'

'It's alright. Sit down and we'll sort this out.'

Alexis paced about the office a few times, and then forced herself to sit.

'It could be a rare side-effect of one of the viruses,' Gerald said, fetching her a coffee from his machine. 'There's always the chance that one or two people out there will react differently to them.'

'He hasn't got anything else on the go? Something like Corona – something that does this for a while before it presents?'

'Not that I know of…but I haven't been working on all of them – it could well be. Having said that, anything new should have shown up on your screen. It must be something you're already wearing.'

'So what am I going to do? I can't get a hold of him. It's only a few hours until the curtains go up.'

'I'll try to get him for you, but I've got an idea. Corona did affect some of the wider testing group in this way and we prescribed them eye drops. Let me get you some – they might keep things under control for now until we can get a hold of Kester.'

'OK,' Alexis said, emptying her coffee cup and shooting up out of her seat, 'but make it snappy. I'm due to update Chen on our progress in half an hour and I need to get down to inspect the site before then.'

'Stay put,' Gerald said. 'I'll look them out now.'

-o-

Cherry sat on a chair by the misted-up window, staring at it as if there was a view. She visualised the baster-style virus applicator, still sitting in the shoe box at Dempsey's and thought through how she had handled everything. There was no way it could be her. And someone finding the virus, putting it on, coming in to V – another agent of the Church perhaps, a backup in case she bottled it? No. Too farfetched. It was co-incidence, she told herself. She had made the right decision and was just freaking.

'You wanted to see me?' Gerald asked as he came in the door.

He nodded amiably to Cherry as he entered. She got up from her chair and guided him by the elbow towards the isolation booths. She could feel his good cheer draining as they walked.

'Can I speak to you privately?' she asked.

'Of course.'

He stepped aside so that she could enter the booth first. Once the door was shut, they both stood for a moment. Cherry looked at the bench and the chair.

'Please, after you,' Gerald said, indicating the bench.

Cherry sat down and Gerald took the chair.

'What's eating you?' He passed a hand over the slick surface of his hair.

'We just had a briefing with Farrell,' Cherry said. She wasn't sure quite how to continue. He had said he didn't want to be involved but she needed to know what he knew. His eyes were wary. 'She was using eye drops.'

'Yes. I gave them to her.'

'You did?' Cherry said, relief readying itself to rush in. 'So they're for something official. I mean, they're for one of the show viruses?'

Gerald stared at her for a long time. The rectangle of the room's daylight ceiling made dramatic windows in his brown eyes. He was considering something. Whether to end the conversation there, perhaps.

'No,' he said. 'They're not.'

Cherry tried not to react, but by Gerald's face it was obvious that she had failed.

'You know what it is?' he asked.

'I don't know – I mean I can't be sure. The Church had me get another virus.'

'The Church…' Gerald closed his eyes as if trying to erase this last piece of the conversation.

Cherry winced. He didn't know she was working for the Church. Hadn't wanted to know.

'That's just what they're calling themselves,' she said, backpedalling. 'My employers. But I can't be sure that's what it is. I was supposed to...' Cherry paused and looked at Gerald's face. She needed to continue, needed him to know it wasn't her. He didn't stop her. Just stared, concerned. 'I was supposed to release it amongst the models for the final show. One of the symptoms was running eyes.'

'But you didn't.' Gerald lowered his head.

'No. I just thought when I saw her eyes...I was worried that someone else...'

'Cherry,' Gerald put out a hand and placed it on hers, 'we use the eye drops for lots of different viruses and so do other companies. It's a common side effect of one of the base viruses. It could be anything – you know what Farrell's like.'

Cherry examined Gerald's expression. He couldn't be more heavily involved than she thought, could he? Was he Blotch's back-up? No. His eyes were clear, sincere.

'And if it is?'

Gerald sat back. 'You know more than me, but presumably your employer will be happy and you'll have a clear conscience. Everyone's a winner, assuming it's nothing that Kester can't fix.' He looked suddenly concerned again. 'What will happen if they find out you've not carried out your orders?' he asked, then looked as if he wished he hadn't.

'Nothing that will affect you. I'm sorry, Gerald. I didn't realise the drops were so common. I just thought you might know what they were for. It just freaked me out a bit.'

'I'm sure we'll find out what it is soon enough. Kester's probably got something new up his sleeve, or rather his...' Gerald coughed and smiled.

Cherry smiled back and allowed the relief to come. As Gerald stood, the door slid open to let them out.

'Probably some new thing he hasn't had the chance to pass on to anyone else,' Gerald said. 'He's been so busy. Though a friend at the PlayPen tells me he was down there last weekend.'

'Really?'

'Yes. Making a bit of time for an old flame by all accounts –

naughty boy. He'd better hope Farrell doesn't find out!'

Cherry laughed. An old flame. The room was hot. The room was cold. She put a hand out to the doorframe as they passed through.

'You alright?'

'Fine.' Cherry slowly became aware that she was shaking her head. 'Nothing that can't be fixed.'

Once Gerald had left, Cherry returned to her seat at the window. *Everyone's a winner.* Gerald's words looped in her head.

Chapter 23

In the knowledge that Alexis wouldn't be there with him, Kester opted to get ready for the show in his apartment. A large mirror sat on his desk, surrounded by Rita's makeup kit and hair products. He examined her work in the mirror as she packed her things into what looked to him like a chrome toolbox.

'I'll take all this backstage in case you need any touch-ups,' she said.

Kester peered at his makeup. It was heavy but reasonably natural-looking, though Rita had gone a bit eyeliner-happy this time. He watched as she finished stowing her gear. All packed up, she walked to the door, listing to one side with the weight of the case.

'Good luck!' she said as she left.

Kester looked back to the mirror and smiled, baring his teeth. Failing to convince himself, he let his face fall straight and then smiled again, tried to look excited. This was the end of it. No more clamouring to sleep with Doctor Lowe, unless you happened to be an ambitious underling. Would he still be a superstar when he started proper work on the screen trials? Yes. A different type of superstar. Would people still desire him? He tried to think of any serious scientists he had ever fancied. He touched the frayed edges of his pocket where the ads had been lovingly sewn on and removed, and then wandered back over to the mirror.

'You look ravishing, dear boy.' Gaunt's voice made Kester jump. 'You ready for your last supper?'

'Alexis told you then?'

'She intimated that you wouldn't be doing this again. I've been saving my pocket money but I'm afraid I still can't quite afford you. Sad that this could be my last chance.'

Kester laughed. 'Sad for you, Gaunt.' He turned and walked through the doors of his living quarters, patting Gaunt on the shoulder as he passed. 'Some of us are relieved.'

'Getting me a gin?'

Kester clattered around at his bar for a few minutes, then re-entered his office with a beer for himself and a gin for Gaunt.

'Better not have too many.' Gaunt nodded at Kester's beer. 'It'll stop my medicine working properly.'

'Fat chance. I managed to get the freeze lifted from my booze account, but I'm on a strict limit – ten units a week; cans and miniatures only.'

'Ouch!'

'Tell me about it,' Kester said, then sighed.

'What's getting you, boy?'

Gaunt was at the window now, taking in the view of the square. Wardrobe had kitted him out in a velvet tailcoat with a high collar. With his shock of white hair, and the shifting red and green glow from the square below, he looked like a ghostly count.

'Just…' Kester struggled to put his finger on it. 'There are bits of all this I like.'

'The sex god status, the access…'

'Creating beautiful things, being listened to, being…'

'Worshipped?'

'Recognised. The recognition.'

'The money?'

'Yes, the money. But that's not going to stop.'

'Who says everything else will. Keep your hand in on the viral side. Creative Director has always been a job title that's captured me – or how about Chief Imagineer.'

Kester laughed.

'You don't think for a moment we're going to stop doing this until it stops making us money do you?' Gaunt said. 'Just because your arse isn't on the silver salver any more – and despite my personal feelings I agree with the decision that it shouldn't be – that doesn't mean we can't keep on selling your wares.'

'No, I suppose not.'

'Don't worry boy, they'll still love you. Come here.' Gaunt beckoned to Kester to join him at the window. 'Lap it up. If you're going to miss it, taste it, drink it in, make the most of it.' He put a hand on Kester's shoulder and gave a squeeze. 'But whatever you do, don't be late. Curtain's up in thirty minutes. Alexis will meet you backstage before the first models go out. I'll see you at the after-party.'

Gaunt slipped a packet of pills into Kester's top pocket and left him standing at the window.

Outside, the square was full. To increase capacity they had installed rows and rows of three-tiered balcony boxes up the sides of the two buildings that flanked the square. The boxes jutted out, angled towards the stage, covering the windows of the bottom fifteen floors with a serrated wall of metal. They were already filling slowly from the bottom up and as they crowded with pinprick faces and waving arms, the buildings started to resemble living coral, hard structure with delicate fleshy protuberances so fine as to resemble a pink fur. At the back of the square, set up as before, was the Stark Wellbury structure, pulsating in its many different ways. The V building itself was the only surface in the square not covered with excited flesh. It was terrifying. Kester imagined them all tumbling out of their boxes down into the square, arms and legs stuck out like dolls, an avalanche of flesh and sweat and hair.

He shuddered. Perhaps this was too much desire for his liking, even for Alexis'. Perhaps. He took the packet from his pocket, popped two pills from it and washed them down with a swig of beer. Time to go.

Kester walked through the central V revolving door into the backstage area. It had begun. The noise was all-consuming. The screams and shouts of the crowd rolled across each other, pulling together, gathering into a great ball of sound that tumbled endlessly, contained by the square. The acoustics were different to the first show. The sound was no longer clattering off metal and glass; it was broken on the jagged lining of screaming fans, jetting into their mouths, eyes, ears and spilling back out distorted.

'They're having trouble with the sound,' Alexis hollered into Kester's ear as he joined her. This time they had a massive display on which to watch the show, a patchwork of different angles of the stage.

'No kidding!' he said. He tried to see her face in the nightmarish backstage light, see if she was looking less done in. 'How are you feeling?'

She sneered at him and pointed to her temples. A headache? The noise was vibrating his bones. He could feel his eardrums fluttering, unable to cope with the bombardment, the pressure in his head building.

'Cover your ears,' Alexis mouthed, pointing up to the top portion of the display which showed the side stage. The first band was taking the stage. The scream of the guitars was painful, but at least it united the sound, drawing everything together. A technician shambled over to Kester and Alexis, head low, as if he was ducking wires, and handed them each a pair of protective headphones.

-o-

Cherry's legs were shaking. This was ridiculous. She wished she hadn't looked out into the square. She was beginning to understand why they had spent so much time practising walking. Her head hurt from the severe up-do wardrobe had imposed on her, the thirty or forty hairpins that had scraped along her scalp during the process of getting it to stay up. The noise made it hard to think, but she needed to figure out what to do. The virus was out there and the Church would expect that to be the case. So what now?

Doctor Lowe would be destroyed if one of his viruses spayed half the City. He would never make his screens. Or would the company manage to clear it up, get him off the hook so he could continue his work? Whatever happened, god knows how many people would still be affected and she would be guilty not because she had caused it, but because she could have stopped it.

But she couldn't reveal herself. If she did, Blotch would know she hadn't held up her end of the bargain and they would find a way to get to her. This wasn't where she had expected to be.

The first models were due to go on in ten minutes. Cherry's mind churned but turned up nothing new. She peeked out at the crowd again and let her eyes wander up the wall of spectators on the east side of the square. Somewhere in one of the boxes, a spectator dropped something – an empty drinks cup. It fell down to the open hands of the crowd below and was tossed along, somersaulting for a few moments, before disappearing to the ground to be trampled. At the front of the crowd, someone threw a handful of fliers up in the air. Cherry watched as a woman near the front, struggling to stay on her feet, picked one of the fliers out of her bouffant hair and read it before tossing it away. That was it.

Fizzing with purpose, Cherry started to cast around backstage. Coming to the bank of hair and makeup stations, she found what she was looking for. The makeshift structure had no built in displays, so tucked into the bottom of the mirror at each station was a paper copy of the running order for the night. Cherry grabbed one or two, then spotted a handful of spares sitting in a messy pile on the edge of the bench and scooped these up too. The second lot of models were starting to arrive for their last-minute prep, already in costume.

Suddenly, there were people everywhere. Rita appeared from behind a clothes rack.

'Thanks, Cherry!' Rita said, as she saw Cherry shuffling the papers into a pile. 'What a state, huh?' She waved her arms at the carnage on the benches and long dressing table.

Cherry looked up at her questioningly. 'Just chuck them?'

'Yeah.' Rita handed her an empty cup. 'This too if you don't mind, love. Then can you tell your lot I'll need them back here in fifteen minutes for final prep?'

'No problem.'

Letting her hand brush over the station next to her, Cherry lifted an eyeliner pen and held it tucked against her wrist. She rushed away and slipped into the wings, eyes clambering along the scaffolding, looking for an obvious viewpoint. The only people around here were the lighting technicians and they were storeys above her where they could get a real view of the square. Their lift was stationary at the bottom of the scaffolding, so they weren't coming down any time soon and she would have a few minutes warning if they were planning to.

Cherry spotted a series of slim ladders leading up to a small landing. She looked around again to check that there was no-one there. Confident she wouldn't be seen, she stripped out of her sheer kaftan, down to her skin-coloured knickers, stuck the paper and pen between her teeth and started to climb.

-o-

The first models were about to go on. Kester went to take Alexis' hand, but she was rummaging in her pocket. He looked back to the display to see six cloaked figures walking down the catwalk. When he turned his gaze back to Alexis, she was looking up, holding something above her face – a tear-shaped bottle – eye drops. He recognised the label. They were the eye drops he used for viral side-effects. He grabbed her wrist.

'Alexis – what's going on?'

With the headphones on Kester could hear himself, his voice soft and rounded, simple-sounding in his head. But Alexis could not. She pulled her arm away and put the drops in her other eye. Kester stood up and, despite her wriggling protests, led her away from the display back into the foyer of the V building where they could hear one another.

'Kester, what's wrong with you? The first models are going out!'

Kester could feel the glass walls booming as if they might implode at any minute.

'What's going on with your eyes? Where did you get those drops from?'

'From Gerald – he said if it was a viral side-effect –'

'We haven't had any of this sort of…' Kester felt a weight in his gullet.

'Look – this isn't the time.'

'Alexis, this could be another attack.'

'What?'

'This isn't one of tonight's viruses. I'm certain of it. We haven't had any side-effects like this.'

'You've given me something new then?'

'No.'

'Nothing's shown up on my screen. You really think this could be an attack?'

'It's OK.' Kester put his hands out.

'OK?' Alexis' voice ripped through the noise in the foyer. 'What am I infected with? What the hell is this?'

'Just calm down – I need to get you upstairs to find out.'

'Don't tell me to calm down, Kester!'

Alexis flipped into efficiency mode. Her face calmed and Kester could see her thinking things through, only tiny movements in her facial muscles, small physical tics, betraying the urgency of her thought process.

'The first models are out there,' she said after a few seconds. 'They're in the exchange booths by now. If I'm infected, who else is? Fuck – I've slept with half of them.'

'Half of who?'

'Half of everybody else! I wish I could tell you that it's only you, Kester – I wish I could – but old habits die hard.'

'We need to get up to the lab now. Call Chen.' Kester grabbed her arm again and pulled her towards the lifts.

-o-

Panting slightly, Cherry dismounted the bottom ladder. She hadn't had time to wait and see what happened. A scream went up from the crowd and she tensed for a moment, but it was just the band starting another song. She checked the running order. It was an unscheduled song. The next lot of models should be on already.

She rushed back through to the waiting area and waved to her fellow models to follow her to the makeup desks. Rita tapped at the time on her Book, then pulled Cherry onto the bench in front of her and started poking at her hair with a pointy-ended comb. Cherry listened to the crowd as the band played. Nothing. Well, nothing besides the normal screaming and singing along. It hadn't worked.

Then she heard one solitary note of fear rise above the clamour.

-o-

'You think she's got what?' Chen was as Glaswegian as Kester had ever heard her.

Alexis was standing at the lab window, forehead against the glass.

'We called it Ladies' Choice. It was a virus I developed at the Institute for export, a population control virus. It's self-administered, normally...'

'Another one of yours – great. What does it do?'

'It's a form of biological spaying. It makes women infertile.'

'It what?' Chen looked up at Alexis.

'Let's not mourn the loss of my ovaries, Chen. We both know I screwed them up a long time ago.'

'It's irreversible,' Kester said.

'It's what?'

'Once it's run its course. It could be another attack and it could be serious. This thing is a registered approved therapeutic virus, so it won't show up on people's screens. We don't know –'

'You'd better have some solutions for me right now, Doctor Lowe, or I'm going to personally throw you out of that fucking window.'

Kester glanced anxiously at the window.

'And I don't care if it doesn't open,' Chen added.

'It's not his fault, Chen,' Alexis said, still forehead-to-glass.

Chen ignored her. 'Where has it come from?'

'We don't know. Alexis could have been infected by anyone she has slept with in the last –'

'Are you infected?'

'I'm running analysis on both our bloods now.' Kester glanced at the machine suspended over the bench opposite. The light was still flashing. 'We'll soon know if it's what I suspect it is. Where the thing's come from is irrelevant for now. The good news is we have some time.'

'Time?' Chen growled. 'The band has played two extra songs. The crowd is getting restless. And if the models are infected, one lot have already done their damage.'

'The infection takes around a week to render the host infertile. It's the deletion virus that causes the weeping eyes.'

'Deletion virus?'

'The product is…' Kester tried to clear his mind of technical terms. '…a bacterium that does the dirty work coupled with a virus that clears up the infection once it's run its course.'

'Which means?'

'Two things. Firstly, we can stop the bacterium before it does any damage if we administer the clean-up virus to anyone who has been infected. Secondly…when I said where it's come from was irrelevant…we can't track it. It's designed to –'

'I don't care how it's designed to function. You can treat it?'

'Yes, inside a week.'

'And all they'll get is runny eyes?'

'Yes. And only a small percentage of them.'

'For how long?'

'Twelve to twenty-four hours.'

'OK.' Chen lifted her Book to her ear. 'You still there, Yule? Tell them to go ahead. But there's to be no possibility of infection outside the guest-list. Get to Hera – tell her to keep it under control – no going over the barriers.'

Alexis looked round. Kester's eyes danced between the two of them.

'Chen?' Alexis walked towards her.

'Everyone who has potentially been infected by us tonight will be there at the after-party. Kester, I need you to put together a "gift pack" for the guests. It's another freebie – infection isn't 100% certain via intercourse, so this is a sort of compensation if it doesn't work for them. They need to receive the clean-up virus, but we need some cover for it – one of the viruses from last time, maybe – anything that's tried and tested. We give them the drops and tell them that the weeping is a rare side-effect of infection. Make Corona the free gift so that the story stands up – it had that effect on one or two test subjects, right?'

Kester went through it in his head. Yes, it would work. This was why she was running the place.

'And the preshow clients?' he asked. 'We'll need to treat them soon. If Alexis is presenting now and she infected me then they may have been exposed.'

'A personal aftercare visit with a free gift. Talk to Yule about it – he's better at these things than me. Just treat them and make sure it doesn't look suspicious.'

'Yes. I'm on it.'

'Alexis –'

'Shit…' Alexis was back at the window. 'Chen.'

Chen and Kester rushed over. Kester's vision of the tumbling walls had come alive. The square was in turmoil, the crowd swelling towards its back corners as if two sluice gates had been opened. The boxes were emptying, their occupants flowing down the metal staircases, some attempting to climb down the outside in their panic. Alexis gasped as a tiny figure fell and was swallowed by the crowd.

'What the fuck's going on?' Chen's Book began to buzz. 'Gaunt?'

Alexis and Kester could hear Gaunt's voice shouting above the echoing rabble.

'Something's spooked them. They think there's been an attack – is going to be an attack – a terrorist attack – a bomb maybe. They're not listening to the announcements.'

'Why aren't the nets up?'

'Too late. The crowd is moving too fast. I'm with the head of security right now. He says our best bet is to shepherd them safely through the exits. The line police and paramedics are dropping down low, ready to grab any casualties.'

Chen looked out of the window at the line police. Alexis pointed to where a stretcher was already being hauled up to one of the platforms.

'Jesus Christ,' Chen said. 'Get all the VIPs into the foyer.'

'Already done,' Gaunt said.

'Tell them...' Chen faltered and then looked up at Kester. 'Get them up to the lab now. Tell them we've got no reason to believe that any attack has happened or is imminent, but that we want to run some tests and administer a clean-up virus which will protect them in the event of one occurring.'

Kester nodded encouragingly as she said it, a panicked grin on his face.

'What?' Gaunt said.

'Just do it.' Chen slammed her Book down on the workbench. She closed her eyes, put her hands over her mouth for a moment and breathed deeply. Dropping her hands, she was back. 'Right you two – rewind – we'd better get our story straight.'

Chapter 24

Alexis surveyed the square from the boardroom window. The cleaners were blasting the ground with high pressure hoses, transforming the muddied paving slabs into slices of reflected morning. Here and there a few men in orange vests were loading the last bits of mangled barrier onto carts. It was a miracle the place wasn't littered with bodies. They had been lucky: five or six broken limbs, two head injuries. Nobody had counted the cuts and bruises.

She continued to watch the clear up and listened as the Board members entered the room one by one through the open doors. She didn't have to turn. Even had they not been announced, she would have known each of them by their little rituals, by the small noises they made as they settled down at their stations. Gaunt's brief chair scrape, jacket fling, pen toss; Agbabi's handbag rummage; Yule's embarrassed chair readjustment as he tried to get it centred underneath his huge bulk; Jones' silent entry, punctuated with small neat coughs and followed by the sorting of papers. Alexis was never sure what the papers Jones brought with her were. No-one else ever brought bits of paper to meetings any more, just their Books, and Jones hardly ever made reference to them. There was a distinct lack of greeting going on today. Then Chen arrived. Her leather-backed Book landed on the table with a fat slap.

'OK,' Chen said, going straight into deliberating mode, pacing back and forth behind her chair. 'Where are we? Alexis?'

Farrell braced herself and then turned to address the room.

'Here's what we know. Another virus has been released, presumably by the same people who released the first one.'

'But the screening on the Pigs – has it not worked?' Chen said. 'How widespread is this thing?'

'There's good news and bad news. The bad news is that they got to Kester. Both he and I are infected and we're processing the results for everyone else. This isn't coming from the Pigs. We don't know where it came from and we're unlikely to find out.'

'Find out,' Chen said. 'You may not be able to track it but it doesn't take much to make a list and get the thumbscrews out. And for fuck's sake, tell me the good news.'

'The good news is that we've treated all the pre-show guests and the VIPs who were at the show. All of them accepted what we called a precautionary "clean-up" virus and didn't even blink at the possibility of having to use eye drops. These people are used to a lot worse than weeping eyes. But there's more bad news. It's more than likely that the Princess is infected.'

'What?' Chen burst up from her chair. She shifted her weight from foot to foot for a moment as if she might take off and then sat down abruptly.

'The virus would have run its course in her before we discovered it. We sent a team to check her out and while she didn't complain of weeping eyes – not everybody does – the virus Kester was supposed to be giving her had presented fully. That makes it more likely she would have contracted both. Pera Pera has escaped infection, possibly due to the fact she spent more time mucking around than actually getting down to business.'

'So the royal line has been cut off. We consider that bad news?' Gaunt asked.

Chen looked round at him and he fell silent. 'Potentially cut off,' she said. 'So what can be done? If she is affected can we cure it?'

'Short of POR, no,' Alexis said.

'And offering to grow her a new set of ovaries might make her suspicious,' Jones said.

'What the hell kind of weapon is this anyway?' Chen asked.

'I can see how it might be used as a weapon,' Alexis said, 'but it's not designed for that. It's designed for private use by women who no longer wish to be fertile. Non-invasive sterilisation. That's why it comes packaged with this "master switch" virus that deletes the bacterium once sterilisation is complete.'

'So the rest of our guests are OK,' Chen said. 'How many other infected persons are there?'

'We don't know. Problem is that it's very hard to trace because it's self-deleting.' Alexis took a breath. There was a solution and she had to offer it, even though she knew Chen would take her head off. 'If we really wanted to make sure we've caught this thing we could tell Stark – they could send out a temporary instruction to the screens, get them to flag any –'

'Hah! Tell Stark?' That was Chen's full appraisal of the idea.

'If someone uncovers this and it gets out that it has come from Kester, we're in big trouble,' Yule said. 'It's going to look like we set this up as a publicity stunt – an attack that goes unnoticed on Stark's screen and threatens to sterilise the whole bloody City, a few days after we announce that we're going to manufacture a rival screen – it'll destroy Kester. And if Kester's destroyed so are our chances of taking his new screens to market. If they can't trust us…'

'Realistically,' Chen said, 'if this gets out V will be shut down and we're all going to jail. There'll be no leniency and it won't matter that it was a mistake, that we've been compromised. We've a duty of care to our clients and frankly if our client is a member of the royal family and we don't carry out that duty – well, under the circumstances it could be considered treason.'

'It won't get out,' Gaunt said. He rubbed his temples. 'This creation is self-deleting. Alexis just told us that. So we shall have no further problems unless someone in this room goes public with the knowledge that we've killed off the royal family.'

'Gaunt.' Chen sounded like she was warning off a dog. She stopped pacing and stared at him. 'It pains me to say it, but you're right. Yule, what's your perspective.'

'I've been keeping an eye on the press. Our so-called "preventative" treatments are being viewed favourably by our clients and, on the whole, by the press. But some people are asking if there has actually been an attack, if we're bluffing, and if so whether we've contained it.'

'Which there has been, we are and we haven't,' Jones said.

'Which we can't,' Alexis said, glaring at her, 'unless we find out where it came from. Yule, what else?'

'The majority of the press has run with the story that it was a bomb scare that spooked the crowd. One of the sites has a picture that the editors seem to think is evidence of this – a squashed piece of paper with some smeary writing on it. And we might not want to disabuse them of the notion. It does seem a likely explanation from what those interviewed have said, and if that was some other joker's idea of an attack, they've done us a favour by providing cover for us. '

Alexis felt a surge of relief as Kester appeared at the door. The sooner they could get to talking about the positive stuff the better.

'Alexis asked me to come –' Kester began.

'I want the show back on,' Chen said, looking around the table. 'I want it rescheduled today. And remember, it's not a big deal – nobody was seriously hurt and it wasn't our fault. Don't apologise for anything. Anyone with nasty injuries can get a backstage and VIP pit pass and a big fat goodwill payment.

'The other thing we need is some good press, a distraction. Yule, I want you to work with Kester to produce a statement about his work on the new screens – they were expecting one at the show, so let's give it to them now – we've already said we're going to do it, but we haven't quite shot our load. We can tell them that we've already got a working prototype and that it's in torso testing now. I want Kester on every news site by lunchtime.

'Kester, I need you to start your in vivo testing. Get your team together. Even better, get a new team together – this is going to be big, it's got to be big – get the best people you can onto it – internal, external, whatever you need.'

Kester nodded, hovering in the doorway.

'And Kester – people we can trust.'

'Yes,' Kester said.

Alexis caught his eye and gave him an encouraging look.

'I have people in mind,' he said. 'Ex-colleagues from the Institute. I know I can trust them.'

'It would be good if we could get them,' Yule said. 'Will they come on board?'

'Some of them, for the right price.'

'Money is no object,' Chen said.

'I'll need nanotechnologists, immunologists –'

'The wine-thrower, Dee,' Alexis said. 'You worked on this together with her. Would she still want to be a part of it?'

'I did – we scoped it out together…'

'What does she look like?' Yule asked. 'Could she be a good face for this?'

'She may not be as keen as the others.'

'She's the one who thinks scientists should help people,' Alexis said. 'She wanted to build the screens too, didn't she – what's changed?' She watched Kester's reaction carefully. This wasn't the time for him to start doubting himself.

'Yes. It's the big business thing. She really wasn't happy –'

'You said you'd made up,' Alexis said. 'Just talk to her.'

'We did make up, sort of.'

Alexis stared at him, willing him to just agree. She knew his relationship with Dee was still shaky. Even Kester wasn't dumb enough to think that an afternoon of running around at the PlayPen would make right a betrayal, but it was a start; they were talking. As for persuading her to shift her moral stance, it would just be a matter of money.

'Make up properly,' Chen said. 'Get on with it.'

-o-

Cherry tried to force herself to relax as Gerald primed the hypodermic gun. He loaded the virus capsule and then injected it into her arm. She glanced away, over her shoulder, as he did so. You'd think she would be used to it by now.

Behind her, a long line of models stood waiting to be administered the control virus, all angled poses, hanging from their hips and shoulders like puppets.

'That was all pretty painless, wasn't it?' Gerald said to her as she turned back to him.

Cherry raised an eyebrow. What was he asking her?

'What started the stampede?' she asked him. 'Do they know?'

'Paper airplanes,' Gerald said. He winked at her and smiled. 'Paper airplanes with bomb threats written on them. Or that's the rumour. I don't think anyone has actually found any of them – trampled to pieces I imagine.'

Cherry took a deep breath and let her shoulders drop. Perhaps this was it. She was out the other side.

'Thanks, Gerald.'

'Don't thank me.'

'Am I allowed to go out now?' she asked him as he went to the door. 'I've got a few things to do.'

'Yes, of course.' Gerald smiled at her, showing even more of his bleach-white teeth than usual. 'I've got a long line of models to get through, but if you fancy a drink afterwards, perhaps we could meet in the refectory and take it from there. Once you've run your errands.'

'Why not,' Cherry said, a small spot of excitement springing up under her ribcage, spinning and enlarging as she held his eager stare. 'I'll see you there.'

-o-

Kester stood on the steps of the Institute. The light was on in Dee's lab. He walked up the steps and in the door. The security man greeted him with a forced smile.

'Long time no see, Superstar,' he said. 'Looking for Dee?'

'Yeah.'

'Up in the lab, burning the late-afternoon oil.' He waved Kester past.

'Thanks, mate. See you later.'

The whole place seemed smaller than before. He had never noticed the appalling colour of the walls, the way it looked like a backstreet hospital. It was a toy lab. A joke. The Institute deserved better. Had deserved better. As he walked along, the walls seemed to distort, pulled out of shape by his nerves. The corridors toyed with new profiles – trapeziums, parallelograms. He felt a defensive disgust.

The lift had been crushed to tin can size. He forgot for a moment to pull across the gate. It was listed, this lift. 1930s he remembered. It predated the floor reconfiguration; it served all of the floors and none of them. You got the lift and then had to take the stairs or ramp up half a floor or down half a floor to get where you were going. The lift was beautiful in its own way, but the fussiness of its interior, its self-conscious old-worldiness grated on Kester's nerves as he waited for it to lift him the mere four floors. He could feel each revolution of the pulley, its slightly distorted shape giving the lift an uneven rise. The lift pinged as he arrived. Kester pulled aside the door and hurried up the stairs and down the corridor.

And he was there. And what now? Kester watched the back of

Dee's head through the small window in the lab door. She was shuffling back and forth, picking things up, moving them around, stopping every now and again to press her hands to the bench and arch her shoulders in a tension-relieving move. He watched for a good five minutes, stuck. Just then, she turned to walk over to the sinks. Seeing his face at the window she stopped and stared. She continued over to the sink, washed her hands, then returned to her bench and sat down with her back to him. Her silhouette looked less sure now, shaken round the edges. She wasn't really doing anything. After a few minutes he opened the door and walked over to his old station on the bench that ran down the side of the room, perpendicular to hers. So small, he thought. He wondered how he had ever got any work done here.

'Dee. You weren't answering your Book.'

'No.'

She looked up at him. Her face was blank, controlled, as if she hadn't yet decided how to act.

'John said I'd find you here. Are you OK? I thought everything would be closed down.'

'It is. They've done all their forensic work, taken everything they need. They graciously agreed we could come in to clear up after them – do all the waiting while our funders come and repossess our equipment.' Her anger slipped momentarily into upset. 'This fucking black dust...'

Kester looked around the lab. It still looked cluttered, though now he saw that all the computing equipment and some of the larger lab machines were gone. Fine black dust made a pattern of fingerprints on well-used areas of the workbenches, doors and shelves.

'I wanted to talk to you about a job,' Kester said eventually. If she was going to be like this he had best get to the point.

'A job?' She swiveled on her stool and looked at him, eyes narrowing.

'It's exciting,' Kester said with a silly grin. 'Do you think you could bring yourself to work with me again? I've spoken to John and he's on board.'

'John? What, you mean a job at V?' she asked. She looked as if he'd offered her a jellied eel.

'Yes, at V – why not?' He spoke quickly. He would try to get the whole explanation out before she could cut him down. 'I'm putting a new team together and I'm poaching people from the Institute. You wouldn't normally approve I know, but it's the screens. They want them now and I need a team to work on them. I know this is just your thing. You're the best. The screens are working but I need someone to run the in vivo immune system integration testing. You'd be perfect.'

'I...' Dee stared at his shirt front.

'I know what you're going to say, but Dee we'd really be helping people. This is what we used to talk about – I mean, I know it's different doing it for a big company, but at least we'd be doing it. And what with the shutdown...' He looked around at the benches again.

Dee looked underwhelmed. She seemed tired, Kester thought, or something. He had done something wrong. It was his default belief when faced with behaviour he didn't get. And it normally turned out to be right.

'Is this about...before...at the PlayPen? I'm sorry, I thought we were cool. You didn't –'

'No,' she said.

Well that was something.

'You probably wouldn't even need to go through an interview if that's what you're worried about.' He tried another tack. 'I haven't discussed it with Alexis, but I'm sure we wouldn't need to.'

'Alexis?' Dee sneered as she said the name. 'I'd be working for her?'

Kester could see her back arching, her shoulders rising as if her back would open up into a set of great black wings.

'Sort of, but it's my lab and you'd have your own team.' He knew she would be hard to win over, but he hadn't imagined she would be this unmoved by the whole idea. 'Like I said, I've already spoken to John and he's on board. I don't know what you think about Betta and Sienna. Betta's perfect but I'm not so sure about Sienna – she could probably do a tech job but that's a bit of a downward step for her. I know the two of them are a bit of a package though. I don't want to step on any toes.'

'Of course not.'

Kester got up and put a hand on Dee's. Her hand jerked but she didn't remove it.

'Just think about it will you? This will have your name on it too –
co-creator.' What else did he need to say? There was something
niggling him. 'And I'm sorry I started the research without you. I'm
sorry about everything, really.' That was it.

'OK,' she said, then took a long breath in through her nose and
looked up at him. 'I'll think about it.' She got down from her stool
and walked over to the sink to fill her water glass.

Kester put his hands in his pockets and let his gaze fall to the
floor. It alighted on Dee's recycling basket.

'Um,' he said involuntarily, swallowing hard, 'I'll go then.' His
throat was tight, his voice struggled to escape. He pulled his eyes
away from the bin and walked to the door. 'I'll call you.'

'Bye,' Dee said, without looking round.

Kester's heart thundered in his ears as he walked away from the
Institute. He moved in a straight line, ignoring everyone around
him. In his head he climbed straight over cars, his feet leaving
burning outlines on their paintwork, straight through traffic that
never seemed to hit him.

Dee. What had she done? He held the image in his mind: nestled
in between the ripped-up paper and food packets of Dee's recycling
basket, a small flattened cardboard box, an eye drop box, Mexodrol.
She was out to destroy him – properly destroy him. And for what?
Nothing. Nothing. A one night stand? Or because she thought he'd
abandoned their 'dream' of making the screens together? He tried to
think himself into her head but all that came was images: her pale
face and black hair an ink blot on the pillow, her earnest expression
in the café, her snarl as she threw wine at him, her figure leaving the
PlayPen, doll-sized.

Buildings flickered past him as he walked, his legs on automatic
pilot taking him back to the City. The lights were coming on. Night
spilled down between the buildings, finding the few slivers left to it.
Each straight fall of darkness was her hair, each bright window her
white staring face hating him as he walked. His heart was expanding,
would crush his lungs, crush itself against his strained ribcage. The
laughing faces in each bar were laughing at him, window displays of
cruelty, his beautiful creations pressed up against scab-infested
cheeks and breasts, faeries and goblins. It should rain. It should
thunder. But the sky was clear, the moon riding above him like
another version of her face, hollow and furious.

He thought of Alexis. Was it all about her? Could it be? Could jealousy grow this malevolent? Was its stranglehold so cold, so unreasoning? Or had Dee been got to? He remembered her attitude to his taking the job at V. Was she against it enough to want to bring the company down? To bring him down? Kester's mind folded in and in on itself, a box of mirrors filled with two faces, Alexis and Dee, reflecting off one another, mixing in shards. He had to tell Alexis. He took his Book out of his pocket, his hand shaking.

-o-

Alexis exploded into Kester's office through the sliding door. He could see she was resisting the urge to smash it, was wishing it could be slammed.

'Jesus Christ, Kester! You said you'd made up.'

He flicked his walls to mist and then stepped behind his desk as if it might shield him.

'I didn't know. I'm angry too, I'm furious she did this, that you were – but at least we know now – the Princess is the only other casualty.'

'Fuck the Princess.' Alexis took a terrifying lunge towards him.

'What's...you said it didn't matter. You didn't care about the virus.'

'You slept with her.'

Kester closed his eyes. His insides were already churning. But where was he? Who was this? He was back in Dee's flat, scrambling to find his pants.

'You slept with her,' Alexis repeated.

'You slept with...everyone.' Kester cursed his brain for not stopping his mouth. 'And what do you care? I told you we'd made up.'

'Made up, made out, fucked – it's all the same to you now, when it suits you. So why hide it from me?'

'Hide it from you? Right, Alexis,' Kester stepped out from behind his desk and went towards her. He had never seen her so angry. 'This is getting silly. I don't know what the problem is.'

'Are you emotionally retarded?' Alexis asked, with a murderous laugh.

'Please sit down,' Kester pulled out a chair.

She grabbed the back of it and flipped it onto its side.

'Do you remember how mad she was with you? How unspeakably angry. She was mad...she was mad because you fucked me – because you did it with me despite the fact that it meant nothing to you but a job. It meant nothing to you but a job, true? Remember how it was?'

Kester nodded, backing away again.

'You remember that? She was mad because with her she thought it meant something.'

'It did.' Kester defended himself, thought he was defending himself.

'Did it? Kester, you'd already chosen V over your screens. You'd already chosen me over her. And she only finds that out when she catches viral seconds and sees the night of her life implode into a one-night stand. You can't see what that might do to someone who doesn't even wear? And now? Does it mean something with her now?'

'Look...' Kester closed his eyes again. Did it?

'Well? Does it still mean something?'

'You want to know how it is now?' He spoke slowly to buy himself more time.

'Kester...' The rage was fading from Alexis' voice. She was starting to sound upset and it panicked him. He wanted to rush over and comfort her. No, he wanted her to turn hard again.

'It's the same,' Kester said. Seeing her colour rise again, her eyes darkening, a storm on fast forward, he realised he had put it the wrong way. 'I mean the opposite – I mean it means something with you; it means nothing with her. I didn't know until afterwards. I'm not sure it ever did. I think I get it, I get it. I'm sorry, I'm an idiot.' Alexis stared at him, hands on hips. Suddenly he did get it, a tiny chink of light. Her face was hard again, reminding him of his interview. He wrinkled his brow, trying to push out the inappropriate memories. 'I don't know. What can I say? She's a crazy bitch – I love you.'

Alexis turned away from him. Kester moved to his chair and sat tentatively, let her pace around, unwinding her rage. Shouldn't she rush to his arms? He cursed himself. He got it, that one little thing, but there was so much more he just couldn't get his head around.

'She knows you know that it was her?' Alexis asked eventually.

'No.'

'You offered her a job?'

'Yes. Well, I said there was a job for her if she wanted. Said interviews would be a formality.'

'Interviews,' Alexis said with interest.

Kester could still hear the shake in her voice, but her focus was turning from rage to revenge.

'Yes.'

'Would she come to an interview?'

'I don't know.'

'She would. It would be suspicious for her not to.'

'Maybe...'

'She tried to take you away from me.' Alexis still faced away from Kester, as if she didn't want him to witness her expressions. 'She tried to destroy everything I've created. She tried to destroy me.'

Kester didn't respond.

'She'll pay.' She turned. Her eyes were glistening. A shadow of a smile played around her blood-red lips.

'And me?'

'You, Doctor Lowe...' She walked around his desk towards him and sat on the edge of it.

'Me?' His voice barely filled his mouth.

She put a hand up to his throat. He wished she would hit him, scream again, something.

'You'll make amends.' She leaned forward and kissed him long with closed lips. 'It's just as well you're my favourite.'

Kester stood and leaned towards Alexis. Anger flexed muscular under the surface of her skin, only just contained. He placed his head against her hard collar bone and slipped his arms around her waist. She didn't resist the contact. Any venom she felt towards him was overshadowed by her rage at Dee. He knew not to apologise again. He knew she would never break down, declare her love for him. This was it – her offering her forgiveness.

'What do you need?' he asked, eventually, lifting his head.

She looked at him for a long time, as if gauging his loyalty and his readiness. Then she looked up at his design board.

'I need a virus.'

Chapter 25

Cherry left Dempsey's and headed straight down to the Thames. She climbed up the steps to the east Hungerford Footbridge and looked down the river. When she reached the old skyline plaque she stopped and swung her backpack down. She took out her new Book and searched for Lady's number. It was easy to find, the Hospital being such a large attraction. The minute it started ringing, Cherry felt closer, connected again.

'Hello?'

'Lady, it's Cherry.'

There was a long silence.

'Cherry. They told me you weren't coming back. I'd guessed it from the way things were going. Seems like you got them what they wanted. I'm surprised they didn't want to keep you in their pockets, but fair enough. I guess it's too risky to keep on trying the same tricks. They've stopped paying me of course, but don't worry, I extracted compensation when I found out you were staying. We saw you in the run-up to the show. Marlene and Tim bullied me into getting the big screen out in the runkroom. Looks like it's quite a change from the Hospital.'

'In some ways. I just wanted to let you know myself. I wanted to thank you, I suppose.'

'Don't thank me, Cherry.'

'Nobody wants to be thanked. Good luck then, I suppose. You'll have heard about the new screens.'

'Of course.' Lady's words became clipped. 'What with those and the designer viruses there'll be no business left for us soon. Except for the original business.'

'I know.' Cherry wasn't sure what to say to this. It would be no different if she were there, if she had never left. 'Will you pass on a message to Marlene and Tim for me?'

'Cherry, I'm not your personal answering service,' Lady said, then paused for a moment.

Cherry imagined her smoothing back her hair, stroking her skirt flat down the length of her thigh, her conscience struggling with her image.

'Call back at three-thirty,' Lady said, as if she were ordering Cherry in to her office. 'I have to see them both about something anyway. You can tell them whatever it is yourself.'

'Thank you. I can thank you this time, can't I?'

'You're welcome, Cherry.'

'Take care –'

'We'll speak later,' Lady said and put the phone down.

Cherry shook her head and tucked her Book away. Reaching into her bag, she brought out an almost empty gin miniature and a lighter. If the alcohol didn't do for the virus, then fire would. She carefully took the top off the bottle, tipped it so that the liquid reached its lip, lit the liquid and placed it quickly back down on the plaque. Her actions caused several passers-by to perform a shambolic stagger-and-duck manoeuvre. Presumably they had expected it to explode. When it proved to be just burning, they fell back into their normal gaits with alarming ease, carrying on across the bridge as if they had defective memories. Cherry watched the plastic melt and buckle, holes gaping it in like panicked mouths. When the flames died down she took off her shoe and knocked the remains of the bottle into the river, leaving a small round scorch mark on the plaque.

Cherry took her Book out again. Her mother's picture smiled from the display, looking past her, somewhere over her left shoulder. She was meeting Gerald for dinner at nine, which gave her plenty of time to start on her next project. The fiscal records building with its forms and queues was the place to start. If her mother was still in the City, imprisoned or not, alive or not, that was where she would find out. She tapped the destination into her Book, held it up against the north Embankment vista to see her route mapped out for her, then tucked it away and started to walk.

–o–

Jesus had a particularly stern look on his face today. His wounds were not bothering him, or if they were, they were a mere irritation against the pain that Blotch had clearly caused him. Blotch knelt in front of his office altar, tracing the sequence of events, explaining, apologising and stopping to curse V in short bursts. Things had turned out a little more complicated than he had hoped. The blasted company had taken Lowe back into their dirty nest and had managed to make themselves look like the good guys in the process. The girl had done her bit, so things might have been recovered, but there had been a stampede at the fashion show, seemingly unrelated – bad luck really.

He could have done with a hand on that front. It was the best chance of getting back into the City that the Real Church had been afforded in years and they'd blown it. Rumours of a viral attack had damaged business at the Pigs for a few days, though, and that had to be worth something. This wouldn't happen next time, he assured the Christ. Next time they would nail it.

'Your forgiveness, my Saviour.' Blotch crossed himself and bowed his head to the altar. 'Unfortunate turn of phrase.'

There went his promotion, just like that. He felt queasy, hot and cold. This had been it; he had been so sure. And he still had one boss to apologise to. He cast a pleading glance at Jesus. Just then there was a knock at the door and it opened a sliver. A small grey head popped in, accompanied by the flash of what Blotch thought was a knitting needle.

'Minister.' Nan's voice went straight through him. 'Ah, you're talking to himself. You'll thank him for the transfer while you're down there will you? It was just the thing.'

Nan pushed in through the door, indicating her new cardigan proudly. Blotch looked back at Jesus, closed his eyes and was silent for a moment, then got up and squeezed round behind his desk.

'Nan,' he said, smiling over gritted teeth.

'I've got a little titbit the two of you might be interested in.' She settled herself opposite him, glancing over her shoulder at the altar with a fond nose wrinkle.

-o-

Alexis turned right then left in front of her mirror and then looked straight at herself. On the dark grey wall behind her, opposite the open doorway to her bathroom, hung Kester's gift. She smiled. The fiery circle around London was reflected just behind her head, giving her a flaming halo. As she stared, the light bulbs at the mirror's edge fuzzed and melted into a luminous frame.

She interrogated her reflection, trying to see herself objectively, critically. Her skin was good. There was no youthful glow, but it was clear and smooth. Her makeup was simple and precise: black liquid-lined eyes, black clump-free lashes, red lips, tidy eyebrows. Her hair was parted exactly in the middle and drawn up in two tight rolls that started above her temples and swept back down to meet in a V at the nape of her neck. She wore simple V logo stud earrings. From the neck up everything was perfect; inhumanly perfect. She nodded, satisfied, and continued her appraisal.

Her simple silk top was a patchwork of logos, all tonally similar, creating a pattern effect on the fabric. It flattered her frame. She looked at where her breasts lifted the fabric in small peaks, then down to where it wafted free over her flat stomach. She moved from side to side and took pleasure in its small movements against her skin, a tropical breeze. Nice, but too feminine, she decided. She tried pinching it in with the waistband of her skirt but it was still too soft. Classy, but the order of the day was not classy – it was professional, sharp, intimidating. She picked up her Book and called Rita.

'Rita, I've got an interview at three. I need to look intimidating. Bring me up something angular, something androgynous.' She hung up without waiting for a reply.

This one she would reserve for meeting Kester afterwards, she decided. He would like it. There was plenty of room for his wandering hands to slide in underneath. Once this interview was out of the way things would be back to normal. She couldn't relax until she had taken her revenge, taken the driver's seat again. Passing a hand across her abdomen, she felt a small tug of rage, buried deep. She had never wanted to have children. Even if she did want to there was always POR. She had lost nothing, but it was the principle of the thing. As Gaunt had put it, it is little consolation to the man whose manhood you've cut off that it can be sewn back on. Campbell needed to see her at her best. She must be powerful, sexy, virulent; she must be indestructible, a perfect bronze of woman. *But she doesn't care about those things*, Kester would tell her.

'Bullshit, Kester,' she said to her reflection, 'everybody cares about those things.'

Dee would care and she would see how complete her failure was. And once she had seen how complete her failure was, Alexis would build her up and destroy her again. There was a tight ball of anticipation at Alexis' diaphragm. She picked up the hypodermic gun Kester had given her, recalled his warning, loaded it and tucked the second vial into her skirt pocket. She looked at herself in the mirror again, and pointed the hypodermic at her reflection like a hand gun.

'Bang,' she said, blew smoke from the needle, and tucked the gun into an imaginary holster at her hip. She had plenty time to visit Gaunt and Yule; a short six hours was all it needed.

A picture flashed up on Alexis' Book. An outfit suggestion from Rita. A clean-lined suit-fabric jumpsuit – sharply flared legs, a high collar balanced by a mid-depth V-neck, a neat line of close-set buttons sweeping down to either hip from the centre point of the V. Alexis flicked to see the back view. A waistcoat-shaped panel on the back was given over to a well-matched montage of logos. Perfect.

And perhaps Kester would like this too, in a different way. Not so easy access. She imagined the struggle he would have wrestling her out of it, could already feel the pull of his clumsy hands at the lines of buttons. Tonight would be perfect. He would be enlarged with ego, her greatest creation, Doctor Kester Lowe; she would be hot with the blood of her enemy. She smiled to herself. There would be buttons everywhere.

-o-

Kester swung his feet up on his desk and gave a happy sigh. The rescheduled fashion show had gone off without a hitch. Everything was new again. He felt safe, elated and confident that his world was under his control. This must be what Lex felt like all the time. He remembered his first days at V, his projects growing, the fervent activity. That was great, but this was better. He knew exactly what he was doing. *Welcome...John Boyd*, said the doors.

'So, Boss, where do you want me to start?' John said.

Kester giggled. It was weird having John there. He felt like he had done something wrong, had got a friend in the back door, even though John was one of the most capable scientists he knew.

'Make us a cup of coffee,' Kester said, holding his face as straight as he could. He let John waver for a moment then laughed. 'Just kidding. I need you to go over my data from the initial torso tests. I want you to question the methodology, interrogate the data – just check I haven't cocked up anywhere along the way.'

'A nice no-pressure start then?'

'Yeah.' Kester expected John would go and start work, but he hung around at the door for a minute before coming back across.

'The booths – the exchange booths...'

'Yes?'

'Is it really OK? I mean is this a trap or something? You can just use them, right?'

'Right. Any time, with anyone. But try not to exchange below your grade too much – stick to the up-and-comers and your seniors if you can. You'll get used to it.'

'So her, over there.' John looked to the window and pointed out a girl with a sleek mousy ponytail a few benches into the room. 'Suppose I feel she's got potential...'

'Yes.'

'I could just go and say to her, "Hey doll, fancy a tumble in the booths?"'

Kester smirked. He'd had trouble getting to grips with the etiquette when he first started too.

'Best way is to use the exchange request on your profile. Just ping her – you can use name, station number, or just point your Book to identify her and a message will pop up. She'll *yes* or *no* you and a booth will light up to show it's free if she accepts your offer.'

'Cool. I meant it hypothetically of course.'

'Of course. And, hypothetically speaking, you won't have to walk back across the room like a tool with everyone watching if she says *no.*'

'Nice,' John said, meandering towards the door. 'Thanks Boss.'

Kester skipped over to his coffee machine and made himself a small cup. He sat down and looked up at his twin display; streams of data tumbled down the wall next to his static design board. Picking up his Book, he flipped through his appointments. There was a heady mix of science and celebrity: a meeting to set up the controlled in vivo trials of the screens, a guest feature on Take It, his first presentation to the Board, a photoshoot with his new team, the first planning session for the show's world tour.

Kester stood and walked to the front window of his office. This was enough vertigo for him, he decided. A happy medium. The odd visit to Alexis' office to make him dizzy would suffice. And he could always look down on the people in the square from here if he chose to. He watched them for a moment and imagined that each one was leaving a different-coloured trail across the square, together creating a giant tangled Beck map charting their encounters and decisions.

One of them might be Dee. He wasn't sure what he thought about that, knowing that she was headed for the building. Would she try something else? He stopped himself. Alexis was in control. It was her call, her plan, nothing to do with him any more. And if it made her happy it was worth it. He made a mental note to shower and get his apartment fixed up before the interview was finished. Though it might be nice if she called him up to her office so they could relive his own interview. He wondered if she would. It was a sort of anniversary for them.

Kester's Book rang. It was his mother.

'Mum, how are you?'

'Kester – my Kester. I can't believe it's really happening. You're really doing it.'

'I know, Mum. I told you I would, didn't I?'

'You did. You did.'

'Did you offload the rest of those panties OK?'

'Don't you worry about that, darling.' His mother shrieked with laughter.

'You alright, Mum?'

'Oh yes, yes, just the dog has just come through with a pair round his neck. He's been sticking his head in my bag again. Oh sweetie…' She descended into a stream of baby-doggy talk.

Kester tuned out and started to scroll through the live data on the display next to his design board. It was satisfying to watch. He could see things progressing before his eyes. It wouldn't be long now until he saw his dream come to fruition, until every member of staff in the building offered themselves up to his needle – he smirked – became a vessel for his creation, came under his protection. Then it would go live to the City, to London, to the other cities and then...a small sadness sloshed in his stomach, the dregs of something that had once tasted fine. He recalled his and Dee's plans, and his drunken promise on the bar at *Brass* that his screen would be free for everyone. Well...maybe...

As he looked out over the lab a piece of equipment unfolded from the ceiling on a multi-elbowed arm. It paused for a moment, seeming to look at him before continuing down to the station that had requested it.

This was a corrupt business. It would only take one member of staff to decide the screen technology should be open source for whatever reason – one person struck by a moral revelation, one person having a noble five minutes. Halfway across the lab the lift doors opened, admitting Gerald's smile. Behind it followed Gerald and a group of models back for the next round of testing: Cherry, Hera and a few he didn't recognise. Cherry looked over and gave him a shy smile. After a minute or two Kester became aware that his mother's tone had changed again.

'Kester? Are you listening, Kester? I said I've booked my tickets to come and see you. Now you're sure you and Alexis don't mind having me for a whole weekend?'

'No, Mum, it's fine – really.'

'It's going to be so lovely to finally meet her. Has Dee met her yet?'

'Em, not quite.'

-o-

Dee entered the interview room. It was on the top floor of the building and as she walked forwards to meet the panel, she could see the whole of London falling away from them in a steep tilting bowl. They were at the top edge, the highest point. She might trip and be sent flying over the edge, skittering down into the centre of the city. It was impressive – she struggled with the feeling. No, it was good to be impressed. She should let herself be taken over, taken in. She needed to seem convinced to be convincing.

Dee recognised the woman in the middle of the panel as Alexis Farrell. Farrell was dressed in a grey all-in-one suit. It was tasteful, sexy, businesslike – a look that bothered Dee. She would never be able to dress that way. She was suddenly very self-conscious about the simple trouser-suit she was wearing.

'Take a seat,' Farrell said.

Dee looked in front of the desk. There was no chair there. She glanced side to side and then back towards the door. Finally she spotted a chair in the far corner of the room, marking the intersection of the two glass walls. She walked over to it, picked it up, brought it back and placed it down in front of the desk. Cheap trick. She had heard about this sort of stupid stunt. It was supposed to unnerve you.

Dee positioned her seat carefully to avoid the wedge of sunlight that was cutting through the room. She seated herself at a leisurely pace and then looked one by one at the panel members, who were all fiddling with their Books. On either side of Farrell there was a man, one tall and thin, one extremely large.

'Delilah,' Alexis Farrell began.

'Please, call me Doctor Campbell,' Dee said. She wasn't here to be patronised.

The thin man laughed and licked his lips.

'I'm sure you remember me –' Farrell began.

'No.' Dee cut her off, then checked herself. She needed to look like she wanted the job. She wanted to be offered the job. It would be good to be able to turn it down. Yes, to turn it down was the thing. 'Perhaps,' she said, 'with Kester.'

'Doctor Lowe's leaving drinks from his Institute job, I believe. A fancy-dress affair.'

'I say.' The thin man spoke again.

'Delilah, let me introduce you to Byron Gaunt, Pharmaceuticals, and Roger Yule, Marketing.' Alexis extended a hand simultaneously to either side, neglecting to indicate who was who.

'Nice to meet you, gentlemen.' Dee smiled. She could feel how unconvincing her smile was. It was uncomfortable across her face, a tight piece of elastic.

'The pleasure is all ours,' the fat man said, mopping his brow. He seemed kindly.

'It'll be all mine, I think you'll find, Roger,' the other man said, inadvertently helping her out.

The fat one was Yule; the thin one was Gaunt. Gaunt stood up from his chair and walked over to her. He was a decrepit pillar of charming sleaze, the sort of which Dee had frequently encountered in the academic world.

'And an exquisite pleasure it will be,' Gaunt added.

He took up her hand and kissed it. She tried not to pull away. No funny business, Kester had promised her. Dee could feel her colour rising. She hadn't spoken to Kester since he came to see her. Couldn't get a hold of him. She had wanted to talk to him about the interview. Had half hoped he might persuade her that working with him was a good idea, that he might say something to make everything that had happened go away. But then there was Farrell. He wouldn't be able to make her go away.

'Gaunt, you're making the poor girl blush.' Farrell's voice was acid. 'Let's get down to business. Tell me about your experience with regards to this role – we'll get on to your sexual experience later on.'

Dee tried to hide her shock and began to talk through her academic career and her areas of special knowledge.

Once Dee was talking she found it didn't matter that she was here, at V. She was in her element. The panel watched her carefully, nodded and listened patiently for a long stretch until –

'That's all very interesting,' Farrell said, with a wave of her hand, 'but I'd like to go back to this first point.'

Dee felt heavy, as if someone had cut the string on her balloon. She talked over the first point again, a comment she had made about her PhD thesis, not really relevant at all. Farrell moved onto another point and then went back again to the first. Then she picked up some more points and revisited them repeatedly. Why had Dee taken a travelling year? Why had she not travelled for longer? What had she learned? Why had she not got a first in every subject – was it lack of talent or laziness?

As they talked, the wedge of sunlight Dee had so carefully avoided moved towards her and broadened, sliding up her shins into her lap. Farrell started to delve into Dee's knowledge about the company – could she give them a potted history of V? What did she know about their other products? Who did she think would be the biggest competitors for the new product?

'I'm sorry,' Dee said, eventually, after struggling through an hour of half-guessed answers. 'This is all way out of my area of expertise. I'm just interested in the immunology angle on the screens project. Kester must have briefed you.'

'Oh, Kester briefed us.' Farrell's tone was strange. Dee was unsure what she meant. 'He said you were an ambitious girl. Fiercely ambitious, I think were his words. Is that true?'

'I suppose –'

'Said that working on this project with him was your dream. Is that true?'

'Yes...' Dee faltered.

That was true. That had been true. Was it still? The thought that she might not even get through at interview, that they might appoint someone else to work by Kester's side and finish what they had started together was beginning to make her feel sick. She looked down into her lap. Her hands were clasped there. She shifted them forward a little and then back again to hide the sweaty patches they had left.

'You know there may be more in this for you than working on the team, if you want it,' Farrell said. 'We're impressed. You don't think we go into this much depth with every candidate?'

The sudden change of tone took Dee by surprise. She was light again, had ten balloons in her hand. What were they going to offer her? She wanted it, she realised suddenly. She really wanted it. Did Farrell matter? Could it all just disappear? Only she herself knew what had happened and it had obviously been dealt with. She had seen all the fuss on the web about the bomb threats and about the 'precautionary measures' V were doling out to their clients. It was all in a day's work for them. To everyone else it would look like she and Kester had had a tiff, she'd gone off the deep end and was back. It would be more suspicious if she didn't...

'You'd still be involved in the screen work of course, but blue skies immunology research is where we're really –'

'I'm sorry?' Dee lifted one hand to shade her eyes from the encroaching sunlight.

'Blue skies research. Immunology is a key aspect in everything we do – designer viruses, the screens, pharma – and with the competition the way it is we need to be at the forefront of the field like never before. Budget is unlimited of course.'

'Unlimited?'

Dee was dreaming. She was dreaming. She was still in her bed and had overslept. They were offering her a job, her dream job. Her mind buzzed. She wasn't here to get a job. She was here so it wouldn't look suspicious, her not wanting a job. Not wanting a job. Not wanting a job. Why? Because she would be working with Kester? But that was all over. He need never know; they need never know. Her dream job – why not? She was at the top of her game. They could obviously see her potential. Anything would be possible. Anything. And she would be working with Kester more closely than Farrell. She thought back to their afternoon at the PlayPen, her thoughts as she had left him there, betrayed. Her regret. If she regretted it, perhaps she could forgive him.

'We're satisfied with your experience.' Farrell sat back in her chair.

Dee smiled broadly at her. It could happen. If she could smile at Farrell here, now, smile and mean it...

'Most satisfied,' Gaunt said with a lascivious smile.

'I've just one more question for you,' Farrell said.

Gaunt was on his feet again. He moved round behind Dee. She felt his gnarled hands slip under the collar of her jacket and begin to guide it ever so gently back off her shoulders. Dee tensed, but didn't stop him. She was suddenly aware of the film of sweat that lay on her skin, the damp gathered fabric of her trousers in the V of her crotch. So this was the price. Yule hauled himself out of his chair and came towards her, a strange smile on his face; excited, regretful.

Farrell stood, turned and walked away from Dee towards the window. Her question reflected back across the room, blood-edged glass, and wedged in Dee's breast.

'Just how much do you want it?'

About the author

Cleland Smith was born in the Highlands of Scotland in 1977 and grew up in Dingwall by the Cromarty Firth. She has a degree in English Language and Literature from the University of Glasgow and an MA in Creative and Life Writing from Goldsmiths College, London. Smith has worked as a supermarket store detective, a telecoms knowledge engineer, a business analyst in the banking sector and as the development manager for an award-winning online learning company. She has published three books of poetry under her maiden name, Angela Cleland. She lives in Surrey with her husband and two sons.

Find out more about Cleland Smith at www.clelandsmith.com.

CPSIA information can be obtained at www.ICGtesting.com
Printed in the USA
LVOW12s1922090314

376635LV00006B/991/P